Grihabhanga

S.L. Bhyrappa (b. 1931) is an eminent Kannada novelist whose works span twenty-four novels, six critical works and an autobiography. With an honorary doctorate from six universities, he is one of the highest-selling authors from recent times in Kannada literature. He received the Sahitya Akademi fellowship in 2015, and was awarded the Padma Shri in 2016. He was also the recipient of the Saraswati Samman in 2010, and most of his novels have been translated into almost all Indian languages, including Sanskrit and English. His most well-known works include *Vamshavriksha, Grihabhanga, Daatu, Parva, Saakshi, Saartha, Tantu, Aavarana, Uttarakanda* and *Godhuli*.

He lives in Mysore.

L.V. Shanthakumari (b. 1938) is a well-known writer and translator whose pen-portraits, poems, biographies, collections of long stories and critical articles have been published in leading journals. Apart from articles involving the incisive study of S.L. Bhyrappa's novels, she co-translated the novel *Mandra* with the author, and also his autobiography *Bhitti* with Dr S. Ramaswamy. Also, she has independently translated the author's novels, like *Sakshi* and *Vamshavriksha,* into English. Her translations from English into Kannada include Pannalal Patel's Jnanapith Award-winning Gujarati novel, *Manavini Bhavai,* and several chapters of Will Durant's *The Story of Civilization.* A life-member of Karnataka Lekhakiyara Sangha, a collective of women writers, Shanthakumari has received the Vishishta Lekhaki and Sadodita awards.

She lives in Bengaluru.

To Neetu
with love
Shakuntala J.
17/3/2021

Grihabhanga

A Broken Home

S.L. BHYRAPPA

Translated by L.V. Shanthakumari

RUPA

Published by
Rupa Publications India Pvt. Ltd 2019
7/16, Ansari Road, Daryaganj
New Delhi 110002

Sales centres:

Allahabad Bengaluru Chennai
Hyderabad Jaipur Kathmandu
Kolkata Mumbai

ISBN: 978-93-5304-125-0

First impression 2019

10 9 8 7 6 5 4 3 2 1

The moral right of the author has been asserted.

Printed at Parksons Graphics Pvt. Ltd, Mumbai

AUTHOR'S NOTE

This novel is an effort to depict life—too vast and complex for the grasp of a single person—objectively.

The story begins approximately after 1920 and ends by 1942, and it is set against the regional backdrop of the Tiptur and Channarayapattana taluks of the old Mysore State. The language carries the local tenor and aroma. However, it should not be classified as a 'regional novel'.

I am certain that the novel will touch the hearts of those who view life disinterestedly, have undergone suffering and joy and who are familiar with the nuances of rural life.

'Grihabhanga'—disintegration of a family—is not the central idea of the novel, but it is an effort to portray the structure of rural life during the aforesaid period, that is, pre-independent India.

S.L. Bhyrappa

S.L. Bhyrappa's *Grihabhanga*, a supreme work of art, is the most popular novel in Kannada and has had nineteen editions till date.

Set in pre-independent India, *Grihabhanga* depicts rural lives, the plight of villagers in the face of famine, the epidemics they suffer and endure—the picture is haunting. There is selfishness, ignorance, irresponsible attitude; the treachery of the characters in the village has been portrayed in the rawest manner. And amidst all this is protagonist Nanjamma, who shines as a symbol of virtue, righteousness and endurance, amidst the most arduous of life's circumstances. Her selfish husband, despite being a Shanubhoga (village accountant), doesn't know how to prepare accounts and the mother-in-law, an incorrigible shrew, makes Nanjamma's life hell. Aside from being surrounded by such unhappiness, there is utter poverty too amidst which she brings up her children. Her heroic effort is ruined by fate when her two children succumb to the plague and finally, she too is swept away by the same.

There are other myriad characters with vivid colours that stupefy our minds: Kantijois, the living legend who is learned in a vast array of subjects; Jangama Maadevayya, the spiritual wandering ascetic; village headmen, Patel Gundegowda and Patel Shivegowda, who have temperaments that are quite opposed to each other; and Narasi, the housewife-turned-prostitute, whose kindness and compassion elevate her to a more humane position. In a novel that is acclaimed as 'a commentary of life by life itself,' these characters come alive in flesh and blood. The story ends on a symbolic note. The aged and wise ascetic Jangama Maadevayya leaves the village hand in hand with the budding teenager who is yet to discover the world.

For the readers who are about to delve into the world of *Grihabhanga*, here are a few things to remember. You will come across quite a few profanities in this book and as a translator, I have retained them in order to be able to stay true to the diction of the characters across the story. Their usage also speaks about the character of the people who utter them. For instance, in Kannada, the word 'munde', an equivalent of the word 'widow' in English, has, contrarily to its use in English, great abusive power. It is inauspicious and derogatory, beyond only meaning a woman who has lost her husband. I could use no other word except 'slut' or 'whore' to convey the exact meaning of this abuse. In Kannada, words like 'donkey', 'thief', 'harlot' and many such words are prefixed with the word 'munde'. Even words such as 'bastard' or 'bitch' precede them. That style has been maintained.

Till the time around which this novel was written, it was a custom in South India to tonsure a woman when her husband passed away, especially so in the Brahmin community. Unless they were tonsured, they were not allowed to cook prasadam for the Gods. Wearing a blouse was a taboo for them. They had to have only one square meal a day and live a life of austerity, wearing only red sarees. As such, to call any woman with a husband as 'munde' was a curse.

Aside from the above, readers will also come across many kinship terms or forms of address following proper names. For instance, you could have Gangamma being addressed as both Gangakka and Gangavva besides being called Gangammanavaru or Gangammanavare by people of the village belonging to the lower strata of the society. While 'Avva' is used in rural areas to address any woman and sometimes used to address little girls as well, 'Akka' or 'Akkayya' is used to address someone as an elder sister. Added to proper names, you will find these forms of addresses being applied to several names in the novel.

Similarly, 'Ayyanavare or Ayyanore' are honorific addressings in Kannada—for example, Maadevayyanavare or Maadevayyanavaru.

Akkamma, Kantijois's mother, is addressed as Ajji by Nanjamma, meaning 'grandmother'. 'Annayya' is a form of addressing an elder brother with respect and affection. It is also used to address any person, either elder or younger to one, with affection. Again, while 'Ajjaya' means grandfather, 'Bhaava' stands for brother-in-law, and 'Mavayya' and 'Attemma' stand for Uncle and Aunt respectively.

'Amma' is used for one's own mother and any elderly woman.

Addresses like 'Shastrigale' and 'Gowdaru' are honorific plurals and 'Joisare' is a way to respectfully address the Jois or purohits.

I have also provided an exhaustive glossary at the end of the book for the convenience of the readers.

S.L. BHYRAPPA

Last, but not the least, I would like to express my heartfelt gratitude to Dr S.L. Bhyrappa for permitting me to translate this novel from Kannada.

L.V. Shanthakumari

CHAPTER ONE

1

Ramanna, the dearly departed Shanubhoga of the Ramasandra village was survived by his wife Gangamma and his two sons, Channigaraya and Appannaiah. Now, Ramasandra was located in the Kambanakere Hobali of the Tiptur taluk under the jurisdiction of the Tumkur District. It had already been six years since Ramanna had passed away; the year of his death the same in which M. Vishveshwaraiah had become the Dewan Bahadur. Then Ramanna's wife Gangamma was twenty-five years old, elder son Channigaraya was nine and the younger one Appannaiah, seven. Since Ramanna's death, the hereditary post of Shanubhoga was being managed by Shivalingegowda, brother-in-law of the village Patel, Shivegowda. Three years hence, when Channigaraya would attain majority, he would take charge of his father's office. Managing the post of a Shanubhoga required suitable education. At least, if one reached the level of understanding 'Jaimini Bharata',[1] he might know how to deal with calculations, khirdi, accounting of the khata, pahani and khaneshumari. Channigaraya was getting his education from Channakeshavaiah, a master in the village school.

Appannaiah, the second son, though already thirteen, had not yet been admitted to the village school and practised writing 'Sree Oum' on the sand. Nor had he undergone the rite of *upanayanam*. His mother questioned him angrily: 'Hey you, Appanna! Are you going to school or not?'

The son retorted: 'Hey, you widow of a donkey! What's it to you, if I don't?'

Mother said: 'You, whoreson, you call me widow? Your lineage will be snuffed out, you'll see.'

While the son was muttering 'Your lineage itself will be destroyed,

---

[1]'Jaimini Bharata' is an epic poem written based on *Mahabharata* and has been written by the mid-sixteenth century-Kannada poet Lakshmisha. It is in a metrical pattern called Shatpadi.

1

you...', Mudda, who was in charge of distributing water to the fields from the village tank, came in.

Gangamma ordered Mudda: 'See, this brat calls me the widow of a donkey. Catch hold of him, take him to Channakeshavaiah master and make him sit there.' As soon as Appannaiah heard this, he took to his heels. But being a tall fellow, Mudda caught hold of Appanna's tuft within ten strides. Appanna whined like a pup, but Mudda did not let go of his hold on him and brought the boy before Gangamma. She commanded Mudda, 'Kick this whoreson twice and take him away.' But how could Mudda kick a brahmin lad? He knew if he did so, worms would pour out from his legs. Instead, he dragged the lad away, holding his arms.

After the younger son left, Gangamma's eyes turned towards the elder one who was lazing at home. 'Hey you, Channiga, how much more should I bicker with you over going to Honnavalli Seetharamaiah and learn to maintain accounts? Tell me, will you leave tomorrow morning itself, or do you need a taste of a beating from a cudgel?'

Her elder son, who was sitting near the pillar, snarled: 'Hey, if you are going to meddle with me, you'll see, I will call barber Rudra and tell him to shave your hair off.'

'Fine, you son of a widow! My head was tonsured when your father breathed his last. If you utter these words to the mother who gave birth to you, worms will pour out of your tongue, you bastard!'

Honnavalli is a village eighteen miles away from Ramasandra. Though these villages belong to the same taluk, the hobalis are different. Ramasandra belongs to the Kambanakere hobali. Honnavalli is central to the hobali. Earlier, it was also a town and a taluk. After the Tiptur town expanded and developed, Honnavalli fell to neglect and was left behind just as Kadur was impoverished when Chikkamagalur developed. Seetharamaiah was the Kasaba Shanubhoga of Honnavalli from the time it became the taluk centre. He was not only competent in accounts, but a well-to-do and powerful person who could make even Amaldars dance to his tunes. Whoever learnt accounting from him, could easily and skillfully manage a Shanubhoga's work. This was the unanimous opinion of the Shanubhogas and the Patels of Arasikere, Gandasi, Javagal and the surrounding areas. But to undergo the training and get experience under him was not an ordinary matter. The apprentice had to endure hundreds of thrashings from Seetharamaiah's ruler before he could master the procedure of properly binding the ledger, writing an impeccable heading on it, and drawing neat lines in red ink in it. Like the masters of schools, Seetharamaiah too maintained: 'How can an idol be moulded without a thousand smites from the chisel?'

Gangamma got angry at her children's behaviour. She felt like crying and her eyes filled with tears. She wept, thinking, 'How scared other children are of their mothers. I don't know what deadly disease has struck these whoresons. Oh, this is my fate!' Then she went into the kitchen straight away, took an iron spatula and put it inside the oven. As it was already past three in the afternoon, there was no burning coal in the oven. Husks of dried coconuts and coconut leaves had already burnt and reached the stage of soft cinders covered with warm ash. Her fifteen-year-old son, who had read 'Jaimini Bharata', understood that his mother was heating the iron spatula to brand him. He took to his heels, shouting in one breath: 'You donkey's widow, tonsured widow, harlot widow, filthy widow, you pariah's widow...!' Gangamma knew it was not possible to catch him now. But she could not accept her defeat. She sat reflecting on how to bring these bastards under control. By then the spatula was slowly getting heated on the weak cinders.

Gangamma was a girl of thirteen when she had entered this household after her marriage. Her husband was forty-five at the time. His first wife had given birth to two children; they had died and she too had followed them. She was also from Javagal and was related to Gangamma's people. Because of that relationship, Gangamma was married off to Ramanna, who was managing the post of Shanubhoga of three villages along with that of Ramasandra. Besides, he owned six acres of wetland, eight acres of dryland, three hundred coconut trees, possessed ample vessels of brass and copper, and had enough silver and gold at home. As such, who wouldn't be ready to give his daughter in marriage to Ramanna? The village people would say, Ramanna was a very mild person—mild in the sense of being as gentle as a cow, like a tender calf—but the same people used to call Gangamma a tigress. When these words reached her, Gangamma retorted and said to herself, 'Old chappals from my left foot should be crammed into the mouths of these sons of bitches.' If only her sons would have been intelligent and obeyed her, no one could have restrained her; she could have caused her chappals to be stuffed into those people's mouths. But these widow's sons had become such duds. She thought: 'I must teach a lesson to these idiots. If I don't, I am not a woman from Javagal. I'll let this iron spatula remain in the fire. Let it heat up nicely. Anyway, they will have to come in the evening to devour food. Then I will brand their legs twice, as it is done to young bulls. Unless you brand the bulls' calves, they never obey your commands. Belura of Kurubarahalli says, "If cattle are not branded they get cattle's disease." All that is false. They are branded so that they become docile and obedient.' So thinking, she held the spatula's hilt with her red pallu, turned the rod once and pushed it again into the cinders.

By that time, Gangamma felt, someone was walking in stealthily, on the tiled roof of the house. Why do these bastards come in such broad daylight! Perhaps it must be the monkeys, she thought. 'How dare these bastard monkeys enter the village!' Leaving the tender coconuts in the garden, she felt as if the monkeys had landed right on top of her head. 'Oh, may there be no one to succeed you!' she raised her voice but soon held her tongue. 'Alas, monkeys are considered God Anjaneya's forms. It is said, they curse if evil is spoken of them.' With such thoughts in her mind, she raised her head and looked above. She felt someone was striking on the tiles with two cudgels. Fifteen to twenty tiles had broken to pieces and showered on her tonsured head and uplifted face.

'May there be no one left to survive him,' as soon as she shouted this, she heard Channigaraya shouting, 'Oh here she is, Appannaiah! Strike, strike—another four or five tiles more...' Both the brothers exhibited heroism with the wooden pestles in their hands, hitting the tiles of their house, in the very part where Gangamma stood. The mother ran out of the house, screaming: 'Wait, you whoresons, wait! I'll inform Patel Shivegowda, and I'll ask him to hang you both!'

Appannaiah warned his elder brother: 'Oh Channayya, she will go to Shivegowdaru.' Both of them left the wooden pestles on the roof, ran over the tiles, then jumped down to the gutter and ran away.

2

Earlier, Ramasandra was a village of five hundred houses. The Shanubhoga's census shows an account of only forty-seven houses now. Each year, mud deposited from the tank water which surrounds the two sides of the village, keeps pushing the walls of the ruined fort, shrinking it further. Earlier, the original lingam of the Choleswara Temple to the south of the village was located in the shrine on the tank bund. At the end of the street in the village and in front of the temple, there was a mantapam for Brahmadeva. There was a shrine of Anjaneya near this mantapam. Outside the village, near the grove, a shrine existed for the village deity, Kaalamma. In the village, there were lanes and by-lanes for different castes like the Banajiga, Nonaba, Ganiga, Kuruba and others. Nonetheless, other castes too lived in the lane. But, it was very rare that Brahmins, Lingayats, Chataalis and others would live in the middle of the meat-eating castes.

The distance between the houses of Shivegowda and the late Shanubhoga Ramanna was maybe two lanes. That meant Gowda's house was nearly twenty houses behind Ramanna's. Gangamma went directly inside Shivegowda's house and said, 'Come quick and see, Shivegowda, our Channiga and Appanna have climbed on the roof of our house and are hitting the tiles with pestles. Look here, the tiles have fallen on my head and blood is oozing.'

'Why did they do so?'

'I told them to attend school. They said they won't and are doing this.'

Gowda's wife Gowramma told her husband, 'They have grown stubborn, naughty and blunt. Go, give them a good, sound beating.' Carrying his big belly and putting on his sandals, Shivegowda set off for Gangamma's house, walking with an elephantine gait. By the time he arrived, the brothers had already run away. At the same time, Maadevayya—who lived in the temple—and ten to fifteen other people, had gathered in front of Gangamma's house. The roof tiles had been shattered, starting from those belonging to the kitchen to those of the back of the roof. To four among those gathered there, Shivegowda said, 'Hey, you go search for them and bring them here.'

Looking at the kitchen, Gangamma's eyes filled with tears. She said, 'See, Shivegowda, those bastards should be caught hold of, brought here, their legs should be broken and they should be made to sit in a corner with those broken legs.'

However, the boys were not to be found anywhere. There was not even a trace of them following that night. Gangamma said to herself at least ten times, 'Where did they go? Let their lineage be snuffed out!' She was alone in the house. The tiles on the back of the roof were shattered. Not afraid to be alone, she said, 'No devil hovers around where I live. But where have these poor bastards gone? They must be sitting somewhere, hiding. What will they do to fill their bellies in the night? Must have drunk the water from the tender coconuts in the garden, eaten the tender kernel from inside. If they have gone to the sugar cane field, they must have chewed sugar cane. But they have crossed their limits. Shouldn't they have come home? Let them come for *roti* tomorrow morning, I'll see...'

The Choleshwara temple was in front of Gangamma's house. The door of the temple was to the north and the door of her house was to the east. That meant the left side of the temple was in front of Gangamma's house. In between the temple and house, there was a piece of barren land. Here, there were still traces to show, that once, it had been the enclosing wall of the temple. Sitting alone in the temple, Maadevayya held the single-stringed iktaara in his right hand for shruti, and strumming it with the thumb and index finger of his left hand, he sang aloud: 'If *rudrakshi* is worn and "Hara Hara" is chanted aloud, the cycles of birth and death are destroyed; the Supreme Lord (Shiva) wore the Rudrakshi...' This was his typical routine. He sang hymns in praise of the Lord until midnight, and would rise before the cock crowed in the morning and again begin the rituals. Nobody knew to which village or country he belonged. It was heard that some twenty years ago, he had arrived at Ramasandra, a little earlier than Gangamma had, following her marriage. He lived in the Choleshwara temple, sang hymns, begged for alms and food—that was the pattern of his life. He was tall and had a round face. Three wide stripes of *vibhuti* adorned his forehead. Between the eyebrows and near the ears too, there were spots of the ash. He had tonsured his head and wore an ochre-coloured dhoti and a full-length shirt of the same colour.

Gangamma couldn't sleep. The boys had not returned home yet. It was already time for Maadevayya to end his hymns. He had started with 'Come, women, wave this mangalarati to Sangayya Basavanna...!' Gangamma got up, closed the door of her house behind her and went inside the temple. The front part of the temple was like a big mantapam, without a door. It was there that Maadevayya sat and sang bhajans. Some villagers would come and sit there in the evenings to listen to the bhajans, beating on drums and snapping their fingers. Some would join him in reciting the hymns.

It was already midnight. There was no one in the temple. Gangamma came, sat near the pillar in front of Maadevayya. After he concluded the last part of the bhajan and stopped strumming the iktaara it, she asked: 'Maadevayyanore, when will these bastards get wisdom?'

'Gangavva, slowly they will. First, you learn to speak good words.'

'What bad words have I spoken?'

'Why do you say, "to these bastards"? Say, "to our boys".'

It was not the first time Maadevayya was advising Gangamma to mend her way of speaking. Though he knew it was not possible for anyone to rectify her, he repeated it whenever an occasion arose. She told him about her children who had not yet returned home.

'Gangavva, why did you drag the Patel into this? You should've punished them yourself.'

'You tell me, how can I catch them?'

Ayyanavaru said, 'It's still your fault.' She became uneasy with Maadevayya's usual words: 'The mistress of the house is the mother. Without rectifying herself, how can she correct her children? You had sent Appannaiah to school; there he abused the master as "bastard" and ran home. Where did he learn that word?'

'You see, it is my fate that made him speak like that. Did the master leave that bastard without punishing?'

'Is it not after running from there that these brothers broke the tiles?'

'Let the lineage of these sons of widow be destroyed! Where shall I get the money to put new tiles for the whole roof?'

'Again you are speaking bad words Gangavva...?' Ayyanavaru was about to say something more, when the sound of several people walking on the street outside could be heard. Some shouted: 'Come! Run, run! The sugar cane field is on fire!' These two came outside the temple and saw the field behind the tank was aflame. The fire was spreading wide and that smoke was also visible.

'Ayyo, our sugar cane is also there. Which home-wrecking evil bastard has done this?' Muttering these words, Gangamma went home, locked the door and ran towards the tank bund with the other people.

The tank is located in front of the village. To reach the tank bund that had surrounded the village on both sides, one had to go around the front of the village. Now the whole village came running, and stood on the bund. Sugar cane was planted in more than half the field and it was being crushed for making jaggery in two areas located on the western side of the sluice of the tank. The fire that had started burning in the field in the east, was spreading slowly to the west and the north. As the sugar cane was ripe for harvesting, the leaves in the bottom had dried; it was, therefore, easy for the fire to spread. The force of the fire would have slowed down if there had been no wind. But, as if it had lost direction, the wind was blowing once to the west and once to the south and the flames were spreading very quickly. People of both the sugar-crushing houses of the western side untied their oxen and drove them towards the tank bund. Servants started to carry bundles of jaggery. Moulds made of wooden planks were carried by two servants together and put on the tank bund. It was certain that the crushing houses, which were built with bamboo sticks, coconut leaves, and dried leaves of sugar cane were going to be scorched in the flames that were reaching the sky, and the houses would fall, burning.

Owners of the sugar cane field were shouting 'alas, alas, ha, ha' when flames spread into their fields as if the fire was burning their own bodies. All manner of guesswork was made and numerous arguments put forth to ascertain the cause of the fire—who started it, who ignited it, and so on.

Gangamma's small garden was located near one of the crushing houses. It was an area of one acre, with forty coconut trees. Another of her gardens was attached to the dry field on the other side. Now fire was pervading all four sides of the garden. The crushing houses beside the garden caught fire and its flame and smoke rose much above the coconut saplings. Then, clearly heard amidst the crackling sound of fire from the centre of the garden, was a voice; 'Ayyayyappa—Oh, somebody come and save me. I am going to die! Come and save me!' Somebody was screaming, beating his own mouth with his palms, in panic. While people stood looking in the direction of the screams with fright and curiosity, Gangamma shouted: 'It is the voice of our Channigaraya. Why did this idiot sit in the garden at this time! I beg you, brave men among you, go and rescue him!'

But who would enter the garden while the fire had spread, and the crusher beside was burning and in flames? The fence in the garden had caught fire too. The coconut leaves, stalks and branches stocked inside the garden were all on fire. Not a single male member dared take a step forward. Maadevayya said, 'The fire can't enter the garden,' and then climbed down the tank bund quickly as if he was sliding; then, crossing the water canal that runs in the middle of the field, he reached the garden.

Gangamma too climbed down the bund shouting, 'Is there no whoreson here who's born to a man? Look! I'm a female, and I'm going.' The fisherman Mudda, the untouchables Belura and Thotamari who used to attend bhajans were then followed by seven or eight other folks who climbed down behind her and quickly outpaced her.

Channigaraya sat on the stalk of a coconut palm sapling in the garden and was still crying 'Ayyayyappa'. Maadevayya shouted,' Come down quickly Channayya, the fire has not yet reached inside the garden'. But he was afraid to climb down. He was lamenting, 'Oh, I am scared, Ayyanore.' By that time Mudda, Belura, Thotamari and all others had come running. Gangamma too had reached the place, panting heavily. She too shouted and coaxed, 'Come down, my child! Where is Appanna?' Channigaraya got a little courageous, and came from the stalk to the stem of the tree, and then climbed down as easily as a monkey. Taking him, they returned, for if they had waited, there was the possibility of fire catching the stock of coconut leaves and stalks. The fire was raging in the sugar cane field on both sides of the canal through which they came. But the flames from the sugar cane crusher were still rising. Now a big pile of dried husk had caught fire.

After everybody had climbed up the tank bund, Maadevayya asked Channigaraya, 'Why did you climb the coconut tree and sit on it at this hour?'

'Didn't Amma say, she would fetch Shivegowda? That's why I sat there.'

By that time everyone had gathered. Patel Shivegowda also came. Maadevayya asked, 'Why did you brothers break the tiles?'

Gangamma anxiously asked, 'Ayyo, let the tiles go to dogs. Where did Appanna go?'

'He ran towards Lingapura. It is he who set fire to the sugar cane field.'

'Hey, why would he start the fire?'

'I said to him, "Come, let both of us climb the coconut tree and hide there." He did not know how to climb the tree. So he said, "I'll be in the field. If we are on this side, the sugar cane crushers will spot us. Saying this, he ran to the other side of the outlet of the tank. He told me that he had lit a match to smoke beedi there and that the dry leaves caught fire immediately.'

The moment Patel Shivegowda heard this, he roared, 'Run now and get him! Bring him before me!'

But Maadevayya said, 'Can we trust what Channiga says?' Then he asked Channigaraya, 'How do you know that the fire started when he smoked beedi?'

'I don't lie, Ayyanore. If you don't believe me, I'm ready to swear on God. He came running to me and said, "You know what happened? Puradappa's sugar cane field has caught fire. Please don't tell anyone. I'll run away to Lingapura. You come with me." I told him, "You've started the fire. You go. I'm not coming." This is when he scooted.' The full import of his testimony had already struck Patel Shivegowda's mind and that of other important village folk. Gangamma didn't really understand anything. But Maadevayya did. It was to thwart any unpleasantness that would follow that Maadevayya said again, 'But how can we believe the words of this mere boy?'

'Oh, of course, we can. Why can't we believe him?' the Patel asked haughtily.

Channigaraya was anxious again and insisted, 'I'm telling the truth, respected Patel,' and suggested that he wasn't at fault. Maadevayya fell silent, lost in thought about how the elder son of the house was talking continuously, and how this fool was trying to show off his intelligence, but how it was a fact, that the Patel and the other villagers would conspire and turn against him.

3

As per the order of the Patel, both the village servant and the village watchman went in search of Appannaiah. He had not gone far in that dark night. He was squatting in the Boothapparayana mantapam near the outlet of the tank on the other side. Fisherman Mudda got suspicious, entered into the mantapam, and Appannaiah was caught. He was frightened, but stubbornly told them that he won't come. He prayed and beseeched. Lastly, he was obstinate. But, just like a lamb is

S.L. BHYRAPPA

carried on the shoulder, its four legs held tightly, Mudda carried that obstinate boy on his shoulder and set off.

Villagers stayed put on the tank bund. By then the sugar cane crushers had completely burnt and only burning coal was visible. The sugar cane in the field was charred and blackened. Though there was no moonlight, everything was dimly visible. When Mudda brought Appannaiah and set him down in front of those people, the boy shuddered. Clean-shaven in the front part, a small tuft of hair was all that was left on his head, and it was tied into a knot in the back; even the top of his head was sweating. Oh God, Gangamma sighed with relief looking at her son's face. In the beginning, she had decided to tell Shivegowda to give the boy a good thrashing. But Gowda's decision was totally different.

He asked, 'Hey, you! Why did you set fire to the sugar cane field?' Appannaiah could not speak out of fear. After Gowda chastised him, roaring loudly, the boy said, 'I don't know, you see.'

Channigaraya came forward all charged up and gave his testimony: 'Ohoho, he says "I don't know". Didn't the fire start when you were smoking beedi? Didn't you come and tell me when I sat on the coconut tree?' Appannaiah bowed his head and stood still. Underneath his short dhoti, his legs were trembling. Ayyashastri who was in the crowd said: 'Silence suggests acceptance. That means it is true—he has set the field on fire. Now decide further action.'

Each of the sugar cane field owners began to talk as was his wont. Kurubara Sannayya grumbled, 'My good juicy sugar cane would have produced jaggery like sugar candy. In the weekly fair on Thursday, buyers would have jumped to take it, though it was two annas per mould. I am now met with a loss of at least three hundred rupees.' Banajigara Revannashetty said, 'It is true, my sugar cane was already crushed, yet I would have got four hundred rupees if the sugar cane was grown on stubbles.' Each one estimated his loss and mentioned the amount.

Ayyashastri did not possess any of the fields. Yet, he too spoke of his loss. 'It is true I do not own any field. But, when everyone would crush sugar cane, fist-sized balls of jaggery, one to each bag, had to be remitted to me for the worship of the Ganapat. If calculated in total, at least five hundred balls of jaggery had to come to me. It would be about fifty rupees. Besides, sugar cane juice, warm jaggery, all these...'

Maadevayyanavaru intervened and said; 'Your calculation of interest is very heavy, Shastrigale. It is right for people who own sugar cane fields to calculate. You should not estimate your loss on the basis of Ganapati Pooja and handfuls of jaggery balls, etc. Revannashetty is taking up account of four hundred rupees for sugar cane grown on stubbles. He owns only one and a half acres of field. He has not earned four hundred rupees for the primary crop itself. Then how can he profit four hundred rupees for the stubble crop? Moreover, he had told me, "I do not leave stubble. I'll clean the field and plant paddy next time. Land is spoilt by sugar cane".'

It was unclear as to how many more people would've given an accurate account of their accrued loss. But because Ayyanavaru had spoken thoughtfully and wisely, his word would be accepted by everybody. Ayyanavaru continued: 'Jaggery balls are made of the size to fit a fist to be remitted in Ganapati Pooja. Who gives fifty rupees for five hundred balls of that size? That means, ten balls to a rupee. Forty moulds of jaggery are available for a rupee. How can one and a half annas be given for the ball the size of a fist?'

Now Ayyashastri was completely tongue-tied. As if giving the final verdict, Maadevayyanavaru stood up and said, 'Nobody gets anything by simply calculating damages. The boy has not done it intentionally. If such a little boy smokes beedi, that means he must be taught a lesson. Take a stick, hit him, and send him away. If not, advise his teacher and tie him in kodanda as punishment.

Appanna humbly requested, 'No, no, look, please, I beg you, don't punish me by tying into kodanda without any reason.' Channigaraya spoke in the middle, 'You punish only him. I've done no wrong.'

But Patel Shivegowda spoke in a different manner altogether. 'Ayyanore, you are a sanyasi, you do not own a house or a mutt; neither wife nor children. Teaching a lesson to the boy is a different matter. But who is going to make good of the damages? I am the Patel of the village. I'll pronounce the judgement. These boys should give a lumpsum amount as reparation for the damage. That should be distributed among those who have suffered loss.'

'That's right, that's right,' many people nodded their heads. Revannashetty and Ayyashastri said loudly, 'Yes, these are the words fit to be spoken by a person truly begotten by his father.' They had spoken only to taunt Maadevayya. But he did not pay any heed to it. Only now did Gangamma understand, the direction this matter was taking. Folding her hands, she said, 'I am a widow. These idiot sons have caused havoc without intention...,' but even before she could continue, Channigaraya interrupted and said, 'I have not done any wrong Amma. You speak only about Appannaiah.' Without heeding her son's words, Gangamma requested: 'You may punish him with kodanda for his mistake I don't have a penny.'

Appannaiah started crying and said, 'Look, don't punish me with a kodanda, you make me pay for the damages.'

There were discussions among the village elders. The worth of the damages suffered was calculated. It was decided that Gangamma should give two thousand rupees, so that, if not fully, at least a small amount could be distributed to those who had lost their crop. It was decided that Ayyashastri be given ten rupees as compensation for the loss of the jaggery balls meant for the Ganapathi pooja, and Revanashetty get twenty-five for the loss of his stubble crop.

Gangamma begged, pleaded and urged with folded hands again and again. No one heeded her. Realizing that it was futile to speak out in her support, Maadevayya too fell silent.

When Gangamma said she did not have even a single paisa, Patel Shivegowda suggested a solution: 'You mortgage your dry field, wet field, coconut garden and house, I'll give you money. When you settle my accounts, I'll cancel the mortgage.'

Gangamma could think of nothing. She looked at Ayyashastrigalu. Why would he lose ten rupees that should be remitted to him? There was no benefit from him to her. Another purohit of the village, Annajois was Ayyashastri's distant brother's son. He would not speak against his own uncle. It was a decision by the village elders. So, Gangamma had to agree.

At the beginning itself, Maadevayya tried his best to avoid payment towards damages. But it was not possible. Yet he advised her: 'Gangamma, don't mortgage your lands and take loans. Whatever gold and silver you have, sell it off. To fill in the deficit amount, sell grains, pulses, coconuts and the other things you have. Do not get documents like mortgage deeds prepared on immovable property. If you take a loan, interest grows rapidly. You do not have any knowledge to manage it.'

Patel Shivegowda interrupted, 'What kind of expertise would that need? ...Am I going to demand interest from her? A mortgage deed is of no value. If jewels, gold, and other valuables given by elders are lost, how can they be earned again? Just because gold and silver are of no use to a sanyasi, it does not mean it is of no use to householders. What do you say Gangamma? Will you listen to the words of this sanyasi, or to the words of wise village heads like me?'

All concurred with the Patel's words. The Patel's brother-in-law Shivalingegowda, who was looking after the post of Shanubhoga then, said, 'A woman does not have the right after her husband's death to sell gold given at the time of marriage. There is no rule to support that. She may mortgage lands.' Ayyashastri approved it. Maadevayya did not have enough legal knowledge to protest the opinion of all these people. Even if he had, what value would his opinion have among these villagers? He was not sure if even Gangamma would listen to his advice. So he kept quiet.

Legal matters should not be delayed. At that very moment, harnessing bullocks to two carts, taking Gangamma and her two sons with them, the Patel and the other village elders started for Tiptur. Shivegowda gave two thousand rupees to Gangamma in front of the sub-registrar. Describing the reason as 'domestic' in nature, all of Gangamma's property was mortgaged. The mortgage deed was drawn up by Shanubhoga Shivalingegowda. He was obstinate that he should be given at least twenty-five rupees for 'bikkalam', or writing the deed, on behalf of an illiterate Gangamma. She agreed, saying that she would give that amount by selling *avare* after harvesting. Shivegowda kept four hundred rupees for himself as damages due to him and distributed the remaining amount among others.

Because Gangamma was a tonsured widow, eating in hotels was a taboo. She was forbidden to eat even parched rice because it had to be first soaked in water before it was fried. She washed herself in the tank, ate two fistfuls of chana, a piece of jaggery and sat in the cart, her saree still dripping water. At a Brahmin hotel, she paid six annas and bought twenty-four dosas and a lump of chutney for her sons.

After returning to the village, Gangamma did not go out anywhere for three to four days out of a feeling of sheer disgrace. She gave sixteen rupees to potters of Sannenahally—a place three miles away—bought five hundred whole tiles and replaced the broken ones on the back of the roof.

Eight days later, she sent for Maadevayya. After narrating her woes and troubles to him, she asked him what she should do now. He said, 'You take Appanna to a teacher, and enrol him in school. He will turn out to be good if he learns a little. Take Channigaraya to Honnavalli. You go with him yourself. Leave him there with Seetharamaiah and tell him, "The office of Shanubhoga, to which we have ancestral right, is in the hands of others. Please make this fellow intelligent and educate him." If you still delay matters, there is no use. Already Channigaraya has completed fifteen.'

Gangamma agreed. Shivegowda heard that Channigaraya would be left under Honnavalli Shanubhoga Seetharamaiah to learn accounts and other matters essential to manage the tasks of a Shanubhoga. The Patel came and said to Gangamma, 'Why do you need to send your son so far away, Gangamma? You can send him to our Shivalinga. He can stay at home and learn. Isn't it possible to do that?'

But Gangamma firmly believed that unless educated under Honnavalli Seetharamaiah, her son would never acquire the required knowledge to run the office of the Shanubhoga efficiently. The rest of them just managed the office of Shanubhoga, but only Honnavalli Seetharamaiah was a worthy teacher for that matter, in these parts. Even Venkateshayya of Halebeedu had the same merit around Javagal. But, he did not belong to these parts. Only a local would know the pulse of a particular place.

Gangamma harnessed a cart with an arched cover and set out to Honnavalli with her two sons. Two days before starting, Channigaraya got his hair tonsured by Bhandari Rudranna and applied sandalwood paste on top of his head. The following day, he bathed in oil. Bundles of fried snacks like *kodubale and tambittu* were prepared for his journey. While Channigaraya climbed into the cart, wearing a coat and a cap, Maadevayya said: 'You see, now you are going to a big place. Hereafter, there should not be any foul words coming out of your mouth. Become an intelligent young man and return.'

Honnavalli Seetharamaiah was acquainted with late Ramanna. So, he heeded Gangamma's request, and agreed to teach Channigaraya the principles of accounting while the latter stayed in his house. After dropping him at Seetharamaiah's place, the mother and younger brother returned in the same cart.

Channigaraya stood weeping. He finally said, 'Do send kodubale and tambittu often with somebody.'

After returning, Appannaiah was admitted to Chaatali Channakeshavaiah's school. To send him to school, the pallu of his dhoti would have to be filled with fried channa, jaggery and half a portion of copra, daily.

CHAPTER TWO

1

Channigaraya completed his apprenticeship at Honnavalli in three years' time. Now, he can roll the ruler stick easily with his left hand and draw lines with his right hand with a steel nib or pencil. He has learnt to write without errors on the left side of the book and to fill the contents on the right side of it. But it is difficult to say whether his education is complete. Seetharamaiah, the teacher, says, 'You have not yet learnt the four anna part in a rupee or one-fourth of what you need to learn.' Though he does not openly contradict his teacher, Channigaraya doesn't believe these words. He means it differently. 'He says so because he wants me to stay here scribbling away on only his accounts.'

Channigaraya used to go on foot to his village twice or thrice a year. As soon as he came this time, he told his mother: 'For how many more days should I stay there? I'll come back to the village and take charge of the post of Shanubhoga.'

'Did you learn accounting properly?'

'Why not? You ask me if you want: Number one is *khatavar*, number two is *banjartakhta*, number three *pahani*, four is *khata*, five is issues related to taxation, six is less and more, seven is *takarartakhta*, eight *inam* register, nine is *jamabandi* estimate gist (assessment of revenue due to government), ten is *rojkhirdi,* eleven is *receipt patta*, and twelve is *khaneshumari*. These are twelve kinds of the Baaraanamune accounts in the post of Shanubhoga.' Channigaraya listed these out in the way that he would the names of sixty years (Samvatsaras)—Prabhava, Vibhava, etc.

The mother believed that her son had indeed become an educated and worthy man. He asked: 'What? Will you simply look on, doing nothing, or will you get me married?'

'Why wouldn't I? Wait, first take charge of the post of Shanubhoga...'

'That will certainly happen. Have I not already crossed eighteen? I am of age. Rest of the people marry their sons off at sixteen itself. What would people say if I remained unmarried?'

Many people had already negotiated about giving their daughters to Channigaraya. Gangamma had not taken these proposals seriously. But now, when her son himself was demanding it, it had to be acted upon. When she asked for Maadevayya's advice, he said, 'Let him learn accounts for two or three years more, and take charge of the post; marry him off later.' Channigaraya got angry and said: 'Oho ho ho, he says I should wait for another two years! Ayyanore, you keep quiet, what do you know! Gangamma had never spoken to Maadevayyanavaru like this. Ayyanore was silent.

Channigaraya didn't return to Honnavalli ever again. One day, on his own initiative, he visited Shivalingegowda and asked, 'Give me my Shanubhoga post back.' To this Shivalingegowda said, 'Certainly. But let the order come from a higher authority in the government.' The would-be Shanubhoga Channagariya didn't know what to say or do further. He did not pay much attention towards acquiring his post as a Shanubhoga too, since negotiations for his wedding were in progress.

One day, a large white horse with a shining saddle and rein stood in front of Gangamma's house. A heavily built and aged individual, wearing a white coat, white shorts, socks and boots climbed down that horse. Looking at the large horse and his physique, anyone could have said he was the master of the district, the Deputy Commissioner. Gangamma could see that too; she went in and informed Channigaraya of his arrival. He came out, bowed with fear and devotion, folded his hands and stammered, 'Mahaswami, your honour should please come in.' He thought that the Deputy Commissioner had personally come to return to him the post of Shanubhoga. Channigaraya asked, 'Shall I send word to Shivalingegowda?'

'Why?'

'He is in charge of the post presently. Respected master should order him to give it back to me. I am Channigaraya, elder son of *baraavardaar* Ramanna, his legal heir.'

'It can be done. Now, go inside.'

The man went inside. There was no chair in the house. Except the one at Annajois's, there was no chair in anybody else's house in the village. So the person who came in, sat on the mattress. When Channigaraya brought the *gangodaka* and placed it before him, the person said, 'We should not drink water now.' Mother and son could not understand what the matter was. Finally, he said, 'You have heard of Nagalapura, haven't you? I am the local priest there. My name is Kantijois, my daughter's name is Nanjamma. Her birth star is Revathi, in the Second Pada. She's eleven years old, running twelve. I've also brought her horoscope. Give me your son's horoscope.'

Gangamma took some time to realize that the person was not the Deputy Commissioner but Kantijois of Nagalapura. The fact that he had come to offer his daughter's hand in marriage to her son raised her self-confidence. But he had come riding a large horse and seemed to be dressed like a Deputy Commissioner. She said, 'I have thought of not getting him married until he assumes the charge of Shanubhoga.' Channigaraya asked his mother to shut her mouth, 'You keep quiet Amma! What do you know? Has he not said at the beginning itself, he would get Shivalingegowda to hand over the charge?'

'I know all those matters. It doesn't take much time to give back your rights to you. I will recommend the same to the Amaldar. Let the marriage be over first.'

Gangamma handed her son's horoscope to Kantijois. Kantijois was an astrologer himself. He looked at it with utmost seriousness, calculated the position of the stars, then said, 'The horoscopes agree beautifully. Now let's take this further.'

2

Nagalapura is a village twelve miles west of Ramasandra. There was nobody who had not heard of Kantijois from that village. As Ramasandra belonged to the taluk of Tiptur, Tumkur district, and Nagalapura belonged to the taluk of Channarayapatna, Hassan district, Jois's name was not much familiar to the people on this side. But everyone was familiar with his name in the taluk of Channarayapatna, Shantigram, Hassan, Kaushika and other places.

Kantijois was quite tall, had a broad forehead and sharp eyes. He got married at sixteen. His wife came home when he was twenty. A son was born after two years. Another two years, a child was born and died. Again two babies, and they too died, and during the delivery of the last, his wife herself passed away. The girlchild that survived was brought up by Kantijois's mother. Jois never married again. Now he had two children. Elder son Kallesha was working at Shravanabelogala as a police constable. The child that survived after the death of the mother—Nanjamma—was to be married off to Channigaraya.

It was not these incidents in Jois's life alone that had made him known among people—such incidents were, after all, common to the lives of many. Kantijois's achievements were aplenty; his renown owed itself to the many dramas he had acted in. No one who had looked at him once, could forget Kantijois's physique; it was like that of Bheema. Nobody who had seen him enacting in dramas, the Yakshaganas, from the beginning, would ever forget his roles. Bhojaraja's role in Kalidasa's play would not suit anyone but him. The dancing steps of Duryodhana in Mahabharata used to be reserved only for him. When he donned the role of 'Veeravesha' in Yakshagana, he would not stop dancing and jumping until he broke two planks. He would sing the Kanda in a high pitch, melodiously and in one breath. He knew how to play the harmonium and tabla. Along with the knowledge of priestly rituals, both auspicious and inauspicious, he knew about astrology, black magic and medicine. Besides, not only did he have the courage to speak in English with the Amaldar but he would speak in Urdu with the Muslims too.

Courage and charisma brought fame to Kantijois. People would say, he had won some cases in court earlier, and had digested even one or two murders. No one knows whether it is true. Jois, however, denies anything like that. Listening to the hauteur in the words he uttered —'I'll kill you'—while quarrelling with somebody one day, it was not surprising if fear occurred in the minds of people, and made them wonder how many murders he must have committed. He is a nocturnal creature, not afraid of the darkness one bit. With a small knife tucked in his waist, he would leave at night to go to Hassan, which was twenty-four miles away, but to do so, he would have to cross the Buldalutittu jungle alone. In fact, it was rare that Jois walked during daytime. His widespread popularity was no surprise for he would bravely confront the firebrand ghosts with white braids, and the spirits called Jademuni, on his way, and scare them away.

The Brahmins of Ramasandra, Patel Gundegowda of Kurubarahalli, which was under the charge of the Ramasandra Shanubhoga, and some other important individuals, attended Channigaraya's marriage. But neither Shivagowda nor Shanubhoga Shivalinga were present. The bridegroom's party had harnessed four bullock carts. The bride's party welcomed those on the bridegroom's side near the tank bund of Nagalapura by blowing bugles and horns, and had brought along Kantijois's white horse for the bridegroom to mount and take him in a procession. But Channigaraya was scared and confused about mounting the horse. If he did not ride it, it would be an insult to the whole of Ramasandra. After Gangamma abused, 'Fie you, effeminate bastard', he stepped on the saddle and mounted the steed. The bride's brother, police constable Kallesha, held the horse's reins and came walking beside it, so that it did not cause any trouble.

The bridegroom's people who attended the marriage, came up against Kantijois's personality. Though not rich, he was well off and had made a grand arrangement of food and other services. A lawyer from Hassan came to the ceremony. Ayyashastri and Annajois acted as officiating priests for the bridegroom. Ayyashastri's priesthood did not extend to conducting rituals beyond monthly shraddhas, *punyaah*, Gowri and Ganesha poojas. Though young, Annajois studied regularly under Surannajois of Sindaghatta and was famous around that place. He had already conducted a number of marriages and upanayanams by now, and was chanting mantras easily like a practised individual. In the bridegroom's rest house, while performing homa, Annajois was chanting loudly: '*Ommbhooragniyee praanayaswahaa; Idamagniyee praanaayaswahaa*'.[2]

The bridegroom's resthouse was beside the bride's house. Annajois's chanting was heard by the bride's people too. As soon as Kantijois heard it, he came there and asked: 'Oh Jois, do chant again that mantra by which you offer oblation to Agni.'

'Why?'

'I want to hear it.'

'Vedic mantras should not be repeated like that.' Annajois looked at Ayyashastri.

'Why wouldn't you chant it again? Will you chant it incorrectly?' Kantijois asked.

'What! Is what I chant, wrong? Is the lesson of Surannajois of Sindaghatta wrong? You ask him, uncle, whether I should officiate this marriage or leave it and go?' so saying, the Jois stood up.

---

[2]Oh, the terrestrial deity Agni, you are the vital force in our body; this offering is for you.

'I know about your mentor. He doesn't know Sanskrit properly. To say "Bhooragniyee" is wrong. It should be "Bhooragnayee". What you chant is not grammatically correct. Shall I open the book and show you? If Vedic mantras are chanted wrongly, your head will be broken into thousand pieces.'

By then Annajois became quiet. The people from Ramasandra were spellbound with Kantijois's knowledge of mantras. People assembled at the marriage hall listened to him as Kantijois himself chanted aloud mantras of *Kanyadaana* at the time of giving away the bride. After marriage, when the bridegroom's party was about to leave, Annajois came to Kantijois and said, 'I have only been taught lessons. In the grammar part, I am a bit weak. As my father died before I finished my studies, I did not pursue my education any further. I came back later and practised the rest only with the help of books. Please excuse me if there are mistakes.'

The marriage ceremony went off very well. The bride's father had given ornaments like nagaru to be worn around the head, a hairpin— the shape of a chrysanthemum flower—made of gold, to be worn on the braid, bangles, a silver girdle and silver chains as anklets. The bridegroom's party had brought earrings, a nose ring and *mangalyam* as per tradition. The bride was beautiful and tall like her father, with a broad forehead and big eyes. The people from Ramasandra said, 'Our Channigaraya was fortunate to get a bride like this.' But Gangamma did not like these words. The people from Nagalapura made fun of Channigaraya for devouring every delicious dish that was served as part of the special dinner served for the newly-weds. Even the people from Ramasandra told him afterwards that he should not have eaten like that. But Channigaraya defended himself, 'I don't know how those dishes, prepared so deliciously and with such aroma, could be thrown away, that too once they had been served and were half eaten.'

3

Shivalingegowda did not give back the post of Shanubhoga to Channigaraya, even after several requests. For a few days in the beginning, Shivalingegowda would say, 'Let us give, let us give.' Channigaraya, not quite comprehending the meaning correctly, would wait for days. When asked again, Shivalingayya would say the same words in reply. One day, he said, 'Year-end accounts—annual accounts—should be settled first. Let us see after that. Year-end meant, "end of April". That meant, another five months. Channigaraya agreed thinking what Shivalingegowda said was true. 'What will you understand if I hand you over the charge without completing annual accounts?'

There was no work at home for Channigaraya. His wife had not yet come of age; the nuptials had not been consummated. She stayed at her father's house. Though Appannaiah attended Chataali Channakeshavaiah's school, he did not learn anything. The teacher decided that Appannaiah did not possess any merit from his previous birth and so, could not be educated, and abandoned him. Now Appannaiah would pass his time plucking beehives on the fences, and pulling down tender coconuts and drinking from them. The Shanubhoga-to-be, Channigaraya, after taking a bath in the morning, would smear vibhuti mixed with water on his head thickly, sit in a wet loincloth, perform *sandhyavandanam* holding *brahmagantu* in his hand and chant the Gayatri mantra a 1,008 times, loudly to be heard, in a monotonous voice: 'Oomtatsattttt...oomtatsattt...'

At the end of the year, when Channigaraya asked Shivalingegowda, he said, 'How can I put you in charge of the post of the Shanubhoga without the order of the higher officials?'

'Where is the need for a higher official to give me what is truly mine?'

'Ho, it is not written down that the Shanubhoga's post is your father's. I have already enjoyed possession of it for ten years. You go away! There is nothing that you can extract from me!'

Hearing these words, Channigaraya felt like weeping. The words 'Go, fuck your mother' came right to the tip of his tongue but he lacked the courage to utter them. Channigaraya went to Patel Shivegowda, brother-in-law to Shivalingegowda, and when he asked him, he said, 'Hey, my little brother, are you capable of running the post of Shanubhoga? Do you think it is a cakewalk? Child's play?'

Channigaraya did not know what to say. How can he be courageous to talk before the Patel who Gangamma would always call only to threaten Channigaraya when he was a child! So, he directly came to his mother and told what Shivalingegowda, and the Patel had said. Gangamma was not the woman to keep quiet. She came out on to the street, stood near the door of the Patel's house and asked him loudly:

'Hey Shivegowda of how many days are you going to eat the shit of other people's wives? Your wife's bangles will be broken[3], and your house will be washed away, do you understand?'

Gowramma, the Patel's wife, was frightened when she heard these words. What would happen if these curses of a brahmin widow were to come true? She told her husband: 'What do we gain by keeping their wooden ruler stick, that bloody stick of a pier? Tell that Shivalinga to throw it away.'

Patel himself came out and said, 'Why do you speak evil words like this Gangavva? Come, sit here and let's talk.'

Gowramma brought a wooden seat and placed it on the platform. After Gangamma sat on it, Patel asked for a pillow, leaned on it and sat. Channigaraya, the Shanubhoga-to-be, stood under the sloping side of the roof. Shanubhoga Shivalinga, the incumbent, came after the Patel sent word to him, and sat, his legs crossed one on top of the other. Patel said, 'Shiva, explain to this Gangavva a little convincingly why it is not possible to hand over the charge.'

Shivalinga asked Gangamma, 'What is your son's age?'

'He is running nineteen.'

'You say that. But in government records he is still sixteen, he has not reached majority at all. How can a government job be given to him?'

'My husband managed the charge of Shanubhoga when Channigaraya was born. Look at the date properly. Did my husband write a false birth date?'

'We don't have with us the birth and death register. A fee needs to be set aside for the government to scrutinize the register. Give me fifty rupees first. Afterwards, I'll go to Tiptur and check.'

Gangamma did not know whether the register of birth and death would be with Shanubhoga or a fee ought to have been given for examining it and even if that was the case, if the fee was fifty rupees. When she asked her son, 'Hey Channayya, what should the fee be? You who has learnt about accounts, tell me.'

He, who stood under the slanting roof began to think with a stupid face. When she asked again to say what it was, he said, 'I don't know, Amma.'

---

[3]The curse of breaking the bangles equals wishing widowhood for the Patel's wife.

'You said you know all sorts of accounts?'

Now Shivalinga said, 'You said you were taught by that Honnavalli fellow. If that pauper of a fellow of Honnavalli had known accounts, he would have taught you. Let it be. Now, you carry on your head the garbage baskets of our house for three or four years, I'll teach you.'

Patel Shivegowda said, 'Let us leave it be, Gangavva, you put here fifty rupees. We will write to the higher officer and confirm his birth date.'

'Why should money be given, Shivegowda?'

'Is it not the government? Is this some boyish prank?

There was no other way out for Gangamma. Unless fifty rupees was given she wouldn't get a confirmation on her son's correct age. Without losing this amount, the post of Shanubhoga would not come into her son's custody. But she did not have that much money at home. She went home and searched in her big wooden chest. There, she found thirty rupees in coins that had on them the Queen's head. She collected six pallas of ragi along with that, delivered it to Shivalinga and said, 'Bring the date of birth of this boy fast. The post of Shanubhoga belonged to my husband's ancestors. I want to see my son take it on.'

Three months passed but there was no progress. When Gangamma met Shivalinga and asked about it, he said, 'It is government work. Does it happen quickly? It will go to the deputy commissioner, from there it would reach Diwan Mirza Saheb and return; it will take its own time. Wait a little, why do you behave as if a gadfly has entered your body?'

Gangamma was helpless. She returned home and told her son, 'Channayya, it seems like these people won't hand over the charge to you. You go to Tiptur, prostrate before the Amaldar Saheb and make an appeal to him. Go now!'

Channigaraya was scared to go alone and meet the Amaldar. What would he do if the Amaldar got angry and abused him? Maybe, he really was only sixteen. His horoscope must be wrong. So, he said, 'Amma, perhaps, I am only sixteen. Let us wait for another two years Amma.'

'Tut-tut, you son of a whore! I, who gave birth to you, I am here—a living widow. Do I not know your age? It is already close on nineteen. You, son of a widow, go and plead before the Amaldar,' Gangamma scolded angrily.

'I feel scared, Amma.'

'Are you not ashamed, you effeminate whoreson? I'll also come with you.' Even though Gangamma said so, remembering that women should not go to the government, she kept quiet. It was prevalent then that if women touched the government account and if that came to be known, they would be jailed. As such, if she herself went and confronted an Amaldar, would she be left alone?

There was no other way. After a month, Gangamma said to her son, 'Whatever happens, just go to Nagalapura and request your father-in-law. He'll do something.'

4

Though it was one and a half years since his marriage, Channigaraya had not visited his father-in-law's house even once. Not that he did not have a desire to visit it, but nobody from there had come and invited him. He didn't know whether it was shyness or fear that had prevented him from going on his own. Now, when his mother told him to consult his father-in-law about reclaiming the post of the Shanubhoga, he felt elated. One day, early morning, he finished bathing and the sandhyavandanam very briefly, ate avarekalu roti, coconut chutney and curd, packed three rotis and chutney for his journey, wore a dhoti and over that a coat given during his marriage, started from Ramasandra and walked twelve miles west to Nagalapura, barefoot, as he was not used to wearing footwear. After climbing down hillocks, crossing sand pits and a jungle of flame-of-the-forest trees, Channigaraya sat near a well, ate the rotis with chutney and drank six handfuls of water. He walked on the tank bund of Nagalapura and reached the place, by crossing the outlet of the village side, and walking through the grove where the weekly fair was regularly held.

Channigaraya felt a sort of fear when he came near the tank-outlet on the village side. He began to ruminate: 'What if somebody recognized me; if they ask why he had come now? If his father-in-law himself asked, what would he say? And this one, his wife, how would she be; would she speak with me or not? If she doesn't speak with me, I'll teach that donkey's widow a lesson. She doesn't know, what'll happen when she comes to our village! Only now she has completed thirteen. Yet how many days are needed for her to attain puberty?' Pondering on such matters, he walked on the tank bund and reached the tank outlet on the village side. While entering into the village he felt fear again. He was now walking on the same street on which he was taken during the marriage procession. If somebody identified him!

As soon as he entered the village in which houses were built in a cluster, the name of the first street he came across was Shanubhoga Street. It was said that Shanubhoga Shamanna of the village ruled haughtily. That is why the street was so named. The house of Channigaraya's father-in-law was in a crooked by-lane. All the houses in the village were built in the same manner. But the house of Kantijois was a little bigger.

Controlling his throbbing heart, when Channigaraya pushed the half-opened door and entered, there was no sound at all. He waited for a minute, gathered courage and shouted loudly, 'Anybody there?'

An old woman from the kitchen asked, 'Who is it? Is it Kalegowda?'

'No, I am from Ramasandra. I am Channigaraya, son of late Ramanna.'

Ajji came running from inside. 'Oh come, come in,' she said. She spread a mat and said, 'Please sit down'. She went in and brought gangodaka in a tall copper glass and placed it before him. When Ajji asked about the welfare of Channigaraya's people, Channigaraya's wife came in from the back door, holding a washed green saree and blouse in her hand. In the dim light, not knowing that a stranger was inside, she stood there to shake water off the wrung saree.

As soon as Ajji said, 'Nanja, your husband has come. He is sitting there, didn't you notice in the dark?', she ran, away from the back door, without heeding that the saree she was shaking was caught in her hasty stride and she was about to stumble over it.

Ajji herself gave water to the son-in-law, for washing his hands and feet, served him hot rice, kadi, papad, pickles, ghee and curd. Though Ajji did not want to serve him ragi balls, Channigaraya asked for a few and ate one and a half ragi balls along with rice.

After lunch, he came to know that this father-in-law did not usually stay in his village for long. He would go on tours to Channarayapatna, Narasipura, Hassan, etc., on his horse. This time, twenty days had passed since. He might return within three or four days. Channigaraya could not go back without talking to his father-in-law about the matter he had on his mind. Ajji also forced him to stay and he stayed. Neighbours took him along for walks, showed him wetlands and dry fields belonging to Kantijois. The next morning, Ajji herself massaged oil on his head and gave him an oil bath. But Nanjamma was not at all visible except on that first day when she had been seen shaking the washed saree in half darkness.

Whether it was out of fear or shyness, but Channigaraya would not visit the neighbouring houses on his own. It was difficult to pass time. Here too, as in his village, after taking a bath in the morning, he smeared his forehead with stripes of vibhuti and while performing the sandhyavandanam, he chanted the Gayatrimantra *a* thousand and eight times. Ajji's joy knew no bounds seeing this.

It was midnight on the fourth day of Channigaraya's stay. Suddenly, street dogs began barking. From somewhere the sound of trot-trot was heard. The barking grew loud. In the middle of the barking, the words 'you sister-fucker' were heard. As the sound of trot-trot came closer to the house, it seemed somebody knocked on the door. Along with it was heard, 'Nanja, open the door.' From that voice, Channigaraya knew this was his father-in-law. He felt a sort of fear to open the door. He simply pulled the blanket over himself, laid still under it and shut his eyes.

Nanjamma, who slept with Ajji in the kitchen, knew that it was her father. But she felt shy to cross the hall and open the door, for her husband was sleeping in the hall. So she nudged Ajji and woke her. Ajji lit a kerosene lamp and opened the door. Kantijois took the horse from the front door to the backyard, tied it there, came back and asked: 'Who is this, lying down here?'

'Channigaraya has come. It has already been four days. He has been waiting for you.'

In a voice that sounded like one's head had been struck with a hammer, Kantijois called once, 'Channigaraya.' Channigaraya kept quiet. Ajji said, "Perhaps he is sleeping. Don't wake him.' As he had finished his dinner already, he did not want anything to eat. Chewing tobacco, he did not call his daughter to lay the bed for him, and pulled the bed to the hall himself, a little away from that of Channigaraya's, removed his boots, coat and shorts, tied on a dhoti and slept.

5

The next day, Kantijois awoke at ten in the morning and enquired about his son-in-law's well-being. Channigaraya informed him about everything and even about Shivalinga exacting fifty rupees from them. Kantijois then asked: 'Was there some wisdom in your head or was it filled with clay? What else can you do—one who does not know rules regarding Shanubhoga's post, wastrel...'

Channigaraya, shivering feebly, bowed his head and sat down. He had informed Ajji of the matter the very day he had arrived there. While he narrated it to his father-in-law, Ajji sat close by. When the father-in-law scolded his son-in-law thus, Ajji intruded, 'What are you saying Kanti? He is only a boy and doesn't know what to do. You always speak roughly. You go there, make them give him back his right.'

Kantijois did not speak again. He took his bath, completed chanting the sandhyavandana mantras. Nanjamma prepared rice rotis and masala curry of brinjal, Ajji brought them along and served the dishes. Kantijois took his breakfast with his son-in-law. Then, chewing tobacco and spitting four or five times, he enquired about the local condition of Ramasandra, asking Channigaraya four or five questions. Channigaraya related whatever he knew. Kantijois called moolemane Honna, who was tilling Jois's wet fields, gave him a letter and asked him to go immediately to Shravanabelagola, give the letter to Jois's son Kallesha, the police constable, and bring back his reply. Jois did not speak about anything with his son-in-law. When they came to know about Kantijois's return, people came and filled the house with questions about black magic and medicines, and to get charms and amulets to check devils and ghosts. Ajji called Channigaraya into the kitchen so that he does not get bored. Nanjamma went into the room of boxes.

The next morning at eleven, Honna returned from Shravanabelogala and gave a letter to Jois. After Honna left for home, Kantijois said to his mother, 'Akkamma, Channigaraya and myself will go to Ramasandra tonight.'

'What are you saying—you are starting today itself! I have not prepared any snacks yet.'

'You do it by the evening. Prepare the payasa for dinner.'

'You wander like a firebrand ghost at night. Why are you taking him also in the dark night?'

'Is he a woman? I have married off my daughter to him because he is a man, isn't he?'

Though Channigaraya was not that afraid of darkness, his heart contracted on remembering that devils and ghosts roamed in darkness. Besides, it was rumoured that hyenas that lived near Choleshwara hillock, and roamed about during the night. He was scared to say this to his father-in-law, afraid that he might scold him. Caught in this dilemma, Channigaraya fell silent.

Ajji deep fried kodubale in a hurry. Nanjamma had ground flour for chakkuli. That too was deep fried. After finishing dinner with payasam, Kantijois wore socks, boots, a pair of white shorts, a khaki coat, and put a khaki hat on his head. A full moustache that was cut and trimmed in the morning, appeared prominently on his face. Harnessing his horse with saddle and rein, he put his clothes into a long bag and let it down on both sides of the saddle. Before leaving the place, Channigaraya prostrated before Ajji and his father-in-law. Ajji called, 'Nanja, come take your husband's blessings.' Nanja did not come. She came after Kantijois called her twice, prostrated from a distance, touched the ground and went inside. Though Channigaraya desired to look at his wife, owing to the presence of his father-in-law, he did not turn his eyes that side, out of fear.

They left home at ten in the night. It was pitch darkness enveloped everywhere as it was a new moon day. After coming out of the village, Kantijois told his son-in-law: 'You too ride on the horse; let both of us sit.' Channigaraya said, 'I don't have practice. I am scared.' Jois said, 'I'll hold,' but Channigaraya said, 'No, whatever you may say, it is not possible for me.' He was obstinate.

Kantijois said, 'Okay, come, let us go walking,' and even in that pitch darkness, he walked as if the road was clearly visible to him. The horse followed him. Channigaraya came running behind the horse at a distance of four to five metres. Father-in-law walked silently. Son-in-law felt not only embarrassment but also fear. The wind blowing in the darkness made a swishing sound.

6

They crossed the tank bund, left behind Hoovinahalli, Kattigenahalli, and were crossing Kemmannuhalli which was found before the slope of Choleshwara hillock to its west. They had already walked eight miles.

Kantijois walked ahead, and behind him was the tall white horse. To Channigaraya, who came half running, half walking, the white colour of the horse seemed dim in the darkness. Father-in-law suddenly stopped. The horse too stopped. Son-in-law was almost crashing into the horse when he too stopped. At a little distance, a light was visible on the right side of their path. Father-in-law called son-in-law, 'Come forward a little.' Encircling the horse, he came near his father-in-law. Pointing his hand towards that light, he said to his son-in-law, 'Look, there.' Channigaraya did as he was asked, and at once, began to sweat, his hands and legs beginning to shiver.

There was an idol of Kali, about waist-high, that stood kneeling. Its blood-red tongue, hanging from its open mouth, seemed as if it was licking blood. A long garland of red oleanders adorned its neck. On both sides, cloth wicks were burning in small cuplike mud lamps. Three cocks, with their heads severed, lay in front of the goddess. There were two halves of cut ash pumpkin and three bunches of bananas kept on the side. Kumkum was cast helter-skelter everywhere. Turmeric and kumkum were smeared abundantly on Kali's body. Raw thread, thin sheets of copper, amulets and bones—either of men or animals—were scattered around the goddess's figure.

It appeared as if burning coal was piercing the passive darkness. Father-in-law asked, 'Did you see?'

Son-in-law's tongue felt heavy to even say 'yes'.

'Look, go there, bring here those bunches of bananas; then kick the chest of that idol once. You will get money.'

Channigaraya trembled hearing these words. He stammered, 'Please no, please no.'

'Then hold the reins of the horse.' So saying, Kantijois put the reins into his son-in-law's hands, and went forward. Upon reaching the idol he took a few bunches of bananas in his hands. For two minutes he looked at the idol as if to examine it, then put his hand on its shoulders, the protruding tongue, the head and the knees, and took something from there—perhaps silver coins. Then he kicked the chest of the idol with the boot of his left leg. The idol broke. From inside it, fell a few coins. There was a gold coin too, or something that looked like one. He picked them all, put them into his pocket, returned to hold the reins of the horse, and said to Channigaraya, 'Come', and went ahead.

Even now, Kantijois was in front, his horse behind him and Channigaraya was trailing far behind. Channigaraya recalled the *moorti* of Goddess Kali. He felt scared to even turn behind and look at it. Even without looking back, he felt it was following him. He was petrified, certain that it'd jump on his back and wring his neck. The silence resonated with eeriness as before. Like a devil, his father-in-law walked on briskly, in silence. Wondering that speech might somehow assuage the deathly fear he felt, Channigaraya asked:

'Wh, wh, wh, what is that?'

'Is not today a new moon day?'

'Wh, wh, wh what have ththey dddone to it?'

'They have practised witchcraft on somebody. There is an individual called Kareegere Veerachari. It is he who does this sort of things. He has done it in front of the people who wanted him to do it, and he has gone away with them. After the ritual is complete, he returns and takes away not only the money kept on the idol, but the bananas also. Let him come back today and he will get a lump of mud.'

'You touched thththat and took away the coins. Will nothing hahahapen to yyyou?'

'You must touch your heart and know. If it is strong, it is not possible even to pull out a single hair. If not, there are effeminate cowards who vomit blood and fall dead.'

Channigaraya was terribly frightened hearing these last few words. By then, they had crossed a hillock and the place where witchcraft was performed was invisible. Channigaraya took courage and looked back once. Nothing was visible except sheer darkness. A descent from the hillock had begun. A valley of fire trees was also about to pass. Father-in-law was walking ahead in rapid strides.

7

It was two hours past midnight by the time father-in-law and son-in-law reached home. Kantijois's son, police constable Kallesha, had come with a Dafedar to Gangamma's house. Gangamma and Appannaiah identified Kallesha. Both of them had come just half an hour ago. They were in khaki uniforms, stockings and police boots. Along with a woollen police coat that hung long from their backs, they had hunters' canes in their hands. Gangamma did not know the reason for their coming at this hour. They did not say anything. She prepared hot rotis for them but did not know how to brew coffee. Moreover, there was no milk at the time. However, Kallesha and that Dafedar brewed a decoction from the coffee powder they had brought along with them and drank the extract, adding jaggery to it. They knew that Channigaraya would come soon with his father-in-law.

Kantijois came with his horse and son-in-law and explained the matter about the charge of Shanubhoga to his son Kallesha. Kantijois said, 'Let's go now ourselves and take back the charge of Shanubhoga.' The Dafedar who had come with Kallesha, asked, 'How can it be taken back?' Kantijois said, 'You simply come with me' and came out, climbed on his horse, and asked his son-in-law to show him the house.

Channigaraya could not understand anything; he felt a sort of fear. This was another kind of fear—if he asked 'why', father-in-law might scold him. So he kept walking in front of the horse that Kantijois rode, and on both his sides walked the two policemen. After they reached Shivalingegowda's house, Jois said to Channigaraya, 'Knock on the door and wake him up.'

When Channigaraya knocked on the door, Shivalingegowda's wife asked from inside, 'Who is it?'

Channigaraya said, 'It's me Shivamma. Please wake Shivalingegowdaru.' Shivalingegowda woke up, opened the door himself and with sleepy eyes, questioned, 'What is it. You are spoiling my sleep by coming at this hour! Don't you have anybody to advise you?' Before he could finish what he was saying, he saw the big man on the horse and the policemen. He felt his heartbeat suddenly stop and could not speak anymore. The horse rider spoke haughtily, 'Hey Dafedar, arrest this fellow.' Both policemen stepped forward and held Shivalingegowda by his arms. Shivalingegowda's wife Shivamma, who was inside, began shouting, 'Alas, I am ruined, oh Shiva! What wrong has my husband committed?' But Kallesha warned sternly, 'If you open your mouth, we will take you too and put handcuffs on you; close your mouth!' She put both her hands on her mouth, pressing on it tightly.

Kantijois climbed down from the horse and said, 'Go inside.' The policemen entered the house, pushing Shivalinga. The horse rider, who came in with Channigaraya, closed the door from inside and asked, 'Saying you will access the government register for his date of birth, you have swallowed fifty rupees. We have received a complaint. We are going to send you to the gallows. You bastard!'

While Channigaraya started stammering 'Th...th...that, let it go, please leave it,' the rider turned towards him and roared, 'You shut up!' Like Shivamma, he too pressed his hands on his mouth. Kantijois turned towards Shivalinga and said, 'This is raja's government. It is an order by Dewan Mirza Saheb. Vile actions won't work. Bravo, you sister-fucking fellow, you whoreson! You have swallowed money in the name of the government. We have received orders from the English officers that you should be sent to the gallows. Hey Dafedar, put on the handcuffs.' Hearing this, Shivalinga trembled. His wife sunk to the ground, prostrated before the rider and said, 'Bring here those fifty silver rupees.' Shivalinga stammered, said to his wife, 'It is in the iron safe. Open the d...door and give it.' She opened the iron safe with the key which was under the mattress, counted fifty silver rupees and handed them over. Immediately, the rider said, 'Inspector, take this money and put it in your pocket. Tomorrow it should be remitted to the treasury.' Dafedar put it in his pocket.

Now, the rider came to the next point, 'You idiot, whoreson, sister-fucking bastard, why do you harass saying you won't give back the charges of Shanubhoga to baraavardaar?'

Shivalinga stammered 'N...n...o.'

The rider ordered, 'Leave his hands.' After the police let go of his hands, the rider said, 'Bring a sheet of paper, an inkpot and a pen, and sit.'

After Shivalinga did as he was told, the rider once roared like a tiger and said, 'Now you must write as I dictate, you sister-fucking bastard. Yes, write. "The charge list, written in the year 1900... by Shivalingegowda to claimant Shanubhoga Channigaraya, elder son of Late Ramanna baraavardaar of Ramasandra village, Kambanakere hobali, Tiptur taluk, Tumkur district, of Mysore state, Maharaja's government, is provided here. I, Shivalingegowda, Shanubhoga in charge of the above-mentioned district, ditto taluk, ditto hobali, ditto village, is writing this. The charge of Shanubhoga of this subdivision, which I managed till now, belongs to you. Till and as you were a minor, I managed the post. Now, since one and a half years, you have reached majority, today, I am giving back the aforesaid charge to you and delivering all registers, accounts, ledgers, as you have thoroughly checked, to your custody and I have no objection regarding this. Not only that, as I am suffering from a severe illness, and as it is not possible for me to manage government work, I am assigning everything to your custody, even before receiving orders from the government. Details of charge list: Khatevar paper No.

1, Banjar takht No. 2, and other Baaraanamune accounts. Signature of Shanubhoga in charge, Shivalingegowda.'

After Kantijois took the charge list into his hands, he said: 'Bring here all account books and registers.' Shivalinga brought the bundle of books in front of him. Then Kantijois said, 'You and your wife carry these, keep them in Channigaraya's house.'

Shivalinga, his wife and the children—who were awake by then and trembling with fear—carried the bundles and put them in Channigaraya's house. Then, Kantijois said, 'If you wag your tail, I'll finish you. Shut both your traps, go home and sleep. Police will be patrolling here.'

Shivalinga returned home with his wife and children, closed the door and lay down. All these incidents which had happened unexpectedly, as if in a dream, had shaken him completely. But his wife consoled him that they had possibly been saved more trouble.

The two policemen slept. Gangamma, Appannaiah and Channigarayaru lay down in the kitchen. Channigaraya did not get sleep. He felt feverish, in shock. Nobody bothered whether Kantijois slept at night. Perhaps he was hungry. By morning, he had eaten two bunches of banana brought at night from that witchcraft spot. He had piled the banana peels near the pillar. At seven in the morning, he called Appannaiah and asked him to fetch the village servant. As soon as he came, Kantijois ordered, 'Beat the drum and make an announcement in the whole of the village that the charge of Shanubhoga has been transferred to the claimant Channigarayaru. Everybody must obey him. If not, it will be an offence. Look there, the police are sleeping inside. Their caps are near the pillar.'

The village servant bowed, folded his hands in reverence, and went away. Within half an hour it was announced alongside drumbeats, that Channigarayaru had become Shanubhoga. The village servant set out to announce this to Kurubarahalli, Lingapura and other villages that belonged to the same subdivision.

The policemen woke up at eleven. They had a hot water bath, coffee with milk and jaggery, and a wholesome meal. Kantijois left twenty-five rupees with the Dafedar who had come with Kallesha. He took the remaining twenty-five rupees, climbed his horse and set out for Kambanakere to meet the Shekhdar to regularize and transfer the charge of the Shanubhoga's post. Kallesha and the Dafedar left for Shravanabelagola after lunch.

Kantijois returned at ten in the night riding the horse, and what did he see? The new Shanubhoga Channigarayaru was running a high temperature, his body was scorching and the heat more intense than live coal. Gangamma had smeared some balm on her son's forehead and tied his head with a strip of cloth. Channigarayaru was mumbling continuously and stammering, 'Aayyyayyayyu...I did not kick...I've erred, you see Avva...' Nobody could understand this gabble. Kantijois knew the reason as soon he came inside. He asked for a dry palm leaf, wrote a 'mandala' on it, rolled, and tied with it thread smeared with turmeric, broke a coconut, brandished its water before him, and then sprinkled some on the patient's face. He then tied the palm leaf amulet to Channigaraya's neck and waved a broom made of toddy palm around him thrice, and struck his head with it four times. Thereafter, Kantijois asked Gangamma to boil a decoction of clove, pepper and ginger and made Channigaraya drink it. The new Shanubhoga slept quietly.

By the next morning, he had been relieved of the fever.

CHAPTER THREE

1

Nanjamma attained puberty. Following the ceremony consecrating the nuptial vows, she came to her husband's home. Shanubhoga Channigarayaru had many desires about his wife. He was filled with an enthusiasm to reign over her. And what did reigning over one's wife mean? Beating her now and then. But that was not possible for him. He was not used to beating even a troublesome cow or young bull. That is why he would show his authority on his wife only through his tongue. So, to the one word 'widow', that came out of his mouth with ease, he would add the choicest of epithets like tonsured widow, whore widow, filthy widow, untouchable widow, and only then would be appeased. Not that he did not have more such words in his vocabulary. Was he not Gangamma's son? However, there was always that fear in his conscience, that if he used more foul language, his father-in-law would come to know.

Gangamma did not have any less a desire of reigning over her daughter-in-law with the help of all of her creative vocabulary. But she too was, like her son, scared of her son's in-law. So she would satisfy herself by merely growling and snarling. During the first year in which the charge of Shanubhoga was transferred under his custody, Channigarayaru prepared accounts and the assessment of revenue due to the government. It was only taluk Jamabandi, i.e. the annual accounts that were to be checked by local officials only, not huzoor Jamabandi of the higher office. Though bribes were offered, the head clerk picked out a hundred and one mistakes in Shanubhoga's accounts. Well, the Jamabandi was not approved. Channigarayaru uttered in his mind, 'Fuck his mother,' but it was not possible to abuse anyone openly. The head clerk said that he would not conduct that Jamabandi, that Shanubhoga himself should come to Tiptur within two months and get the signature of the officer. Channigarayaru was not used to being scolded by the officer.

Shanubhoga Dyavarasayya of Timmalapura had come to the same

taluk office for Jamabandis. He was known for impeccable accounting which did not have any errors. Except for the post of Shanubhoga, he did not have any other means of living. He used to say that the post of a Shanubhoga was akin to pickles, which merely adds taste to a meal and is not the meal itself. Indeed, the mere post of a Shanubhoga was insufficient to fill the belly. Channigarayaru sought Dyavarasayya's assistance. He said, he would prepare not only this but all other accounts too, but in return Channigaraya should give him an annual remuneration of fifty rupees. Channigaraya's annual payment from the subdivision of three villages was a hundred and twenty-two rupees, seven annas and eleven paise.

From this amount, twenty-two rupees, seven annas and eleven paise was allocated for paper and ink. At the end of the year, when the annual remuneration and expenses would be drawn up, ten rupees would go to the Shirastedar. The Amaldar would get six rupees, the head clerk two rupees, the Hobali clerk two rupees, the cashier one rupee, and the servants, eight annas each. A total of seventeen to eighteen rupees would be spent. Alongside this, when officers came to the village, there would be expenditure related to their food and other services and also those for the filing of the Jamabandi that had to be taken care of. After these, if Channigaraya gave fifty rupees for writing out the accounts, how much would remain? There was a practice of farmers paying a rupee or eight annas or four annas towards ink, when revenue was collected. Those farmers who paid a revenue of over ten rupees, would give a rupee, those that paid an amount lesser than that, would give eight annas, and those that paid a revenue of two rupees would give four annas. But, the Patel himself would swallow the ink charges in Ramasandra. Nothing came from Lingapura. From only Kurubarahalli, a total of forty rupees could be received. Any extra income depended on Shanubhoga's knowledge in writing partition deeds, sale deeds, mortgages, objection takhta, darkhast petitions, etc. How could Channigarayaru, who could not manage the accounts of *khata, khirdi,* have written registration letters neatly? Hence he could not have access to that income also.

Dyavarasayya of Timmalapura visited Ramasandra and stayed there for fifteen days. While Nanjamma and Gangamma took care of his bed and board during his stay, Channigarayaru took care of other things. After the accounts were completed, Dyavarasayya took Channigaraya to Tiptur, 'honoured' the head clerk and Shirastedar with two rupees each, managed the Jamabandi and got the signature of the officer. Wearing a coat and cap, and placing a piece of cloth on his shoulder, Channigarayaru visited the taluk office and returned. Through he stood with folded hands when the officer put his signature on the Jamabandi, luckily the officer did not ask him anything. He put his signature in the place the head clerk indicated.

While returning by cart from Tiptur, Channigarayaru first dropped Dyavarasayya in Timmalapura and then came to Ramasandra. That very afternoon he called his wife. 'Hey slut, my whole body is aching after completing Jamabandi. Come, put some castor oil on my head and massage my body.'

Nanjamma was tall, a girl strong build. She drew water from the well in the backyard, filled a large metal cauldron with it, and then burnt coconut leaves and shells in the bathroom oven. Thereafter, she rubbed oil on her husband's head, and then rubbed oil on his back, his arms, over his legs and feet, afterwards leaving him to soak in the oil. This was followed by pouring hot water on him, and rubbing his scalp and body with soapnut powder, ground into a smooth paste. Later, when he wiped his body, she tied a towel around him, spread the bed, put on it a fresh sheet and blanket, covered him with the latter, sat beside him stroking his body, hands and legs gently, until he said 'enough'.

2

Appannaiah's marriage should have happened two years ago. But, just then, Channigarayaru had gotten married. Afterwards, to get to begin on his responsibilities of the post of Shanubhoga had taken much time. Now, though a little late, Appannaiah's stars in relation to his marriage were shining bright.

It was true that Appannaiah had attended Channakeshavaiah's school for two years. The teacher had himself said that education was not in Appannaiah's destiny, so how could it be his mistake? His nails wore out practising the alphabet on the sand, but the letters would be lost in it. Nobody felt sorry about it. Anyway, why was he sent to school? Only to prevent him from going to the sugar cane field, smoking beedis and causing another fire, isn't it?

Shyamabhatta, the purohit of the Nuggikere village of Kadur region, was the one to give his daughter's hand in marriage to Appannaiah. Shyamabhatta had learnt about Javagal. He came to Ramasandra, saw the bridegroom and fixed the marriage. Shyamabhatta had only one daughter and no sons. Along with performing religious rites, rituals and maintaining traditions, the girl could embroider the image of Krishna on banyan leaves. That meant she was a very 'civilized' girl. But Shyamabhatta did not tell this to Gangamma. If he had done so, Gangamma would not have agreed to make this fashionable girl her daughter-in-law.

Shyamabhatta performed the marriage ceremony with aplomb. He gave his son-in-law, among other things, a silver cup weighing one seer, a silk dhoti, a pair of wedding dhotis and a lace turban. In place of the bridegroom's parents, Appannaiah's sister-in-law Nanjamma and brother Channigarayaru officiated the ceremony of 'accepting the bride'.

Saathamma attained puberty six months following the marriage. The sixteenth day from her first menstrual period, the ceremony consecrating the nuptial vows was performed and she came to her husband's home.

In the beginning, prevailing over his wife posed a problem to Appannaiah also. He had willed that he should rule his wife just like his elder brother ruled over his. So, the very morning his wife came, he shouted, 'Hey, you slut, you widow, come here, rub oil on me.'

Saathamma did not understand for whom these words were meant. She continued to sweep the floor unknowing, that the words had been meant for her. When her husband said, 'Hey you Saati[4] widow! I asked you to rub oil on me. Didn't you hear?' She looked at her husband, bewildered. He again shouted, 'Why do you look like that, you widow of a donkey, didn't you hear what I said?' Saathu felt like crying. She left the broom there itself. She went near her mother-in-law and said, 'Did you hear the words of your son, Amma? Who taught him to speak like this to his wife?'

Gangamma had not imagined that being a daughter-in-law, she would be so courageous. Did not Channigaraya speak to the elder daughter-in-law Nanjamma in exactly that language? She remained quiet. But, how could this shrew come before her and question her like this?

'You harlot, you whore, what else should a husband call his wife?'

---

[4] A short form of Sathamma

'Why should I be a whore? Perhaps, he who says so, must be one.'

Gangamma was enraged hearing this. 'Hey, effeminate son of a whore, did you hear what your wife says to your mother who gave birth to you? Am I a whore? Will you take care of your wife properly or not? You bastard eunuch!'

Appannaiah's manhood raised its head. He went near Saathu, held her neck and hit her twice with a thudding sound. Saathu fell down, dizzy. While Appannaiah roared, 'I'll kill this whore widow!' Nanjamma, who had heard everything, came out of the kitchen. Until that day, she had not spoken loudly before Appannaiah. Now, she said, 'Appannaiah, if you torture and persecute daughters-in-law who have come to your house, your hand will shrink! Tell me, what wickedness has entered into you?' Nanjamma brought water, sprinkled it on Saathu's head and patted her. Appannaiah felt calling his sister-in-law a slut, widow, etc., too. But with a sort of fear, owing perhaps to the memory of her father Kantijois, he kept quiet. Saathu was not fully unconscious. She got up, sat and said, 'If he was born of a virtuous family, only then could good words come out of his mouth.'

'Don't speak Saathu, come quietly,' so saying, Nanjamma helped her to climb the steps and took her to the attic.

Gangamma said, 'Oh, that senior shrew is taking this one to tell her tales,' Though Nanjamma heard these words, she went away pretending she hadn't. Saathu sat on a wooden plank in the attic and asked Nanjamma, 'Should this sort of words come from his mouth, being a brahmin?'

'It is new to you. The behaviour of the people of this house has always been like this.'

'If that is so, does Bhaava also call you so?'

'I have gotten used to it since I came here two years ago.'

'Why did you keep quiet, hearing such words? That is why my husband has become courageous.'

Nanjamma did not respond to Saathu's words. She began to ruminate within herself. Saathu asked again: 'Your father is such a respectable person. He had attended my marriage also. People assembled in the ceremony were scared of him. My father also said that he is very noble and great. It is heard that Bhaava got back the post of Shanubhoga only because of your father. So, you threaten my Bhaava that you would inform your father. These people will shut their mouth. If not, you tell your father about this. She will teach these fellows a lesson.'

'Saathu, you are still young. You do not know. A woman should never tell her father to teach a lesson to her husband,' said Nanjamma. Nanjamma did not fully explain her father's character to Saathu. If her father were to be angry with anybody, he would usually first rush towards him, hold him by the tuft of his hair and slap him so that his molar would shake off, and only after that, would he speak to him. He did not know any other way. Nanjamma knew that her husband had not kept up his dignity as a son-in-law. Her father never respected a person who was not brave and courageous. That was his nature. But, being a woman, a wife, if she did not guard her husband's dignity, what would it be like?

Saathu said, 'If that is the case, you yourself advise my husband not to call me using such words henceforth.'

By then Channigarayaru's voice could be heard. 'Where did she go? Let her lineage be ruined! Haven't you yet made roti and ground chutney?'

'Did you hear your Bhaava? I'll go and prepare roti. You come and grind chutney. If not, go and put oil on your husband's head,' saying that, Nanjamma got up.

Saathu thought, 'I'll grind chutney. If he wants, let him ask his mother to rub oil on him.'

CHAPTER FOUR

1

When Nanjamma was seven months pregnant, one day, Kantijois came to Ramasandra, riding his white horse. This time, he came while daylight was still there. Later, two hours following his arrival on the horse, a cart with an arched cover and pillows came. Kantijois had arrived to take his daughter back home for the impending delivery of the baby and also convey the news of Kallesha's upcoming marriage. The marriage would take place at the bride's house in Hassan, fifteen days from then. He invited everybody to come to Nagalapura for the ceremony, and from there, they could all go together in carts.

On their return journey, Nanjamma sat in the cart while Kantijois rode the white horse befitting an army general, ahead of the cart.

Even today, Ajji stayed in the Nāgalapura house alone. It was she who had brought up Nanjamma since the time of her birth. Nanjamma cried looking at her Ajji Akkamma. Ajji could not understand whether the tears were for having left Ajji for so many days or for some other reason. Akkamma had wished to bring her pregnant granddaughter here much earlier. But Kantijois, who had gone on tour, had returned only the previous night. That too, he had fixed the marriage of his son, and also the date of the ceremony. He had already delayed to get his son married and had not paid enough attention to the matter. It's only when he heard from a constable, that of late, Kallesha's wanderings were not of a respectable nature that he fixed the bride within two days and decided the *muhurtha* in a hurry.

Nanjamma too began to supervise the preparations of her brother's marriage. She took responsibility for directing the servants' tasks of lime-washing the house and drawing coloured lines on the lower part of the walls inside the house. It was against Kantijois's temperament to stay in his village for a continuous period of time. As was habitual, he went off, riding his horse, and returned after eight days. Kallesha came home in police uniform, when there were only six days left for the marriage.

He was clever. He helped his sister and Akkamma in preparations for the marriage ceremony. Kantijois's close relatives were people from Ramasandra only. One day, before the worship ritual involving the family deities and mass feeding, Channigaraya, Appannaiah and Saathu arrived in a bullock cart. Gangamma had sent word that she wouldn't be attending the ceremony since she was a widow.

After the pooja and mass feeding of people were complete, everybody had to start in the night for Hassan. But Nanjamma, being pregnant, had been feeling tired since the afternoon itself and had come feeling feverish. By the evening, she lay down. It was decided that travelling twenty-four miles at night in a bullock cart would not be safe for Nanjamma. So Akkamma and Nanjamma were to stay back in the village.

Nanjamma was naturally scared a bit as it was her first pregnancy and now, it was only herself and Ajji who were at home. Therefore, she thought it would be better if her husband stayed with them. She sent for him to meet her. Channigarayaru, who was looking for a comfortable place to sit in the cart and to sleep at night, arrived. He growled, softly enough to not be heard by others in the vicinity, 'What?'

'I don't know why but I am feeling out of sorts. There is no other male person at home. Let Appanna and Saathu attend the marriage. You please stay here.'

'How is that possible?' Channigarayaru asked, as disappointed as one would be if chitranna—served like a tower—and packs of obbattus were being snatched away from his dining leaf.

'Why not? I'll tell Kalleshanna and father that you should stay here.'

'No, that is not needed. If you want, keep Saathamma here with you.'

Nanjamma did not speak again. Having led two years of family life with him, she knew his nature and said, 'You go, it doesn't matter.' Channigarayaru went away, acquired a warm place in the middle of the arched cart and sat leaning against it. Saathu came of her own accord and asked, 'Shall I stay with you Akka?'

Though Nanjamma said, 'No, no, you go and attend the marriage', Saathu did not heed her advice. She went to Akkamma and said, 'You are a lone old woman. No one else is at home. Let me stay back.'

Akkamma forced Saathu: 'There would be no female member from our side to look after the traditional shaastras of marriage. At least you go and take care of the auspicious wedding dias. I'll take care of Nanja, there's nothing to worry about.' Saathu set out.

At eight in the night, four bullock carts were harnessed. Kantijois wore boots, shorts and a coat, and rode the horse in front of the carts. Kallesha sat in the last cart with his constable friends. Nanjamma got up, stood near the door, and looked on until four carts disappeared from her sight.

That night, Akkamma said, 'Look Nanja, two of your children are like the udders of a goat. Your father knows that you are seven months pregnant. Yet he has fixed this marriage now. Do you think he has any wisdom?'

'His nature has always been like that—always—rash and haphazard.'

'Since your mother delivered you and died, I have been alone here. Kallesha was a boy. When you were born, he was seven years old, wasn't he? Boys somehow grow up. Your father stays here for about three days; for three months he will not be here. You went away to your husband's home after marriage. I am fed up, staying alone. I had a desire to see your children and nurse you after childbirth. God has granted that. However, after marriage, how can daughters visit their mother's home, whenever we wish them to?'

'Hereafter, you need not have to worry. Kalleshanna's wife will give you company.'

'It is only your wishful thinking. Kallesha is in the police department. He goes wherever he is transferred. His wife too will have to go with him. Besides, she is a girl from Hassan town. Did your father ask me while setting up the alliance for his son? He acts as per his whims and moods. I don't know what should be said about the merit of my womb for giving birth to such an obstinate fellow.'

Nanjamma's mind began to ponder over her father's nature. By then, Akkamma asked, 'Does your mother-in-law really treat you well?'

'Yes. She treats me well.'

'Ah, it is enough. What else is needed by daughters?' Akkamma said and then kept quiet.

After some time she spoke again, 'Look here little one, you were singing a song about Sita's exile to forest and one about the battle of Lava and Kusha. Do you still remember them?'

'After I went there, not even once did I sing. One day at dawn, grinding ragi, I began to sing. People there told me not to disturb their sleep and I began grinding silently.'

'From tomorrow, you sing every day. I feel like listening to those songs,' Akkamma said. She also remembered something. 'No, don't sing that. You are pregnant. You should not sing songs that speak of Sita's exile to the forest and all.'

After two minutes, Akkamma said again, 'Look, after you left, there are no girls in our village who can sing. If there is some function like *aarati* in anybody's house, it seems dull and dry. Everyone says that. You forgot to take your music book also. One day, Kanti got it. He has kept it somewhere and said, this book is Papu's. Search it first thing in the morning and practise; else you will forget.'

2

On the day of Kallesha's marriage in Hassan, a rat fell at Fisherman Street in Nagalapura. That meant the plague, Maramma, Goddess of Epidemics, will be coming to the village. She destroys those who do not fulfil the religious vows they owe to Maramma. Villagers should leave their homes, put huts made from coconut fronds outside the village either in their dry fields or gardens, before she enters the village. She stays in the village for three or more months and after she leaves, people may return to their homes.

The next day, came *Goodemarammanavaru*, brandishing a jute whip of about a metre long and as thick as someone's arm, lashing his body with it. Turmeric and kumkum smeared abundantly on his body, Maramma's man came carrying the round basket. Behind him, his wife was predicting: 'Amma has been sighted in sixty-four villages! She is razing everything to dust! She swallows babies! She pulls away mothers of children! She swallows virgin girls! She has broken the shafts of the bridegrooms who were indulging in nuptials! She takes away lives of pregnant women.' The man laughed as he shouted all this, while lashing his bare body with the whip, the sound of 'chateer, chateer' heard from time to time.

Goodemaramma's coming around and predicting ominous things like this was not rare. But Akkamma was scared hearing that Goodemaramma had taken away the lives of pregnant women. She put turmeric, kumkum, rice, toor dal, coconut, a gift worth three paise in a winnowing fan made of bamboo and offered these to 'Amma', ahead of others; she also bought kumkum prasad and smeared it on Nanju's forehead.

The following day, more rats fell. They appeared in other streets of the village too. News spread that people of surrounding villages were already leaving their homes. Now, the people of this village too had to build sheds as early as possible. Shamanna, the Shanubhoga of Nagalapura, came home in the evening, sent word that one person from each house should attend the Panchayat he was going to convene. The Panchayat then decided that before Monday, everybody must vacate the village. The next day, from morning itself, people began putting up sheds in their drylands, gardens, and those who did not have their own lands, put up sheds in lands belonging to others. People who owned small businesses also transported their commodities.

By the time Kantijois returned following his son's marriage, many people had already started to transport their luggage among other belongings. Thus, trouble came when he wanted to rest after the hectic schedule and commotion of marriage. A newly whitewashed house had to be vacated. It was a custom to consult the village purohit, when the village had to be vacated. Kantijois had engaged a poor brahmin Puttabhatta of the Yedatore region to look after minor rituals of purohitya of the village, and left the income from that to Puttabhatta. But now, Shanubhoga Shamanna did not consult either Kantijois or, in his absence, Puttabhatta. He took all the decisions by himself. From the very beginning, there was enmity between Kantijois and Shamanna. Besides, last year, a quarrel had ensued about water concerning wet fields. Since then, Shamanna had wanted to do something to vex Jois. So Kantijois decided to protest Shamanna's decision.

On the day immediately following the return of the marriage party, Kantijois performed the rites of *Kamboli* and finished the ritual of shaking the pandal symbolizing its removal. Channigaraya, Appannaiah and Saathu set out for their village on a bullock cart.

What should be done this Shamanna? His decision should be protested. But villagers had already transported their luggage, locked their houses and were moving to sheds after writing on their doors 'come tomorrow'. Nobody listened to Kantijois when he said, 'I have examined the shaastras. No harm will come upon our village, none of you need to leave the house.' Someone asked him, 'If that is so, would you stay back in the village?' Feeling challenged, he spoke in a fit of obstinacy, 'Yes, I will stay here.' He decided to stay alone in the deserted village to keep to his word.

Akkamma violently disapproved this decision: 'Granddaughter has come here for her first delivery. How can only one family live in this desolate village? We must also leave. If not I will send her to her mother-in-law's house. Let them say, "They have sent back the daughter having no means to take care of both mother and child." If need be, I too will go there and nurse the baby and the suckling mother.'

'I have boasted courageously that I won't leave the village. If I leave now, what happens to my reputation?'

'What sort of prestige is there in it? Come quietly.'

Kantijois did not agree to give up on his honour. After some more argument, it was decided that a shed be put in his dry field outside the village, that Akkamma and Nanjamma should stay there, and that the delivery and nursing of Nanjamma should take place in that shed. But Kantijois decided to stay alone in his house. Akkamma reiterated. 'From the very beginning, yours is a crooked mind. Why will you stay alone here? Shouldn't you also come with us?'

'I am a man, I'll stay here only. That plague Maramma can't touch a hair on my head.'

There was no other choice. Ajji and her pregnant granddaughter went to the shed along with their belongings. But Shamanna called for a panchayati order and brought upon a restraint on Kantijois that he should not visit his mother and daughter often in the shed, as he stays in the deserted village and Maramma resides in his body. That meant, that all the hardship of Nanju's delivery and nursing fell completely on aged Akkamma.

3

Only Kantijois remained in the whole of the deserted village. He sent a cow to the shed and kept another cow and calf for himself. He cooked his own food, and kept his home clean by sweeping and mopping it regularly. He would sit on the tiger skin placed on the floor of his house, read palm leaves related to astrology and meditate upon the power of mantras like 'Hreem', 'Dheem', 'Oom' and figures such as circles, triangles, squares and pentagons, or he would walk in the backyard chanting some mantras loudly. If he felt too bored, once in a way, he would ride on his horse towards far off Channarayapattana and then return.

He had never stayed in the village at a stretch in this way. Even now there was no need for him to stay. But because of the challenge of Shanubhoga Shamanna or of the villagers, who, without heeding his words, had deserted the village in fear, he stayed alone in that desolate village. It was not in his blood to be afraid of things like darkness, loneliness, thieves, robbers, murderers, snakes and lizards.

One day, a man came to that deserted village. About fifty years of age, the front portion of his head was shaved in the shape of an arch. A tuft of hair, white, was tied in a knot at the back of his the head. He had on a red shirt, a soiled black coat and wore a dhoti in traditional pattern. The empty space that once held two teeth in front of his mouth indicated the habit of chewing tobacco. There was a sorcerer's ring woven in golden threads on the middle finger of his right hand. Though he could not identify him at once, after a minute, Kantijois remembered and said: 'Oh! What, Veerachaari, you have come into this deserted village?'

'In the past two years, I have come nearly four times to meet you. But nobody knew whether you were in the village or not. Today, I came again just to see if I could meet you.'

'Come on, come, sit inside.'

Veerachaari came inside and sat. Kantijois had put four old chappals near his seat. Veerachari asked, 'Sir, do you believe in the power of old chappals?'

'Oh yes. If you take it in your hands, anybody will obey your words.'

'I didn't know that. It is said that old chappals drive away ghosts and goblins.'

'That too may happen. But I keep them for people.'

Talking for a while about some general matters, Kantijois asked, 'What business brings you here?'

'I just came. Two years ago, an incident had occurred. I had performed witchcraft for a man from Kattigehalli near Cholanagudda. It was a new moon day. Someone stole the money placed on *Chowdamma* as *dakshine*, and three bunches of bananas. I came to ask whether you know about this.'

'Doesn't a person who has learnt witchcraft, know that he needs to look at the shaastras by casting shells in order to find that out? Why do you ask me? Do I have more knowledge than you in interpreting the shaastras?'

'Shaastra or otherwise, nothing is required to find out who was behind this. As soon as I came again and saw the condition of the place, I knew. No one else has the power, the strength to digest bananas offered to her, break that Chowdamma I made and take the money placed upon her. Who else has gall enough to go there on a new moon night? At once I understood that around here, no one other than you has the guts to do this. Tell me the truth, joisare.'

'Oh, Achaari, you too have some sense. What, have you now come to claim that money?'

'Oh, let that money go to dogs. I don't want it. Hereafter, you should never set foot in a place where I have done something. I fold my hands before you, Sir.'

'Okay, I haven't started cooking yet. I'll cook a meal now for the both of us. Stay, finish lunch here and go.'

Veerachari stayed for lunch till four, then went away. That night, suddenly, Kantijois remembered his daughter. Perhaps the delivery date was close. 'I haven't gone to see her at all. Why should I be cowed down and stay here, without visiting her, just because that badmash Shamanna put a restraint on my movements through the panchayati? Tomorrow I'll go and certainly see my daughter. Let me see, what the hell is he going to do to me. This shed is located near our fields. I'll go before him openly. If he even snarls, I'll peel the skin off that motherfucking fellow. I did not go there until today and that was not right on my part. That Shamanna must have thought that Kantijois is scared of my panchayati, that's why he didn't turn up. Shamanna must be twirling his moustache at the thought. That whoreson's moustaches must be shaven clean with my urine! Jois thought, turning turned in his bed. By then he felt something fall on the tiles of the roof above his head. Again, within a minute, there was another sound of two stones falling on the tiles. A sudden thought passed in his mind—what if this was the handiwork of Veerachari? Then at once was heard the thud of around twenty to thirty more stones falling on the roof. Kantijois thought, 'There is no connection between Veerachari and this. Perhaps some from this village are doing this to threaten me. Let it be, I'll teach a lesson to these impotent bastards! He got up, opened the backdoor silently and went to the backyard. Silently, he jumped over the backside wall, and reached the neighbouring house, went onto the street and hollered: 'Who is that, you son of a whore, I'll kill you!' Four to five people began running helter-skelter. They were shaking with fear, when Jois roared again, rushed forward and caught one of them. The remaining managed to escaped.

Juttaga was the one caught by Kantijois. He was a tenant working on Shanubhoga Shamanna's wetlands. True, he was brave. But now he began to tremble with fear. Juttaga had heard that it was sure that Maramma living in the deserted village. He was unable to distinguish Kantijois and Maramma; he could not make out who held him and caused him to fall. In fact, Juttaga could not believe that Jois was not Maramma.

He folded his hands and said, 'Llleave mmme sssir!'

'Hey, who are you? Did that Shamanna send you?'

'Yes.'

'How dare you come here?'

'He said, that yyyyou will not be in the village.'

'Even if I am not in the village, from where did you get the courage to pelt stones on my home?'

'He said, if you don't go, he would throw me out of my land and tenancy.'

'Who are the others?'

'Gidda of Thimmakka's house, Gulliga from the upper-street and village watchman Siddura.'

'How did they have the nerve to do such a thing?'

'Shanubhoga said, if we did not do as he said, he won't recommend government lands for us at the *darkhast* price.'

'Okay. Do you want that your wife becomes a widow?'

'Please, I beg you ayya, do not cause that to happen.'

'Tell me, how are you going to survive, after pelting stones at my home?'

Juttaga stood trembling without uttering a word. Kantijois thought of going at once, pouring kerosene on Shamanna's shed and setting fire to it. But near Shamanna's shed, there was the shed in which Kantijois's mother and daughter were staying. The flames may spread to engulf that shed too; so he let go off that idea. Another question also rose in his mind: 'If a lesson is to be taught to that mean cur, it is to be done in broad daylight. He has acted during the night. So what difference is there between him and myself?' Juttaga still stood there with folded hands.

Kantijois asked, 'Did you go near our shed?'

'I didn't go inside. But I went near it.'

'How are my mother and daughter?'

'Nanjavva gave birth to a girl child this afternoon. Mother and child are doing well.'

Kantijois was happy and satisfied hearing this. He decided to go there tomorrow morning to see them. Besides, that Shamanna too had to be tackled. He said to Juttaga, 'Well, you can go now.'

But he remained without setting off. Kantijois asked, 'Why are you still standing?'

He said, 'I am afraid to go alone. Please, you must accompany me for some distance.'

'Vah re vah, you son of a whore! You were not afraid to come here. Now, when I ask you to leave, you want me to come with you? Will you leave quietly or shall I strike you on your back?'

'No, no ayya I'll go,' he said and walked rapidly more than two hundred to three hundred steps through the lanes and by-lanes to get out of that plague-stricken village. It took him much courage to leave the lane of Kantijois's house. All of a sudden, an agitated cry 'Ayyoayyayyappa' was heard, along with the sound of a man running from a distance. It was Juttaga.

As the front door was bolted from inside, Kantijois jumped the backyard wall, and went inside the house through the backdoor, just in the same manner he had gone out of the house. But he could not sleep immediately. Several plans and thoughts went round in his head regarding what was to be done to Shamanna the next day. Since his father's time, there had been hostility between these houses. Shamanna's father Narasimhayya had boasted: 'The job of a Shanubhoga is actually the work of the palace. He's the representative of the king himself.' This bastard also boasts like this—I'm a purohit. Is my profession lesser than his in any way? If he thinks his work is the work of the palace, it is my responsibility to provide guidance to the palace. Earlier, the folks at the palace used to threaten the purohits and pocket their money. But in my time, that has stopped.

Kantijois thought: If we live by obeying them, they like us and need us. But they cannot play with a brave Jois like me. Do they know what is meant by Kantijois? Kanti means Ranadheera Kanteerava. I am the paramour to all these palaces. I'll teach these important whore sons a lesson tomorrow. Kantijois went to sleep by dawn.

It was already ten in the morning when Jois woke up. He had intended to go to Shamanna's shed, and so went to the toilet to freshen up. By that time, he saw a constable standing before the house. As soon as Jois asked what the news was, he said: 'Your son Kallesha has contracted plague. A lump has been sighted in his left armpit; you must come at once.'

'What! Where?'

'He is in Belagola now. He is conscious. The Dafedar has sent me to bring you. When Kallesha went on his regular beat in the village, he was struck with Plague Amma. Come, move quickly.'

Jois couldn't talk; he was petrified. He went to the backyard, untied all the cattle in the cowshed, drove them out of the village and asked someone he met to drive the cattle to their shed. He locked his house, asked the constable to sit behind him on the horse and they went riding towards Shravanabelagola.

This time, the plague had not struck anybody in Nagalapura. All the surrounding villages lay devoid of people. Though Ramasandra villagers had put their sheds outside and vacated their village, three persons were already dead. It couldn't be said that Plague Amma had not received even one life as sacrifice. Juttaga, who had gone into the village at night to pelt stones on Kantijois's house and had been caught by him, developed a fever after some time. He told his wife that he had been to Nagalapura. When he returned alone from there, he felt as if a huge, black woman was waving the black-coloured edge of her saree at him. His temperature rose quickly and would not come down. By the evening, he was slightly awake. Soon he told his wife, 'You go to Kantappa Jois, ask him to perform some ritual or chant some mantra.' She sent her uncle to the village. As the door was closed and locked, Kantappajois's whereabouts could not be traced. The next morning too, the door was found locked. Juttaga gained consciousness once again and asked, 'Has Jois come?' When he realized he had not, Juttaga closed his eyes. He did not regain consciousness and died after two days. Nobody could ascertain whether the plague had developed in him or not. But is there a rule that a lump should emerge and be sighted, if Plague Amma were to strike and cause a death? Juttaga's wife became a widow. Juttaga had trembled, had begged Kantijois to stall this from happening. But no avail.

The afternoon following Nanju's delivery, Akkamma sent their tenant Honna to inform Kantijois about the safe delivery of a girl child and that both mother and child were well. Honna returned to say that the door of the house was locked. Gidda of Thimmakka's house, Guliga of the upper street, Siddura, the village watchman—none of them opened their mouths before anybody about their going into the village to pelt stones on Kantijois's house. So, Akkamma and Nanju did not come to know about any of this. As the cattle were sent to the shed, Akkamma understood that her son had gone out on some tour and had not yet returned. The village priest Puttabhatta's wife assisted Akkamma. Akkamma asked Puttabhatta to go to Ramasandra, inform about the birth of the girl child, and invite Channigaraya to come for the naming ceremony. When Puttabhatta hesitated about going there from a deserted village, Nanju, lying in the labour room, said: 'They would have also left the village. Our shed might be behind the shrine of the deity in front of the village, behind the red-wooded fig tree. Our groves are also there. You please go.' Puttabhatta travelled East.

Following the cleansing of the afterbirth in the shed, Channigaraya walked to Nagalapura on the tenth day. He could have taken with him Saathu and Appannaiah, harnessing a bullock cart. But now Saathu too was pregnant. She was still suffering from morning sickness. Besides, she was not on talking terms either with her husband or with Gangamma. One day, she retorted and returned all the abuses hurled at her by her husband and mother-in-law. From the beginning itself, she did not talk much with her brother-in-law. He too would not speak with her of his own accord. As such, Channigaraya set out alone for Nagalapura.

By eleven in the morning, he left Marulahalli, crossed Cholanagudda and Kattigehalli, and passed through Hoovinahalli. Clusters of ripe bananas were hung in a shop in front of the village. Channigaraya bought three bunches at three annas per bunch. He decided that these bananas could be put with betel leaves and areca nuts on a plate for the naming ceremony. He saw in that shop finely ground sugar in an open box. He bought a quarter seer of that too, tied it in a paper packet, put it in his bundle and started on his way.

A thought came to his mind while he walked the two miles to reach Nanjamma: *Nursing after childbirth meant oil bath once in three days, a ladle full of ghee for meals, some tasty and fragrant lehya, and always sleeping comfortably. But for me there is nothing. After 'she' went to Nagalapura, nobody has smeared oil on my body and bathed me with hot water. Doesn't my body ache? Akkamma—that old woman, Nanji's Ajji—she would prepare whatever her granddaughter desired for she was pregnant, and her granddaughter was a motherless orphan. Ajji would always attend on her. When Puttabhatta came to invite me, he said so. Did Ajji send anything to me? Did she send word like 'We are preparing this dish, please do come'? They should be slapped with my chappals.*

Channigaraya reached a banyan tree. He saw a pond at a distance of about forty yards. Without being aware, the Shanubhoga sat in the shade having put the bundle beside him. He thought: *Why should I take this pounded sugar and bananas to the house of those wretches?* As soon as the thought occurred to him, he opened the packet of sugar, peeled the bananas one by one, dipped them each in sugar, and even before chewing them, gulped, them one at a time.

After eating thirty-eight bananas and a quarter kilo of sugar, Channigarayaru felt thirsty. He drank water from the pond, put down his bundle by his side and using it as a pillow, snored away until evening. After waking, he walked towards Nagalapura hurriedly. It was not difficult to find the shed as Puttabhatta had explained precisely where it was. Akkamma was expecting Channigaraya to arrive anytime now and went inside to prepare a fresh meal for him. The food cooked in the noon had gone cold by then. Nanju lay down with the baby in the portion of the shed built for the nursing mother. When Channigaraya went near the door, she asked, 'Food prepared for you in the afternoon has become cold. Why did you sleep under the tree instead of directly coming here?'

Channigaraya was surprised to hear this. 'Who said so?'

'Shopkeeper Chinnayya of Hoovinahalli belongs to our priesthood. After you bought three bunches of bananas and a quarter seer of pounded sugar in his shop, he too started for this place for purchasing provisions for his shop. On his way, he saw you sleeping beneath that banyans tree, with peels of banana beside you.'

'Did he say so? Scoundrel...'

Nanjamma stopped him and asked, 'Why do you utter such abuse? You felt hungry on the way and ate fruits. Is it not what others do? Shouldn't you have come early and had lunch here?'

No answer came to Channigarayaru; neither did any abuse come instantly to his mouth.

With the assistance of Puttabhatta and his wife, Akkamma invited ten or twelve people for lunch and performed the naming ceremony. Shanubhoga Shamanna's family also attended the function. As the first girl child of the family, it had to be named after the grandmother Gangamma. But she was still alive. So, the child was named Parvati for the convenience it availed and also because it was in concurrence with the baby's birth star. Channigarayaru stayed there for eight days. Akkamma treated him with affection and served him hot meals. Copra and jaggery brought for the nursing mother appealed to his taste buds too. She would smear lime on betel leaf, fold it and give to Nanji's husband. Akkamma desired to prepare a variety of dishes for her granddaughter's husband. However, being an old woman, she was not strong enough. Moreover, she did not have the money to buy the required provisions. Nobody knew where her son Kanti had gone.

One day, Nanju told her husband, 'There is work for the Shanubhoga in the village. What will happen if you stay here for so long without informing even the Shekdar?'

He asked, 'Shall I send a letter to Shekdar now, informing the matter?'

'The time for revenue collection is drawing close. If you are not in the village, what will that Dyavarasayyanaru do? Besides, revenue collection is your responsibility, isn't it? Today is the fifteenth or sixteenth. Already the first rains have started. Shouldn't you see what has happened to the lands in the village?'

There was no other option for Channigaraya except to start for Ramasandra. So, the next day, he finished his breakfast, carried the packet of mango chitranna prepared by Ajji in a bark made of betel nuts, and set out. After he left, Akkamma asked her granddaughter, 'Nanju, why did your husband not even once hold the child close to his bosom? Is he unhappy because it is a girl?'

Nanju did not speak. Her eyes filled with tears. She did not speak out, though the words came on her tongue—'Even if it was a boy he would not have held it to his bosom.' She remained quiet and wiped off her tears as if she had not heard her Ajji's words.

4

By the time Kantijois came back, the tumour in Kallesha's armpit had swollen further and the pain had increased. The government doctor had prescribed him medicines and said, 'It is better if some expert treats him. But it will be difficult to transport the patient in this condition. I will do my best.' As soon as Jois reached there, he took responsibility for his son and said to the Dafedar, 'You engage a van for me. I will take Kallesha to Hassan.'

The Dafedar went to Channarayapattana, hired a van, came back, and then Kallesha was made to lie down in the van and taken to Hassan. There was the possibility of Kallesha dying on the way, but he did not. Doctors at the Hassan hospital admitted him. Ranganna, Kallesha's father-in-law, was serving as a postman for the last twenty-five years in Hassan. The doctor at the General Hospital and Ranganna were well-acquainted. The doctor put all the effort he could. He opened up the tumour in the armpit, squeezed out the pus, scraped away the rotten parts. He applied medicines and bandaged the wound. There was no danger to his life now. But Kallesha was weak and emaciated. The doctor said, 'Let him stay in the hospital for at least fifteen days.' So Kantijois stayed in his in-law's house and took care of his son.

Even by the day he was discharged from the hospital, Kallesha did not get control over his left hand, in the armpit of which he had developed a tumour. The doctor said, 'Let him stay in town. We will continue the medicines.' But Ranganna took his son-in-law home. Kantijois rode on his horse and set out for his village. His horse had grown feeble and ruffled in the twenty-five days during which Kantijois had stayed at his in-law's house. Kantijois's meals were provided by his in-laws. Although in a household like Ranganna's, who was a mere postman in Hassan, it was not possible to get the quantity of milk and ghee Kantijois was used to eating, nothing hindered the latter from getting a bellyful of the same. But from where could Ranganna gather fodder for Jois's white horse?

By the time Kantijois reached his village, even the hint of plague had vanished, and the surrounding areas had received two rounds of rain. The Nagalapura villagers had left the sheds and returned to their homes. Through rumours, Akkamma and Nanjamma came to know that Kallesha had been attacked by the plague, had been taken to Hassan, cured there and Kantijois had stayed on there to look after his son. So it was not possible for Akkamma to wait until Kantijois returned to move back to the house. There were farmers who worked on their lands to help them. Puttabhatta was there too. Akkamma decided to transport luggage with their help and take home the mother and the child. First, she went into the village, sent for the blacksmith and asked him to break open the lock on the main door of their house. She went inside and saw that rainwater had leaked from the roof, and the floor was totally wet and slushy. The strips of bamboo from the attic too were still wet from the leaking water. Without anybody having to tell her, it was clear to her that some mischievous individuals had pelted stones upon their house. Now, it wasn't the time to enquire who those were. Honna, the tenant, climbed a ladder to reach the attic and adjusted the tiles. He opened both the doors of the house so that air from the sides could help dry the floor. Yet, the floor had to be stamped upon and beaten down with fresh mud and sand. So Akkamma entered the house with the child and the nursing mother four or five days later than the other villagers. It had just been a month since Nanju's delivery. Akkamma did not allow her granddaughter to do any household work though Nanju insisted. Akkamma herself did all the household tasks from sweeping to dusting the house to milking the cows.

Four days after Akkamma and Nanju returned to the village, Kantijois came home riding on his horse at three in the afternoon. After informing them of Kallesha's well-being, his attention went towards the floor.

He asked, 'What's that? Why have you redone the floor? Was it that urgent?'

Akkamma said, 'Look, I don't know what happened. Somebody must've thrown stones on the roof; perhaps the eagles must've pulled out the tiles, or whatever. But rainwater had completely soaked everything inside, the floor was like a paddy field watered and ready for planting saplings. It was impossible to step inside the house. Only after finishing work on the floor could we transport our belongings here.'

'I'll teach that bastard a lesson! The bloody pariah, let him go fuck his mother.' Uttering these words Kantijois left at once. Neither Akkamma nor Nanju could understand what he was referring to or why.

It was the habit of some village chiefs to gather on the big platform in front of Shanubhoga Shamanna's house after lunch and play dice until evening or nightfall. Kantijois knew Shamanna would be there at this hour. He went there directly, climbed on the platform and asked, 'Hey, you badmash cheat, did you pelt stones on my house during the night? If you were half the man you are, you should have come in broad daylight. That too, you should have come when the village was full of people. Did you get what I said? I am a man, you bloody nincompoop, and know, I am your mother's paramour!'

It was not only with the unexpected arrival of Kantijois but also with this kind of unexpected proclamation of war that all the generals of dice were dumbfounded. Shamanna too was befuddled. Kantijois directly entered Shamanna's house, took the wooden pestle kept leaning against the wall near the stone mortar behind the door, held it in his right hand, and then taking hold of the bamboo ladder, came out to place it against the sloping side of the roof. Thereafter, he climbed on the tiles and began to strike them with the pestle. The tiles above the platform where the village elders were playing dice, were powdered by the time they had received four or five beatings. Then, Kantijois climbed to the upper part of the roof.

As soon as one blow of the pestle fell on the tiles above the platform, the people below got up and came out onto the street. Kantijois stood upon the roof, looked at them once, and thundered, 'Hey, you impotents, stand there! I'll make sure that your wives' heads are tonsured and they are left bereft of their *talis*.' Saying that he bent, took out two tiles and threw them towards the people standing below. The tiles hit two of them; blood dripped from one's hand and another's shoulder. They were stupefied and ran helter-skelter. Shamanna thought of climbing on the roof and teaching Kantijois a lesson. He too was strong enough. But his mind cautioned him. Climbing on the roof like that would be risky. By then, his mind was working on another strategy.

In less than half an hour, Kantijois pounded nearly ten thousand whole tiles. Then he slowly climbed down, put the ladder and pestle back in their respective places and came out. He stood before Shamanna's wife who came out on to the street, fearful, and stood with her children on the platform situated on the opposite side of the house, and said, 'Look here, sister, I tell you this, because you are Toobinakere Thammayya Jois's daughter. Thammayya Jois is equal to my Guru. When I was living alone in the deserted village, your husband sent his servants in the middle of the night and made them pelt stones on my house. But look at me, I've done this in broad daylight. Kanti means "a valiant man". Tell your husband, "Hereafter, don't act like eunuchs, act like a man." I don't want to talk to that bastard born to a paramour.' After saying this, he went back to his house. Shamanna's wife stood confused.

Reaching the house, Kantijois entered the kitchen. By then, the red mungesari rice in the pot, that Akkamma had put on the stove, was boiling. Close by, there was sambar in the tinned utensil Akkamma had brought from the neighbouring house. Jois went to the backyard, drew water from the well, filled two pots with that water and finished his bath. While bathing, he chanted the mantras of sandhyavandana loudly in his high-pitched voice, wiped his body and wore the dhoti. From the coconut shell kept near the niche of the space where the idol was kept, he took kumkum and applied it to the middle of his forehead. Then, he washed his hands and sat for lunch. A seer of perfectly boiled and very hot rice was ready. Whatever remained of the ghee from after being used on the nursing mother, was poured on it. The first time, the sambar and rice fully mixed and laid on the betel nut tree bark, was partaken off in three minutes. Next, the rice was mixed with pickles and oil. Then Kantijois asked Akkamma, 'Is the milk this cow gives enough for the nursing mother?'

'Oh, more than enough. I have stored one full container of ghee.'

'Well, while she completes the nursing period and leaves for her home, collect three, four containers of ghee and send it with her. Let her eat and live comfortably. Which of the castor seeds did you crush? Were they small or big in size?'

'She is a tender nursing mother. Who smears small castor seeds? She will catch a cold.'

'Well, did you celebrate the naming ceremony?'

'Yes, Channigaraya came. The child was named Parvati.'

By that time, Kantijois had finished the curd rice. Belching loudly he came into the room where the nursing mother was lying down and asked, 'Nanja, hand me over your daughter. Let me look at her.'

He took the baby, placed her on his lap and sat on the threshold of that room. The child was chubby, fair and excited. 'Nanja, she too is like you. Look at her forehead, how wide it is. What is her birth star?' he asked.

'Puttabhatta told the name of some star. He said that the horoscope should be written after Kantijois returns, that you write it more proficiently than he does.'

'It is all right; remind me tomorrow. Have you noted down the time of birth correctly? Well, give me some betel leaves; since morning I've not chewed tobacco.' So saying, he went into the kitchen holding the baby in his arms, and asked Akkamma, 'Amma, what did you do for the money needed to get pepper, ayurvedic medicines like lehya, etc., for the nursing mother? I had forgotten about you all for a while. Just wait...' Then he came out, took thirty rupees from his coat pocket and said, 'If you have taken any loans, pay them back. Hereafter, I'll stay in the village. After twenty days, I should go to Hassan; if Kallesha has recovered, I will bring him here.'

He chewed the betel leaves folded by his daughter, placed the baby back in her lap, put a little tobacco on his left palm, rubbed it with the right hand thumb, filled his mouth with it, went out five or six times, spat into the gutter, and then spread a mat, put a plank under the head, and slept for a while. In the evening, he went to the paddy field, came home, dined on hot rice, sambar and ragi balls and slept warmly.

5

It was midnight when somebody was heard knocking on the door. Kantijois woke up and asked, 'Who is it?' The answer surprised him, 'Your father-in-law's descendants. Open the door quietly.'

'Who the hell is that? You *haivan*, are your brains not working?' saying that, he loosened the bolt angrily and opened the door. Four police constables rushed forward and held his arms tightly. They did not let go of him even though he shrugged and tried to escape. The Dafedar whistled once. Two constables who were waiting outside the backdoor, came around the wall and joined these policemen.

When Kantijois asked, 'Why, why have you held me so? What for? What have I done?'

The Dafedar said, 'Whatever it is, you may ask in the station. Move now,' and proceeded. Meanwhile, Akkamma and Nanjamma woke up, came outside and began crying. Kantijois said, 'Akkamma, don't cry. This seems to be the mischief of that bastard Shamanna. I'll go to Channarayapattana and return. You shut the door while I am not here. If any dog comes, send it away hitting it with chappals.' He then set off in the police van which stood outside the village. The police van went towards Channarayapattana. Shamanna remained in the village.

When Kantijois had left for the paddy fields that evening, Akkamma learnt that her son had pounded the tiles of Shamanna's house and also knew the reason behind that. Now, that Shamanna had sent for the police and had made them take away her son. This made Akkamma intensely angry. In the middle of the night, she went off on her own and stood before Shamanna's house; then scooping balls of heaped mud from the street in her hand, she began to curse the winnowing mud: 'Ayyo, effeminate whoreson, let my shit be put in the mouth of your parents! Did you send servants during the night to pelt stones at our house, you impotent, widow's son? I had given birth to my son—a—man and put him in winnowing bamboo fan. That is why he came in broad daylight and pounded the tiles of your house. Scared of him, you went to the police? Have you worn a saree? Let your lineage become extinct. Let your children be destroyed and your wife become a widow. You see, your wife too will be tonsured and she will wear a red saree like me. What do you think the power of the curse of a widow who has lost her husband can do...'

By then, many people from the surrounding houses had woken up and gathered there. Everybody knew what had happened but nobody spoke openly. The door of Shamanna's house did not open. Remembering that Nanju was alone with the baby at home, Akkamma concluded her cursing with the choicest of another ten or twelve words and came home.

When they reached the Channarayapattana Police station, the Dafedar said to Kantijois, 'You stay the night here. Tomorrow morning, the sub-inspector comes and takes your statement.' But Kantijois did not agree. He argued forcefully, 'You send for him now in haste. Let him ask me whatever questions he wants to. I have not stolen anything or robbed anyone to spend a night at your station.' The police were afraid to silence him through violence. They had heard enough about this person. The sub-inspector came immediately. Shamanna was a Shanubhoga; that meant he was a government official. He had made a complaint that

Kantijois had not only broken the tiles of Shamanna's house, but also entered the house and carried away ledgers and account books from the Shanubhoga's office. It was doubtful if the police would have taken immediate action for breaking the tiles. But the complaint on which they could take prompt action was that of carrying away government account books. Shamanna submitted a copy of this complaint to the Taluk Amaldar also.

Kantijois gave his statement: 'I do not know anything. I did not go into his house. All this is false.' The following day too he gave the same statement before the Amaldar who was the local magistrate. The Police registered a case against him. But since the local municipality member had paid for a bail, the Police released Kantijois from their custody. After coming back to the village, he walked around all the streets in the village, twirling his moustaches and then came home.

Kantijois had often thought of catching Shamanna on the wrong foot, of crushing him. But he kept quiet thinking that it would not be wise to do so when a case was booked against him. Within a few days, he received a summons from the Holenarasipura court. He engaged the famous lawyer Venkataraya. For three months Kantijois travelled on horseback to Holenarasipura and Hassan.

On the day the witness was to be called for investigation, Kantijois had to meet his lawyer in the morning itself. He left his village in the night, rode on his horse, crossed Channarayapattana and upon reaching the tollgate, he realized there were floods. Now, at this time, floods were unexpected. But Kantijois had to cross the stream and reach Narasipura early in the morning. It was already midnight. It was a full moon day and the stream was in full flow with the floodwater engulfing the two banks. It was not possible to ride on the horse. He went to the travellers' bungalow near the bank of the river, woke the peon there and enquired about the floods. The peon said, 'Since two days, even rafts have not been allowed. The river has been overflowing.' But Kantijois could not stop. He told the peon to take care of the horse, gave him a rupee for expenses, and tied his cash bag containing silver coins tightly around his waist. He then removed his coat, shirt and shorts, tied them on his head and bound a towel around the head. Though the peon tried to prevent him from going any further, Kantijois went a little above the boundary and began swimming.

Nearly half a mile down, he finally reached the bank of the other side. Only his body and loincloth were drenched. A small portion of clothes tied to his head was wet. Thereafter, he had walked half a mile away, by which time his body dried. He wore a pair of shorts, a shirt and coat, and started walking rapidly barefoot. Only a distance of eight miles was left to be covered. He reached Narasipura by the time the cock crowed; then he finished his toilet, took a bath, completed the sandhyavandana on the river bank and reached the lawyer's house at daybreak.

There were two important witnesses on that day. One was Shamanna's wife. When the lawyer told her to touch the Nandi idol in front of the court and swear and say, if she lied her husband and children would die, all of Akkamma's curses came to her mind and she was in a state of half-crying. When the lawyer insisted that she tell the truth, she was scared, and at once uttered: 'It is true, Kantappa Joisru entered our house, took out the wooden pestle and pounded on the tiles. When the village was deserted, the man of our house sent Guliga, Juttaga and others to pelt stones on Kantappa's house. That is why Kantappa did this to us.'

Shamanna, who was present there, looked at his wife as if he would devour her. The lawyer on Jois's side asked her, 'Look here sister, tell us the truth. You have sworn on God. Is it not a lie that Jois entered your house and carried away account books of Shanubhoga's office?'

'No, he did not take the account books. I was there.'

It was reported later that after going back to the village, Shamanna beat his wife brutally.

The Police Dafedar of Shravanabelagola gave evidence in favour of Kantijois and said that on, that day, at three in the afternoon, he had been to Hassan and had seen Kantijois there. And Shamanna's complaint contrarily stated that on the same day and at the same time, Kantijois had entered his house and stolen the account books apart from breaking the tiles.

The Judge stated that the verdict would be delivered after eight days. That day, Shamanna too came, as did Kantijois. Sharp at one in the afternoon, the Judge read out the verdict: 'Complainant's wife herself says that the accused has not touched the account books of the Shanubhoga's office. Plaintiff had caused stones to be pelted on the accused's house. Perhaps to avenge it, the accused broke the tiles of the plaintiff's house. But the chief charge is that the accused carried away government account books. But during the time and the day as recorded in the complaint, the accused was in Hassan. Dafedar of Shravanabelagola has given witness that he saw the accused in Hassan at that time. Given this, it is observed, considering all the aspects, that there is no strength or truth in the accusation. Small quarrels might have occurred because of mutual enmity between the two. The case is dismissed.'

6

Kantijois had brought fifty rupees to pay his lawyer. He would have to give it to the lawyers at his house. The lawyer had some work in his office. Kantijois said to the lawyer that he would have his lunch in a hotel and then go to his house. Jois came out of the court, untied the horse that was fastened to the tree, rode on it and had gone for nearly a furlong when he saw Shamanna walking alone. Suddenly, his anger hissed.

'Hey, you, fucker...what hell of a difference did you make to my life by going to court?' he said. Then, mounting down his horse, he stood before Shamanna, who panicked. Jois took off his boot from his right foot and struck on Shamanna's head. Shamanna attacked him back but the force with which Kantijois struck using all his strength, made Shamanna bend. Kantijois struck him using his boots. Shamanna rolled down on the earth, blood oozed out of his mouth till he became unconscious. Kantijois had lost all his senses. But when Shamanna fell down unconscious, he got scared. Meanwhile, he heard someone shouting from a distance, 'Maybe, it is murder. Catch him immediately!' Kantijois looked back. The person shouting was the judge who had delivered the verdict on Jois's case. He said this to the constable who was accompanying him as his bodyguard. Suddenly, Jois began to sweat. The police rushed forward. Jois jumped on his horse like lightning and whipped it hard. If he was closer by even ten feet, the police would have caught him. By then, the horse leapt and galloped like an arrow. Jois did not even turn to look back.

Kantijois rode on the horse speedily on the motor bridge and turned to the path on a lower level. Rushing, squeezing into any path that he could find, he came near Baragur by the evening. He argued within himself: *The police have surely been following me. The state would have given an order to arrest the murderer, wherever he would be. The gallows are waiting. As the judge had himself been witness, no lawyer can do anything.* He decided, he should leave this state, though he knew that riding on this horse would be risky. A thought arose: Where should he leave this horse? He turned four miles towards the right, stopped the tired horse, drove it towards his village, Nagalapura, which was five miles from there. It was a familiar path for the horse. No matter which direction he took there, it would reach home; or if someone found him, let him rear the horse, ride it, Jois thought. From there, Jois took a left and went into a village he saw. He knew it was Bevinahalli. There was a shop there selling clothes. He bought a thick dhoti from there. From a grocery store beside that shop, he brought turmeric powder and a matchbox for one anna and left that village. He drenched the new dhoti in a garden well, squeezed the water out of it and rinsed out the starch. He then put turmeric powder on the dhoti. He took out lime from his box of betel leaf and betel nuts, mixed it with the turmeric powder and converted the dhoti into an ochre-coloured robe. Thereafter, throwing the dhoti over his head, Jois walked north. By midnight, the ochre robe had dried completely.

In a sandpit he came upon, Kantijois dug up a certain quantity of sand. He now wore the ochre robe, removed his shorts, shirt and coat that he had been wearing, gathered some dry leaves and sticks and set fire to them. After they turned to ashes, he covered it with sand and evened the surface. He tied the money he had with him into a small bundle and pocketed it in the inner loincloth. If he walks eight more miles, he will reach Arsikere. It would be risky if he delayed. He strode rapidly, reached Arsikere and enquired in the railway station about the next train. He was informed that a train would be starting towards Hubballi following daybreak. He waited in the station without fear, and set out at daybreak in that train. If the last border of the state of Harihara could be crossed, one would reach areas under the Company Government. Jois was sure that after crossing the state border, those bastards would not be able to touch a hair on his head.

7

Although treated with medicines and nursed continuously for eight months, Kallesha's left hand did not regain strength. The hand shook visibly and it was impossible for Kallesha to hold anything tightly or

S.L. BHYRAPPA

manage anything with his left hand. It was impossible for him to use the bicycle since he could not balance it using only his right hand. Besides, he could no longer continue his service as a police constable. Owing to unsatisfactory physical fitness, Kallesha was terminated from the job.

When he served as a constable, although it was the lowest level of job in the police department, Kallesha would display arrogance and exercise a kind of authority suitable for a highly placed government official. Now all this was a memory. There were the wetlands, the dry fields, the garden and house in his village—more than enough to live a life in comfort; if he could take care of this properly, he would not have much to worry about.

Meanwhile, Kallesha came to know that the Narasipura case had been decided in his father's favour, after which his father, in a fit of rage, had caught hold of Shamanna and hit him so hard with his boots that owing to the force of his blows, two of Shamanna's front teeth were broken, blood had poured down his mouth and he had become unconscious. In fact, Shamanna was not dead. The judge who had witnessed this had sent for a doctor. But, before the doctor arrived, Shamanna had regained consciousness. He had not agreed to file a case against Kantijois for the second time. By filing the case, Kantijois might have been forced to pay a fine or he might have been put in jail. But Shamanna kept wondering, what if after coming out of prison, Kantijois, as a means to avenge that insult, locked him in his house from outside, poured kerosene from above and burnt the house at night? Who in this village would protect this Shamanna?

Kantijois's horse reached home. Akkamma sent for Honna and asked him to tie the horse. Where did her son go; why did he go?—weren't known either to her or to Kallesha. In the meanwhile, Kallesha came to his village and began his treatment with the application of iguana's ghee to his left arm. He too had little information about his father's whereabouts.

By then, Kallesha's wife Kamalu had attained puberty. The families waited for six months, but there was no clue about where Kantijois was. So Akkamma said, 'Let us not wait for him. The ceremony consecrating nuptial vows must be performed and daughter-in-law must be brought home. It is not proper to sit tight.' An auspicious date was fixed for the ceremony after which Kallesha went to Ramasandra, brought his sister, her child and brother-in-law along. They harnessed a bullock cart and went to Hassan, along with Akkamma.

Kamalu did not give to her husband any opportunity at all to touch her when the couple were left in the room assigned for the first night. She spent the night stubbornly lying shrunk. Kallesha was not a man who had not seen a woman before, nor was he innocent. As he stayed in their house for seven months, he was well-acquainted with Kamalu. But now, neither did his enticing words and cajoling work on her nor did she utter a word herself. The next night, when they were together, she opened her mouth: 'It is impossible for me to come and stay in that damned village.'

Her desire was at once clear to Kallesha. But he was not in a position to do anything. He cajoled her, whispering, 'What if it is a village? There are two milking cows. There is no scarcity of milk and ghee, as is often the case here. Pulses, paddy and all other crops grow there abundantly. Everything comes in the form of donation and gifts in the village.'

'It is not possible for me to stay in a village.'

'I had a government job. My luck turned against me. What could be done? There are lands and that house in the village. Let us live happily looking after them.'

'Try to get some other government job,' she turned towards the wall grumbling.

'Let us see, when one department has certified me as medically unfit, it is doubtful if other departments will take me.'

'I don't know all that,' she said, and never gave her husband a chance to speak. Kallesha's right hand moved, ready to slap her on the cheek and make it swollen. But father-in-law's relatives were all outside the room. Besides, there were his Ajji, sister and brother-in-law too. He kept quiet, thinking it would not be proper to create a ruckus then.

Another factor that was weighing on Kallesha's mind was that his in-laws had nursed and served him all these days, keeping him in their house while he was ill. His father-in-law especially had taken such good care of him that he could regain control of his left hand. Kallesha felt that it would be a little unfair to cause him pain.

The next day when everyone was busy in preparation, for Kamalu's ensuing departure, she told her mother, 'I won't go there.'

'You shouldn't speak like that. People will laugh.'

Her mother did not say anything more than that. She thought, it was not unusual for daughters to speak in such a way while leaving for their in-laws' house, and kept quiet. Kamalu's parents, younger brothers and younger sisters came to Nagalapura in bullock carts. They all stayed there for four days, and after the feast and gift exchange, they returned. The same day, Nanju also left for her village with her husband and child.

That night, when Kamalu again said the same thing, Kallesha said, 'You have seen everything here; what is lacking in this house? Is there this amount of milk, curd, ghee, grains and greens in Hassan?'

'I don't know all that', she said, turned towards the wall and sat with his knees bent her knees.

As long as his in-laws had stayed, Kallesha had retained his patience. Now he could not control himself any more. He raised his hand and slapped Kamalu on her face. She began to sob. Kallesha had served in the police department, and as was habitual of him, he struck her on her back again and again. Akkamma, who was sleeping outside the room asked, 'What is this? What are you doing?'

'This worthless slut behaves as if I have never seen or enjoyed a woman,' he said while he brought his bedspread outside the room, placed it there and lay down. When he informed the matter to Akkamma, she went into the room and started to console Kamalu. 'Why do you speak in such a way? What do you think you lack here? Is there not enough to eat? You should not behave so stubbornly. We will not give you any trouble. Be happy here.'

She said sobbing, 'I cannot live in this damned, useless village.'

Akkamma did not know how to comfort her. She had had her doubts even before the marriage took place, about bringing this town-bred girl to this village. But without asking anyone, her son Kantijois had fixed this girl. However, what had to happen had happened. Akkamma felt that somehow the girl had to adjust to this life.

Kallesha, who was outside, said, 'If "that" girl behaves obstinately, you don't go about coaxing her. Just come back here quietly.'

Akkamma tried her best to reassure Kamalu and then went to bed. After a while, Kallesha was fast asleep too.

Kallesha woke up early in the morning, too his bath and had his breakfast, rode on his father's white horse and went to Shravanabelagola. A woman, his former acquaintance, lived in a nearby village.

CHAPTER FIVE

1

Saathu was pregnant. During her fifth month of pregnancy, her father came and took her to his house to have the baby delivered. Nanjamma too was pregnant again.

Dyavarasayya of Timmalapura, who wrote accounts of Shanubhoga's office, was more than sixty. It was becoming increasingly difficult for him to do Channigarayaru's work, as he had to also write accounts of the subdivision he was responsible for. Apart from the fifty rupees he received, Dyavarasayya had developed a certain affection for this house. He respected Nanjamma, the eldest daughter-in-law of this family, as a person. The others were all foolish in their own way.

One day, Nanjamma was home alone. Channigarayaru had gone to the temple opposite his house to listen to bhajans by Maadevayya, all the while chewing tobacco. Appannaiah had gone to Mata's house on the Fisherman Street and sat there smoking beedis. Gangamma had gone to have the oil from sesame seeds extracted from an oil-crusher who used to live opposite 'Ganigara' Eerakka's house.

Dyavarasayya said to Nanjamma, 'You see child, I am also aged. After all, I may only be able to write accounts for you people for the next one or two years. Our Channigarayaru did not learn to write accounts by himself. What will happen in the future?'

'You teach him properly, showing him one by one, Mavayya.'

'What's so tough in these accounts, my child? If he didn't learn even after staying three years with Honnavalli Seetharamaiah, it simply means that he'll never learn. During the time I'm here, I write the accounts. He leaves everything to me, roams around or snores away. But if he sits with me and writes, he might learn something. But then, he can learn only by practising the actual writing of accounts. All he needs to do is to ask me what he doesn't know. I'm more than willing to teach. Can't he even manage his own profession? How long does he think he can give money to others and ask them to write accounts?'

Nanjamma had thought about these matters two years back. But what could she do now? She said, 'Mavayya, you know my fate. You tell me what should be done.'

'Look here child, you know so well to read and write. I've seen your music book. Your handwriting is so neat, clear and beautiful. I'll teach you. You learn everything. You write everything sitting at home and give to Channigarayaru. And wearing the coat, tying the turban, let him go and conduct Jamabandi. If not, he will not prosper.'

'Can women write government accounts?'

Dyavarasayya too did not immediately know any answer to this doubt. He did not know what the government rule regarding this matter was. Yet he said: 'Look here, you are not going to take charge of Shanubhoga's post. You are only going to sit inside the house and write accounts. How will higher officers know whether it is written by a man or a woman? You simply learn.'

Dyavarasayya moved the book in which he was drawing the lines forward and said, 'Now, put rules on this. Look here, this ruler stick should come at an equal level to the red line of the heading. The ruler stick should be moved lightly with the fingers on the left hand. You should take care that ink does not jump out from the steel nib. Now draw them, let me see.'

Nanjamma drew the lines exactly as told by Dyavarasayya. Though not as fast as Dyavarasayya, the lines Nanjamma drew were straight and in the right place. He said, 'Beautiful! You draw the lines in the whole book. It will be good practice.' That said, he went towards the tank. It was a new experience for Nanjamma. She had drawn rules in her music book with the frame of her slate when she was a young girl. But now, with a ruler stick, that too to draw rules in a government book! She was feeling a sort of excitement. Besides, the first time itself she learnt to draw the lines without a mistake. She did hear Shanubhoga say, 'What is meant by the work of Shanubhoga? To draw the lines correctly one should bear beatings for at least six years from ruler sticks on the joints of fingers until they are swollen. Writing accounts can't be learnt free of cost.'

While Nanjamma was drawing the rules, Appannaiah came home. Looking at what his sister-in-law was doing, he was startled. He got very angry. He dashed off to Ganiga Street and said to his mother. 'See

Amma, she is ruining the account book.'

'Who is that?'

'Your elder daughter-in-law. She is drawing rules in the book.'

'What did you say? What is it! let her lineage be destroyed, that slut, widow of a donkey!' Shouting these expletives, Gangamma came running home in one breath. By the time she came home, Dyavarasayya had returned from the tank and was sitting on the platform preparing snuff. Daughter-in-law was drawing rules in the book, inside the house. 'You harlot, is your mind not right? What are you doing?' Hearing Gangamma's words, Dyavarasayya came in and asked, 'Why? What happened?'

'Can she touch the account book and do this?'

'Not like that, sister. I myself asked her to put the rules. I am not feeling well. Accounts should be completed under the stipulated time. Channigarayaru does not do anything at all.'

'Does anybody allow the account book to be touched by this slut?'

'Why do you utter such bad words, sister? Nothing will happen if she touches it.'

'It is the office of Shanubhoga my husband was managing once. What, may she touch the account book, Dyavarasayya?'

'Is she not daughter-in-law to your husband also? She is not any third person.' Meanwhile, Nanjamma let go of the ruler stick and steel nib, and went inside. Dyavarasayya called her and said, 'Nanjamma, why did you get up and go inside? Come, do your work; I've told your mother-in-law.'

Gangamma went to the temple and brought her son. By then, Nanjamma was again drawing the rules. Pointing to Nanjamma's work, Gangamma said to her son, 'Hey look there, your wife has started to do the work of the Shanubhoga, asserting the rights you have.'

Dyavarasayya volunteered, 'Look here, Shanubhoga, I am not feeling well. I've developed a backache sitting, drawing rules continuously. I never accepted that my duties would include binding books, putting rules and writing accounts. If you finish all these tasks, I will write the remaining accounts. Your wife draws rules neatly; her handwriting too is clear and beautiful. Now you allow her to do this or you yourself sit and do it. Tell me, if not, I will quietly leave for my village.'

Now Channigaraya was in a fix. He thought for a minute and said,

S.L. BHYRAPPA

'You ask this slut to do this. I must go listen to the bhajans.' That said, he went away. Scolding her son, Gangamma went to Ganiga Street. Appanna felt insulted to remain there and walked back to Fisherman's Street.

Dyavarasayya told Najamma: 'From the beginning, I know about this family, my child. When the first wife of your father-in-law died and he married Gangamma, he might have been more than forty years old. Your mother-in-law's mind always works in this way. Let her say whatever she wants. You learn the accounts and all other related tasks with interest and concentration. If not, this family will not survive. In the past, your father-in-law helped me in my difficult time. That is why I will teach whatever I know about accounts to you. You learn everything.'

2

Three months after this incident, the annual year-end accounts had to be completed. This was the most important of all the tasks the Shanubhoga's office was responsible for. If this was written without errors, there would be no possibilities of errors recurring in the coming years. Dyavarasayya told Nanjamma, 'Child, God has given you so much intelligence. Some of the people writing these accounts don't know what should be written on the left side and what should be written on the right, and write correctly, even after studying accounting for four years. Though you feel it is difficult, you write all this like I am teaching you. Afterwards, I will teach you how to prepare the annual year-end accounts.' Dyavarasayya entrusted Nanjamma with what she had to write and went to his village. She had to complete everything by the time he returned.

Nanjamma was six months pregnant now. Saathu had gone to her mother's house for delivery. In Ramasandra, one did not know yet if she had given birth or not. To have to finish all the household chores and then write accounts, sitting continuously, was too tiring for the pregnant Nanjamma. Gangamma was obstinate, refusing even to cook, saying, if this slut—being a woman—sits writing accounts like a man, why should she work?

One afternoon, after lunch was over, Nanjamma was writing. Channigarayaru and Appannaiah were sleeping in the same courtyard and were competing with each other in snoring. Gangamma sat near the door and was sifting green grams to prepare *usuli* for her night-time snack. Little Parvati was sleeping inside. That day, nobody had untied the cow, which was tied outside, and taken it out for grazing. None had bothered to put hay for the cow or kept water for it. The cow cried out aloud and began to go back and forth around the place at which it was tethered. There was a thud. Nanjamma called her husband, 'Did you hear that?' He did not wake up. Appannaiah turned aside. She called him and asked, 'Appannaiah, are you awake?'

'Yes,' that said, he pulled the sheet over his face.

'We have finished our lunch. But this cow, Gomaata, is starving. Couldn't you have taken it to the garden for grazing?'

'Umm...,' he again breathed loudly.

After ten minutes, Nanjamma said, 'Cows are to be milked twice a day. But nobody is taking care of that. If we are so lazy, how will God provide us with food to eat!'

Gangamma got angry at these words and asked, 'Hey, what is it you are barking?'

'I have not said anything wrong. The cow is starving and has been tethered to the post for long.'

'If you feel so, go yourself and take them out grazing.'

'Who is going to write the accounts here?'

'Aha ha ha, what a shrew. Because you write accounts, have you developed the arrogance of a Subedar? You thieving slut, are you affected with rut and dancing?'

After Kantijois suddenly absconded and the possibility of his return came to be severely dim, there was not a bit of fear in Gangamma about her daughter-in-law. Nanjamma had gotten used to hearing words like slut, widow, whore, etc.

Appannaiah awoke to his mother's shouting, but was angry because his afternoon nap had been disturbed. He turned and asked, 'What is it Amma?'

Gangamma said, 'Look, what she is ordering about—"I am doing the work of a Subedar, while you have eaten and are lazing here quietly... Get up, go, take the cows out to graze, go bastard."' Appannaiah was enraged; he sat up and asked, 'How dare you speak thus; where is your mind?'

'Amma, why do you speak such falsehood. Swear on God and say, did I say such a thing?' Nanjamma asked.

'Look, hey Appannaiah, should I swear on God? To speak lies what have I eaten? Ragi balls or shit? She called your mother a lying widow. What are you looking at, kick this slut!'

Even before Gangamma had completed her words, Appannaiah got up, raised his right leg and kicked his sister-in-law's back. At once, she rolled down on the floor. Again he raised his leg and was roaring, 'Look here, if you call my mother such names, I'll dig a pit and bury you in that.' By then, the police came from outside. They were wearing khaki trousers, khaki hats, boots, black coats and carried leather bags. That surely meant that they were police. Two more people like them came wearing khaki turbans, with leather bags, chains and iron rods among other things. Appannaiah is heart skipped a beat. Shouting 'Alas, Ayyayyappo, I am ruined,' he rushed out of the door and ran to the street. From there he rushed into the lane on the side, and seeing his speed, all the dogs of that lane started barking. Gangamma too was taken aback. She stood up trembling. Channigarayaru too woke up and sat still for some time, listening to Appannaiah shouting and running like that. The child inside began to cry. Nanjamma turned with difficulty, saw who came, and tried to get up, go inside and take her child in her arms. But there was severe pain in her waist, as if from a sprain or dislocation. By the time Nanjamma went inside with a hunched back, Channigarayaru got up and spoke with the individuals who had come, fearful and with respect, 'Mahaswami...galu please...do come in.'

'What? Are you Shanubhoga Channigaraya?'

'Yes, Sir.'

'Who was it who kicked that woman? Is it your younger brother?'

'She is my wife, sir.'

'Oh, then was he kicking his sister-in-law?'

'No, Sir.'

'What is this? Being a government official you are telling lies? Can't you look after your wife properly?'

Gangamma was sweating. The government people didn't say anything more. Channigarayaru spread a mat on the platform, requested them to be seated and himself stood with folded hands. At the same time, Gangamma slipped out of the house and went straightaway to Fisherman's Street. There she went to Mata's house and asked him where Appannaiah was. He whispered, 'I have concealed him in the attic amidst the bunches of fallen dried flower bunch of coconuts and betel nuts!'

Gangamma herself pulled a ladder, climbed up to the attic, came near her son and whispered, 'Did you see what the police have brought? They have brought chains as thick as rope. There is a rod as long as a crowbar. If at all you are caught, they will tie your hands with the chain and dig a pit with a crowbar; they may even hang you. Her brother Kallesha was a policeman. These people are from his side. You take to your heels from the garden side. Don't show your face here for five or six months. Go towards Javagal.'

Appannaiah opened his eyes wide and said, 'What will happen to me, Amma?' Gangamma said, 'Oh my child, start immediately. This slut with her wicked feet entered into our house, we became poor; we both have had enough! Look at our misfortunes.'

Appannaiah came out from in between the pile of coconuts and betel nuts, rapidly climbed down the ladder, came to the front door, peeped around, bent down near the fence by the side of a narrow lane of haystack, slipped into the backyard and ran away. Gangamma was looking through the chink in the backyard fence until her son climbed down the tank bund and vanished. Following this incident, she got a little courage.

The people in khaki who had come here were the government land surveyors. The revenue commissioner had ordered to prepare a new index of all agricultural lands in the state, and measure, according to the accounts of its tenants, their areas, forms and taxes. The surveyor who was appointed for measuring the lands had arrived at Ramasandra with his staff. His major task was to camp in Ramasandra for three months and measure the lands of the surrounding villages. It was the responsibility of the Shanubhoga to give him every kind of assistance possible, arrange for his stay, and provide him with help from the village watchman, servants and others.

3

Akkamma herself came in a bullock cart to take Nanju home for her second childbirth. Now Kallesha's left hand was better. Clasping the tree between both hands he could climb the coconut tree and work a little in the fields also. He still couldn't get a government job. He did not desire it also. However, whether it was because of Kamalu not being able to adjust to village life, or her nature itself, there was no peace and happiness for Ajji and her granddaughter.

When Nanju came home for the delivery, two-and-half-year-old Parvati too came with her. Kallesha was fond of the child. One day, when Kallesha went to work in the paddy field, Kamalu uttered loudly as if speaking to herself, 'Is it all right to get pregnant in quick succession, like sows? Why should one become pregnant when people from the husband's side are not capable of taking care of the nursing mother and child? They are assured that people here will take care of the maternity expenses, so they become pregnant. However much our blood is sucked, it is not sufficient for them.'

Nanju heard these words. She thought: *I did not get a good mother-in-law; and likewise, I could not get a good sister-in-law. It is my fate. Seven months are still left to go. I have to stay here for another five to six months till the delivery and then another three months after the baby is born. It is better to leave this place quietly and go to my village. But there, I have to endure mother-in-law's harassment. She will not let me be without pricking and taunting if I return before the delivery and nursing period. And my husband? Would he speak even a word in favour of his wife? I have only to curse my luck.* Warm tears trickled down her eyes.

Akkamma also heard Kamalu's words. Till then she had kept her patience, but looking at the tears in her granddaughter's eyes, she was enraged. She went to Kamalu and asked, 'You—who do not have even the capacity to become pregnant, though it has already been a year you came following the consecration of nuptial vows—why do you call her a pig? No water in the pond, no child in the belly; how can the womb be fertile in a sinner like you, tell me?'

'Hey, you old woman, if your grandson goes and sleeps with depraved whores and sluts, how can the wife at home get pregnant? This kind of lecherous whoresons could take birth only in your house.'

'Don't talk shamelessly, you slut of an ass! If you could learn to sleep with your husband properly, why would your husband go out for it? Were you even born amid species of respectable females?'

From these words, Nanju came to know matters she had not. Yet she came near Akkamma and said, 'Akkamma, please speak at least in a low voice. What if the neighbours hear these things?'

'What about neighbours! Everybody in the village knows the story of this harlot. She ruined the honour of our family within the month she came here. Whenever she goes to the tank for bringing water, she spreads scandals on everything concerning our home among the people here. If only "it" was a woman born and bred in a respectable family.'

'Hey you, old widow, do you abuse my father's family? You will earn punya if you bathe in the pit of our gutter.'

Nanju took Ajji inside saying, 'Akkamma, come inside, don't speak any further.' Again, she came to the courtyard and said to her sister-in-law, 'Sister-in-law, why can't you be a little patient? If matters of our house are known to others, they will make fun of us and laugh behind our backs.'

'You have come here for giving birth to your baby; there is a dearth of ragi balls in your husband's house. Don't come to advise me; you go.'

Nanju went inside quietly. Kamalu went into her bedroom, lay down on her stomach on the mat just like Kaikadevi[5] lay down in the chamber of anger. Kamalu rummaged through her hair until it became dishevelled, erased the kumkum, and puffed her face up still more. Nobody spoke to her.

By one in the afternoon, Kallesha came home and took his bath. He did not notice Kamalu's absence. But how could Kamalu keep quiet? She began grumbling abuses from inside. His attention turned towards her.

He stood near the half-opened door of the room. Her grumblings, which had the speed of at least a hundred words per minute, were heard clearly: 'Let these bastards' house be ruined. Let their lineage be destroyed. Let their house be swept away and annihilated. Let all these bastards die struck by plague. Slut sons, slut sons, slut sons, widow, widow, widow, widow's sons...'

Kallesha had come home after a very long day of toil at the paddy field. He asked, 'You whore, who is it that you are abusing?' Chanting, as if a mantra, of 'slut sons, slut sons, slut sons, slut sons', she joined both her hands, cracked the joints of her fingers while cursing, making the sound of a chain of firecrackers. Kallesha roared, 'You mean fellow, sister-fucking whore,' and raised his hand to punch Kamalu on her back.

She turned her face and said, 'You widow's son, did you hit me? Just as your left hand has shrunk, let your right hand shrink too. What

---

[5]The reference is to Kaikeyi from the Ramayana.

do you think my curse means!' Another punch fell on her back. She continued in the same breath, 'You vile fellow, you devoured all that was given to you for eight long months at my father's house, laid up with sickness. How could you raise your hand to hit me? Let worms infest your hand!'

By then Nanju came there running. Child Parvati started crying in the kitchen to the sound of the beatings. Nanju pulled her brother's hand and said: 'My dear brother, my Annayya, do you have any control on your brains or no? Could anybody beat his wife like this? If something untoward happens, what will be the consequences? Come quietly and have your lunch.'

'You leave my hand, I'll put an end today to this diabolical sister-fucker,' he said, and shrugged his hand away.

Kamalu, who had been lying down like a bow, got up, as if plucked out of its bowstring, turned her back towards him and challenged, 'What? Do you want to hit me? Bloody fellow! Go on, hit me, hit me till you break your arms. Today I am going to send you to the gallows. Today is the final day. Come on, hit me!'

Nanju began to pull her brother's hand, holding it more firmly. She too was a strong woman. Kallesha was no less strong. Both were Kantijois's children. She did not let go of his hands, but then, Kallesha raised his left leg and kicked Kamalu on her waist. She fell. 'You sister-fucker! If you do another vile thing, I'll teach you...,' he said and went out of the room. She shouted from inside, 'I'll send you to the gallows.'

Kallesha sat inside and was partaking of his lunch. The incident that happened today was not new in that house, but today it had crossed its limits. Not knowing what to do to control Kamalu, Kallesha silently broke a ragi ball, rolled it into the sambar and swallowed it. Nanju had not accompanied him at lunch. She said, 'I will take my lunch afterwards,' and was washing clothes in the backyard. Akkamma was filling water into the vessel in which she would be kneading the ragi flour, to wet it. Suddenly, Nanju shouted from the backyard, 'Annayya, come, run! Sister-in-law fell into the well!'

'Ah, what the hell has she done!' Kallesha uttered and, in a single stride, rushed near the backyard well. Akkamma too came running, straightening her bent back as best as she could. With the rope that was nearby, Kallesha lowered himself into the well and told Nanju to hold it tightly. Nanju held the rope tightly, supporting her legs on the structure of the well.

Kapinipatayya's wife from the neighbouring house had heard Nanju's shouts. Telling her husband 'Kamalamma fell into the well, hurry, you go,' she too came, running. Kapinipatayya too came adding to the clamour. Hearing this, all the neighbours gathered. Rumour spread like lightning and people from the neighbouring streets also collected.

In the well, Kamalu came up to the surface once and then went in again. When she came up the second time, she began to wave her hands asking to be saved. She did not fall into the well with the intention of dying. She attempted this to achieve the purpose of sending her husband to the gallows. But once she drowned and rose above the surface of the water, her desire to live and the fear of death filled her mind and she yelped for help. Before she was heard by Nanju, the water dragged her inside the second time. Again, letting her drink water, Gangammathayi—mother-water—lifted, her giving her a final chance. Kallesha held Kamalu's braid firmly. By then, Kapinipatayya and others had gathered above. Kallesha shouted from the bottom of the well, 'Pull the rope a little.' He held the rope with his left hand and Kamalu's braid was in his right hand. Now he had come above the water, which rested lower than the level of his chest. Kamalu's shoulder touched the rim of the water in the well. Kallesha's left hand did not get enough grip, and that hand did not have strength enough to sustain her weight for a longer period of time. He searched for hallows that were left to get down into well, put his legs there, and stood firmly. Kamalu started to gabble. 'Ayyayyappa, I feel scared! Pull me up, fast.'

Meanwhile, the people who were standing above, brought a wooden cradle, tied it with a strong rope and lowered it slowly into the well. Lowering it closer to the water, Kallesha raised Kamalu and seated her in the cradle. When he shouted 'pull the rope', she began to gabble 'Ayyayyappa, I feel scared, I don't want to sit here.' Kallesha thought, 'When the cradle would be moving upwards, if she leaps and dances like a monkey, falls on me standing down, I would not survive her force.' So he untied his dhoti and tied her with it to the frame of the cradle. He took off his undershirt and wore it as a loincloth. The cradle went up slowly. Sitting in the cradle, tied with nine cubits of dhoti and pulled by four men, Kamalu came up like Gowramma on the day of the Gowri

S.L. BHYRAPPA

festival, from inside the well, as if it was a village that had no tank.

Kallesha too climbed up behind her. Kamalu's stomach was swollen, for she had swallowed a lot of water. Her eyes were red out of fear, alarm and shame. Besides, blood trickled from her shoulder, back, and a side of her head; she had brushed against the inner walls of the well when falling from above. Kallesha made her lie down on her stomach and slowly pressed her waist. Water gathered in her stomach, came out of her mouth. He ground some leaves of lantana shrub, wiped out the blood and smeared the paste on the wounds. Kamalu started screaming.

Kallesha turned towards the villagers gathered there and said, 'What work do you have here? You can all return to your homes.' But people stood without leaving. Kallesha, Akkamma and two men from the neighbouring houses drove them away.

Kapinipatayya's wife, Puttamma, said, 'Give her a cup of hot coffee.'

'Coffee, why? It is an utter waste for this one born of a slut. Let the bloody cobbler screw her mother...,' that said, Kallesha went in to wear a dhoti. As he had worked in the police, he had learnt to drink coffee, but he did not have the habit of drinking it every day. But Kamalu, who lived in a town like Hassan and was a daughter of a postman, how could she be without coffee even if she currently lived in a village? They had coffee powder at home. Nanju went inside, prepared a cup of coffee and gave it to her sister-in-law. Kamalu sipped once, put the cup down on the floor and said, 'Tut-tut, these stupid villagers, do they know how to make coffee? If they had drunk it ever...,' Kallesha heard this. He came near her, took the cup and poured the coffee on her head. Kamalu did not open her mouth again. He went inside.

Akkamma said to Kamalu, 'Get up and change your saree.' The two men who were present, went inside and now there were only women. Kamalu did not get up and neither did she change her wet saree. With her hair all wet and rumpled, she sat stubbornly near the well.

Kamalu did not dine that night too. Kallesha finished his dinner. Akkamma forced Nanju to eat something since she was pregnant and served her food. Nanju refused to eat. As a tonsured widow, night meals were a taboo for Akkamma. Moreover, she was aged and could not digest food if she ate any at night. Since ten years, she had stopped eating snacks at night.

Kamalu lay down in her bedroom that night. Kallesha suggested to

Akkamma and Nanju that they lie down adjacent to the front and back doors of the house respectively. He, with his experience in the police department, suspected that Kamalu might get up in the night and again attempt to fall into the well. Since Akkamma and Nanju would sleep near the doors, it would not be possible for anybody to open the doors and step out. Kallesha spread his bed near the door of the room and tried to sleep, but could not. Several thoughts haunted his mind. He got angry at his father for fixing such a girl to him. Besides, memories of many outsiders came. After a long time, he fell asleep.

Suddenly, though, he awoke. He thought he saw a light in the kitchen. When Kallesha raised his head and looked inside the room, Kamalu was not there. He quietly got up, stepped like a cat noiselessly towards the door of the kitchen and saw that she was sitting before the oven, her hair still dishevelled. A small lamp was burning in the niche of the wall where the deities were placed. It seemed she was eating something. He took another step forward and saw that she, who had adamantly refused dinner at night, was now devouring whatever was left. She had poured sambar into the vessel containing rice and there was the pot of buttermilk beside her.

He returned as silently and lay down. Just like today, there were several occasions when Kamalu had obstinately refused to dine. But after everybody slept, she would finish her dinner in privacy, and, pretending ignorance, would come and sleep. Next morning though, she would continuously grumble, crack the joints of her fingers and curse, 'The whole night they made me starve. Let your house be ruined!' The rice, that would be left over from the previous night, would have vanished by morning. That was ample evidence for Kamalu's secret mischief. But today Kallesha saw this with his own eyes. He was thinking that he should get married a second time and kick away this wicked woman when there was a sound outside, either of a bus or of a car—which was it? For whose house? While he was still thinking, people got down from a car and knocked on the door of Kallesha's house. He got up, lit the lamp, awakened Akkamma who was sleeping by the side of the door, and opened the door. It was his parents-in-law and four of their other relatives; who the could driver was though, Kallesha did not see. He was surprised to see them at that hour.

'How is Kamalu?' Kamalu's mother came in sobbing.

S.L. BHYRAPPA

Kallesha said, 'Go and see for yourself in the kitchen.'

When she went there, Kamalu was not inside. There was the smell of a lamp that had just been extinguished. Fie, where did she go? When he went inside the room, he saw that she was lying on her stomach on the mat, eyes closed, as if she had not gotten up at all.

'Look here, when you came, she stealthily devoured rice and sambar in the rice vessel itself. Now putting out the light, she has come here and is sleeping as if she does not know anything. Come and see for yourself,' he held the lamp in his hand, took them in and showed them.

His father-in-law asked, 'Leave that now…What happened? Are you all in good health?'

Former police constable Kallesha asked, 'Why have you come now? What's the matter?'

'You yourself sent news through someone, who called us to say that Kamalu had fallen into the well.'

'Oh yes, yes…who telephoned you, by the way, tell me…I forgot in this confusion.'

From inside the room, Kamalu suddenly shrieked, 'Why does it matter to him, whoever it is…'

However, everybody knew that it was she who had sent news through someone, asking that person to phone up her parents. But who it was that had worked in her support, was not known. Kallesha did not rake the matter up further for it would not be difficult to find out. He went to the neighbouring house straightaway and knocked on the door. They too had been awakened by the sound of the car. Kallesha brought Kapinipatayya and Puttamma home. Likewise, he awakened the people from another neighbouring house, brought them along too, and started to speak: 'If we speak, you may think it is a lie. You ask these people. Kapinipathi uncle, you tell these people what the matter actually is.'

The neighbours did not speak on their own accord. Kallesha narrated what had happened. He said he beat her but did not say he kicked her. Neighbours opened up and conceded, that what Kallesha said was true. Yet Kallesha's mother-in-law spoke, 'Yet, we have sent our daughter to your home here in this village. We have brought up our daughter affectionately. You too must adjust.'

However, the postman Ranganna, Kallesha's father-in-law, did not raise his bowed head. Kallesha asked him, 'Now you tell me. Who was the bastard that phoned you?'

'Lies won't come from my mouth. The call came from Channarayapattana. From the electric camp there, they spoke to the Hassan camp. They said, "Postman Ranganna should be immediately informed." I go there daily for the delivery of letters. I am well-known there. The electric foreman came and informed me of this matter. He said, one Kallesha by name, phoned. Wondering what misfortune might have befallen our daughter, we arranged a car, renting it for twenty-five rupees, and rushed here.'

'However, you have come now. There is the car too. Your daughter feels too bored. Take her with you.'

At once, the mother-in-law said, 'Yes, let her come and rest for a few days.'

But father-in-law immediately said, 'No, no, when husband and wife have quarrelled, we should not take our daughter home. Both should come when they are happy.'

His wife said, 'What obstacle might there be to take our child with us?'

The husband said, 'What do you know? You be quiet! Not at this time.'

For the first time, Kamalu got up from where she had been lying down, came out and stood beside her mother saying, 'Certainly, I will come.'

She disliked what her father had to say to that: 'Look child, you heed what I say. You should not come now.'

He thought he should not delay further and got up. To those that had accompanied him till here, he said, 'All of you get up, go sit in the car. We should start at once.' He urged them to hurry. His wife was repeating, 'Our daughter...', to which he said: 'All my life, I have obeyed you, and this is the result. Now, you shut up.' Everybody sat in the car. Kamalu tried to squeeze herself into car stubbornly. But Ranganna himself held her hand and did not allow her to stay. Nanju came running and held the kumkum before her brother's mother-in-law. The driver, who understood the situation, started the car and moved it forward. Nanju heard Ranganna saying, 'Twenty-five rupees...a sheer waste...one month's salary. From where will I earn back such an amount of money?'

The car stopped after going some twenty or twenty-five yards.

Ranganna called, 'Kalleshanna, come here please.' Kallesha came and stood beside the car. His father-in-law climbed down, held son-in-law's hands and said, 'Do not be angry. Even if a wicked cow is brought, it should be allowed to graze, be managed. Do not think of her. Look at my face, think of me.' When he said these words, tears fell from his eyes.

The wife asked her husband, 'What is it? You behave like a child. What wicked deed has she done?'

'There is no use speaking,' that said, the husband again sat in the car. The driver quickly moved the vehicle forward.

The neighbours went back to their houses and slept. People in Kallesha's house too slept off. Though there were matters piled as high as a mountain, they could not be talked about. 'She is a shrew like the thorn plant,' Akkamma said four times. Nanju, as usual, was silent. As Kallesha too kept quiet, Akkamma did not get any opportunity to speak. Father-in-law's tears on his hands impacted Kallesha's mind deeply. When he was struck by plague, his father-in-law had nurtured him and taken care of him like he was a child. Kallesha had developed a respect towards his father-in-law, his character, and his heart felt that sentiment deeply. The thought to simply get up and break his wife's back was gathering strength in his mind. But his father-in-law's tears bound him and made him lie back down on his bed.

CHAPTER SIX

1

After nearly six months, one dark midnight, Appannaiah knocked on Mata's door on Fisherman's Street. Mata came out, saw him and asked, 'Where did you run away *saami*⁶?'

'Are the police searching for me?'

'What police, saami?'

'For what happened, that day...'

Now Mata remembered everything and said, 'They were not the police. They were land surveyors who had come to measure fields. They stayed in our village for three months. Why did you hide for so many days, saami? Your amma was worrying about you, wondering where her son had gone.'

'If so, shall I go home?'

'Yes, go at once, saami.'

'You also come with me. I am scared.'

Accompanied by Mata, Appannaiah knocked on the door of his house with half courage. Gangamma shouted from inside, 'Who is this fellow knocking the door at this hour?' Mata answered her query. Lighting a kerosene bottle lamp, Gangamma came out. Looking at her son, her eyes filled with tears and she said, 'Oh my child, where had you gone for so many days? Where all did you wander, being scared of that unlucky slut?'

Mata came in and sat down. Nanjamma had gone for childbirth to Nagalapura, and Channigarayaru was fast asleep and would not be awakened so soon. Gangamma enquired where her son had been and what he did for food and shelter.

Her hero-of-a-son narrated the story of his adventure: 'I was not scared. I managed well everywhere. From here I went towards Javagal. On the way, I went to Bidare Sannegowda's house and said, "We are brahmins, please get us provisions for cooking." He gave two seers of rice,

---

⁶The word 'Swami' is pronounced here as 'Saami' which means 'Sir' or 'Master'.

avare dal, chilli powder, butter and other things. I cooked, had my lunch, packed the remaining provisions, and then headed to Javagal. I stayed there for a month. It is there that that coquettish slut, Venkataramu's wife, lives. She asked me why I had come now, how you all were in the village, why you all didn't come, etc. One night, I started from there and set out towards Arsikere. Then wandering, I crossed Banavara, Kadur and went to Shivamogga. There, on the bank of the river, is a mutt called the Bekkina Kallina Mutt. I put up there.'

'What did you do for food?'

'People of that mutt taught me. They were lingayats, I was not supposed to have food there. In that town, there is Dodda Brahmins street. Affluent people live there. I used to go out for bhikshanna every day there. Amma, whatever you may say, with no matter how much care you prepare your food, no food is as tasty as what you get through bhikshanna. I would bring rice in the square cloth bag hung upon my shoulder and a pot full of sambar. I would wash clean a boulder near the river bank, pour everything on it and devour it with relish.'

Mata asked, 'What does bhikshanna mean?'

Appannaiah answered: 'At meal times, we have to go, stand before every house and say "Bhavathibhikshamdehi".' Then people will put rice into the cloth bag, put rasam, sambar, curry, gojju and all into a metal vessel. Then we mix everything and eat. Do you know how good and tasty that is.'

'Why won't it be tasty? Is there not a proverb, "Sambar of several houses is tasty; the daughter of an adulteress is beautiful?"' His mouth watering, Mata smacked his lips.

'Amma, I am bored eating only rice in that dammed Shivamogga. Cook some ragi balls for me, I feel hungry,' said Appannaiah.

'What? At this hour?'

'I've not eaten anything tonight.'

'If any of those sluts were here, I would have asked them to get up and cook. But nobody is here. Appannaiah, your wife gave birth to a girl child. They had come to invite us to the naming ceremony. Perhaps, it is four months now. Go and bring her. I am fed up and tired of cooking.' That said, Gangamma got up.

Appannaiah walked courageously with his head held high in the village for four or five days and then started for Nuggikere to bring home his wife and child. He set out with a bundle of roti and chutney on his shoulder, walked sixteen miles to Tiptur, and went to Kadur by train; thereafter, he walked nine miles from there and reached his father-in-law's house. The baby had already completed four months, and was named Jayalakshmi.

It was evening when Appannaiah reached the place. Saathu was still in the nursing mother's room. He went inside, took the child in his arms and caressed her. He spoke to his wife too. After dinner, a bed was laid out for him near his father-in-law's bed. When he sat on the bed with a dull face, his father-in-law asked, 'I sent an invite for you for the naming ceremony. Where had you gone then?'

'To Shivamogga...no, to Javagal.'

'Didn't you know it would be time for your wife's delivery? What was so important, that, without informing anybody, you left your place?'

'There was some work.'

Saathu shouted from the nursing mother's room, 'What sort of momentous work did you have? Why do you utter such shameless lies? Tell the truth. You kicked your sister-in-law and then absconded out of the fear that the police might arrest you, didn't you?'

Appannaiah did not answer. He sat with his head bowed. Saathu asked, 'Your mother said "kick her" and you kicked? Unless that damned worthless woman dies, you won't learn anything.'

Appannaiah was immensely angry because Saathu was abusing his mother. But it was not the right time to display his anger. Besides, Saathu was not a docile woman like his sister-in-law. So he kept quiet. Saathu continued from inside the room, 'I don't want the company of or any sort of association with your mother. There is an empty place in the backyard of your house. Build a small outhouse there, arrange for us to stay separately. After that, come and take me and the baby.'

Trying to clear his throat, Appannaiah asked, 'How is that possible?'

'Why is it not possible? You build a small house for us. You brothers divide the things. Utensils and other things needed to run a house are there, they were given in my marriage. If it is not enough, I'll bring some more.'

He did not utter a word even now. Saathu continued, 'I don't want you both to be living apart from each other. You brothers be together. I'll stay with my sister-in-law. But your mother should live elsewhere. You build for her a pent-roof and send her out. After that, you come— take me and the child.'

Appannaiah got angry at Saathu abusing his mother again. He frowned. Having noticed this, his mother-in-law said, 'Saathu always says that our Appanna is a very good person by nature. He is as good as gold. But mother-in-law and daughter-in-law won't get together. You live separately. If need be, Saathu will help in your mother's house too.' Now his face began to light up a bit.

Finally, the father-in-law said, 'However, it is important that husband and wife must live with mutual affection and love. You should not be uttering words like widow, harlot, slut, etc., as soon as you wake up in the morning. To sum up, you make the arrangement for living separately and then take your wife and the child. Saathu is our only daughter. There is no other sibling.'

Appanna stayed in father-in-law's house for eight days. He did not abuse his wife verbally during that time and would fondle the child happily. However, all of them felt awkward at his sudden bursts of anger, irritation, roughness and arrogance triggered by no reason whatsoever. One day, he was peeling a coconut husk; the shell was hard and would not come off easily despite the fact that he was pulling hard at it. Appannaiah quickly uttered, 'Fuck its mother!' Another day, when a cow in the shed brandished its horn, he said, 'Ayyo, fuck whoever begot her!' Mother-in-law, who was close by, heard it. She knew it was not easy to mend him. She sighed, thinking about the fate of her beloved daughter.

On the day of Appannaiah's departure to his village, Saathu once again asked him to make separate living arrangements and made him say 'yes'. Appannaiah walked to Kadur, from where he reached Tiptur by train. He had to walk another sixteen miles from Tiptur to his village. Though the Mudaliar Company had started a bus service, it was running only on alternate days—Mondays, Wednesdays and Fridays. Appannaiah had already enjoyed the excitement of travelling on it once. He was not scared of travelling in it at all. When he had travelled alone by train, what was there to be scared of a bus? But it was a Friday evening. There was no bus service the following day and on the day after. It was difficult to walk, but the happiness of the bus journey was lost.

Since it was already evening, he stayed back in Tiptur. He consumed a sumptuous dinner comprising rice, sambar made of onion and potato, brinjal curry, papad, rasam, curd, and other condiments. All of this for just six annas. He slept on the platform of a choultry, a hall for conducting auspicious ceremonies like marriages. At daybreak, he went by the village tanks, to relieve himself, revisited the same hotel and ate masala dosa. He had eaten masala dosa for two days while in Shivamogga. But that was not as tasty as this. Green chillies, coriander leaves, potato curry with onions and coconut chutney were stuffed inside the dosa. He finished the dosa, which was a little hot, smacked his lips and ordered for six more. Served hot, he ate them all paid a total of seven annas and walked towards Ramasandra, taking a shortcut. Within two miles of walking, he felt thirsty. *What the hell! Eating those dosas has made me thirsty*, he thought and then his eyes fell upon a coconut garden on the right side of the road. There was nobody there. He squeezed himself slowly through the fence, went inside the garden and plucked out three tender coconuts from a small tree. Then he pierced their eyes with a stick and poured the water from those at once into his throat. Though he desired to eat the tender soft kernels inside them, he was afraid that he may be caught. So he left the coconut shells there, went around the fence, reached the road and strode towards his village. On the way, a gowda grazing cows gave a beedi to Appanna. He had never bought beedi following the incident at the sugar cane fields. But if anyone gave it to him for free when he asked, he would smoke and throw the stub.

3

By the time Appanna returned to the village and reached home, it was already four in the afternoon. Just then Patel Shivegowda, his brother-in-law, ex-substitute Shanubhoga Shivalingegowda had all arrived together and were seated. Shivegowda began to speak as soon as Appannaiah came.

'You see Gangavva, Appannaiah too has come as if he was sent for. What did you decide about my money? Have you completely forgotten about that?'

For about two minutes, Gangamma couldn't recall which money he was referring to. Shivegowda said, 'The principal amount is two thousand. Interest for seven years is one thousand eight hundred and eighty rupees. If interest on the interest is calculated, it is six hundred rupees more. That means it will be four thousand six hundred and eighty rupees. Within a month, settle my money. The time time limit for repayment is ending. If not, I'll go to court.'

'From where shall I bring such a huge amount for the deed done so long back, that too by the ignorant boy?'

'Maybe it was done by the boy, but is it a lie that I gave you the money? What are you saying Gangavva? Hey Channayya, you are looking after the work of Shanubhoga, you tell me. Is it a lie that I shelled out money to your family then?'

Channigarayaru sat quietly. 'If you do not repay me within eight days, I'll file a case. Don't blame me afterwards, yes?' Shivegowda warned and then went out with Shivalingegowda. Gangamma asked Channigaraya, 'What shall we do now, Channayya?'

'What do I know Amma?'

'What? Being a Shanubhoga, shouldn't you know?'

Appannaiah spoke, 'Let us see, what the hell is he going do to us. Tell him, "we won't give".'

'Shall we say so?'

'Yes, that's right, Amma.'

'Amma, I am feeling hungry. First, serve me food. Let us think about this later,' said Appannaiah. Gangamma hurried in to serve him food.

Gangamma wondered who might be the proper person to consult regarding this matter. Immediately, the name of Revannashetty flashed in her mind. Many people in the village called Revannashetty a lawyer. He would often visit Tiptur to argue in some cases. It was said, he knew things not known to even big lawyers. Gangamma directly went to his house. His wife Sarvakka said, 'He is not at home; he has gone to Kodihalli.'

'Oh, what's the business?'

'Don't you know Gangammanore?' she hesitated, and said, 'To play cards. What is it that has made you come this far? Please sit down. I'll put out a seat.'

Gangamma sat on the wooden seat, narrated to Sarvakka the

purpose of Shivegowda's visits to her house and the context for the land to be mortgaged. The mortgage of Gangamma's land was known to the whole village. Sarvakka said, 'Shouldn't you have returned his money by now? Why did you delay it for such a long time?'

'Did we eat that money? Did we enjoy it? How can we give it?'

Sarvakka did not have the knowledge required to suggest any solution to this problem. Sarvakka was about thirty-three. She had five children, of which, three were dead. She had not been pregnant since the past two years. She knew that her husband had demanded twenty-five rupees, as loss of the crop, which he could have gotten out of the sugar cane stubble. Revannashetty had earlier said that he would not grow sugar cane again with stubs, but now he took money for it. When Sarvakka said it was unjust, he beat her on her jaws.

While these two women talked about sundry matters, Revannashetty arrived. He had on a dhoti as white as the feather of a crane, rubber chappals, ironed shirt, a gold chain visible on the neck, three shining rings containing red stone studs on his fingers, and his moustache was cut to a perfect size—seeing Revanashetty look so stylish, like a dandy, Gangamma believed she already had won money from Shivegowda.

After listening to Gangamma, Revannashetty said, 'Whose free money does that crook think it is? He said he'll go to court? Tell him to go. Tell him to snatch whatever he can from you. I know many lawyers in Tiptur who are close to me.'

Gangamma was emboldened. 'Revanna, shall I go and tell him to go to court?'

'Oh yes, Ammavre, you don't be afraid. I'll look after all further proceedings.'

'You also come with me.'

'My accompanying you won't look proper. I should work from behind. What fear do you have? People say, in the surrounding sixty-four villages, no male bastard has as brave a heart as that of Gangamma. Why do you fear?'

These words had the desired impact. 'I am not such a coward widow,' and that said, she got up and went straight off to Shivegowda's house, standing before which she said: 'Hey Gowda, when my husband looked after the office of Shanubhoga, you were like a cur. But now, you are unjustly causing me to be fined, threatening me that you would go to

S.L. BHYRAPPA

court against me? Go up to the Dewan, if not to court. I'll also engage a lawyer. You cannot take from us even a single pie. Although a woman, I am not scared.'

Shivegowda came out and said, 'What is this, Gangammavre? Just two hours ago, you spoke justly. Now you speak like this?'

'Yes, why shouldn't I speak like this? I too have people who help me in my difficult times. I am not a destitute,' she said, and returned home.

By the time she came home, Revannashetty was already there. Seeing her face he knew that she would have told everything on the face of Shivegowda. Revannashetty said, 'Ammanore, you and your two sons should come to Tiptur four or five times in bullock carts. If you request and plead before the judge and explain the injustice, the case will be decided in your favour. In all, you have to spend five hundred rupees.' Appannaiah asked, 'If we go to Tiptur, what shall we do about meals, snacks, etc.?'

'Are there no hotels there?'

As soon as he heard the word 'hotel', Appannaiah's mouth watered. *Oh potato, onion sambar, curry, the flavour of coconut chutney, mixed with fried Bengal gram, curds, masala dosa for snacks!* In a firm voice, Appannaiah said, 'Yes, it is right, Amma, let us go to Tiptur and file the case.'

When the mother asked the Shanubhoga about what he had to say, Channigarayaru said, 'We should consult some intelligent person.'

Shivegowda filed a case. Mother and sons went to Tiptur with Revannashetty and engaged Mahantayya as their lawyer. Shetty himself narrated the case of his clients to the lawyer, 'Some villagers put fire to sugar cane fields, and put the blame on these stupid boys and collected money from these people. When they were minor, the sons had signed this paper.

'What is mortgaged is ancestral property. The paper is written and bikkalam has been put by the brother-in-law of the man who gave the money and mortgaged the property. When there are so many points, can't we win the case, sir?'

Lawyer said, 'Why shouldn't we?'

For the first day expenses, they had to sell some gold that was at home and amounted to two hundred rupees. Revannashetty said, 'Lawyer would not take money if given in front of everyone.' Having said that, he took a hundred and seventy-five rupees, went separately and on his own to the lawyer's house, finished the accounts and came back. Appanna, besides having had lunch at the hotel, also ate three masala dosas. Shanubhoga Channigarayaru was familiar with the hotel. At least four times in a year he would come to Tiptur with Dyavarasayya. Channigarayaru ate hot snacks, rave unde and Mysore pak until his stomach was full. Gangamma, being a widow, finished her snack by eating fried ragi flour and some bananas.

4

Nanju delivered a boy. Channigarayaru came for the naming ceremony and as suggested by his mother Gangamma, named the child after his father—Ramanna. This time, he did not stay long. He felt a sort of fear inside seeing his brother-in-law. That aside, Kamalu, Kallesha's wife, would always be peevish.

Nanju came to know about the case with Shivegowda in the court on the very second day she came to the village after completing three months of nursing. She knew all about the loan these people had taken from Shivegowda within a month of her entering the house as daughter-in-law. She heard at the village tank while washing vessels that her people had mortgaged their lands to Shivegowda, taken a loan of two thousand rupees, and given that as fine to a few villagers for the boys had set fire to their sugar cane fields. But she could not ask anyone in the house. Yet, when one day she asked her husband, she received the reply: 'Why do you want to be the master? Learn to sit quietly.'

After Nanju started writing the accounts of the Shanubhoga's office, she got a clear idea of what might be the outcome of this mortgage loan. Nanjamma kept quiet out of the fear that she would be lambasted in the form of 'why do you want to assume headship', if she started to inquire about this matter. Meanwhile, she went for delivery. Now, by the time she had returned, the matter had reached the court.

One day when she asked her husband very subtly, he boasted, 'I won't give a single pie to that fellow. I will make him retch that money out in court.'

'Who said you will win the case?'

'Revannashetty.'

'How can you trust Revannashetty's words? Don't you know what sort of a person he is?'

'You widow of an ass, do you abuse him? See, I'll tell him tomorrow that you abused him thus.'

That her husband was indiscreet and a fool, was not new knowledge to Nanjamma. But stupidity and ignorance of this level brought tears to her eyes. She stopped talking about the matter but the thought was drilling itself into her mind. Revannashetty played cards, drank and the manner in which he looked at women while he walked on the street was not palatable. Sarvakka too was not happy at home—Nanju knew all this. Every villager knew about it.

Next day, when Nanju went to the tank to wash vessels, she saw Rudrani, Revannashetty's eldest daughter, sitting on the stone beside Nanju.

Rudrani, is your mother at home?

'Yes, she is.'

'Your Appaji?'

'He has gone to Kodhihalli.' Everybody knew it was to play cards.

'If so, go home at once, and will you bring your Amma for a minute? Tell her I've called her. Let your vessels be here, I'll take care of them. You stay at home and send her.'

Sarvakka came within ten minutes. For a few minutes, they exchanged remarks on mutual welfare and then Nanjamma looked around once, making certain nobody was there. She asked, 'You see, I ask you in secret about a certain matter. You must tell me the truth.'

'Tell me, what is it?'

'Your husband has taken a stand that he would manage the case about our house. Will we surely win?'

'Nanjammanore, it is a matter concerning menfolk. What can we understand of it? Leave that matter. Why should we worry about it?'

'No, you must tell me whatever you know.'

Sarvakka, looked around once and said, 'If it is known to my husband Shettaru, he will kill me. You must swear touching this Gangammathayi.'

'I will not utter a word about this to anybody.'

Nanjamma held the tank water in her hand and swore, 'I swear in the name of *Gangammathayi*. I won't speak of this to anybody.'

'My husband worked as a lawyer in the dispute of brothers in Valagerehalli Ningappa's family. Assuming he would surely win the case, my husband swallowed the money. But they lost the case. One day, that man came home and abused us cursing that our children's lineage would be destroyed. He threw mud at our house and went off. My husband holds a brief for other people and gets them money so that they can play cards.'

Sarvakka said the exact words Nanjamma had anticipated. Nanjamma became quiet, thinking how to get rid of this court affair and the means by which one could save the existing lands. Sarvakka sighed and said, 'Nanjammanore, mine is the same fate as yous. My husband knows how to break houses, but your husband knows nothing. No one is happy. I'll move. Don't tell anybody what I have told you; you swore on Gangammathayi.' She then put her vessels into the basket and went home.

Nanjamma did not sleep the whole night. Following daybreak, she took a sheet of paper and wrote to her brother: 'Here, these people had mortgaged all lands. Now they have filed a case in court. You should come at once'. She then took the vessels near the tank, wishing in her heart that she meets someone at the tank who would deliver the letter to her mother's place. But there was nobody. Only Jangama Maadevayya of the temple was coming towards her to wash the flowers and bilwa in the tank water. Nanjamma had great respect and devotion towards this Ayyanavaru. Though Maadevayya did not visit their house often, he had developed respect towards Nanjamma. Nanjamma called him: 'Ayyanore, please come here...' Then she looked around once, took out the folded paper from her waist, threw it towards Maadevayya and said, 'You read this and you yourself will understand. Whatever you do, this letter should reach my brother. But no one should know about this.' She then started cleaning the vessels with her head down, as if she had done nothing.

Maadevayya took the letter, put it in the pocket of his ochre shirt and said, 'Yes, I'll do.' He then dipped the flowers from the cloth bag in the tank water and went away. He did not beg for alms in relation to *Gurukarunya* on that day, but went to a couple of villages of Shivagere.

The following day, Kallesha came on foot to his sister's house. There was no place where she could tell everything to her brother. So Nanjamma decided, instead of going to some other place and speaking of this situation, it was better to speak of everything in front of everyone and narrated to her brother all that had happened until now, asking his advice about the future course of action.

Gangamma suspected that Nanjamma must have sent word to her brother through somebody and had made him come here. But she kept quiet thinking she rather not speak before the in-law who had held a police post. Kallesha did not know precisely what these people had written in the mortgage deed. When he questioned his brother-in-law, the Shanubhoga, he answered, 'I don't know what it is that Shivalinga wrote.'

Kallesha asked, 'How did you file your case in court without knowing anything?'

Channigarayaru said, 'Revannashetty and the lawyer know what it is. Would they lie? The case will be decided in our favour.'

Nanjamma courageously explained all about Revannashetty: 'If we depend on him, we will be completely lost. Our family will become bankrupt. Now we must act according to our discretion. Let us not talk about others' advice!'

Kallesha said to Channigarayaru, 'Brother-in-law, come with me. Let us go to Shivegowda's house and ask him what he has written in the deed.'

But Shanubhoga was afraid to go to Shivegowda's house. Fear that Shivegowda would deride him by perhaps saying something on the lines of 'Oh, why did you come to me now? Go, decide whatever that is, in the court itself', was gnawing at his mind. So he said, 'Why should we go to that bastard's house? We surely have a winning case on our hands. Don't I know even that much?'

Kallesha went alone to Shivegowda's house. The latter responded as Channigarayaru had expected and sent him back. Nanjamma told her brother to go to Dyavarasayya of Timmalapura for guidance.

Kallesha, wearing chappals, started, enquiring the route to Timmalapura. Not ten minutes had passed after he had left home, that Gangamma started abusing her daughter-in-law: 'With whom did you send word to bring here your paramour? What, you whore, are you going to sleep with him tonight?'

Nanjamma got terribly angry and assumed an audacity she did not possess before. She retorted, 'Perhaps you must have done such a thing. That's why these words come to you so easily. Hold your tongue! If you had been brought up properly when you were young, would you be like this? Would your children turn out to be such imbeciles?'

'Channayya, did you hear her? Get up, kick once on that harlot's waist.'

'Dare you come near me! My brother returns in the evening.'

Whether he did not have it on his mind to get up and kick his wife, or he felt lazy even to do that, Channigarayaru, however, did not get up. Gangamma did not ask her second son to act on her orders. Even if she had asked him, he would not have dared to do that again!

Kallesha did not return the next day, but came on the second day and Dyavarasayya was also with him. The previous day, Kallesha had stayed on in Dyavarasayya's village, then taken Dyavarasayya to Tiptur and met Shivegowda's lawyer. The lawyer informed them that all lands of Channigaraya were annexed due to the mortgage. If these people agreed to give the principle amount, interest and court expenses, the lawyer said he would somehow make Shivegowda take back the case.

Kallesha called his brother-in-law, Gangamma and Appannaiah and clearly explained: 'Nobody will let go off that much money; court expenses too are not going to be let off. We may request him to leave some amount of interest. However, if it could be settled at five thousand or something, either by selling a large piece of land or making a sale deed to Shivegowda himself, the rest of the lands can be saved. Let us go to his house, come with me...'

Gangamma did not consent to this suggestion. But Kallesha did not let go at that. Besides, Dyavarasayya advised Channigarayaru. The mother, her two sons, Kallesha, Dyavarasayya—all five went to Shivegowda's house. As these people went there voluntarily, Shivegowda would not budge. But Kallesha and Dyavarasayya were patient in speaking to him and were providing solutions to each of his questions. Shivegowda turned once towards Gangamma and asked in the tone of settling his vengeance: 'What Madam, you abused me as a cur, and said I could not pluck even a pie from you. Now you have come to my door. Are you not ashamed?'

Dyavarasayya said to Gangamma, 'Amma, you must be patient now.' But by that time Gangamma, who was burning like fire, retorted: 'What, you Gowda, are you going to taunt me? What are you, what is your status? You fucker of a bitch!'

'If so, let me see what you can take from me.'

'If you don't give what we want, I'll take from you what I will, in court itself. You son of a sinning widow! Get up you Appannaiah, Channayya. Let us go home. Why don't you get up? What, are you not sons born to your father?'

At once, Appannaiah got up and stood beside his mother. Gangamma rebuked Channayya: 'You Channayya, are you going to remain seated there? Are you not born to your father? Get up, you bastard born to a paramour!'

The honour of Shanubhoga Channigarayaru was hurt. What if he couldn't actually prove that he was indeed born to his father? In the presence of all these people—his brother-in-law, Dyavarasayya, his opponent Shivegowda, and his wife who stood watching from the inner door and the servant who stood near the outer door? He too got up, went back to his home with his brother and mother. Kallesha and Dyavarasayya stayed there and tried to negotiate further, but Shivegowda did not give them a chance: 'If that woman has such arrogance and thoughtlessness, what of me? Know this, if I don't bring these bastards begging on the streets for food, I am not a son born to my father. If I don't win the case in the court, kick me with chappals on my chest. You call me sister-fucker. Let it go to the chief court or go to the Maharaja himself.' That said, he held the casket holding linga in his right hand and swore: 'They have taken the support of that Banajiga bastard Revanna and stood against me. I'll show them what sort of Nonabanna I am.'

Knowing there was no use talking about compromise now, Kallesha and Dyavarasayya left the place. Gangamma sat on the pyol of her house and was boasting about her bravery. Shanubhoga was slowly chewing betel nuts and tobacco, and Appannaiah, devoted as he was to his mother, was speaking of tonsuring Shivegowda's wife's head. Kallesha was enraged. He stood beneath the platform and said, 'Fie, you stupid fools, you don't have your wisdom, or common sense. If people like us try to find some way, you behave so stupidly and stubbornly. You oldie, until you die, this house will not survive. My father should be slapped with chappals for giving his daughter to such a house as yours.'

Gangamma had already been excited. She became even more enraged, for he, who had to prostrate before her when he came here, had uttered these words: 'You bankrupt bastard, whoreson, dare you call me so? Who invited you to come here? Did you come here to sleep with her stealthily; is it why she sent for you? You Appannaiah, hold him and slap him on his cheeks.'

It was impossible for Appanna to gather that kind of courage. Kallesha retorted, 'You sinning widow, your tongue will rot and fall for the words that come out of your mouth. Where was your prowess, manliness, when you were anxiously running about to take back Shanubhoga's post from Shivalinga?'

Kallesha crossed the threshold to go inside the house and said to his sister, 'You, Nanju, what kind of family are you running in such a bastard's house? Take your children and start at once. You will partake of the food, whatever God has given me, in my house.' Nanju stood calmly. Kallesha asked again, 'Why are you still standing? Move!'

'Annayya, oh my brother, we should not do anything out of anger; come inside and sit.'

'I won't even take a glass of water in this harlot's house,' Kallesha said, and then taking his handbag from the peg, put on his chappals and went away. He did not stop though Nanju shouted, 'Oh brother, why are you behaving like this?' Dyavarasayya thought that if he conveyed to Nanjamma what had passed in Shivegowda's house, those people sitting on the platform would get angrier and so, he too left for his village.

5

Nanjamma was now more courageous than ever. She hoped that if she informed Saathu's father of all that was going on, he could come and advise these people. Kallesha was her own brother though and so she wrote him a letter. Besides, how could she write to Saathu's father? Of course, he was also like a father to her. Thinking thus, one afternoon, while the rest were sleeping and Parvati was playing outside, Nanjamma wrote the letter. She knew the address: Sri Shyamabhattaru, Nuggikere village, Kasaba Taluk, Kadur district.

The postman, Vasappa came to the village once a week. He had to take the signature of Shanubhoga Channigarayaru as proof of his coming to the village. Nanjamma knew this. That week when Vasappa came, except the children, nobody was in the house. Nanjamma asked him: 'Vasappayya, I want an envelope. I do not have money. I will give you two copras. Would that be enough?'

Vasappa said, 'Amma, you offer me snacks whenever I come here. Shall I take copras from you to give you an envelope? What is that trivial thing worth? Take it.'

'Please you should not speak of this to anybody. You too know the case regarding our house. I have written to the father-in-law of my brother-in-law to come here.' She gave the letter to Vasappa and told him the address. He kept it in the pocket of his khaki dress and said he would put it in the post box. He knew that the Shanubhoga would be chewing tobacco either near the furnace of Veerachari or before the shrine of Maadevayya. So, he said he would take Shanubhoga's signature there, and went away.

After Vasappa left, Nanjamma felt she had done a wrong thing. Appannaiah related to his mother after his return to the village that Saathu's people had asked him to take his wife and child, only if he gave up his mother and lived separately. Gangamma shouted and raged for a few days: 'Oh, has this vile Jois of Kadur region planned to break my house?' After that, owing to the Tiptur tours and other topics, the matter concerning Appannaiah's in-laws, did not occupy Gangamma's mind. Already there was enmity brewing between the two parties; in such a scenario, surely she would not stay quiet if Shyamabhatta intervened in their domestic matters. Nanjamma felt that by inviting him to come here, she herself had paved the way for a quarrel. Yet, there was a sort of awareness—that what she was doing was not completely wrong—which consoled her.

Shyamabhatta came alone by four in the afternoon, on the twelfth day from receiving Nanjamma's letter. Gangamma had gone to the stream in the garden to pluck some greens; Appannaiah followed his mother like a calf behind a cow. Channigarayaru was home. Nanjamma asked Shyamabhatta to wash his hands, freshen up and rest, while she narrated to him the matters regarding the court case. She spoke of her brother's visit while serving him meals. However, Shanubhogaaru was getting angry all the while, while his wife was telling Shyamabhatta their family matters. But whether out of the lack of courage to scold his wife in front of Shyamabhatta or out of shyness, he simply sat on the platform and was struggling to keep the juice of tobacco from spilling out of his mouth.

By the time Shyamabhatta finished his meals, came out and was rubbing snuff, Gangamma had returned with a basketful of honna gone leaves. Appannaiah followed her and went towards the cowshed holding the rope of the cow. Looking at Shyamabhatta, her son's in-law, Gangamma was enraged. *This bastard, ruiner of my family, who asked my son to have a separate house, has come and is sitting here. Let him sit; I will teach him a lesson.* With such thoughts, she went inside, put the basket with a thud on the floor of the kitchen, came out, stood before Appannaiah's father-in-law, addressed him in the singular, and burst out, 'You Jois who lives by eating shraadha meals, have you come to separate me from my son?'

Shyamabhatta knew that his son-in-law's mother did not have much control over her tongue. But he could never imagine that she would talk to him in this manner, standing in front of him. He turned dumb, stared at her for two minutes and said, 'Look here, you must speak with patience. We won't be envious if your son stays with you. The urgent matter of my coming here now is that you should not lose the ancestral property by going to court. You must act with discretion...'

She went towards the kitchen door, turned her neck towards her daughter-in-law, and raged, 'You adulteress, you slut! You sent for your brother and asked him to sleep with you! Now you've sent for this old Jois? What, do you want to roll with him tonight? And what're YOU doing with this slut,' she came near her son. He merely spat the betel juice from his mouth. She sat on the platform and said, 'You impotent bastard, are you really born to your father? Your bitch of a wife has written a letter to this person, asking him to come here. So, you sleep right here on this platform. Let her sway with him in the attic!'

Meanwhile, Shyamabhatta pressed his hands on his ears. His mouth was chanting, 'Raama, Raama', but he stared at her in disgust. After talking thus, Gangamma instantly came out, took Appanna with her and went straight to Revannashetty's house.

Shyamabhatta removed his hands from his ears and told Channigarayaru, 'You see, I am compelled to tell you this as you are the master of the house. If the elderly person of a family speaks in such a waywardly manner, how can the family live in peace? Our Saathu too praises the character and intelligence of your wife Nanjamma. If our son-in-law's mother abuses that child—that too the elder daughter-in-law before me like that—I can understand in what words she might abuse the younger one, my daughter. Since people from Javagal, who are our relatives, recommended it, we gave away our daughter to this house. However, now, whatever happens, both parties should adjust. Do you understand what I say?'

Shanubhoga ordered his wife, 'Bring a couple more betel leaves.' After Nanjamma brought them, he smeared lime juice on them, put one in his mouth, and rubbing tobacco on his palm responded, 'Yes.'

'We do not desire to separate you. But you being a man and the master of the house should use some discretion. Now you settle your business affairs, negotiating with your creditors. As Nanjamma says, sell him one or two lands and make him write off the mortgage deed loan. Try to run the family with whatever remains thereafter.'

Shanubhogaaru was enjoying the betel leaf juice that was rippling around his jaws. When Appannaiah's father-in-law waited for his answer and said, 'Is it not so?', Shanubhoga lifted his face towards the attic and opened his mouth, but the words would not come out. He went out and spat the juice. Shyamabhatta asked again. 'Now you ought to talk.'

Channigarayaru was afraid to say anything. Finally, he came to a decision with difficulty and said, 'I don't know anything. This is only between you and my mother.' Then he went away.

Bhatta asked Nanjamma, 'Did you hear him, daughter?' Nanjamma came out and said, 'You are not aware of this man's nature. You catch hold of your son-in-law. If Appannaiah is obstinate and demands for his share and says that he would clear half the loan, I am hoping this issue may get settled.'

'Don't you know what he is worth? I did not know about this court matter. But even before this, we had decided. She is my only daughter. We will look after her somehow. God will not deny her two meals a day. How can I send my child to live here, with such a mother-in-law? That's why we have kept her with us even after the nursing period.'

Not knowing what to say, Nanjamma stood quietly. Meanwhile, Gangamma rushed into the house. As soon as she saw her daughter-in-law, she blazed, 'Did you finish your dalliance with your paramour? Has your husband left the house and sitting quietly in the shrine?'

Nanjamma was not only enraged, but she gained courage also. She retorted, 'Perhaps you have done such deeds. That's why you call all chaste wives with these words. Let worms fall on your tongue! Will you shut your mouth now?'

'You filthy slut! You've the guts to call me names? If I am not going to have your mangalasutra plucked by telling my son, I am not a woman from Javagal, you mind it!' Roaring, Gangamma went to the temple, stood before her son and thundered: 'If you are a son born to your father, come, slap her so hard that she loses her molar teeth, and pluck out her mangalasutra. That adulteress said, "Let worms fill your mouth".'

Maadevayya, who was strumming the one-stringed instrument and singing, 'Awaken, oh brother awaken! Before you are smitten by the snake, awaken!', now stopped at once and sat gaping at them. Gangamma again challenged, 'You tell me whether you are born to your father or not. If it is certain that you are your father's son, you will come and pluck her tali.' Channigarayaru was struggling to prove the sanctity of his birth to his mother. Finally, he got up. Maadevayya, who sat near him, held his hand, pulled him, made him sit and said, 'You see Shanubhoga, you listened to my bhajans until now. What happened to your discretion?'

Not knowing what to do, Shanubhogaaru said, 'Let it go, sing the bhajans, let me listen to them.' Maadevayya, started strumming the one-stringed instrument and began the same bhajan. At once, Gangamma rebuked, 'This bankrupt son of a widow, without having any regard for his mother who gave birth to him, obeys the words of this bastard sanyasi,' and again went to Revannashetty's house.

Here in the house, Shyamabhatta said to Nanjamma, 'Look here daughter, my coming here was of no use. I'll take your leave. However, I have the priesthood of eighteen villages. I will look after my daughter and granddaughter.'

She pleaded, 'Whatever happens, you please send Saathu.' To which, Shyamabhatta replied. 'Why should I send her? Don't you know everything?'

Nanjamma did not speak again. She touched Shyamabhatta's feet. He blessed her, 'May you live a "sumangali" long. Let your husband live long. May good and pure befall you,' so saying, he left. Nanjamma came near the door and said: 'There is a village called Timmalapura towards Tiptur. There lives Shanubhoga Dyavarasayya. You go to his house, stay there tonight and start tomorrow morning. Do not walk to Tiptur after nightfall. There are thieves at Bukkanathittu. Though two or three carts full of people travel at night, they catch them, strike them and rob them of everything.'

S.L. BHYRAPPA

CHAPTER SEVEN

1

Ramanna completed one and a half years. Nanjamma again conceived. She came to realize in her heart that all their landed property would be lost due to the court dispute. Often she grew weary thinking why she should beget more children and bring to fore their umpteen worries and problems. She remembered that her brother did not have a child even after many years of marriage. Perhaps it was not in his fate. However, she consoled herself, 'When God gives us children, we should not refuse and say we don't want them.'

During this period, two events occurred in the village. The first one was that the village was stricken with plague. It was not uncommon for these villages. People here were habituated with staying in the sheds outside the villages once in two or three years. The second rare event was the entrance of moneylender Kashimbaddi Sahukara into that village, and starting his business. He was a Mapillai Musalman from the Malabar region and gave loans against gold, silver, copper, brass and other articles, charging an interest of one paisa per one rupee per day. About fifty years old, he wore a striped lungi like the skirt of lambanis and put a cap with a cluster. Shivegowda himself explained the generosity of Kashimbaddi's moneylending business to the people and said, 'Oh, what is this one paisa worth? Does he not give us money when we are in difficult circumstances?' Shivegowda himself had accommodated this stranger from faraway Malabar. Shivegowda owned three houses in the village. Kashimbaddi started his business in the small house that was beside the street, brought a big iron box and put it in that house. It was heard that he used to give eighteen rupees per year as rent to Shivegowda. He told everybody that there was no connection between his business and Shivegowda.

More or less, all the villagers started to take loans from Kashimbaddi Sahukar, within one or two months of his coming to the village. It was believed that even Shivegowda had taken a loan from him on interest.

The calculation was accurate; no lies, no cheating. Calculating interest also was not difficult. It was only one paisa for one rupee per day. As such, Kashimbaddi Sahukar was of much use to the villagers. When the village had to be vacated during the plague, Kashimbaddi too put his shed in Shivegowda's garden next to his shed. The iron safe of money too was installed in that shed.

As usual, Gangamma's family too put its shed in their garden in front of the village. Nanjamma was in her third month of pregnancy and was still suffering from morning sickness, but all the tasks from packing up household things to transporting them to the shed, fell on her. Maadevayya too had to vacate the village temple. The original *lingam* of Choleshwara Temple was situated in the shrine on the tank bund. That shrine on the tank bund was made of stone. According to legend, it had been built by the famous sculptor Jakkanachari. Everybody knew there were plenty of snakes in that shrine. 'After all, what is a snake? Is it not Shiva's necklace? What will it do to me?' so saying, Maadevayya took his one-stringed instrument, his drum, his *jolige* hung from the shoulder, wooden sandals, ragi and pulses stored in the temple, and went to that shrine. Gangamma's shed was a bit far away from the shrine on the tank bund. So Channigarayaru's visit to the shrine was rare. Kashimbaddi chewed tobacco too; so Channigarayaru went to his shed. Sometimes, Shivegowda too came there. They were still on talking terms. They were Shanubhoga and Patel, weren't they? The quarrel was ongoing between Gangamma and Shivegowda. But Gangamma scolded her son to her heart's content when she heard about his visit to Kashimbaddi's shed.

Except the six elders and two children who died of plague before vacating the village, there weren't any casualties this time in the village. Villagers performed the ritual of worshipping Goddess Maramma and vacated the village. Though the villagers left their houses and all of them were happy, for they were outside the grasp of either plague or death, they felt bored to live outside the village without any valid necessity. All of them had one topic on their tongue now: What would rid them off their boredom?

The dispute between Gangamma and Shivegowda in court reached its final stage. Lawyers on both the sides argued strongly, putting across interesting legal points. Revannashetty's words spread through the village: 'The judge staggered to the point of our lawyer's argument.'

S.L. BHYRAPPA

Shivegowda said, 'Gangamma and her party were relieved there alone at the argument our lawyer presented.' Both the sides would go to Tiptur and return with great enthusiasm. Appannaiah would get down first from the cart and go to the hotel in Tiptur. Channigarayaru would never be behind his brother. Shivegowda would finish his court work with ragi rotis, sesame powder and parched grain, and return home.

Both the parties harnessed carts and went to Tiptur on the day of judgement. Gangamma put her hands on her chest and listened to the verdict of the judge: 'It is true that these people have received money from Shivegowda. They have to remit to the court five thousand and five hundred rupees as the principal amount and the interest on the principal amount along with court expenses. If they fail to remit the amount, the court will auction all the lands and settle the amount to the creditor.' Though Gangamma felt like abusing the judge and the words, 'let your wife's bangles be broken, you bastard' were on the tip of her tongue, she kept quiet, remembering the police near the court hall door.

After coming out of the court, lawyer Mahantayya said, 'You may appeal to the district court at Tumkur. Money is required. Have you brought some?'

'Hey Lawyer Sir, I have pledged gold, silver vessels and whatever I had in my house. Now being a widow, from where shall I bring money?'

By then Shivegowda's lawyer arrived there. Both of these lawyers said something in English and then Gangamma's lawyer said, 'Look here Amma, this lawyer sir says if you write off all your lands to Shivegowda, the lawyer sir will request Shivegowda to give you some money which you need. If you settle your loan, we have no objection? Let there be no injustice to you.'

Gangamma asked, 'Lawyer Sir, what shall I do for my survival after losing the lands?' Channigarayaru was silent as tobacco juice filled his mouth.

'If that is not possible, you should appeal to the higher court. That requires thousands of rupees. If you have courage to adjust the money, it is a different matter.'

No other solution came to her mind. Shivegowda was brought there. He agreed to pay two thousand rupees more to Gangamma. In fact, he was scared since if the lands were auctioned through court, someone from the village or another village may bid for these lands. Gangamma was bewildered. Shivegowda went to the copra wholesale shop, brought two thousand rupees and gave it to Gangamma. Both the lawyers wrote the deed and settled matters. One hundred rupees had to be given to Mahantayya as the last instalment of his fee. He said that Revannashetty had not paid his fees.

Gangamma swore and said, 'Oh! Lawyer Sir, I have given eight hundred rupees in total as your fees.' The lawyer replied, 'I have received only hundred and fifty rupees in all.'

Revannashetty said on the judgement day, 'You people go by cart, I'll come by bus tomorrow morning', but he did not come. However, Gangamma gave hundred rupees to the lawyer. The next day, after the sale deed was registered, Gangamma and party harnessed the cart and left for their village; Gangamma kept one thousand and nine hundred rupees in the fold of her saree and sat without blinking, and reached the village.

After arriving in the village, Gangamma did not disclose to anybody the verdict of the court. But why would Shivegowda be silent? As soon as the news spread, all the creditors who had paid fifty or hundred rupees on promissory notes for court expenses, rushed to his shed. A total of eight hundred rupees was taken away by the creditors. Gangamma put the remaining amount under the sheet of her bed and would be careful, even while sleeping.

One day, she went to Revannashetty's shed and asked, 'What's this Revanna, you have not given the full amount to the lawyer? He took one hundred rupees from me.'

'Who the hell said so?'

'The lawyer himself told me.'

'Damn that son of a bastard! Come, if he says so before me, I'll strike that thief, my wife's bastard son!' Revannashetty rolled his red eyes at that. Somehow Gangamma did not feel like speaking any further. Either it was fear or weariness or doubt in his truthfulness—but she kept quiet.

She asked, 'Revanna, the lawyer had assured that he would win the case. Why did we lose the case?'

Revanna replied, 'You know, they bribed the judge! Yes, they made the judge eat the shit of another's wife. That Shivegowda, it seems like he gave two thousand rupees to the judge on the day prior to that of the judgement. Didn't he go a day earlier, harnessing his cart? Then itself I knew. If we had two thousand, we too might have bribed. I knew you did not have that much of money. That's why I did not come on judgement day.'

Gangamma returned to her shed silently.

2

Many people visited Gangamma's shed, rebuked Shivegowda and the court judgement, and expressed sympathy. One morning, Ayyashastri came to her shed, abused Shivegowda and said, 'Gangamma, my wife wants to speak to you; come, you may return later.' He took Gangamma to his shed. Shastri and his wife again cursed Shivegowda. Shastri scrutinized the almanac and prophesied, 'That judge's wife and children will certainly die.'

Shastri's wife Subbamma insisted, 'Gangakka, take your bath here. Wear silk cloth or any cloth made of plant fibre. Have your meals here. Indeed, who's there in this world to feel compassion for you?' At this, Gangamma started to abuse her daughter-in-law wholeheartedly.

'You see, that quarrelsome slut stepped into my home and troubles too started. Now all the lands have vanished. Is this adage a lie, that it is the merit or fortune of the children born and the fate of the daughter-in-law while she steps into her husband's house that makes or breaks a house?'

Gangamma took her bath, wore silk cloth, smeared vibhuti and finished her *aachamana*. By that time, Ayyashastri went to Gangamma's shed and brought Appannaiah. Then Annajois, grandson of Shastri's uncle, too came. Subbamma had cooked for them also. Buttermilk sambar of ash pumpkin, ragi balls and rice were served on betel nut tree barks. While Subbamma was serving them, Ayyashastri started speaking: 'Ramanna should have lived. Matters would have been totally different. Often I tell with my wife how I worry about you. His death was like the dome of our village falling down.'

'How can he be alive when I am fated to have these kind of sluts as daughters-in-law?'

Subbamma asked, 'Gangakka, isn't it two years since your menopause began?'

'Yes, it has already been three years.'

Shastri said, 'Is it? You see, you led a virtuous and meritorious life.

There is no charity, *vrata* or any religious rites you have not performed. After menopause, women should perform *Rishipanchami Vrata*. By performing this, all your problems will be solved.'

Annajois was more learned and efficient than his uncle in shaastras and mantras. He was taught by Suranna Jois of Sindhaghatta. He recited the efficacy of Rishipanchami Vrata along with mantras.

Subbamma said, 'Whatever happens, you finish this one vrata. Whatever help you need I'll give. Venkatalakshmi, Annappa's wife, is also here. If a separate pandal is put for this, it would be enough. Let us put a big pandal before our shed. There is the problem with people from other castes near your shed. It will not be convenient for observing religious purity and rituals.'

Gangamma asked his son, who had finished swallowing ragi balls and was mixing rice in buttermilk sambar, 'What do you say Appannaiah? Shall we perform this?' Appannaiah had attended the feast when Venkatachalayya's mother from Chennenahalli had performed Rishipanchami. Obbattu, mango chitranna and other dishes he had eaten there were very tasty and mouthwatering. At once, all of that came to his mind. Instead of buttermilk sambar and ragi balls, heaps of mango chitranna and packs of obbattu appeared before his eyes.

'Yes, let us do it, Amma. In what way we are lesser than that Venkatachalayya?'

So, it was decided that the vrata will be performed. Subbamma said, 'What do you think of Gangakka? If she utters a word, it is done. She will not alter her word even if Brahma's father were to intervene.'

Gangamma didn't change her decision. If she had changed it, her reputation and fame would have been tarred. After lunch, Annajois scrutinized the Almanac. He counted using the fingers of both his hands and fixed a date. But then it wouldn't befit the honour and stature of Gangamma to perform a mere trifle of the ritual like Rishipanchami. That ritual was for people like Venkatachalayya of Chennenahalli village who had gotten it performed for his mother. No—in this case, provisions had to be bought on a large scale. The list of provisions was written down using a pen and ink prepared with charred ragi. Silk dhotis and cotton dhotis sporting the Melukote border[7] were to be offered to the

---

[7]These were dhotis with red or dark pink borders worn by temple priests.

two purohits of the village and then sarees costing fifty rupees each for their respective wives were to be bought. The cow that they owned had to be donated as daana. Fine quality rice, pulses, sugar and rava— now a cart had to be harnessed for going to Tiptur to buy all these. So it was fixed: Annajois and Ayyashastri would accompany Gangamma. Appanna, once again, had a chance of going to Tiptur.

3

The Rishipanchami Vrata was performed on a grand scale. It was decided that people should enter the village after eight days. Sugar, ghee and rava brought for the Vrata were still left. One day, Gangamma told her daughter-in-law, 'On the day you stepped into this house, everything was destroyed! You are a shrew. All our lands have gone. When we go into the village, you and your children stay separately. We will stay in our house.'

Nanjamma could not understand immediately the meaning of her mother-in-law's words 'you and your children'. She questioned, 'In which house are you going to stay?'

'Which one? In the house built by my husband.' The words came to the tip of Nanjamma's tongue, 'Only if that Shivegowda allows you to enter into the house!'—but she did not openly say that. Her insightfulness had already told her that the lands of the family would be lost in court. She did not expect that two thousand rupees would be given by Shivegowda himself. Even when money came, Nanjamma did not feel like advising her mother-in-law about it. If she said something, there would be an unnecessary quarrel; she should have to listen to evil words. Pregnant women should neither listen to bad words nor should entertain evil thoughts. They should always be listening to good words and be happy and pleasant. Nanjamma had heard this when she was a little girl. These words had not come to her mind during her first two pregnancies. Now, suddenly this thought occupied her mind. Sometimes, she engaged her mind in reciting songs like *Dhruva Charita*, *Bhakta Prahlada*, and those speaking of the coronation of Rama, etc.

That afternoon, when her husband lay down to sleep, she informed him of her mother-in-law's order and asked, 'Mother told me that we stay separately. Where shall we go? What shall we do for a living? Have you thought about this?'

'My mother said so knowing fully well your wicked nature. You and your children may do whatever you like.'

'The whole village knows what I am. Now, this need not be discussed. Tell me, what should be done now?'

'Haven't I told you? I will stay with my mother,' so saying the Shanubhoga covered himself and started snoring.

Nanjamma got angry. 'What are you saying? Do you have your wits under control or not?'

'Go away, you widow of a donkey! Do not ruin my sleep.' Nanjamma did not speak again. She knew for sure that they had to live separately. But, she had not imagined her mother-in-law would separate her son and daughter-in-law. She wondered how long his mother would maintain this son after the lands were lost. She knew for sure that she alone would have to shoulder the responsibility of bringing up the children. But how could she? The answer did not present itself to her. She was determined not to cry or disturb her mind since she was pregnant.

After her husband fell asleep, she took her child Ramanna with her. As her stomach was fully bulging, she did not carry the child on her waist; she carried him upon her shoulder, took Parvati by hand and walked towards the tank bund. The tank was dry and the sedimented area of the tank was hot. Dust on the tank bund and the heat of the sun were striking hard. As she was panting, she walked slowly and when she entered the door of the enclosing wall of the temple, Maadevayya had just finished his bath and was spreading his ochre dhoti to be dried. Rice was boiling in a pot on the brick oven. Maadevayya said, 'Come, daughter come, I thought of coming into your shed, but kept quiet because your mother-in-law will speak harshly.'

'Hereafter, mother-in-law can say nothing. I came myself.'

And it was not just Maadevayya. There was nothing—no small detail—about this family that was unknown to anybody in the village. So, there was no need for Nanjamma to explain the situation. She told him only two things: Her mother-in-law's order to Nanjamma to stay separately with her children and her husband's reply to that. 'You people got two thousand, and one thousand was left after repaying all the petty loans. When that woman unnecessarily spent on celebrating Rishipanchami Vrata, listening to that Jois, why were you silent?'

'I kept quiet Ayyanore, thinking, while everything had gone, let this also be gone. Even if I said no to the Vrata, she would not have agreed. Why should there be a needless quarrel?'

'Yes, you are correct.'

Maadevayya put some of the boiled rice and beans sambar into an aluminium plate and ate. Every day he would finish his begging in Veerashaiva homes, cook and then finish his meals. But he would not set out to get alms after the Sun God began to wane in the west. Today it was Monday and he had gone to distant villages for begging alms. As it was late when he returned, he cooked for himself. Maadevayya gave pieces of coconut and jaggery to Nanjamma and Parvati and sat pondering for a while.

Nanjamma said, 'Ayyanore, I don't know whether you are aware of anything about my mother's house. Why should we disclose to others internal matters of our house? I've not told this to anybody. My sister-in-law, by nature, is not friendly or good. Hereafter, I will not go there either to deliver, a baby or in trying times. If I request Ajji to come here, she would come and help me. She has already crossed seventy-five. She is also weak. Yet, she works. But, I need a place to stay, a fistful of grain to eat. Moreover, if this man, my husband, too forsakes me, what shall I do?'

Maadevayya thought for a moment and said, 'You don't worry about Channayya. He will come searching on his own for you, like an ass to the old pillar. You are acquainted with Patel Gundegowda of Kurubarahalli, don't you? If you pursue him, he won't let you down. There is none in this village to help you.'

Kurubarahalli was a village that came under the jurisdiction of Shanubhoga Channigarayaru. All forty houses of the village belonged to one caste: Halumatha shepherd. Gundegowda had been the Patel of this village since forty years. Nanjamma had even heard the people of the surrounding villages praising him as 'Dharmaraya Patela'. During his regime of forty years as Patel, there had not been a single theft or adultery committed, and none had left the village due to starvation.

Maadevayya said, 'There is a house that belongs to him in the lower street of this village. It is vacant. You request him saying that you will reside there. He will not refuse.'

Now Nanjamma remembered that in Ramasandra itself, there was a house that belonged to Gundegowda. Nobody was living in it. If he agreed to let her live there, the problem of lodging could be solved. Nanjamma had seen Gundegowdaru, but was not well-acquainted with him. As he was the Patel attached to the jurisdiction of Shanubhoga Channigarayaru, he had come several times to Nanjamma's house. Sometimes she had served him lunch too. He had a thick white moustache, broad face and a gold bracelet as thick as a finger on his right wrist. Though he wore a coat, he would wind his dhoti high up so his knees were visible, and had on hard slippers made by the cobbler of Koppalu.

'You go to Kurubarahalli tomorrow by around nine in the morning. I'll also reach there by then asking for alms as I usually do, and will talk with Gowdaru. He will not say "no". But don't tell him that Channayya will stay with his mother.' After Maadevayya said so, Nanjamma returned to her shed.

Gangamma chided, 'Oh! The harlot had gone roaming on the streets', but Nanjamma did not reply. The next morning, Nanjamma woke up, took her bath, bathed the children, prepared rotis, herself ate and fed the children, then combed her hair, applied *kumkum* and *chandra* on her forehead, put Ramanna on her shoulder, held Parvati's hand and left the shed. Gangamma, sitting beneath the tree in front of the shed, shouted loudly, 'You slut, to which paramour's house are you going now?' Nanjamma went ahead without reacting. After walking a little distance, she turned back to check whether her mother-in-law, brother-in-law or husband were following her to see where she was going.

Kurubarahalli was two miles from Ramasandra. In the middle, a mound had to be crossed. Nanjamma was not afraid of walking alone. But being pregnant, while climbing the mound with the child on her shoulder, she found it hard to breathe, and was panting. Parvati, who had not completed four years, was crying for her legs were aching. Yet the child continued to walk, holding her mother's right hand. Suddenly Nanjamma too burst out with grief. She put the child down, sat on the earth, wept to her heart's content and then wiped her eyes with the edge of the saree.

The thought of pushing the children into any tank or well and to drown herself, sprang in her mind. But she recalled that she, a pregnant woman, should not nurture such evil thoughts nor should she cry. She got up. Now she put Ramanna on her right shoulder, held Parvati's hand in her left and walked ahead. After climbing the mound, she could see Kurubarahalli at a distance. Basavanna's shrine could be seen in the middle of the village. Gundegowda's house was located beside that shrine. Nanjamma walked down and prayed to God that Gundegowda should be kind to her.

Gowdaru sat on the platform in front of his house chewing tobacco. Seeing him, Nanjamma easily traced the house. Gowadaru got up and said, 'Come in, come on in Avva, you've come here like Goddess Lakshmi. Did you come in this hot sun carrying this child?' He peeked inside and called out, 'Hey! Our Shanubhoga's wife has come. Spread a mattress for her.' He took Nanjamma and her children inside. Nanjamma sat leaning on the wall with the children. Gowdaru sat against the pillar. Lakkamma Gowdithi gave copra and jaggery to Parvati who stopped crying immediately.

Nanjamma asked, 'Gowdare, do you know the state of our house?'

'Yes, I heard everything Nanjavva; your mother-in-law is a burning torch shorn of all restraints. Until there is binding and restraint, the torch burns and also survives. But after the binding is torn, what remains? Your father-in-law was a blockhead—like me. This shrew came, you see, this great lady hurled a spade to the very base of the house. Now it is left to you to save the house.'

Gowdaru turned towards his wife and said, 'Hey, you see, it is this woman who writes all accounts of Shanubhoga. Is it possible with that Channayya? He is only a bull. If you ask, "Oh bull, would you like to drink water?" he'll say yes. If you ask him, "Would you like to graze on the grass," he'll say yes. If you ask him, "Would you like to graze on crops?" he'll say yes. But if you ask him, "Would you like to be tied to the yoke to till the land," he'll brandish his horns, shake his head and run away. Don't get upset Nanjavva because I abused your husband.'

Gowdamma said, 'Why will she get angry? That man behaves in this very way.'

Even as they enquired their mutual well-being, Gowdamma went inside and brought three full glasses of hot milk mixed with jaggery and three spoons of ghee. She placed the glasses before Nanjamma. Nanjamma said, 'I don't want milk now,' but Gowdamma objected, 'A pregnant woman should not refuse milk; you drink it.'

Nanjamma spoke, 'I do not refuse milk from your house Gowdare, but you must promise me that you will not forsake me.'

'What is it? Speak Nanjavva.'

'Yesterday my mother-in-law ordered me to live separately. We do not have any shelter.'

'Why do you worry about shelter? Is there not my house? Stay there. Now drink this milk.'

Even before she requested, Gundegowda had granted what she wanted. She had no need to beg or beseech, for anything. He gave as if donating was not difficult at all for him. Nanjamma asked the children to drink milk and she drank her fill too. Gowdaru said to his wife, 'Wasn't I telling you? Look at the lustre on this lady's face. It is like Goddess Seethamma's face. Isn't it?'

By then Maadevayya came for his *karunya bhiksha*. Gowdamma offered him a seat. As if he did not know anything, Maadevayya enquired about the cause of Nanjamma's coming to Kurubarahalli. After he heard Gowdaru's promise of giving his house as a shelter to Nanjamma, Maadevayya asked, 'Well, Gowdayya, you provided her a shelter to dwell in. Should she stretch her legs in the house and sleep? What should she do for her food?'

Gowdaru said, 'Aren't there the tasks of the Shanubhoga? What more than the work of Shanubhoga is needed for a man who works hard?'

'Don't you know what sort of a man he is?'

'He is a eunuch bastard. Let it be. In a pair, if one is weak, it is all right if the other is strong.' Turning towards Nanjamma, Gowdaru said, 'Ask your bull to obey you. There will be no problem for food.'

Ayyanavaru said, 'Is he the sort of a fellow that listens to any advice?'

Gowdamma said, 'It is the fate, Ayyanavare; one has to suffer.'

It was already noon. Gowdaru and Gowdamma would not send these people without offering food. Gowdamma went inside and brought some brass vessels and two pots. Though Maadevayya said that he would return to his village, Gowdamma did not let him go. Cleansing the vessels with tamarind, Maadevayya and Nanjamma drew water separately. Gowda's son set stone ovens separately. Both of them cooked rice separately. With coconut scrapping, mixing salt and curds, they finished their meals. Children were given milk again. Gowdaru harnessed his cart, seated the pregnant and the children in it and Maadevayya too sat in the same cart with his begging bag.

After leaving the shed, Gangamma entered the village and opened the door of her old house. She had not yet entered the house and swept the dust off the hall with Appannaiah when Shivegowda's servant Muruva, with a big lock in his hand, came and informed them, 'Gowdaru said, you should take your things and move out. I have been instructed to lock the house.'

Gangamma said, 'Who is that bastard Gowda that said so?'

'It is Shivegowdaru, Avva.'

'Ayyo, let his family be ruined, the entire land gone. Now does he want me to give up this house too? Does he think it is his father's hoarded money?'

Gangamma uttered these words, and went straight off to and stood before Shivegowda's house, shouting: 'Hey! Gowda, do you think this house is your father's? It was only the lands that were settled in the court.'

'If you want, go to Tiptur and enquire Gangavva; the sale deed that is written by you and your sons is in the iron safe. Shall I bring it and show you?' so saying, Gowda came out.

Gangamma did not know how to respond. 'Ayyo, let his family be destroyed!' For a little while she stood stunned and then she asked, 'If that is so, where shall we go and die? You being the Patel of the village must tell me.'

'I am not working as a Patel to build houses for homeless people; go away from here quietly,' Gowda said, then went inside and shut the door with a thud.

'Let his home be harrowed and ruined. This evil schemer of a bastard flaunts, acquiring property by fraud. I am not without anybody to help me.' So saying, Gangamma directly went to Revannashetty's house, told him what had happened and asked, 'Your cowshed is large enough. Give me some place there, my sons and myself will stay there, putting a bamboo partition on one side.'

'There is no place there to tie even my buffalo calves, Gangavva. Where are you going to stay? Ayyashastri of your caste is there; why don't you ask him?'

'This bastard wanted only to loot me.' Abusing him, she went to Ayyashastri's house and asked him. But there was no place in his cowshed also.

'You needed me when you were in dearth of food! Now do you refuse me four cubits of place, you begging Jois?' Gangamma stood in the middle of the street and asked.

Jois felt a little irritated but he did not like the idea of giving her a place in his cowshed. At the same time, he did not want to be the fodder for Gangamma's tongue. At last, he called his uncle's son Annajois, spoke with him and suggested a plan. In the eastern corner of the village, there was Lord Hanuman's shrine. Annajois was the priest there. There would be no impediment for this mother and her sons to live in it. But he was also concerned with the opinion of the villagers. Who did he mean by villagers? Chiefly the Shanubhoga, the Patel, the chairman and members of the Panchayat. It was not difficult to get others to agree. But being the Patel as well as the chairman of the village, it was doubtful whether Shivegowda would give his consent. Ayyashastri said, 'Look here Gangamma, you must speak with good manners. Standing in the street, you should not call Shivegowda bastard, widow's son, etc.' When Ayyashastri said so, Gangamma replied, 'Oh! you be quiet! of which bastard do I need be afraid?' Both the Jois went to Shivegowda's house for negotiation. It was not certain whether he would agree, but his wife Gowramma had a fear; Gangamma's tongue was not auspicious. It was said that there was a black speck on it. Whether the time was auspicious or evil, she would stand on the street, throw mud hurl and abuses. Moreover, the shrine of Lord Hanuman belonged to Brahmins. Let the people of that caste live there. This was Gowramma's opinion. She took her husband inside and whispered her wisdom in his ears. Whether Shivegowda believed all that or not, he was not losing anything from it as such; he came out and said, 'Well, you may stay there.'

There was some benefit to Annajois because of their arrival at this shrine. Five acres of dry land and an acre of wetland were left as endowment to the priest for his daily attendance at the shrine. But although the priest Annajois enjoyed profits the lands accorded, he didn't really like to come to the shrine to do the hard work every day: sweeping it, cleaning the hall, tidying the enclosure of the shrine and performing the puja and ablutions by pouring water on the deity. Moreover, when he went to the village for donations or pecuniary gifts,

Lord Hanuman would neither get worshipped nor water. Many days the hall of the shrine would be filled with excreta of birds, and the place would be reeking of stench. The Patel of the village wrote a complaint against Jois. If you peeped inside from the hole in the front door, you could see clearly whether God was being worshipped or not. The villagers too tested this and on the days the Jois did not offer flowers, or pour water on the idol, they would curse him.

Now Annajois told Appannaiah: 'Look here, I have allowed you people to stay in this shrine. You must sweep and wash the hall and the whole enclosure daily. There should not be even a little bit of dirt. After you bathe, you must wash the idol, bring bell flowers and worship him. But if you disclose this to anybody, I will oust you from the temple. I too will come some day and perform the rituals.'

Appannaiah agreed and Gangamma too would not object to worshipping God. Her devotion to God was great. Channigarayaru, however, knew mantras used for performing the puja.

5

Gold ornaments with the image of the cobra, which would be worn on the rear of the head, gold jewellery the shape of chrysanthemum flowers worn on the braid, a pair of gold bangles and silver anklets—all given to Nanjamma in her marriage from her mother's house were kept by Channigarayaru in a corner in the lower part of the wooden box, where important documents concerning Shanubhoga's administration were stored securely. When Nanjamma asked about them, her husband did not reply satisfactorily. When she asked for them again, he said, 'Will they stay there because they were given by your father's house? They were spent.'

'Why were they spent? What did you do with them?'

'They were spent for court expenditure.'

'What did you do?'

'They have been pledged to Kashimbaddi for fifty rupees. If you want, repay the loan and get them back.'

'When did you pledge the items?'

'During last Deepavali.'

That means it has already been seven months. Interest would have gone beyond fifty rupees. Now paying back hundred rupees and getting back the jewels would not possible even in a dream.

Nanjamma asked, 'Without my permission, how did you touch the jewels given to me by my father?'

'Mother told me to take them and use them as pledge. I did so.'

Nanjamma's resolve that she should not lose patience at any cost, did not last.

Gangamma did not give any vessels to her from the house. Mother-in-law even refused to give brass and other utensils given as gifts to Nanjamma in her marriage. At least, if those little bits of gold were there, it would have been useful in these troubled times. When she had to start her family afresh now, there was not a jug to hold water and not even a quarter seer of ragi flour to make rotis for children. Under such circumstances, she would have to take care of delivering the baby, and nursing the child for a few months beside herself. She gave up the idea of going to her father's house for delivering the baby. Her brother did not have a woman of such good quality for a wife.

Nanjamma was now enraged and asked her husband, 'Any husband should earn and bring jewels and sarees for his wife. But you and your mother together have stolen and squandered the jewels that were given by my father's house, that too without my knowledge. Are you not ashamed?'

That godly husband did not speak. He stood there rolling his eyeballs like a sheep. Nanjamma asked, 'What are you going to do to fill the bellies of our children? How much did I entreat you, not to go to court. I tried to persuade you like you were a parrot. But you went to court and swallowed all the lands. Now you sit like a pauper.'

Channigarayaru did not know how to answer her. So he got extremely angry. He felt like abusing Nanjamma. No new words of abuse came to his genius. So he uttered, 'You widow, widow, slut, slut of an ass, tonsured widow' three times in a plain tone harshly and went away. Nanjamma too got angry. She sat there for ten minutes and wiped her tears.

On the same day, Nanjamma went to Maadevayya's shrine and took a loan of five rupees. The next morning, she left the children in her husband's care, instructing him to look after them. She went to Sannenahalli with Puttavva of the weaver caste. Sannenahalli was entirely a potters' village and was three miles away from Ramasandra.

Nanjamma bought two small earthen pots, two big pots in which to draw water, one big earthen cauldron, earthen pans to bake rotis and other things needed for the family from a potter's house to which Puttavva took her. As Puttavva bargained wisely, all they had to pay was twelve annas only. Puttavva carried three fourths of the burden and Nanjamma carried the rest. By the time they reached the village, it was already noon. The Sun God had its peak reached its peak. Nanjamma kept the articles in Gundegowda's house in the village, locked it and went to the shed. By then, her mother-in-law and brother-in-law had transported their luggage to the temple of Lord Hanuman and vacated the shed. The child Ramanna lay there weeping before the shed, Parvati was not there and Channigarayaru too was not to be seen. Nanjamma took the child, washed the mud smeared on its body and hands in the pond nearby. Luckily the child had not gone near the pond. Suddenly, Nanjamma's mind recalled Parvati. Everybody was vacating their sheds and transporting luggage to the village. *Where did this little chit of a girl go? What had happened?* Carrying Ramanna on her shoulder, Nanjamma came again into the village. Maadevayya was transporting his luggage to his original temple which was in front of their earlier house, and Channigarayaru was sitting on the platform of the shrine and gargling tobacco juice. Nanjamma came near him and asked, 'Where is Parvati?' He got up, came to the street the spat chewed up pan and said, 'What do I know? Go and search.'

When Maadevayya asked Channigarayaru, 'Hey! What's that? You are sitting here since morning. Where is the child?', he said, 'This damned unlucky girl, where did she go! That girl never sits quietly in one place.'

Nanjamma went in one direction in search of the child and Maadevayya started in another. Somebody said they had seen the child on Fishermen Street. Nanjamma rushed there. Luckily the child was sitting and playing beneath the platform of a shed. Everybody was busy in moving their things from their sheds. None had noticed the child.

Nanjamma took Parvati by the hand and walked to her home. Maadevayya, who knew the condition of this house, brought two seers of ragi flour, a small measure of beans, chilli powder, salt, tamarind, and coconut scrapes that had remained after his cooking. The children were screaming aloud out of hunger. Nanjamma too was very hungry. Having walked in the hot sun, she felt like swooning. Though she was a strong woman, she had not walked six miles at a stretch before. Moreover, she walked the distance with the burden of the child in her womb.

It was not possible to sit quietly though she was suffering from pain and weakness. Nanjamma got up and drew water in the new pot from the well. An oven was there in the house. She sprinkled water on it. Maadevayya brought dry coconut leaves and the fibrous coverings of coconuts as firewood. Nanjamma washed the pots. Though she knew that food would smell of mud, she put avare pulse in one pot and water for ragi balls in another. By one in the afternoon, cooking was completed. When she served the meals, Parvati, unable to resist hunger, rolled pieces of ragi ball in sambar and swallowed them. But Ramanna, who had not yet completed two years, did not like the ragi balls. When he bit on one of those once and it stuck to his jaws, he shouted out that he did not want it. Nanjamma had put away half a seer of ragi flour. She quickly took a fistful of flour, added a pinch of salt, mixed with water, flattened the dough on the earthen pan and baked a roti. The child rolled pieces of roti in sambar, ate that and became quiet. Yet half the roti remained.

By then her venerable husband came home. He stood at the kitchen door and looked inside for a moment. Straightaway he went out, cut a piece of plantain leaf from somebody's backyard, came back and spread the leaf before Nanjamma who was sitting near the oven. Nanjamma had not thought while cooking that her husband would come for lunch. Her mind was totally consumed with the thought of her children who were screaming with hunger. Now, they had become silent. *He had said he would stay with his mother; why had he come here now? Had the ragi balls not been prepared in his mother's house, or had she told her son to go and eat in his wife's home, or had he come of his own accord?* He had not enquired about his wife whether she lived or died. He did not care about his children either. He did never offer to draw a pot of water to cook flour and dal, donated by Maadevayya. Now, he brought a plantain leaf, that too only one piece for himself and sat for lunch. The thought of whether to serve him or not, did not enter Nanjamma's mind. But she felt disgusted to keep sitting there and came out with the children.

By then, both the children were sleepy. There was not even a mat to spread for them to lie down on. Nanjamma spread her old saree and made them lie on it. She too was tired. She placed her right hand down by her side and lay beside Ramanna. Once again, a thought occurred to her. *Shall I go and serve my husband*? But another side of her saying, *Let him call me* took an upper hand. So, she did not get up. Soon she was asleep owing to weariness and the hard work she had done since morning, and also due to hunger.

When she woke up, she felt she had slept for more than an hour. Sunshine and heat were already decreasing outside. She pondered if her husband had partaken of his food. She went inside and saw: A ray of sunshine had fallen on the cooking pots; beside that, the plantain leaf on which her husband had eaten was also there. Nanjamma had prepared a total of five ragi balls. Parvati had eaten only half a ragi ball. The remaining four-and-a-half balls had been in the pot. Now only half a ball remained and a ladle of sambar was left at the bottom of the pot. Nanjamma did not know whether her husband had saved it for his wife or there was no more space left in his belly. She was so hungry that she felt someone had put fire in her stomach. Her hand stretched itself to eat that remaining ragi ball. But what would she give the children in the night? However, there was still a quarter seer of ragi flour left; she could make rotis and feed them. But she felt disgusted to eat that half ball that had been left by her husband after he had swallowed four. She got up quietly, came out and sat leaning against the pillar.

The children were still sleeping. It was already time for sunset. They should not be sleeping at this time. Nanjamma woke them up. Now she remembered that neither she nor the children had bathed that day. She had not washed her face or put fresh kumkum on her forehead after she returned from Sannenahalli. Even the casket of kumkum was in her mother-in-law's house. She did not know whether her mother-in-law would give her even that. There was not even a kerosene bottle lamp to light during the night. Still, four and a quarter rupees were left with her. She took the children with her, locked the door, went to Channashetty's shop on Weaver's Street, bought two bottle lamps, one bottle full of kerosene oil and a match box. It cost three and half annas. She bought sugar candy for six paisa for the children. After coming home, she tore a piece from the edge of her old saree, made a wick from it, filled a bottle with oil in the dim light and lit it. In its light she filled oil into another bottle and put a wick in it. Nothing else came to her;

there was no strength left in her body. So she leaned on to the pillar and sat quietly. Both the children put their heads on each lap of their mother and stretched their legs. It was a new and unfamiliar place; the children too felt a sort of fear.

After a while, Nanjamma took the children inside, served the remaining ragi ball to Parvati and half roti to Ramanna. He ate a piece and said 'enough'; Parvati too left a little of the ragi ball. Nanjamma felt terrible pain in her stomach. She ate what remained of the roti and ragi balls, rolling them in sambar. She thought of preparing rotis from the remaining ragi flour and eating them. Somehow, with a sort of weariness and contempt, she got up, took the children with her, held the lamp in her left hand and came into the hall. At the same time, her husband too came home, carrying the bedroll on his shoulder. Nanjamma felt a bit consoled, for her husband had at least done this much. She was worrying on what she should make her children sleep. She opened the bedroll. There were two beds, two carpets, pillows and a black blanket made of sheep wool, given to her in her nuptial ceremony from her father's house. One bed was in a worn-out state from Parvati and Ramanna's urine. The blanket was half worn-out. She put a bed up for the children, spread a carpet beside for herself, and put on it a pillow. She spread another bed for her husband in a separate square.

The husband who stood looking at this, at once, asked angrily, 'Why haven't you put my bed also with that of yours?'

Nanjamma did not speak. She was patting Ramanna to put him to sleep. 'Did I carry the bedroll from there with so much of difficulty that you should put it separately?'

She did not speak even now.

'You slut, why do you keep silent?'

Nanjamma determined as she was not to lose her cool, said, 'I've already completed six months.'

'What if you have completed that?' so saying, he drew his bed from the separate square near Nanjamma's carpet. He held the burning lamp, went inside the kitchen and shouted from inside, 'Hey, you have not kept any food for me. Why?'

Nanjamma replied from outside, 'What had you saved after you took your meals at noon to keep for you food?'

S.L. BHYRAPPA

Channigarayaru did not respond to that. He mixed salt and water to the remaining ragi flour, lit the oven, flattened two thick rotis on the earthen pan, baked as per his knowledge, ate them hot, drank some water from the pot and came back to the hall holding the lamp. Children were asleep by that time. His wife too had closed her eyes and laid down. The husband lay on the soft bed beside his wife. Nanjamma could not get sleep. It was not possible for her to get sleep. Not having had any food since morning, she felt fire burning in her stomach. She felt grief, agony, tiredness. She questioned herself, 'Why does this damned stomach wail so much if it does not get food for a single day?' She remembered how her belly was so heavy even though she was hungry. A pregnant woman should not go hungry. Somehow, we may survive, but how can the baby inside the womb get food? She thought she should have eaten at least the half ragi ball her husband had left behind. But if she had eaten that, nothing would have remained for the children. Thus she felt what she had done was correct. She should have made rotis with the remaining flour and eaten them. But she was thinking what she would give them in the morning when they'd cry due to hunger. Now, the father who begot these children had prepared rotis from the same ragi flour and eaten them. How could he have been hungry so quickly after swallowing four ragi balls in the evening? She remembered, that some people had very strong appetites. While taking his food alone on a plantain leaf, he did not even think about his wife's hungry stomach. Even while eating the rotis, that thought did not occur to him. And now he had come to sleep beside her. He did not think about his wife's health nor did he want to know by how many month she was pregnant, whether she had eaten anything since morning, if she felt any strength or was suffering. Nanjamma felt like telling him to get up and lie down at some distance.

But her husband who had boasted that he would stay with his mother, had come of his own accord at noon, swallowed ragi balls, had now eaten the rotis and had carried the bedroll to sleep with her. If she now refused to abide by his wishes, he might again go to his mother. Perhaps this was the meaning of Maadevayya's words, 'He will not stay with his mother. That is all for a couple of days!' Nanjamma kept quiet. Her mind decided, if she had to save her family, she had to undergo this act—a wife's duty towards the husband. Her body was much exhausted from the tiredness of walking to Sannenahalli, toiling in the noon, not having had a mouthful of food, and to top it all she was six months pregnant. But there was no reason for Channigarayaru to feel tired.

All of a sudden, her father's picture came to Nanjamma's mind. Her father was a giant by nature. He wouldn't care for anything. If he was angry, whether it was his wife, children or mother, he would beat them like Yamaraya[8], without caring whether they lived or died. But he was kindness personified when his heart melted. When the plague attacked Kallesha, the father put his son on his lap and sat the whole night. Oh God, it was all right even if the husband beat his wife, but if he did not have the heart to care or to ask if the wife ate or starved and what she did for the children's food, what kind of a family was it? Nanjamma's mind questioned, *why should she live in such a family?* Her grandmother Akkamma came to her mind. Nanjamma had not suckled her mother's milk. The child was born and soon, the mother had died. From then on it was Akkamma who had brought her up. *She is the only one who is affectionate with me. She is already more than seventy-five. I must at least send for her. But there is nothing for us to eat, what will I do asking her to come here? Who is going to take care of my delivery, the nursing and child after birth? The matter of going to Nagalapura was a foregone solution. If Akkamma comes here, for one month, she would give oil bath to me and the child. But if she comes, there is nothing at home to eat. Not a drop of castor oil or a pinch of soapnut powder.* Alongside these thoughts, she remembered that the pots would be empty by the following morning. She became aware that she too was feeling hungry. But her current problem was with what she should feed the children in the morning. Lying on one side, she felt pain in the right side of her stomach. When she turned to change to the other side, she saw her husband sleeping on his back beside her and snoring. She felt disgusted. She got up in the darkness, took her carpet and pillow, spread it beside her children, put her left arm on Parvati who was asleep and went to sleep.

6

---

[8]Lord Yama, the god of death

Nanjamma got up in the morning, poured water in the pot, washed her face and the children's also, and wiped theirs with her saree. She went inside the kitchen, took out ash from the oven, cleaned and mopped the mud oven, and washed the pot in which she had cooked yesterday. As she had forgotten to fill the pot in which she had cooked ragi balls with water, flour was stuck in its bottom. So she filled water into the pot and came into the hall. Her husband, happily snoring, had stretched his legs towards the front door. She half opened the front door and sprinkled water in the courtyard. But she did not have rangoli powder. She asked her neighbour Channashetty's daughter-in-law for a coconut shell of *rangoli*, drew some lines and designs on the threshold from the powder lent, kept the rest inside and sat silently. There was no further work to do. She did not know what the plight of the hungry stomach would be that day.

Because of the loud mooing sound of a buffalo in the street, Channigarayaru's sleep was disturbed.

He got up uttering, 'Fie fuck its mother', sat on the bed, said '*Kausalya Supraja Rama*',[9] rubbed both his hands against each other, chanted '*Pancha Kanyah Smarennityam*',[10] got up and went towards the tank bund. By the time Nanjamma rolled back the bed, Maadevayya came carrying a bag on his shoulder, put it down near the pillar and said, 'I am going for bhiksha to villages. Here, there is twenty seers of ragi and four seers of beans. You make use of this.'

Though Nanjamma felt happy for the grain and pulses while she was worrying for that day's food, she said, 'Ayyanore, yesterday too you brought us flour and beans and again today you have carried for us these bags of ragi and beans. You roam around villages, ask for alms. How can I repay you?'

'Avva, you well know how I spend this, don't you? When sadhus and sanyasis like me visit this village, I cook and serve them from this. If you and your children eat from this for a week, what great loss would it be to me? You cook and have food. In the meanwhile, Shiva will surely show a way,' he said and left.

---

[9]The first line of the morning hymn addressing the Lord.
[10]Names of five chaste women in mythology, which are chanted in the morning—Sita, Mandodari, Tara, Ahalya and Draupadi.

The winnowing fan Ayyanavaru had brought the previous day, was still there. Nanjamma cleaned two seers of ragi, and sat to grind it. The grinding stone, round stone for grinding and stone mortar were fixed to the floor in that house. Nanjamma felt exhausted much before she could grind the whole quarter seer of ragi. She remembered she had not eaten anything the previous day. She sat quietly for five minutes. Her husband came. He did not enquire from where she had got the ragi or what she might have had to do to get it. He just leaned on to the pillar, took out a betel leaf from his pocket, folded it and began rubbing tobacco on his palm.

Nanjamma asked him, 'I feel too tired, I cannot grind. Will you at least grind some of this?'

Her husband did not speak. When she asked again, he roared, 'Hey, do men ever turn a grinding stone? What? Do you take me for a woman or a man?'

Nanjamma remembered her resolution not to lose patience, and kept quiet. She went to Weaver Street, requested Puttavva to come and grind ragi. Puttavva agreed to grind a winnowing fan of ragi for an anna and sat before the grinding stone. Nanjamma brought chillies, coriander seeds, salt, oil, etc., for a rupee from Channashetty's shop, and began cooking. By eleven, beans sambar, ragi balls, and ragi roti for Ramanna were ready. Nanjamma had not bathed the previous day also. She drew water from the well, bathed the children and washed herself too; she then wore a clean saree and came inside. Today too her husband had spread a plantain leaf and was swallowing ragi balls; she did not ask him to save some for herself and the children. But he left three-and-a-half balls and got up. Nanjamma had made a total of seven balls. She sat for lunch with little Parvati, poured sambar and swallowed one and a half ragi balls. Parvati could eat only half of a ragi ball. Ramanna, after four bites of roti, drank water and started crying for rice. Nanjamma finished her meal thinking she should have brought a seer of rice in the shop for one and a half annas. Soon after she had had food, Nanjamma felt too tired, came out, spread a carpet and lay down.

There was no firewood to cook food for the night. Whatever little Ayyanavaru had given was spent. Nanjamma's husband was also lying on the floor. She said, 'Go and bring firewood from somewhere.'

'Hey, you go! From whom shall I beg firewood?'

'If so, what can we do now? You go to the garden, ask somebody and bring some coconut stalks and dry leaves.'

'If you need them, go and bring them yourself. I cannot,' he said and inviting sleep to digest what he had swallowed, he turned to the other side and slept.

She did not go to anybody's garden for firewood. Upon request, Chinnaiah's wife, her neighbour, gave her a big basket full of coconut husks, fifteen coconut leaf stalks and four pieces of coconut leaves. Then she went to Channashetty's shop and asked the price of rice.

He said, 'Fine rice is nine seers for a rupee and coarse rice is twelve seers.'

She gave a quarter rupee, bought three seers of rice and cooked half a seer of rice for the night. Parvati and Ramanna ate happily. Besides, Chinnaiah's wife Rangamma had given her buttermilk. Channigarayaru came for the remaining rice and buttermilk after the children had finished their meals. Luckily, he had not come before the children had finished their dinner.

The grains Maadevayya had given may have sufficed for eight or nine days. The thought of what she would do afterwards was plaguing Nanjamma's mind. But still no solution was before her. The next day, there would be a fair in Ramasandra. She decided to buy some plates and glasses and other utensils she needed, from there. After lunch, by three in the afternoon, she went to the fair with the children. She knew that Muslim traders would bring aluminium utensils to the fair that would take place in the grove, nearly a mile from the village. She bargained with the trader and bought four dinner plates, glasses, a ladle and a mug for bathing. In all, it cost a quarter less to two rupees. She purchased three sticks of sugar candy and rattles for the children. When she was returning home, she met Patel Gundegowdaru. He asked, 'Is everything all right, Avva?'

'Yes Gowdare, please come, let us go home.'

Gowdaru took the aluminium utensils. Nanjamma put Ramanna on her shoulder and followed Gowdaru. After she opened the lock, he inspected the inside of the house and asked, 'What will you do for food?'

'I thought of asking you about that.'

'If you had asked on that day itself, I would have given you twenty-five seers of ragi.'

'For how many days will it last?' At once, an idea flashed before her. She said, 'You don't give it for free. I'll suggest one thing. If you do so, there will be no trouble for you and it will help us too.'

'What is it, tell me Avva?'

'Your total tax on lands is eighty rupees. Isn't it?'

'Why?'

'Please do this. You take a receipt from my husband that fifty rupees towards your tax for this year has been remitted. And for that fifty rupees you give us ragi, cowpeas, chillies and if you have at home, some amount of paddy. It would be enough for us.'

'If I take a receipt from him now, how can you remit the government money later?'

'Our annual payment would be a hundred and twenty rupees. The government would deduct this fifty rupees from that.'

Gowdaru thought this was a brilliant idea. He agreed and said, 'Avva, you have a brain sharp enough to become a diwan.' She knew her husband would be chewing tobacco in the shrine of Maadevayya. She sent Parvati to inform Channigarayaru about Gundegowdaru's visit and bring him home. After coming home, the Shanubhoga took betel leaf, betel nut and tobacco, and chewed again. Then Gowdaru asked, 'Where is your accounts ledger)? Come, bring it here.'

'It is not here.'

'Then where have you kept it?'

'In my mother's house.'

'Hey, what's this? Do you think the post of a Shanubhoga is a useless and perfunctory job? You should keep your ledger where you live. I have given this house to you to keep your account book safely, haven't I? Do you know the government rules? Get up, run along and bring the ledgers here.'

The Shanubhoga went to the Hanuman shrine. But Gangamma did not give the bundle. When she heard that Patel Gundegowdaru himself had asked for the books, she came over herself. When Gowdaru said, 'Government rules are like that, Avva', she agreed and said, 'If so, I too will stay here.'

'Yes you can. What do I lose?'

But Nanjamma at once responded, 'No, no. That is impossible. Since once you threw us away to stay separately we will stay here on our own.'

'See Gundegowda, how this slut of a shrew speaks?'

'See Gangavva, I have given this house to keep the account books of Shanubhoga's work, and to this Avva who writes the accounts and not to others. You don't have to abuse anyone without reason.' When Gundegowdaru uttered these words, Gangamma returned to the Hanuman shrine abusing loudly. The Shanubhoga himself carried the ledgers on his head, walking around four times. But Gangamma did not give the wooden box in which the ledgers were kept.

After all the ledgers were brought home, Gundegowdaru asked, 'Hey, you nitwit, all these years you managed the work of a Shanubhoga. Don't you know why the government has appointed the village watchman and servant?'

The Shanubhoga did not reply. The Patel himself asked, 'You carried all these ledgers on your head and brought them here. Couldn't you call the village servant and order him to bring these account books here? What sort of administration are you going to carry out? Do you think it is child's play? Well, bring paper and the ink pot and write what I say. You tell him, Avva, what to write.'

Shanubhoga Channigarayaru held the pen. His wife dictated, 'Fifty rupees have been remitted by Patel Gundegowda of Kurubarahalli *firka*, in connection with his revenue tax of this year. At the time of collecting taxes, this amount will be debited, and rest of the amount will be collected and written in your receipt. Shanubhoga Channigaraya. Date...'

He wrote as she dictated and handed it to Gowdaru. Only ten minutes later, the meaning of what he wrote flashed before him. Later, as if he remembered, he asked Gowdaru. 'Oh, where is the money?'

'Hey keep quiet, don't ask me. Where does the money go?' Gowdaru asked, but Channigarayaru did not stop grumbling.

The next day, Gundegowdaru came with a cart load of provisions, lowered the bags and said to Nanjamma, 'See Avva, there are four quintals of ragi that cost twenty-four rupees; one quintal of cowpeas—eight rupees; a measure[11] of chillies that was for three rupees. How much is it it—a total of thirty-five.'

'Now, take this five rupees. It is forty altogether. I'll pay another ten rupees after I sell copras at Tiptur. We don't have even a little paddy in our house. You need to purchase rice from the shop.'

---

[11]Five kilograms

Nanjamma took heart. She tied that five rupees and another two rupees she had in a piece of cloth and hid it between the beams of the tiled roof.

7

In the eighth month of her pregnancy, one afternoon, Nanjamma was drawing rules in the account book maintained by the village accountant. As it was during an advanced stage of pregnancy, it was difficult for her to put the rule in squatting posture. Yet she struggled and worked, changing her position. Channigarayaru was asleep on the other side of the hall and snoring.

All of a sudden, Gangamma entered the house. She had never come here except on the day Gundegowdaru had been here a couple of months ago. She did not say or ask anything to anyone. She opened the cap of the big basket, started filling ragi from it to the bag she had brought. Nanjamma was quiet for two minutes, not knowing what she should do, but then she asked, 'What is it Amma? What are you doing?'

'Hey! What am I doing? I am taking out ragi. Who the hell are you to question me?'

'Keep that bag down first and speak from a distance. How could you touch our grains, coming here all of a sudden without being invited?'

'Oho ho, she says it is her house. What? Did your father build this house? Hey, you son of a eunuch's whore, did you hear? I did not light the oven since this morning as there was nothing to cook at home. If I come here to take a little ragi, she behaves as though her father has brought it here. That Kurubarahalli Gundegowda is our Patela; he is not your paramour to give you grains freely.'

By then Channigarayaru was awake and said, 'Hey leave it! Let her take ragi! Fuck your mother!'

Nanjamma said, 'Gundegowdaru has not given this as charity to give it to you. I requested him to send the grains and have the amount equal to it be debited from the tax amount to be paid.'

'Aha ha, the post of Shanubhoga was my husband's. It is not your father's, you harlot,' the mother-in-law said. Daughter-in-law retorted, 'Yes, it was my father who could give it back to your son. You understand this, otherwise, you could never have got it back. Moreover, it is I who is writing the accounts, struggling day and night. If you break into my house and touch the grains again, I will send for Gundegowdaru.'

'Oh you son of a bastard, I've not eaten since morning! What shall I do?'

Nanjamma herself replied, 'Go and request either Shivegowda or Kashimbaddi. If not, ask that Revannashetty.'

Gangamma could not understand the taunt in Nanjamma's words. She left the bag there and went straight to Shivegowda's house. After she left, Nanjamma felt restless and uneasy. She thought she should not have sent her mother-in-law without grains after hearing that she was hungry since morning. She went in, filled three seers of ragi flour in a winnowing fan, told her husband to take it to his mother. The son went to his mother holding the winnowing fan filled with flour.

Gangamma directly went to Shivegowda's house and asked, 'What hey Patela, I have not lit the oven since morning. Give me twenty-five seers of ragi.'

'Oh what is it? Are you kidding? From where can we get twenty-five seers of ragi?'

'You evil-minded, bastard who breaks families, dare you speak to me in this manner after swallowing all my property? Your lineage will not survive!'

'Hey filthy slut, have I not poured money for the property? Will you control your tongue or shall I push you out holding the back of your neck?'

Shivegowda's wife Gowramma came at once and told her husband, 'Why do you speak in that manner even if that woman speaks like that? You go to the garden, leave now.'

Gowramma was scared that some evil or misfortune would come upon her house if this old woman would hold mud and curse standing in the street. The Patel too did not want to have a quarrel afraid of Gangamma's tongue. It was enough for him. He obeyed his wife's words. He put on the chappals and left for the fields. Gowramma filled two winnowing fans full of ragi, poured them into a clean basket, placed it before Gangamma and said, 'Please don't get angry because he speaks like that. You take this.'

Gangammaa was burning with anger and perhaps she would have refused it. But when Gowramma pressed insisted again, she hoisted the basket on her head and went off to the shrine where she lived.

Channigarayaru had given the winnowing fan full of flour to Appannaiah and had left for Maadevayya's temple. Nanjamma, with a bent neck, was drawing lines with red ink on the account book. She felt a shadow of someone coming into the house. Even before she could raise her head and see who it was, Gangamma entered with the winnowing fan full of ragi flour poured it down on her daughter-in-law's head, struck her head once with the empty winnowing fan and roared: 'Hey you begging slut, do you think I will eat ragi balls begging from your house? What do think of this Gangamma?' and walked off hastily.

Nanjamma's head, body, hands, the books, the red inkpot—everything—was covered in ragi flour. Nanjamma felt like getting up, following her mother-in-law and holding her, so she could show this to one or two people. But she kept quiet thinking that if she took such family quarrels to outsiders, she and her family would become the laughing stock for the villagers. Perhaps, many people already make fun of her family. She got up, shook the flour off her saree. Luckily, the flour had fallen on the toddy-palm leaf mat on which she had been sitting. She shook the ragi off the book also, heaped the flour, sieved it and put it away. She washed her head and rinsed her hair. Then she washed the inkpot, brought two packets of red ink powder for three paise from Channashetty's shop, prepared ink and sat again to draw the lines on the account book.

8

The third day following this incident, around ten in the morning, while cooking in the kitchen, Nanjamma thought she heard someone calling 'Nanju' from outside. She recognized the voice, and was sure it was Akkamma's, and she came out excited. Yes it was true. Akkamma stood there with a bundle on her head and her bent back. Two male servants stood behind her, carrying two gunny sacks. Akkamma told the servants to put down the gunny sacks as soon she saw her granddaughter. She asked, 'Oh what is this Nanju? Shouldn't you have sent word to me that you were pregnant? Shouldn't you inform us of your plight, and what happened here?'

'Yes, I was thinking of sending for you. Now come in…Have you finished your bath?'

S.L. BHYRAPPA

'I will bathe later. If cooking is over, first serve these two. They have to return soon to their place.'

Sambar was boiling and the ragi balls had to be made. Nanju went in, turned up the flame, and within fifteen minutes she prepared sambar and ragi balls. The servants went to the village tank to wash their hands and feet. Nanjamma served them. Akkamma asked, 'Don't you have buttermilk?'

'Where shall we get it from?'

After the servants finished their meals, Akkamma called one of them and said, 'Look Honna, let not that Lakka open his mouth about this—you tell him again. And soon after you reach home, tell him one more time. Also, inform Kallesha that there is no milch cow here, and there will be no milk for the nursing mother. There is that breed of our white cow that has a calf just a month old; let Kallesha send it here. The mother of that cow was given away to Nanjamma in her marriage. Later we did not send it here. Now at least her daughter can be sent here. Inform Kallesha that Akkamma has asked for it.'

The servants left. Akkamma bathed in cold water, wore the wet saree, put vibhuti on her forehead, did her aachamana, came into the kitchen, and sat before the oven, drying her wet saree. Nanju asked, 'How did you know all this?'

'Don't you know that our village's weaver Thammayya Shetty's wife is from this place? Nearly a week back, I met Thirumalamma when I went to the village tank. She told me everything in detail. She said you were now staying in the house belonging to Kurubarahalli Patel. You are pregnant and in the seventh or eighth month. Your mother-in-law did not give you even a glass in which to drink water. Kallesha had said all the lands would be lost.'

'When did you start from home?'

'Yesterday itself. But by evening, it started to rain heavily. The three of us took shelter on the platform of Hoovinahalli Patel's house beyond the hillock. Patel's people served food to those two and gave me scraped coconut and jaggery.'

The children returned home after playing. Parvati had not forgotten Akkamma. It was not possible for Ramanna to remember her. However, within half an hour, the children were acquainted with and became familiar with their great grandma. Channigarayaru came home. Except asking, 'How are you?' he did not speak much with Grandma. Grandma too did not pay attention to him much. After lunch, he did not lie down at home but went to the platform of Maadevayya's temple. Now Akkamma opened the two sacks she had brought. One bag contained copper and brass vessels, four small and big basins, two brass jugs, one pot, five brass glasses, two copper glasses, two pots to cook rice in, two vessels to keep sambar in, etc. Another bag was filled with rice flakes, parched flour, jaggery balls and fifteen seers of mungesari rice.

'Oh, why did you bring all this, Akkamma?'

'Hey Kallesha himself told me to prepare rice flakes and parched flour, as there are children here. Moreover, the sugar cane crusher is set. Three large bins are full of jaggery. He gave jaggery and a bag of rice also.'

'What about these vessels?'

'See, while Kallesha was working in the police department, I had filled all these vessels and other things given as gifts and donations in a corn bin and put it in the attic. None had any idea about how many there were. When I heard what happened to you here, I took some from there and handed them to Honna's wife when Kamali went to the village tank. I had instructed Honna to ask Lakka to carry them without being noticed and wait near the outskirts of Chowdenahalli, when we left home yesterday.'

'Anyway, you shouldn't have brought them Akkamma. Will Kalleshanna keep quiet when he knows this?'

'Hey, you keep quiet. He will not know. Moreover, all these gifts and donations were received when Kanti was here.' When the old woman remembered her son Kanti, her eyes filled with tears. She said, 'Oh that unlucky fellow, I don't know where he went or what he is doing. From the beginning, his life has been strange. He tries his hand in so many things. He won't be satisfied and live happily at home, enjoying what God has given him.'

Tears filled Nanju's eyes too, remembering her father. She asked, 'Is there no news of father?'

'No, Nanju, nothing is known; people say, "where will he stay; he must have died." But how can he die? Oh! He was like King Bhojaraja.'

'No, he is not dead. All that is a lie,' when the granddaughter assured her so, Grandma was comforted.

Akkamma was tired. There was no mat in the house. Being a tonsured widow, she couldn't lie down on a mat of toddy palm leaves. So she lay on the floor. Nanju asked, 'How is sister-in-law?'

'Do you think bad habits go away so easily? Can evil, spiralling hair be destroyed by shaving?'

'I don't know what can be said of your father's madness. He was not cautious enough...did not discuss with people. He came here impulsively and got you married into this house. And just like that, he went there and brought that girl as his daughter-in-law. She devours food. She pours milk from the vessel and drinks. She swallows solid ghee, digging into it with her fingers. Once a week she takes oil bath. No, she does not allow me to pour her water. But though she takes so much of care about her health and nutrition, this wench of ill luck did not conceive.'

'Let it be so...Are the husband and wife happy?'

'Oh what sort of happiness is it? For four or five days they will be whispering with each other, lying down in their room. Another four days he beats her black and blue. She curses me, accusing me of carrying tales against her and instigating my grandson to beat her. If I advise him, that he should not beat his wife in this manner, he retorts and shouts at me: "You keep quiet! If I do not strike her, how would this slut be cured and become straight?" Do you remember that Kempi[12], the daughter of that Paraiah's daughter?'

'Oh yes, don't I?'

'There is a rumour that Kallesha is often with her in the sugar cane fields. There was that Mayaga from the Fisherman's Street. You know him? He died three years ago. His wife stays with her two little children. They say, this fellow goes to her house and keeps sitting there. People say many things about him. One day I asked him about this and chastised him. Do you know what he said? "Who is that bastard that carried such tales to you? I'll slap him on his head with my chappals until his hair falls." I kept quiet thinking that it was best not to rake up the matter.'

'Tell me Akkamma, though he has a wife at home, why does he behave in this manner?'

'Oh, he is a luckless poor fellow. If this one had behaved properly with her husband after marriage, why would he go elsewhere?'

---

[12]Kallesha's concubine

Grandma enquired about the plight of her great granddaughter. She took the responsibility of cooking. Nanju had already completed eight months. She began sleeping near her great grandmother at night, spreading a mat. The children slept on both sides of their great grandmother, hugging her. Grandma and granddaughter would be talking about mundane matters until they felt sleepy. Channigarayaru felt bored to sleep at home. One night, after meals, he carried his bed and went to the platform of Maadevayya's temple.

Kallesha came with a white cow and calf eight days after Akkamma came. He stayed for two days in his sister's house and then went back. After nine months were over, Nanjamma gave birth to a boy. It was healthy, good looking and chubby. There was no money to perform the naming ceremony. But the custom, the shaastra, could not be left out. Akkamma had brought jaggery and rice and she had five rupees with her. She spent that amount, sent for two Joisas and invited four houses of brahmins for dinner. She completed the ceremony and named the child Vishwanatha. On that day, Gangamma and Appannaiah were not in the village; they had left the place and had gone to another village.

CHAPTER EIGHT

1

Akkamma nursed the mother and child for four months. Though she took care of her granddaughter with affection and never allowed her to do any domestic chores, she could not stop Nanju from preparing the summary of accounts of the village accountant, the details of which her husband brought by surveying wet lands, dry fields and gardens. She had to start putting rules in the account books and write the accounts from her second month of nursing itself.

Kallesha came to escort Akkamma back to his village. They had to start the next day, but that evening the village servant called the Shanubhoga and said, 'The Panchayati—the council of the villages—is arranged in the house with the *angadi* belonging to Channashetty. You are asked to come.'

Nanjamma questioned, 'What panchayati is that?'

'It is said that Channasetty has an illicit relationship with his daughter-in-law. His son has asked for a panchayati to settle the matter.'

'Whatever that is, you tell them to conduct the panchayati with other village elders. We have some guests at our house. You inform them that Shanubhoga cannot come.'

'No, they have said Shanubhoga ought to come. Everyone has said that I need to bring Shanubhoga with me.'

It was customary for the Shanubhoga to be present in the judicial panchayats of the village. Everybody knew that if Channigarayaru sat as a judge, he would not be able to distinguish between the flour and granules, the right from wrong. But whatever sort of a person he may have been, being the Shanubhoga, he had to be present. Channigarayaru started and Kallesha too followed his brother-in-law.

All important persons from the village had gathered in the inner courtyard of Channashetty's house. Along with Patel Shivegowda, his brother-in-law, ex-Shanubhoga Sivalinga, Revannashetty, four members of the panchayati and two Joisas, there were ten to fifteen people more. Betel leaves, betel nuts, tobacco and beedis were placed before them. Before starting the panchayat, a question arose, 'Who should be appointed judge?' Somebody said, 'Shanubhoga.' Patel Shivegowda said, 'What does that simpleton know?' Another person suggested the name of Patel Shivegowda. Revannashetty opposed this. Then the petitioner Giriya suggested, 'Nobody from this village should be the judge. Let Kalleshajois, the brother-in-law of the Shanubhoga, judge this dispute. He was in the police department.' Everybody agreed to this. As per the opinion of the majority, Kallesha sat in the middle, chewed tobacco and asked: 'Now, what is the dispute? Who has met with injustice? Come and relate it to this gathering.'

Giriyashetti said, 'My father has kept my wife. Both of them should be fined.'

'Who is your father?'

'Look, it is he, that deceiving bastard sitting there,' said Giriya, and pointed towards Channashetty who sat with lowered head near the pillar.

When Kallesha enquired in detail, he came to know this: 'Giriyashetty goes to work in the fields. Channashetty always sits in the shop and trades. The shop is on the platform of the house. Giriya's wife Narasi stays at home. It's been eight years since her marriage.'

Kallesha said, 'It is important to ask in detail everyone's statement in these disputes.'

It's been twenty years since Channashetty's wife died. He did not marry again. Giriyashetty grew without a mother's care, a child of weak build.

Kallesha asked for Channashetty's statement. With head bowed low, he stated, 'Oh look here sir, it seems I have begotten this wicked bastard. He has gathered this panchayat based on the words of slanderers, with the sole purpose of destroying my reputation. I will never give a paisa from the earnings of my shop to this pauper bastard and will not give him a share in my lands also.'

Giriyashetty swore, 'See, I swear on my mother, I don't tell lies. I am myself a witness.'

'Well. I should listen to the statement of your wife also. Call her here,' Kallesha ordered from the judge's seat.

Ayyashastri called loudly, 'Come here Narasamma.' She did not come out. Ayyashastri insisted. 'The Judge is calling you. You must come.' As there was no tobacco juice in the mouth of Shanubhoga Channigarayaru he said, 'Yes, yes.' Narasi came and stood near the kitchen door. Nobody was there in the village who had not seen her. But Kallesha was stunned as soon as he saw her. She was a woman of tall build, red complexion, a round face and heavy-breasts. Looking at the very style of her standing, Kallesha did not know what judgement he had to give. When Narasi stood there, Ayyashastri said, 'Look Narasamma, a father-in-law is equal to your father, a daughter-in-law to a daughter. Can such things happen anywhere in the world? And if they do happen, will rains arrive on time? Will crops grow on the earth? Do you get what I'm saying? Yes, what do you say, Channashetty?'

Annajois chanted mantras and began commenting on the discrimination between *dharma* and *adharma*. The rest were nodding their heads to this purohit's knowledge of the varied nuances of dharma. Shanubhoga Channigarayaru was enjoying the taste of the tobacco he had just filled into his mouth, but Revannashetty said, 'Please don't listen to others' words. You ask that woman what she has to says.'

'Yes, yes, tell us Narasamma, what do you say?'

Narasi questioned those two purohits: 'See, Sir, you are chanting mantras and commenting so much. I'll ask one question, will you reply?'

'Oh yes, surely. You ask,' both of them said together.

'If you lower down a rope of thirty-six feet in length into the well that's seventy-two feet in depth, does the rope reach the bottom?'

'What?' Ayyashastri was baffled and did not know the answer. Other members of the panchayat also were stunned. Then Revannashetty persuaded Kallesha, 'Sir, now you give your verdict.'

Giriyashetti put his condition, 'I won't live with this harlot.'

Kallesha thought for five minutes and announced his verdict, 'The husband says he will not live with his wife hereafter. It is not just to compel him to stay with her against his wish. And he says, there is an illicit relationship between the father-in-law and daughter-in-law. But Channashetty has sworn that all this is false. However, we should not blame a man for the crime he has not committed. Yet it should be decided that the father-in-law and the daughter-in-law must live separately, so that the son finds consolation. Now, the husband has already stated that he will not live with his wife. So, let her stay alone in a separate house. As she is his daughter-in-law, let Channashetty build a small house for her. Then the father and son may live according to their will and wish.'

The rest of the members couldn't understand the nuances of dharma regarding this verdict. They were confused.

Patel Shivegowda questioned, 'What sort of a verdict is this?'

'We have requested Kalleshappa to deliver justice and made him sit on the judge's seat. We must accept whatever he decides, without a second word,' said Revannashetty, turning towards Narasi.

Narasi agreed to the verdict given by the judge and said; 'How can I refuse the words of the elders of the panchayat?'

Before any controversial talks could begin, Revannashetty got up. Kallesha too got up from the judge's seat and everybody left.

After reaching home, Channigarayaru asked Kallesha, 'Narasi said something—what was it?'

'Didn't you understand?'

'No.'

'That's why you were not selected to give the verdict. It doesn't matter if you don't understand. Leave it, don't bother.'

Channigarayaru once again rubbed tobacco and put it in his mouth.

2

Revannashetty used to visit Kodihalli to play cards. There was a convenient place for playing cards on the loft of the cowshed in front of the house of village Patel, Chikkegowda. Lingadevaru, the Chairman of Kambanakere, toddy contractor Chinnaswamy and leather merchant Hayat Saabi would assemble there along with Chikkegowda and Revannashetty.

One afternoon, Revannashetty asked Chikkegowda, 'Lend me fifty rupees, brother. After the sale of copras, I'll return it.'

'Do you know how much you have already borrowed? Now, I have no money with me.'

'No, please don't say so. Lend me, brother.'

Chikkegowda did not lose by lending money to Revannashetty. One part of that money would return to him in the card game. As Chikkegowda was in the moneylending business, he would have with him revenue stamps and promissory note forms. He wrote on the form the amount of fifty rupees, deducted six rupees as interest for a year and gave Revannashetty forty-four rupees after taking his signature. But

Revannashetty did not pocket the money at once and leave; he directly pledged the money in the game of cards. Because forty-four rupees was a very small amount, he did not agree to throw down the cards. And so they began to play the Twenty-Eight game with one rupee as the bet amount at the table. Since nobody turned up, it was just Revannashetty and Chikkegowda who played that day. By six in the evening, forty-four rupees landed in Chikkegowda's pocket. But Revannashetty was adamant. He simply had to play again and win that money back. But Gowda refused to lend money without the promissory note. 'Whatever may happen, fie, this sister-fucking money! Lend me another fifty. I'll write the note.' He put his signature on the promissory note, took forty-four rupees, played until eleven in the night, lost it to Gowda, shook off his towel, put it on his shoulder and returned to his village.

By the time he returned, Sarvakka and his five children were sleeping. He knocked on the door, awakened his wife and demanded her to serve him food. She served on a bronze plate cold ragi balls and sambar of greens. He chastised his wife, 'Why couldn't you cook and serve it hot? What's wrong with you?'

'I had cooked it fresh and kept it warm. But you've come so late. It's gone cold.'

'Yeah? Who the hell gave birth to you? Who the hell is she? Who are you to question me what time I need to come, you harlot, sister-fucker! I'll kick on your chest and kill you,' he screamed. When he broke the ragi ball, rolled it in the sambar and swallowed it, he found that it was hard. He stood up, kicked his wife once and commanded, 'Cook some rice now!' Between sobs and crying in pain, she said, 'There's no rice, what shall I do?'

'No, no, no! Whatever I ask you, that's your answer! You damned slut!' he kicked her again, swallowed the dry ragi ball that remained on the plate and lay down on the cot. Sarvakka washed the plate and lay down next to the youngest of her five children, Rudresha.

3

When Nanjamma had any doubts about the accounts, she would visit Timmalapura, with the village servant Ninga carrying the account books. Dyavarasayya, who had taught her the method to solve a problem, would tally the accounts. While collecting the revenue, usually the village Patel would be present. Shivegowda said that the collection of Ramasandra's revenue was exclusively his. He took a haughty stand, 'The collection of revenue is exclusively the right of a Patel. The Shanubhoga should obey the Patel and keep quiet.' As none had the power to oppose him, it continued in that manner in the village. Customarily, the right to the Shanubhoga's money was to go to the Patel, and Shanubhoga Channigarayaru was not entitled to even an anna. If there had to be sales, mortgages and other registrations, the villagers would go to the ex-Shanubhoga Sivalinga who worked on a temporary basis, but never hover near Channigarayaru. The reason for this was that Channigarayaru did not know how to write documents correctly. Another reason was that the Patel had threatened the villagers: 'Let me see who will secure or possess the records if they are written by that fellow.' Though Nanjamma was well-versed in drafting registration deeds better than Sivalinga, there was a belief that if government papers—deeds—were written by a woman, they will not prosper. As such, there was not even three paise worth of income from Ramasandra.

The income from Kurubarahalli was the only guaranteed source. Although Patel Gundegowda would be present there on the revenue collection day, the actual collection was done by Channigarayaru. Gundegowda would tell each farmer to also pay the ink charges to the Shanubhoga for writing the land records. He would also give him two rupees on top of this. That village generated a total income of forty rupees. After Nanjamma began living separately, Gundegowda had promised her that in the harvest season, he would collect one quintal of ragi and fifty seers of cowpeas from his village. He had continued to keep his word. But because land sales and mortgages were rare in Kurubarahalli, no income flowed from writing such deeds.

Lingapura, with thirty villages, was another place in Shanubhoga Channigarayaru's subdivision. People were sufficiently well off there. Shivegowda of Ramasandra had a distant relation in Lingapura. Shivegowda's contention was 'why should ink charges be given to the Shanubhoga' and this had spread to that place also. Patel Puradappa was obstinate that it should belong to him only. When Channigarayaru's father Ramanna was the Shanubhoga, there was a custom of giving a rupee per house to the Shanubhoga. Some elders of the village are witnesses to this even today. Now times had changed and there was no extra income from this place for the Shanubhoga.

Nanjamma would visit Kurubarahalli for collecting revenues. The Patel himself was supervising two other villages. Nanjamma would write the accounts at home. Channigarayaru would go to the fields, call the particular farmers there and mark the khaneshumaari. But it was Nanjamma who managed everything, from the abstract of the accounts to Jamabandi—assessment of the revenue due to the government. She would go to Timmalapura when she did not understand something and consulted Dyavarasayya. Channigarayaru would wear a coat, wrap a turban around his head, put on a folded upper cloth around the neck, go to the Jamabandi, pay the honorarium to the head clerk, take the signature of the officer and would return to his village like a man of great worth. When the Amaldar visited the village, Nanjamma prepared rice, sambar, rasam, curry, papad and served tasty food with ghee, which she had not even served the children, and said, 'We are poor. If there is any mistake in accounts, Sahebs should somehow adjust.' But she would never let out the secret that it was she who wrote the accounts.

Along with all these, managing her husband was a task for her. The whole year Nanjamma struggled and wrote the accounts. At the end of the year, Channigarayaru went to receive the annual payments and did not return home for fifteen days. Then he came back and said only five rupees were left. He did not even give this to Nanjamma but put it in a tin box he had brought from Tiptur, locked it and hung the key to the string worn around his waist. And even if advance tax was deducted, he should have brought at least fifty rupees back home. Channigarayaru said, 'Hey, you slut, my taste was lost and destroyed by eating the ragi balls and cowpea sambar you cook! So, I stayed happily for fifteen days, daily eating onion and potato sambar, vadas, dosas, Mysore pak, etc.'

'You stayed back to eat tasty food. The children at home have not seen Mysore pak even once. How could you swallow it, and your tongue bear the taste of it?'

Channigarayaru did not have an answer. He started his usual stream of abuse: 'You slut, tut tut, you slut, harlot, mother-fucking slut, don't talk, shut up you stray slut' and headed towards Maadevayya's temple.

Nanjamma pondered: How could she manage the whole year? The third child Vishwa was now eight months old. If the annual payment was squandered in this manner, the children would starve to death.

Even for the grownups, if there are not more than two ragi balls per day, how could anyone even survive? What will the government say if she requests it to give the annual payment to herself? What support is there for her? Where is the refuge? She reflected on this for two days. At last, an idea flashed in her mind.

The next morning, she bathed herself and the children, gave them roti and chutney, left Ramanna and Parvati at Puttavva's house on Weaver Street and then carrying little Vishwa, went to Kurubarahalli. When she entered the house of Gundegowdaru, there she saw Gangamma sitting in the inner courtyard on a seat. Lakkamma, Gowdaru's wife, was pouring ragi into the red saree spread before Gangamma. Gowdaru leaned on the wall fumbling for something in his small purse of betel leaves and betel nuts. Gangamma felt angry seeing her daughter-in-law there. Peevishly she asked, 'What hey! You quarrelsome slut, I am carrying on my living by begging. Have you come here to stop that too?' Nanjamma stood there speechless.

Gowdaru called her, 'Come here, Avva, sit here.' She sat on the mat. Gangamma made a bundle of ragi from the saree, got up and left.

Lakkavva asked, 'Your mother-in-law blamed you a lot. Oh! Two baskets full of abuses. She said you are burning with anger against her, you have made a puppet of your husband and made him dance to your tunes. You roam about the street as if you are the man who is earning. You don't give her any share in the post of Shanubhoga. So many things she said.'

Gowdaru said to his wife, 'Let that woman say whatever she wants. You keep quiet,' and then asked Nanjamma, 'What is it that has brought you here, Avva? I presume the annual payment is over?'

'Yes Gowdare, I have come to discuss about that with you.' Then she explained what her husband had done with the amount.

Lakkavva said, 'That fellow should be held, his neck must be bent and he must be beaten.'

'No, that fellow won't learn by beatings. What should be done now, you tell me Avva. Do I know better than you?'

'The amount of annual payment should not get into his hands. Then everything will be all right,' said Nanjamma. 'What do you say? Will the government agree to give it into my hands? No, that's not necessary. The total amount of annual payment is one hundred and twenty rupees. Fifteen rupees is all that will be spent for paying the Amaldar, Shirastedar and others. Let us leave that. You ask my husband to write a receipt for that remaining hundred rupees, as you did last year, saying, "I have taken from him the revenue in advance". You have to pay a revenue of eighty rupees. Somehow you ask him to write a receipt for twenty rupees for any other taxes. That would be cut while giving the annual amount. Then he would not be able to get any money. From that hundred rupees, you continue to give me ragi, grains, chillies, and five or ten rupees when I ask for.'

'Yes, that is good. You have a brain to govern like a dewan. If you learn to rule that stupid bull, it will not be difficult to rule the Mysore state. I'll come there tomorrow or the day after. Let us make him write the receipt. You don't worry.'

Gowda's wife Lakkamma insisted on cooking her food in Basavanna's temple and finish her lunch. But Nanjamma reminded them that she had left her two children in the village. Lakkamma gave two copras and two balls of jaggery for the children. Nanjamma tied the edge of her saree around them. She drank the milk mixed with ghee and jaggery that Lakkamma put before her and gave it to the child also, and returned.

Channigarayaru did not enquire where she had been early morning, but was angry since lunch was not ready yet. When he sighted copra and jaggery, he took them and started eating them. By the time Ramanna and Parvati returned from Puttavva's house, two copras and balls of jaggery were over and he had washed his sticky hands.

The next day itself Gundegowdaru came to Ramasandra. Nanjamma placed the receipt paper, inkpot and pen before her husband as instructed by Gundegowdaru. He ordered the Shanubhoga, 'You write as Avva says.' Nanjamma was dictating: 'Only eighty rupees has been remitted regarding the revenue tax of Kurubarahalli by Patel Gundegowdaru.' Shanubhoga put down the pen and remonstrated, 'I don't know why I should write that; I will not get anything in the annual payment.'

Gowdaru got angry. 'Oh ho, he doesn't get anything. Hey, will you shut your trap and write, or else...' But the Shanubhoga did not touch the pen.

Gowdaru said, 'What? Won't you write? If you step into our village, I'll break your leg. What do you think I am?'

What shall I do for my expenses?'

'First you write. I'll plan for your expenses.'

Finally he wrote a receipt for having received hundred rupees and put his signature. When Channigarayaru asked, 'Now, give me something,' Gowdaru took two rupees out of the fold of his dhoti around his waist, threw that before him and said, 'Take this. I have given the amount of ink charges now itself.'

The Shanubhoga eagerly took the money and put it in his pocket. Gowdaru returned home. The following day was Friday. Channigarayaru finished his breakfast of roti at home and went to the fair at Kambanakere. People from the hotel at Tiptur would come there and pitch the tent. They will prepare masala dosas, potato curry, Mysore pak and raw banana bondas.

4

Nanjamma very soon realized that the mere post of a Shanubhoga will never be a good source of livelihood. People without lands cannot manage their family with this profession alone. What other job could she do? When she had visited Timmalapura, she saw a neighbour of Dyavarasayya had made a bundle of leaf plates used for eating food, from leaves of the flame of the forest trees and joined them with pieces of broomsticks. Nanjamma heard that the bundles would be sent to Tiptur and six annas per hundred plates would be given in the shop. Nanjamma thought of joining fifty or sixty leaves per day in the time left after finishing her domestic chores and writing accounts.

Ramasandra Brahmins bring leaves from the flame of the forest leaves from the sand pit near Choleshwara hillock, which is three miles away from Ramasandra, and it is on the way to Nagalapura, Nanjamma's father's village. She too went to bring the leaves in the month of *Phalguna*, the season during which these leaves bloom. She thought it was not proper to go alone so far and called her husband to accompany her. But why would he come? He said, 'Let her go! Who wants to go? What itching desire do I have for this?'

She thus took Puttavva of the Weaver Street with her, left the small children at Channashetty's house, packed roti and chutney, took a gunny bag, and started even before the cawing of the crows. She had to give three annas as wages to Puttavva. Both of them would walk rapidly even before sunrise, pluck the leaves swiftly and catch the falling leaves, pressing them close to their chests. At eight, they would eat rotis, drink water from the stream, pluck some more leaves, press them neatly into gunny bags, tie their mouths tightly, carry them on their heads and return home as fast as possible. After coming home, she would open the bags and shake them off. Then she would put a string to a long, thick needle, little Parvati would prick the leaf near the stem and then begin to string the leaves. Ramanna too would slowly string the leaves. By then, Nanjamma would finish cooking. Her husband would present himself during lunch time. He liked dining on the green leaves from the flame of the forest trees. He would take big leaves, join them, sit cross-legged and devour the food heartily. When he lay down to rest, Nanjamma washed the plates and then stringed the remaining leaves, make a chain of them and put the remaining ones to be dried in the evening sun. By then, the whole day would have been spent. In the night, she had to prepare rotis for the next day for her husband and children at home, to pack for herself and Puttavva, and grind chutney. She had to go to bed early, as she had to rise before dawn.

But with the onset of monsoon, the rain began to make holes in the leaves. Even so, she could collect a hundred and fifty strings. If all these leaves could be properly joined and readied, there would be two hundred bundles of hundred leaf plates, per bundle. At six annas per bundle, she would get seventy-five rupees. To get this money she had to slit broomsticks the whole year, split the skin of the palm and sew the leaves. How could living be managed without enduring hardship? By the time she would finish bringing home the leaves, it was already time for tax collection. Kurubarahalli farmers give ink-charges in the fourth instalment. She was six-months pregnant then. Although her husband scolded and tried to prevent her, saying 'I don't know why you have to come', she went along with him on the day of tax collection. Gundegowdaru collected the amount for ink-charges and kept it with him. He gave five rupees to Channigarayaru and said, 'When you need money, come to me. Why do you need it now?' Channigarayaru gave a furtive look to Gowdaru as if he would swallow him, but he did not have enough courage to reproach him. After returning home, he calmed his anger by falsely slandering Gundegowdaru and his wife for having alliances with another man and woman of the village in adulterous relationships. Anyway, now he had with him five rupees. He was swelling with joy in his mind by imagining the pleasure and happiness he could experience when he would visit Tiptur for the remittance of land tax to the Government. He had heard that Gubbi Veeranna's drama company had camped in Tiptur. The sceneries would be like that of a palace itself. He thought: *I must shell out four annas and watch the play. That day, instead of dinner, I must eat only Bombai bondas. That bastard Gundegowda made me write the receipt for one hundred rupees. After distributing to the people at Taluk office, perhaps four or five rupees would remain. Along with it, there is this five rupee. How many days can I eat with this ten rupees? One Mysore pak costs nine paise. If I give four annas they will give six pieces. Bastards, what does his father lose if this fellow gives two or three more pieces? Tut, tut, fuck his mother...*

Meanwhile, a government primary school was sanctioned to be set up in Ramasandra. As no building was available immediately to run the school, the government asked the villagers where the school should be run at present. Patel Shivegowda suggested Hanumantharayas' temple. In that case, Gangamma and Appannaiah had to vacate the temple. Gangamma stood before Shivegowda's house with a handful of mud. Temple priest Annajois also strongly opposed the idea of running the school in the temple premises, and the obstacle for Gangamma's staying in the temple vanished. One of the houses of Shivegowda was vacant. He saw to it that the government would take it on rent, at thirty-six rupees per year and start the school. Surappa of Kikkeri area was appointed as a teacher. Some boys were admitted to the school. The discussion on whether to admit girls too was on. The teacher said, 'You admit girls too. In big cities, nowadays, girls also study in schools.' But the villagers did not agree. The teacher said to Nanjamma, 'See, if the girls are a little educated, they can get a salary of at least twenty rupees. You are an educated woman. Should I explain this to you?' Then Nanjamma, without heeding anybody's warnings, admitted Parvati to school. The villagers whispered among themselves. 'Look, how dare she also!' Nanjamma sent Ramanna to school along with Parvati. In this school, the teacher did not beat the students, nor did he make them practise letters on the sand; instead he asked them to write on a slate.

This time too Akkamma came to nurse the mother and child. But Nanjamma gave birth to a child that died within half an hour. 'Nanju, can the body of a pregnant woman bear the strain of carrying such a large amount of leaves and the fatigue of sitting for long hours and joining them? We don't know what happened to the child; perhaps due to excess heat, it died as soon as it was born.'

Nanju did not say much but she was simply crying. 'Don't cry Nanju, your health will be affected. If something untoward happens, what will happen to these children? Who will take care of them?' Following Akkamma's advice for two days, Nanjamma consoled herself. Gangamma stayed in the temple, far from the defilement caused due to the birth and then death of the newborn, but did not come and console her daughter-in-law. Though the baby died, Akkamma nursed the mother for three months. Before she left for her place, Akkamma told her granddaughter, 'Nanju, your husband is such a worthless fellow. He doesn't love the children he begets. He is concerned only with himself and his food. It is hard for you to bring them up. Hereafter you don't allow him to come near your bed.'

Nanju did not speak. Akkamma spoke again, 'You don't bother even if he gets angry. Keep him away.' Then Nanju said, 'Akkamma this is my fate. If I do so, he begins abusing me in extremely foul language, standing in the middle of the street. He doesn't bother about decency or honour. I have already experienced it.' Akkamma repeated, 'It is your fate,' and became silent.

Akkamma was already seventy-eight years old, yet she said she would walk to her village, and asked only to send a servant with her. But how could Nanjamma send her grandma on foot? She bought a red saree for three rupees for her, and then hired a cart for one and a half rupees to send back Akkamma.

5

One afternoon, at about one o'clock, Revannashetty's wife Sarvakka came visiting. She asked, 'Nanjamma, there's absolutely nothing at home. Can you please spare two seers of ragi flour?'

Nanjamma measured two seers of ragi into the tin basket Sarvakka had brought and without speaking much, Sarvakka left. That evening, when Sarvakka came again, Nanjamma was joining the forest flame tree leaves. Sarvakka sat close by and said, 'I was worried whom to ask. The children were hungry today. I too am tired due to hunger. You gave ragi and helped us have food.'

'What is it, Sarvakka? What do you want to say? How can I believe it if you say that despite having so many pieces of land?'

'Please tell me the truth. Don't you really know anything?'

'I've heard only a little. But I did not know there was not even enough money for buying a small measure of ragi for meals.'

'It is my lot. I had not worshipped Shiva properly in any of my previous births.' Sarvakka shed tears and narrated everything.

The total value of the promissory notes that Revannashetty had written favouring Chikkegowda had grown to three thousand rupees. Now Chikkegowda demanded that Shetty transferred the dry field in the village outskirts to his name. Else, said Chikkegowda, he would thrash Shetty with a cudgel. So, Shetty directly went to Tiptur with Chikkegowda and registered the field on his name and cancelled the promissory notes. There remained some wet fields. If the rains were good and the tank was full, and the land was ploughed well, at least twelve hundred seers of paddy would have grown there. But how could this foot-lawyer Revannashetty, wearing a white dhoti, with shining, striped chappals on, plough the wet fields? If the fields were given for tenancy, at least four hundred kilos of paddy would have come in hand. But Revannashetty had mortgaged that too to Kashimbaddi Sahukar and taken eight hundred rupees against that.

'What urgent expense was there to take a loan by mortgaging the wet fields? Has he fixed the marriage of Rudrani?'

'Ayyo, Nanjammore, if he was aware that he had a daughter who had come of age, it would be quite different. That adulteress! The one who left her husband and slept with her own father-in-law! That daughter-in-law! Now she has built a small tiled house near the grove in front of the village and has started a shop. Do you know where she got that money from? This eight hundred rupees was poured into the mouth of that harlot.'

Apart from these, Revannashetty had a garden of fifty coconut trees. Before they were ripe, he plucked the coconuts off and sold them off. If not, there would be no money for soap to wash his white dhoti and white collared shirts, blades for shaving his beard off and to smoke elephant cigarettes[13].

---

[13]A brand of cigarettes

S.L. BHYRAPPA

Now, Narasi had built a three squares[14] house in front of the village near Amma's groove[15] and has opened a shop. There is nobody who does not know about her. Her father-in-law Channashetty left Ramasandra out of disgrace and has set up a shop at Channapura beyond Tiptur. Her husband Giriyashetty also left the village and went somewhere. Some say he is looking after domestic affairs in a place near Arasikere. There was nobody to advise Revannashetty. Besides, no one liked to face his wicked tongue. Sarvakka had brothers in her parents' house. They had helped her and her children as far as they could. But they had their own families and problems to take care of. Moreover, how much of her hardships could she convey to them? Once when her elder brother came to advise his brother-in-law, Revannashetty abused him using rotten words in conjunction with his mother. After that, her brother said he would never speak with Revannashetty.

Sarvakka said, 'Nanjamma, I have to somehow bring up the children for the mistake of giving birth to them. We are not skilful as you people are in joining these leaves. You please teach me. I'll learn. I will come with you this year when you go to the valley of Cholanagudda to bring these leaves.'

'Will your husband not object if you come along and carry the leaves back?'

'What else will he do except keeping quiet? Didn't he quietly swallow the ragi balls like a dog this afternoon? The same ragi that I took from you, ground and cooked?'

The following day onwards, Sarvakka began coming daily for a while and started learning to join the leaves to make plates. Nanjamma taught her how the broomstick should be split, how the stem of the leaf should be broken and water should be sprinkled. Then later they should be neatly arranged and put under a weight of a round stone. Then the round leaf should be put in the centre and a leaf should be patched beneath it, the stick being, in the meanwhile, neatly pierced and broken. Nanjamma assured, 'You will begin to join the leaves faster after a little practice.' Sarvakka got some hope.

---

[14] An area of three hundred square feet
[15] A groove which belongs to village goddess.

One afternoon, Nanjamma had gone to draw drinking water from the government well in the village. The noose of the rope severed and the copper pot fell into the well. That was the only pot in the house. She could get that pot out of the well only when Kashimbaddi of Kambanakere came to clean the well. Nanjamma thought of returning home and bringing an earthen pot. She felt shy to carry water in an earthen pot from the government well. But what else could she do? When she returned home, Kallesha had come. The children were enjoying chewing the peppermints Kallesha had brought them.

He asked, 'You had gone to get water. Why is it that you came back empty-handed?'

'The rope cut off and the pot fell into the well.'

'Come, I'll get it out.' He got up and Nanju followed him. The children too were excited to see their uncle diving into the well and followed him. Nanju locked the door and went.

The water in all the other wells in the village was tasteless. But in this well, it was tasty and clean. This well had been dug two years ago by the government and was built in stone. Except those from the divisions of the scheduled caste, people from all other castes used to take water for cooking and drinking from that well. Women of upper castes like Lingayat, Akkasaali and Chaataali would bring their own ropes and before lowering the rope into the well, splash some water brought from their homes on the pulley and purify it.

Kallesha lowered the water-drawing rope into the well and tied the upper part of the rope firmly to the iron rods of the pulley. He removed his dhoti and shirt, put them down, and asked his sister to take care of them. Holding the rope, he descended into the well. The water in the well seemed as if it was in the patala itself. The well was six-feet high and six-feet wide. But there were some stone steps on the corners of the stone wall of the well. Kallesha reached the water, dived once, and when he came up he had brought up a pot. He tied it to the noose of the rope and made a sign to haul it up. But it was not Nanjamma's pot. Kallesha shouted, 'Keep it there and don't give if anybody comes and asks you to. Lower the rope again!' He dived again. He got another pot. There were ten or twelve pots at the bottom. Kallesha took them all out and sent them up.

Holding the rope, he climbed up with the help of the cornerstones. By that time, more than twenty men and women had gathered there.

Kallesha told his sister: 'Nanja, you take your pot and keep it separately,' and he told the others present: 'See, the owners of the pots should give me eight annas per pot and take them. If not, I'll take them with me to my place.'

Some went to bring money. Ex-temporary Shanubhoga Sivalinga, who had arrived there, questioned, 'Who gave you authority to dive into the well of our village and take away the pots?'

'If that's the case, I will fill water in them and drown them again in the well. Is it an easy job to hold one's breath and dive deep into a well?'

No answer came to Sivalinga. The owners of the pot gave eight annas each to Kallesha. Kallesha earned, all-in-all, six and a half rupees. He put the money into his coat pocket, held his dhoti, shirt and coat in his hand and came home in wet drawers.

Nanju thought of preparing some special dish as her brother visited rarely and would stay for a couple of days. She bought provisions to prepare rice vermicelli. After finishing lunch that afternoon, Kallesha took a nap. When he awoke, he asked, 'What have you brought?'

'I thought of preparing vermicelli. It is your favourite dish. Isn't it?'

'No, I won't stay. By evening I will start from here.'

'Oh, what brought you here? You came and are leaving so suddenly. Please stay.'

'No, I have some urgent work. I came here only to see how you are. Give me a cup of coffee. That is enough.'

Nanjamma sent Ramanna to bring coffee powder for six paisa, made a bronze glass full of coffee with jaggery. Kallesha drank it and left. Already the sun had set and darkness was spreading. But Kallesha too was like his father—not one bit afraid of darkness.

A little while after Kallesha left, Sarvakka came by and said, 'Nanjammore, the leaves of the flame of forest trees are like golden leaves. Maadevayya of the temple had gone for bhiksha to Hoovinahalli and has brought some along, not being able to restrain himself. I myself have seen them.'

'What, Sarvakka, *Maaghamasa* is not over as yet?'

'There were good rains in the *Maargasheera* month this year. That's why leaves have sprouted early. Come, let's go tomorrow.'

Nanjamma reflected upon the advice. If they did not store during the season of leaves and if there was an early monsoon, it would be difficult to get leaves. So she agreed. Sarvakka said she would be ready even before the cawing of the crow and left. It was going to be her first day. She could not sleep properly. She spent the night somehow and soon she heard the cawing of the crow, got up, held the gunny bag and packet of rotis, covered her head, and knocked on Nanjamma's door. Nanjamma too was ready and came out. The moon was still shining and Nanjamma suspected whether the crows had cawed, looking at the moonlight. Yet Sarvakka walked forward, said; 'No, it will be hard if the weather becomes hot; come.' By the time they had crossed the village, they saw that the door of Narasi's newly-built shop near the groove in front of the village was open. Somebody—surely a man—came out, softly, saying 'sure', and walked rapidly on the path in which these two were going. Narasi closed the door.

Nanjamma immediately recognized the man as Kallesha. As both of them walked covering their heads with the edge of their sarees, and had put gunny sacks on their shoulders, Kallesha could not recognize the women. He strode rapidly, without bothering who these women were. Nanju slowed her pace and remained a little behind. She was silent, thinking she ought not to state the reason behind her slowing down to Sarvakka. After the man, who was walking forward, vanished from their eyes, Sarvakka asked, 'He is your elder brother. Isn't he?'

'No, I don't know who that man was.'

'Yes, Nanjammore, it is your brother himself. It is said he visits this place once in ten days or fortnight. He comes in the night and leaves before the cock crows. It seems that Narasi herself said so to somebody.' Nanjamma did not speak. She walked silently as if she had not heard these words.

CHAPTER NINE

1

If any person stays at a place for a long time and comes to enjoy it, that place becomes the possession of those living there. Likewise, the temple of Hanumantharaya became Gangamma's and Appannaiah's. However, the authority of Annajois on the right of worship in the temple was not altered. Now, many people call it Gangamma's home instead of the Hanumantharaya temple.

Now and then, Gangamma and Appannaiah go around the villages. Earlier, Shivegowda-of-Ramasandra's name was not known beyond three miles around. It is now famous for around twenty miles. This mother and son visit each and every village, and beg at each house, saying, 'A wicked bastard cheated us and swallowed all our property. We have nothing for our livelihood; please give us something,' and Gangamma would spread her red saree on the floor. Villagers would bring ragi, cowpeas and chillies in the winnowing fan and pour them on the saree. She would make a bundle of it all and give it to Appannaiah. He would then put it into a gunny sack, carry it on his head and bring to his village.

Maadevayya also does the same thing. But he doesn't have any reason for begging. After all, he is an ascetic jangama. He is a sanyasi wearing a red shirt, red cloth and red turban, and has vibhuti smeared on his forehead. His job is to stand outside the threshold and say, *'Bhikshaa Guru Revannarabhiksha'*[16]. In each house, a handful of ragi falls into the square piece of cloth slung from his shoulder as a bag. But Gangamma reveals all the unnecessary details in every house she visits and curses the lineage and progeny of Shivegowda. Some people give her at least half full of winnowing fan; those who do not give, get her curses.

Gangamma too has a large box in her house, and it is filled with ragi; she also has two bags of cowpeas. There is one big tin full of chillies. Gangamma speaks about dharma-karma and says neither Shivegowda has prospered much nor has she been ruined.

---

[16]Seeking alms in the name of Guru Revanna.

An afternoon, around two, bullock carts stood before the Hanumantharaya temple. One was of oil miller Shingashetti's, another was of Uppaara[17] Mukkanna's. Both the carts were full of vessels, beds, boxes, umbrellas, wooden seats, mats and other domestic articles. A widow of nearly fifty, a woman of twenty-five, a seven-year-old girl and a boy of four, followed. Appannaiah saw them first, went behind the temple like a thief escapes and from there squeezed himself through the haystalks and vanished somewhere. Mukkanna lowered the cart, and said: 'Avva, this is the house of Gangavva,' and began to put down the articles. The elderly woman among them entered through the door hesitatingly. Gangamma could not recognize her. That woman herself said, 'We are from Nuggikere. My husband died two years ago. Saathu and the children wanted to come here and stay, serving you, so, I brought them here.'

It took two minutes for Gangamma to realize the full meaning of the woman's words. Meanwhile, Saathu came holding the hands of two children. In a trice, Gangamma's imagination flashed like lightning. 'Hey, you slut. This girl is born to my Appannaiah. You were pregnant with her while you stayed here. From whom did you beget this second child? Come out with it, you adulteress. Did you come here to defile the lineage of Shanubhoga Ramanna? See what I am going to do,' Gangamma got up, took the broom from the corner and stood ready. Her in-law said: 'Why do you speak such bad words? Your son himself had come to our place. My daughter is not a girl of bad conduct. You call your son and ask him. We wrote a letter and invited you to attend the ceremony; why didn't you come?' But these words did not enter Gangamma's ears.

Saathu came out of the temple. The children were scared and they stood behind their mother, holding the edge of her saree. Saathu's mother too came out, saying to herself, 'Nowhere have I seen such a woman!' Perhaps she would have told the cartman to drive back. But Saathu said, 'Amma, let us not return without speaking to my husband. We learnt that my sister-in-law stays in a separate house. For the time being, let's go to her house.' Mother too agreed. Mukkanna and Shingashetti harnessed the carts again and drove them to Nanjamma's house. Lowering the carts, they put down the luggage one by one. Nanjamma did not inquire about

---

[17]Title of a caste

the reason for their coming. Looking at the tonsured widow's dress of Saathu's mother, one knew she had lost her husband. Who knows, what hardship they were enduring.

Nanjamma decided of first inviting them inside. Only later, after lunch, could other things be asked about. She invited them all and sat with them. She too was surprised looking at the boy. However, she did not lose confidence, as no woman would dare bring so courageously the child not belonging to her husband. Saathu sat shedding tears. Her mother Thangamma said, 'See Appannaiah had come twice and stayed for fifteen days each time. It was then that Ramakrishna was born. But her mother-in-law shouts, so as to be heard by the whole street, blames her as if she has committed a wrong deed. Oh! That woman is a chandali.'

'Well, first get up and take your bath. When did your husband pass away?'

'It has already been two years. Till he lived, our life was going on comfortably with the earnings of his priesthood. Now without a male support, who calls us or takes care of us? Anyway, a wife should live with her husband. When Appannaiah had come and stayed, he had promised to come and take his wife. Of late, he has not come. So we decided to come here. We came by bus from Tiptur and got down at the roadside. These two cart-men had come to the dry fields, with carts filled with manure. They took four annas per cart and carried the luggage in their carts.'

Nanjamma was saying, 'Saathu, first bathe the children. They are hungry.' At that moment, she heard Gangamma come there thundering. 'My name is not Gangamma if I do not drive away these adulteress sluts out of this village, slapping their heads with chappals until all their hair fall.' Then Gangamma thundered again, addressing Nanjamma: 'Hey you adulteress, have you taken her to your house to start prostitution along with her? See, you harlot widow, if I do not get you punished according to what you deserve, I'll cut off my nose!' Before she finished her words, Ayyashastri and Annajois were seen standing behind her. Within a minute, Shivegowda and Sivalinga came in too. By the time one counted ten, Revannashetty had come too. Yet another five or six people gathered to see the excitement as if a bear was dancing inside. There was no doubt that Gangamma herself had brought all these people.

Nanjamma got so angry that she felt like asking why they had come to her house and who had asked them to come there, but she was patient for she did not want to antagonize these village chiefs. She did not invite any of them to come in, nor did she spread a mat for them. Channigarayaru, who was sleeping until then, woke up and spread two mats. Separate mats were placed to the two Jois. Saathu, her two children and Thangamma went into the kitchen.

Gangamma shouted, 'Oh why are you escaping inside! Hey come out, you harlot slut, come and justify yourself before the villagers.'

'Yes, justice, justice! You people come out!' Revannashetty commanded, taking the role of a representative of dharma. Gangamma shouted again, 'Hey, come out you, Revannashetty himself is calling.'

Nanjamma could not tolerate Revannashetty coming here and speaking of justice like a staunch righteous man. But no idea came to her to make them shut their mouths and send them away. However, she found a way. At the same time, Parvati and Ramanna returned from school, holding a slate and a book. Nanjamma said, 'Hey Parvati, run and bring Maadevayyanavaru and your teacher here. Say to them "Mother has sent for you."' Both the children ran.

Revannashetty asked Nanjamma, looking at her face, 'Why Madam, will it not be proper if we deliver justice?' Nanjamma went inside without speaking.

Gangamma shouted, 'Hey, why did you go inside, you lawyer?', but Nanjamma did not come out.

Now, Annajois and Ayyashastri started to reveal their knowledge of Dharmashastra. Annajois chanted some mantra.

'It is stated in Manudharmashaastra that a woman who has committed adultery should be beheaded. Also, it is written in the Vedas that by spending one thousand coins, atonement must be performed. Nanjamma has committed a wrong by taking them inside, before they had atoned,' Ayyashastri explained.

By then Maadevayynavaru came. As Gangamma had shouted loudly and roamed the streets, villagers had known about the matter and a big crowd—like one finds in a fair—had gathered in front of Nanjamma's house. There was no need to explain the matter to Maadevayya when he had to squeeze himself through the people and came there. Looking from the inside of the door that Maadevayyanavaru had come, Nanjamma opened the door and came out, and said: 'Ayyanore, you have knowledge of dharma and karma. You should judge this matter. The rest of the people gathered here should not speak as they wish. Those people sitting inside say Appannaiah had come and Saathu got pregnant by him only. Even now they are swearing on God and saying so.'

By then Maadevayyanavaru could gauge the situation. He said, 'First, send for Appannaiah. Later, justice may be demanded.'

Gangamma intervened, 'No, there is no mistake from my child's end in this. He is not such a bad fellow.'

Maadevayyanavaru consoled her, 'Let us see whether there is any mistake. If a husband has gone to the house of his wife, is there any wrong in it?' Then he said to the people standing near the door, 'Go, search for Appannaiah. Wherever he might be, bring him here without allowing him to escape.' Ten to twelve enthusiasts went in search of him. Meanwhile, both the Jois started to speak again. Ayyanavaru said, 'Nobody need speak until Appannaiah comes,' and made them shut their mouths.

Within fifteen minutes, Appannaiah came. He had been hiding in the narrow lane of Basappashetty's hay stalk in a small hamlet. When he tried to escape, two men of the search party leapt on him, held his hand and brought him. He lowered his head and stood near the central pillar of the hall where the villagers had gathered. A knot of his hair had loosened and hair covered his face. Maadevayyanavaru did not ask him any question. He told Nanjamma to light the lamps and bring them along with a photo of God. Nanjamma lit twin lamps, brought them along with the photo of Sree Rama and placed them on a wooden seat. Maadevayyanavaru asked for a casket of kumkum. When it was brought, he took a pinch of kumkum, put it on the forehead of Appannaiah, asked him to hold the photo of God and said, 'Look brother, if you tell lies, God will cut your limbs off. *Sunklamma Maari* will strike you dead. Now come out with the truth. Had you not gone to your wife's place without the knowledge of your mother?'

Appannaiah did not speak, but Gangamma shouted, 'Hey Jangamayya, why are you making my child swear falsely?' But as if Maadevayyanavaru did not hear her, he said: 'You ought to speak, Appannaiah. If you do not tell the truth, your hands and legs will be paralysed. The lamp burning there calmly, will become a big flame and burn you. Have you not watched Shanimahatme. Your limbs too would be cut off as that of Vikramarka's in that play. Yes, now speak up.'

Fear struck Appannaiah. The picture of Vikramarka howling with his thighs cut off in the Shanimahatme Yakshagana played by Dombidaasaru appeared in his mind. Before Maadevayyanavaru could repeat 'If you tell lies, Shanidevaru…', Appannaiah blurted out, 'No, I won't tell lies Ayyanavare, I had gone twice to Nuggikere'.

'How many days did you stay there each time?'

'Once I stayed for fifteen days. I don't remember how many days the second time.'

'Since how many days had you gone there?'

'Plague had struck the second time, you know, then. That means, more or less it was six years ago.' Nanjamma went inside and came out holding the hand of Saathu's son; she made him stand there. The face of that five-year-old boy resembled that of Appannaiah.

'You bastard, husband of a widow, telling me "I will go to Javagal", you have done this? From tomorrow you go there only. I won't serve you food. Tut, tut, you bastard, born of adultery…,' shouted Gangamma, and then she got up and left. One by one, the Jois and the village chiefs too left, thinking that there was no further interest or fun in this matter.

2

On the same day, Gangamma took her son and went around the villages. It was not the first time she was doing so. As Annajois had another key to the door of the temple with him, it was convenient for him too, so that he could open the door and complete the worship rituals.

Saathu, her two children and Thangamma stayed at Nanjamma's house. Nanjamma had the stock of ragi and cowpeas in her house which would be sufficient for these people too. But they would suffer from loose motion if they ate ragi and acidity if they ate cowpeas. It was beyond Nanjamma's ability to adjust rice and tovar dal daily. During festivals, she would cook red rice and when some higher officials and Shekdars visited, she cooked fine white rice and rasam of tovar dal. But now there was no other option but to cook rice. Without expressing any dissatisfaction, Nanju cooked rice and tovar dal sambar and served them. If there was cooked rice, her children too would demand rice only. And then there was Channigarayaru—why would he eat ragi balls? If everyone eats rice only, why should Nanjamma alone swallow ragi balls? And what of the savings? To sum it all up, it would have been hard to manage all the expenses.

After fifteen days, when the mother and son returned to the village, Nanjamma came to know this. After lighting the lamps in the night, Nanjamma called Parvati and told her, 'Go and bring your uncle here. But don't ask him to come here in your Grandma's presence.' Parvati, an intelligent girl, understood the subtlety of the situation. She brought Appannaiah with her. When he saw his wife, he was pulled between desire, fear and a sort of shame. He came and stood silently near a pillar. Nanjamma asked him to be seated. Saathu was cooking inside.

Nanjamma said, 'Appannaiah, have your dinner here.'

'What about Amma...?'

'She won't say anything. She will, however, have some rotis at night. Get up, wash your hands and feet.' Appannaiah washed his hands and feet. Channigarayaru too got up. Nanjamma told Saathu to serve the children alongside the elders. Appannaiah felt embarrassed even to say 'enough or don't want'. Saathu felt a shy disdain, and felt insulted to ask whether he wanted anything. When they were dining, Nanjamma and Thangamma remained in the courtyard. Then the brothers chewed betel leaves, betel nuts and tobacco. Nanjamma went inside and whispered something to Saathu for a while. Widow Thangamma too joined in that conversation.

In that house, there was a dark room in which the bins of grain were kept. It had a door also. Nanjamma swept that room, spread a mat, and put two beds that Saathu had brought with her together. When Appannaiah got up, Saathu asked him to sleep there that night.

This unexpected invitation caused in him joy along with alarm. Without being aware, he said 'Amma...'. Then Nanju said, 'I will send Parvati and Ramanna to stay with her. Moreover, she is not afraid to be alone. You go and sleep in the room where the grain bins are kept.' But Channigarayaru stared angrily at his wife and said, 'Why should you make such unwanted mediation?'

Nanju, glaring at her husband, who spoke as if a bear was let loose in the midst of Shivapooja, said, 'Please close your mouth and sit here. Thirumale Gowda's buffalo has calved and his wife has given the milk, and payasa is being prepared. Do you want it or not?'

Hearing of the payasa from the recently calved buffalo's milk,

Channigarayaru immediately got up and went into the kitchen. Appannaiah entered into the room with the grain bins. Nanju came into the kitchen and said to her husband, 'We will finish cooking and call you. Till then, you chew tobacco,' and sent him out. She sent Saathu to Appannaiah's room and closed the door.

On the spur of the moment, Nanjamma had spoken about the milk from the recently calved buffalo, and managed the situation. But now, which cow or buffalo she could cause to calve and bring milk and prepare payasa from for her husband? The usual sharpness of her mind came to her rescue. She spread the beds for the children in the courtyard and made them lie down. Then she came into the kitchen, scraped a coconut, ground it with a little rice, boiled it, put two balls of jaggery in it and then mixed it all in some milk. Then she sent Thangamma outside and called her husband to come into the kitchen. Shanubhogaaru was awake and waiting; he came as soon as called and squatted in front of Nanjamma. Then Nanjamma put before him the large-mouthed vessel of payasa, placed an aluminium plate and said, 'You serve yourself; it was already fifteen days since the buffalo of Thirumalegowda had calved. So, the milk did not split at all. Yet the payasa is nice.'

Channigarayaru put a ladle into the plate and licked. It was very tasty; he smacked his lips. Nanjamma asked, 'Shall I move now. Will you have your payasa?' He did not have time to say 'yes'.

Appannaiah got up in the morning and went towards the village tank; then he went to the temple and asked his mother, 'Amma, shall we bring them here too?'

'Who?'

'The Nuggikere people.'

Gangamma was speechless. In a minute, everything became clear to her. 'Ayyo, ayyo, you bastard, I thought you had been to see the orchestra in the night to Dyavalapura. Had you gone and slept with that harlot?'

Appannaiah stood with a lowered head. Gangamma, after 'blessing' him in her own language asked, 'Did that adulteress herself ask you to bring them to your place?'

Appannaiah gathered a little courage and said, 'Why should she ask? I suggested that myself. Let us bring them. Why should we leave them there?'

'Hey, you bastard, born to a paramour, have you already told her

"I will take you there"? Wait, I'll tell Annajois and teach you a lesson!'
At once she got up and went directly to Jois's house, stood beneath
the eaves and called, 'Joisare, please come out!' Owing to the force of
Gangamma's voice, seven to eight people gathered from around. She
informed the Jois, who came out, 'Look here, Joisare, this—my son—
has slept with that harlot and come home. He says he will bring her
to our home from today. Now tell me, can the husband and wife live
together in God's temple?'

The God, Hanumantharaya, is a known celibate. Husband and wife
living together in this temple is prohibited in dharma. So Annajois said,
'That fellow seems to have lost his senses. If he does that, I'll expel all of
you from the temple.' He came to the temple, warned Appannaiah and
left. Now Appannaiah's face became pale. However, upon remembering
the pleasure he had experienced during the night, he felt it impossible to
be away from his wife. Somehow he took heart, went to his sister-in-law's
house and explained what had passed. Meanwhile, Gangamma, who had
followed Appannaiah, stood outside the door and abused Channigaraya
and Nanjamma to her heart's content. Channigarayaru, who was still
digesting the payasa he had partaken at night and was sleeping, got up.
Perhaps he would have scolded his wife, but as he felt an urgency to
go behind the village tank bund, he went off rapidly, almost running,
without speaking a word. Gangamma felt as if this son too had turned
hostile towards her and returned home, without staying there.

3

Appannaiah stayed in his sister-in-law's house that day too. Within
two to three days, they came to a decision: Appannaiah should live
separately with his wife and children, and his mother-in-law too
should stay with their family. And now, what was to be the means of
livelihood? Appannaiah spoke of his ability and strength. He had all
these years roamed around villages with his mother and had experience
of mendicancy. So he said, 'I will look after my wife and children, even
if I have to beg. Am I not a man?' But a place should be arranged for
them to reside in.

There was an empty place in this village belonging to Kurubarahalli
Gundegowdaru. It didn't have a fence and nobody was using it to
stock hay or firewood. It was at a distance of nearly forty metres.

Nanjamma took Appannaiah with her, went to Kurubarahalli and requested Gundegowdaru. He agreed and said, that he had no objection to Appannaiah's erecting a hut at his own expense and staying in that place. Appannaiah was no shirker when it came to work. He had the enthusiasm and the physical strength to work if someone flattered him with compliments and guided him. The association with his wife that he had not had for a long time, gave him the zeal to work. He got Nanjamma's guidance. Saathu sold a silver vessel she had brought with her for twenty-five rupees and gave him money. Only ten bamboo poles, ten cartloads of mud and two stone pillars were bought from that money. Appannaiah himself dug the foundation, raised a wall of bamboo frames, fixed two stone pillars, tied the bamboo poles and split the bamboos. He brought seven hundred coconut leaves after having begged for them from several people's gardens and covered the roof. A carpenter made a door that was four-feet high and fixed it along with a latch to the hut. Grihapravesha was performed by boiling milk in an earthen pot; until then, all of them had their food in Nanjamma's house.

Now, a means for livelihood should be found. Appannaiah went around the villages, without being accompanied by his mother. He cursed Shivegowda and requested them to give him something. He was not a beggar with the square cloth hanging from his shoulder. So villagers gave him alms not less than half a seer in winnowing fans. Meanwhile, there came the harvest season. He would visit threshing floors, where ragi would be threshed, winnowed, piled and worshipped. It was believed that if donated in winnowing fans to those who came there, the pile would rise. So Appannaiah would get a winnowing fan full of ragi. Many times Gangamma and Appannaiah met at the same threshing floor. She did not speak with her son and the son too didn't raise his face and look at her. A few farmers taunted them. 'Have you two come pretending you are from separate houses? How can we give you both?' There were, of course, some who gave to the both of them.

The same situation would arise in other villages also. And so, now either the mother or the son would go. Some villagers asked, when one of them visited after a few days: 'What is it, if you pretend mother and son are separate and come two times, from where can we give you?' Gangamma came to know this and she went around the village before Appannaiah. She was the only person to eat. Expenses were less. As such, she had a store of provisions of ragi, pulses and chillies sufficient for three years. Appannaiah had to provide for five persons. Besides, villagers could not pity a strong young man when he asked for ragi, as they pitied when an old widow beseeched them. There were some who told Appannaiah: 'Hey, why don't you work and eat? Have you lost your limbs?'

Appannaiah was very enthusiastic at his wife's arrival in the beginning. After a few days, the enthusiasm decreased. It was not comfortable and pleasant to roam around the villages the whole day stepping on to the thresholds of everybody's house, and the plight of being scolded by them. When he was going around with his mother, begging was her work. She would make a bundle out of the ragi or grains in a red saree and pour it all into one place. Appannaiah's burden was to fill it into the gunny bag and carry it on his head. Now he was fretting in his mind by the irritation of himself begging.

One day, Nanjamma came to Appannaiah's house. He had gone around the villages. While speaking about this and that, Nanjamma said, 'Your Jayalakshmi too is already of our Parvati's age. Admit her to school. Admit Ramakrishna also. What will be the plight of the children if they are not educated at least a little?'

'Yes, we must admit them.'

'I thought of telling you another thing. I learnt you are selling ragi that is brought home; you should not sell it. Only during the harvest season and after two months, the farmers give ragi. After the Jyestha and Aashada months are over, they will not give even a grain. If you lose grains now, it will be very difficult during the rest of the months. You purchase a couple of earthen grain bins and store some.'

The widow Thangamma said, 'What can we do keeping that damned ragi? Who will eat it?'

Nanjamma knew that ragi would not suit their body. But how many people were there in the village who could eat rice rather than ragi? If one practised eating, they would become immune to it. To live without adjusting to ragi is possible only by wealthy landlords. Nanjamma advised them how she thought best. She had in her mind to tell them some more. Saathu and her mother had the habit of drinking coffee. As they belonged to the Kadur region, from a very young age they had been addicted to it. When Saathu had first come to Ramasandra, she had somehow controlled that habit because of her mother-in-law's fear. Now even in Ramasandra the number of coffee-drinking people was increasing. If they were well-off they could afford to drink. But for the four persons of Appannaiah's family, coffee was needed twice a day. But from where it could be brought?

'If you give up that habit, a lot can be saved.'

'No, not possible for us. How can we stay on an empty stomach in the mornings? You eat just roti and keep quiet. We cannot live like that,' Thangamma said. Nanjamma dropped that topic.

One day, Saathu came to her sister-in-law's house and was talking to her. Nanjamma was breaking broomsticks quickly and joining the flame of forest tree leaves, one leaf every two minutes. Saathu said, '*Akka*, how hard you work. Along with household chores you write the accounts of a Shanubhoga and you carry these leaves and join them. No, it is not possible for us.'

Nanjamma said, 'Look Saathu, since three or four months I have felt like saying something to you. But I kept quiet thinking you may misunderstand me!'

'Please tell me what it is.'

'In your house, there are five members to feed. But only one is earning. Besides nobody can earn a livelihood by begging. Something should be done on our own. Anyway, why would this family have fallen into such a situation, if they had some knowledge of working independently? At least you people do something. There are two women in your house. After finishing household chores even if you join these leaves, leisurely, you may join three hundred of them per day. Now the rate of leaf plates is seven annas per bundle. However much may be the number of bundle, it is said, they send them to Bangalore in lorries from Tiptur. If there is thirty rupees per month, it helps a lot.'

'Does not the body get overheated by joining these leaves continuously?'

'No, nothing happens if we practise it. Anyway, if the body gets heated excessively, it will become all right if castor oil is rubbed on the soles of feet, before going to bed.'

Saathu decided that she too should join the leaves. The following day, Saathu came to her sister-in-law's house. She too broke the sticks along with Nanjamma. Saathu had joined eighteen leaves while Nanjamma finished hundred and twenty. Nanjamma encouraged Saathu and said, with practice, she too could join leaves quickly. But by the next day, Saathu's hands and feet began to have a burning sensation. Thangamma consoled her daughter with caring words, 'The husband should take care of his wife and children. You don't have to join those leaves, daughter; leave it.' Saathu stopped of joining leaves. Meanwhile, she had not had her periods and morning sickness began.

Saathu's father Shyamabhatta was a priest and they belonged to a family of priests. As such, Thangamma had more knowledge about orthodox concepts such as purity, pollution customs, rites, etc., from the very beginning. Gangamma was less orthodox concerning matters of purity. Nanjamma was observant of these rituals outwardly, but inwardly, she was not bound to these concepts of orthodoxy. She cooked sambar in an earthen pot. When she cooked rice, she preferred cooking in an earthen pot, because it was cooler for the body than the rice cooked in a metal pot. It was okay with Vokkaligas or non-brahmins. But could brahmins do so? Many days, Nanjamma's children would eat whatever Maadevayyanavaru gave them. That third boy, Vishwa, used to eat, sitting on the lap of Maadevayyanavaru, whatever he would bring by kantebhiksha from the houses of his caste. Though Nanjamma aware of this she never taught her children not to do so. All these were not acceptable to Thangamma. Saathu too did not like it.

The wives of Ayyashaastri and Annajois, the village priests, were staunch followers of purity, pollution and all orthodox customs related to these. Annajois's wife, while she had her periods, was not even seen by her husband. But Nanjamma, even during her periods, cooked stealthily; Annajois's wife Venkatalakshmi said that Nanjamma would weave lies and say, 'Our Parvati cooked'. Hearing this, Thangamma decided not to visit Nanjamma's house. She thought, 'Women of other castes bathe themselves the very day they get their periods, go into the kitchen and cook. Being born as brahmins, if she behaves thus, is it not worse than lower caste? Tut-tut!'

Thangamma and Saathu visited Annajois's house one day. The Jois himself began saying, 'When it is ancestral property, both the brothers should share equally, shouldn't they? All the other property is lost; what justice is there in Channigaraya enjoying the post of Shanubhoga alone and nothing being given to Appannaiah? There is this government rule that the annual salary of the post should be divided between the brothers. For how long are they going to cheat you this way?'

Thangamma's ears perked up. Saathu's mind was full of anger and jealousy against her sister-in-law, Nanjamma, who was conducting herself so cleverly, never opening her mouth about what should belong to her brother-in-law's family too. Saathu said to herself, 'She only pretends; she is a fraudulent woman!' Annajois suggested: 'Appannaiah and you demand your share. If they refuse to give it, go to Tiptur, prostrate before Amaldar Saheb and request, and he will help you.'

When Appannaiah returned home from the villages in the evening, Saathu explained to him what Annajois had remarked in the morning and said, 'Don't we have children too? Shouldn't we get a share in the ancestral property now? The annual salary of a hundred and twenty rupees is fixed for Shanubhoga, half the amount, that is sixty rupees, belongs to us. Besides, what about the ink charges they get?'

Appannaiah could not decipher her logic. He knew that the posts of Shanubhoga and Patel were always inherited by the eldest son, and he had seen it happen. But now, he thought, 'Government rules must be different. Moreover, what more do I know than Annajois?' Pondering this even though it was already night, he went to Jois's house to discuss the matter.

Jois explained to him that the brothers should get an equal share in the annual salary of the Shanubhoga; he spoke like a well-wisher. 'Alas, you stupid one, all these years they swallowed your money and cheated you.' Hearing this, Appannaiah was enraged; he stormed to his brother's house. Channigarayaru was not at home. Nanjamma was teaching lessons to Parvati and Ramanna by the light of the dim kerosene lamp. Appannaiah stood before his sister-in-law and demanded angrily, 'I won't stay quiet anymore if you cheat us like this. You must give us half the share in the annual salary of Shanubhoga.'

Nanjamma could not understand his words, 'In which annual salary? What are you saying?'

'From the annual salary of Shanubhoga's post. My father did not beget only Chinnayya. He begot me too. If an equal share is not given, I will go to the Amaldar himself, yes.' He said so and then went to the temple of Maadevayyanavaru, knowing well that his brother would be there. He kept blabbering on his own loudly, so everyone could hear all along the street. 'My father had sired me too. Half the annual salary of the Shanubhoga should be given. These bastards swallow the entire amount and live comfortably. I have to roam around the villages and beg.'

Nanjamma did not know that he had gone to Madevayyanavaru's temple. She thought of completely, enquiring what the matter was, got up and went to Appannaiah's house. But he was not there. Nanjamma asked her sister-in-law, 'What's the matter? Appannaiah came to our house and shouted "We too must get half the annual salary of the Shanubhoga" and other things.'

Saathu said, 'If there are two brothers, should it not be shared between us? As my husband is innocent and lacks knowledge, you have enjoyed everything all these years? Nobody can be believed in these times.' Nanjamma countered, 'See, Government rule is not so. It is true, the annual salary of Shanubhoga is one hundred and twenty. What about the expenses? Paper for the account book, charges for the ink needed to write—do you know how much it costs? What about the hard work of drawing rules in the book and writing accounts, straining our eyes. Could Appannaiah go shouting on the street without bothering about any of these things?'

'After all, what great work is writing accounts? I too can write it. "Only by soiling our hands we can have curds in our mouth", goes the adage.'

Nanjamma decided not to prolong the discussion and went home. Channigarayaru was not in the temple. He had gone to the tank bund, returned home and was performing sandhyavandana. Nanjamma did not want to talk and disturb her husband in the middle of it, so she went in, swept the kitchen, lit lamps for the deities and prostrated in front of them out of reverence. Appannaiah's nature was known to her. But she was surprised at Saathu's behaviour. *She herself had carried tales to her husband. Who might have instigated her? Whoever it might be, she shouldn't have changed thus. Nanjamma sat brooding. We shouldn't help anybody in these times. People do not remember the favour and aren't grateful.'*

By then, there was the sound of Appannaiah coming again. It seemed another eight or ten people also accompanied him. Gangamma's loud voice was also heard. Nanjamma came out and saw that there was every important person in the crowd included Annajois, Ayyashaastri,

Revannashetty, Shinga of the Ganiga caste, the former Shanubhoga Sivalinga and others. Only Patel Shivegowda was not present. Channigarayaru, who was performing sandhyavandana in the hall, put the vessel by the door of the kitchen and draped a dhoti around him. As soon as Nanjamma came out, Gangamma started, 'In other lands, they do keep a portion for grandmothers? That good man begot these two, true. But was it a lie he had tied tali to me? In the annual salary of the Shanubhoga, I should also get a share. You explain, Revannashetty.'

Revannashetty said, 'Sivalinganna had managed the post of the Shanubhoga earlier. He knows everything. Let him be a judge now.'

Immediately, Sivalinga got up, sat near the pillar and asked, 'What do you say Chinnayya?' By then Channigarayaru had understood the situation. But nothing came to him. He pointed towards his wife and said. 'Ask her' and sat as if he had saved himself. Revannashetty was staring at Nanjamma's face and said, 'So, what is it? You yourself tell us,' and after a minute said, 'you need not be scared.'

Meanwhile, Saathu and Thangamma had come and were standing near the outer door. Nanjamma's anger rose. At once, she addressed the gathering in a warning tone, 'Who asked all of you to come here? You come out of your houses to reckon other people's problems. Look after your own problems. Mend your own problems and be decent. Will you all now get up and go out or you need some more "honour"?'

Nobody in the gathering had expected this sort of retort. Shinga, Guruvayya of Horakeri and others did not know anything about the matter. Appannaiah had walked through the street shouting, 'All of you come, there is a Panchayati'. So they had come. Whatever it may be, the village Shanubhoga's accounts were with Nanjamma; why should they be unnecessary hostile to her? Thus they got up quietly and left. After they left, the remaining people too lost courage. When Nanjamma again threatened in a strict voice, 'Will you people quietly leave the place or not?', Sivalinga, Revannashetty and others too, left. Nanjamma again asked Appannaiah: 'Appannaiah, which evil-minded, ruiner of family instigated you to act in this way?' Appannaiah did not answer. But when Nanjamma started this topic, Annajois got up and said, 'It will be late for sandhyavandana. This is the dispute between your houses. Though I told Appannaiah not to call people, he called all the villagers. I don't know when he will get some sense,' and went away. Ayyashastri too adjusted his shawl and followed Annajois.

'Appannaiah, the post of Shanubhoga always belongs to the eldest son. You may go to Tiptur and inquire,' Nanjamma said. On that, Appannaiah immediately got up. He felt as if he was drowned in water, when the people left the Panchayati. Only Gangamma left the place shouting, 'Oh look at the tongue of this slut! What cheek she has. She spoke opposing all the villagers. Let her say whatever she wants. I will not forego my share.'

Channigarayaru did not utter a word about this matter while dining. When Nanjamma asked, 'Did you understand what sort of people they are?' He only said, 'Let them say whatever they like' and poured green sambar prepared in the afternoon, as though the matter was not connected to him. Nanjamma could not sleep that night. Her mind was unhappy and she felt agony seeing the fickle behaviour of her sister-in-law. At the same time, she had a suspicion as to whether they had to give a share in the annual salary. By midnight, the idea of going to Timmalapura and asking about this to Dyavarasayya came upon her and grew stronger in her mind.

She tried to wake her husband up at dawn and told him her idea. But he grumbled inside the blanket. 'No, I won't; you go alone!' She woke up Parvati and Ramanna, washed their hands and feet, gave them some parched flour and jaggery to eat, and took them with her to Timmalapura.

As Dyavarasayya was aged, of late his health was not in a good condition. He would get up late in the morning owing to the chilly weather. He was surprised to see Nanjamma coming just an hour after sunrise. She had not been to Timmalapura for two years. Dyavarasayya was relieved when he came to know that she was managing the accounts of the Shanubhoga independently. He learnt why she had come now and said: 'Yes, there is no doubt about it. I am clearly aware of it. Only the eldest son has a right on the annual salary of the Shanubhoga. Is not the royal throne also like that? Is the kingdom divided between the elder and younger brother?'

After Nanjamma and her children bathed and finished their breakfast, he said: 'You want to be fully sanguine, don't you? If so, Kambanakere is not too far. It is only three miles from here. You walk a little distance and inquire with the Shekdar himself. Then there will be no thorn of doubt piercing your mind.'

He sent a servant to show her the way. Nanjamma walked with the children towards Kambanakere, the headquarters of the hobli. She was acquainted with the Shekdar. She had served him white rice, rasam and chutney, whenever he had visited Ramasandra. He was of a very calm and peaceful nature, and had always spoken with her gently, calling her 'Amma'. Hence without any fear or anxiety, Nanjamma went to his house. When he saw her, he said, 'What, Nanjamma, have you come here to inquire whether a share should be given to the younger brother from the annual salary of the Shanubhoga?'

Nanjamma was surprised and stood speechless. He said to her, 'Half an hour has not passed yet that your brother-in-law Appannaiah and his wife had come here. Both were afraid of speaking to me. They stood outside the door with folded hands. Two persons, Annajoisa and Shivalingegowda, spoke for them. I reprimanded them all and sent them away. I gave them a good dressing down before they left. You need not worry; who does not know that the annual salary is for the eldest son only? Why did you come this far, that too on foot, to inquire about this?'

Nanjamma took heart. The Shekdar said, 'You have walked this far in the hot sun. Come in,' and he asked his wife to serve food to Nanjamma and her children. After their meals, when the heat of the sun had reduced, Shekdar permitted her to go and his wife offered muttaide betel leaves, betel nuts, a coconut and a blouse piece, along with arisina and kumkum. *She also* gave pieces of jaggery to the children.

It was around five miles by this direct route to Ramasandra from Kambanakere. The children complained of their aching legs on the way. Nanjamma's mind was satisfied hearing the Shekdar's words. She held the children by their hands, walked slowly, cajoling them and reached her village before nightfall.

4

Gangamma felt an unbearable loneliness since Appannaiah had started living separately with his wife; she got the feeling that her children, born out of her womb, had disowned her. How could she tolerate this defeat? She thought that her elder daughter-in-law had helped Appannaiah build a hut to separate the son from his mother.

It was a year since Appannaiah's wife and mother had come.

Appannaiah was fed up roaming around villages, begging for grains and listening to the taunting words of the villagers. One day, he went to Kallegowda's house in Kenchegowda's hamlet. Though Gowda was at home, he did not offer a wooden seat to Appannaiah. Yet he sat on the floor and begged him to give him some ragi. Gowda got angry and at once exploded: 'Hey, do you have rumbling in your belly to purge or to emit gas? Just now your mother came and took some away. Now you have come begging. Does ragi grow freely? Come, we will feed you roti, come, work in the field. Then you can take two seers of ragi.'

Appannaiah sat unmoved. Gowda snarled, 'Hey, will you go out quietly or should we push you out by your neck?'

Appannaiah felt sorrow pressing him from within. He had heard such words many a time in the last one and a half years. But nobody had spoken of holding him by his neck and pushing him out. He got up, took his dhoti and small gunny bag and came out. By then his eyes had filled with tears. Wiping them, he had walked about ten steps when he saw Gangamma walking in front of him, her saree pouch full of ragi. Her heart was pricked seeing her son shedding tears at that age. She asked, 'Why do you cry so, my son?' Appannaiah's sorrow only increased. He narrated what happened and asked, 'Amma, should Kallegowda say such things?'

'Appanna, come. Let us talk in Basavanna's temple.' She took her son to the temple in front of the village, sat with him on the platform and said, 'See Appanna, if both the mother and son go begging, what else will they say? Why did you come here for ragi?'

'If I do not come here what shall I do for a living?'

'Oh! Alas, my fate, oh poor fellow! Born from my womb should you worry for your livelihood? Was I not taking care of you like a prince all these days? Why should you get into this sort of misfortune to feed that widow and an adulteress of a wife, going around villages and begging for grains. You should bring home ragi by begging, that too sighing without a grub for the belly and those sluts would sell it, buy fine rice, tur dal and fill their stomachs to the full. Along with that, those damned things need that coffee-peepi also. Look at the colourful sarees that widow wears and look at your torn dhoti. Does the prostitute look after the well-being of her paramour who is sacrificing her own happiness?'

Appannaiah felt that his mother's words were true. He had not begged in anybody's house before the arrival of his wife and children. Begging was his mother's job. He used to loiter around chewing tobacco, in the end only filling up the gunny bag with grains that his mother heaped up, and carrying it home, as was his duty. Besides, since they were only two people, if they went around the villages for three months, they could comfortably live without the problem of food. Gangamma asked, 'Anyway, you are taking care of her as she is your wife. But why should you provide food to that widow, your mother-in-law, who has come here and camped shamelessly?'

Appannaiah did not go begging to any house that day. He put into his gunny bag what his mother had got, tied the bag and placed it on his head. The load was not heavy for him. On the way, Gangamma said, 'See, that Maadevayya is a mother-fucking bastard. Could you believe him when he made you swear falsely? You might have visited her place once or otherwise. How do you know that child was begotten by you and she conceived it by you?'

Appannaiah was carrying the load in silence. When they neared the village, Gangamma said, 'You just come with me. Be happy and comfortable as you were before.'

The son again started living with his mother. He did not do any work. He lay down and slept. Gangamma cooked tasty meloogara sambar of dehusked cowpeas adding a mixture of ground onion and garlic, prepared hot ragi balls and awakened her sleeping son. When he sat for lunch, he felt the heaven-like life he enjoyed one and a half years ago, become a reality again. He always relished ragi balls. Moreover, what can be tastier in this world than the sambar of dehusked cowpeas? Neither his wife nor his mother-in-law were adept in cooking round ragi balls in the house. For them, cowpeas were gastric and eaten only by other castes. He cursed them in his mind, 'damn those abominable whores' while gulping ragi balls and devouring ladles full of sambar.

From that day onwards, he did not return to his wife's house. The first day they thought that maybe he had not returned from the villages; then they learnt that he was staying in his mother's house. But how could they go and call him back? The third day they sent Ramakrishna, the little boy. The temple of Hanumantharaya was locked. For another fifteen days, mother and son did not return. Saathu faced a tough time.

There was no ragi at home to sell. There was no rice or coffee powder; there were only a few little pieces of jaggery given to Jayalakshmi and Ramakrishna in the sugar cane crusher behind the village tank. But coffee could not be made only from jaggery. The villagers were aware of Appannaiah staying with his mother, before his family came to know about it. They did not get provisions on loan in the shop and it was impossible to starve. Without drinking coffee their headache would not subside. So, they pledged a silver utensil containing five cups—panchavala—with Kashimbaddi Sahukara and got two rupees. Eight seers of rice for a rupee, coffee powder for two annas and milk for an anna were purchased.

The mother and son returned to the village, but Appannaiah stayed back with his mother; he did not go to his wife's home. Saathu was running her fourth month and sent word through little Ramakrishna for him to return home. Gangamma said, 'Tell her he won't come. Do tell her this also, "let her demand that person to provide provisions to run the household, who she slept with and gave birth to you"', and sent away the boy.

The boy returned home and reported the same words to his mother. Saathu was enraged. Her mother Thangamma flared up as if she would spit fire. Though her daughter prevented her from speaking anything, she did not heed her, went to the temple of Hanumantharaya, stood in front of it and shouted, 'There has not been a handful of grain in the house all these days. This fellow who is not capable of looking after his wife and children, to what happiness and prosperity should he have married my daughter?'

Gangamma retorted: 'Hey, you wife of a petty priest, my son can never spend his life with an adulteress of a wife.'

'Oh oho, why would my daughter become an adulteress? You yourself must have conceived your son through adultery. Why are you showing your bitch's mind, even when we respect you?' While Thangamma was still going on, Saathu came there. 'Amma, why have you started talking to her? Let her say whatever she wants. She will suffer for her sin.' When Saathu was consoling her mother, Gangamma started her tirade again: 'Hey, Appannaiah, do you hear what this hypocrite witch is saying? First, she has instigated her mother and sent her here. Now she blames me, saying, what I speak is sin. Oh ho ho, is it not a sin to give birth to a child when the husband is not living with her?' Gangamma had not yet finished when Appannaiah got up, came out like a hero and asked his wife, 'Hey, you slut, look, I will hit you with my chappals. Do you think I do not know your character and conduct?' Scared of this force of anger, Thangamma and Saathu ran towards their house. Gangamma roared, 'You stupid fellow, why do you stand still? Pluck away her mangalya and turn them out of this village. That hut is built by you. Set it on fire.'

Appannaiah chased them. Saathu had bent down and was almost going into the house when his hands reached the neck of his wife. His hands got hold of the mangalasutra, stringed with black beads. By the force of the pull, the thread gave way and the black beads scattered on the ground, leaving only the mangalya, the gold beads and the small gold tubes in the thread. There was a cut on the right side of Saathu's neck and blood oozed out of it. Saathu fell down screaming 'Ayyayyamma!' Appannaiah broke into the house. The kitchen stove was burning. He took the burning frond of a coconut tree and torched the roof made of dry coconut fronds. Flame and smoke engulfed the house. In the meantime, villagers gathered upon hearing the commotion.

Thangamma screamed, 'Ayyo, all the articles of our house are burning! Oh, help us save them!' People rushed inside, salvaged whatever they could lay their hands on—vessels, clothes, winnowing fans, baskets, wooden seats, the grinding stone—and brought them out. It was impossible to put out the fire with water as it was a thatched hut. Besides, there was no water near the house. Within half an hour, the house, which was built by Appannaiah himself, had turned to ashes. The four walls around and two pillars were blackened by fire and stood there. 'Hey, you widow do you see what I have done?' Appannaiah thundered like a tiger. Thangamma was cursing, 'Let your hand be paralysed!' By then Saathu recovered consciousness and remarked, 'Amma, I swear on myself, don't speak another word.' Appannaiah held high the mangalya in his hand and went around the streets and lanes of the village shouting, 'I have plucked out the taali off that slut! Hereafter she is not my wife, nor am I her husband, tut-tut, damned whore!'

Nanjamma too had rushed there, when the house was set on fire. She joined others, rushed inside and saved any articles she could put her hands on. She too did not know what could have been done further.

She was aware that it would not be wise to speak with Appannaiah in this context. And to speak with her mother-in-law Gangamma, was unthinkable. She asked Saathu, 'What can I do? Tell me.'

'We will stay in your house for a few days now. Later, we will do something.'

It was impossible for Nanjamma to say no. She requested the men to carry all the things to her house and she too lent a hand.

The materials were dumped in a corner of her house. Nanjamma entered the kitchen. They would not eat ragi balls so, she took out the rice reserved for the feast and soaked it. There was no tur dal. She sent Parvati to bring a seer of tur dal for four annas.

Gangamma became restless when people again helped them and carried things to her elder daughter-in-law's house. Her calculative mind said, 'That whore is a scheming slut. She will plan something and again trap my son.' Immediately, she rushed to Annajois's house and asked, 'Oh Joisare, did you hear the news?'

'What is it? I don't know anything at all,' he said, desirous of listening to everything in graphic detail from Gangamma herself. She picturesquely described the prowess her son had displayed by plucking out the *tali* off his wife and asked, 'Nanjamma has taken her into her house, she being a woman whose *tali* has been taken away. Shouldn't she be called for a panchayati and be fined? You tell me.'

It so happened that Gangamma taught a new point of *Dharmashastra* to the Jois. His mind too reflected on pressing Nanjamma for a panchayati, and making her shell out a fine of at least twenty-five rupees. But he hesitated for a minute, remembering how she had reprimanded them the last time—as if slapped their faces in the panchayat—relating to the case of sharing the annual salary of the Shanubhoga and how, the very next day, he had gotten a further dressing down from the Shekdar. It was an insult to him. Now he gathered up his courage and decided to take revenge. He told Gangamma to wait and went to the house of his uncle, Ayyashaastri. In these situations, this old shastri was not a man to sit quietly. This question concerned brahmins. Should *brahmana dharma* survive or die?

These two guardians of dharma, with other four brahmins of the village, came to Nanjamma's house. Along with them, there were Gangamma and Appannaiah. Nanjamma did not know that these people had come to conduct a panchayati and give out a verdict. Annajois started, 'A woman without a mangalya is equal to a widow. But how can she become a widow while her husband is alive? So, she is as good as a dead woman. One should not see her face.'

'You have committed a crime in taking such a woman into your house. There must be expiation. You must pay fine.'

Channigarayaru got scared listening to him, hand said: 'I don't know anything about this. It is she who brought them into our house. If you want, even now I will kick them out, holding them by their necks.'

'That is all right, but a fine must be paid first for them having been brought into your house.'

'How much should be paid?'

Annajois asked, 'How much is it, uncle?'

Ayyashastri answered, 'They are poor; twenty-five is enough.'

'From where can we bring so much money? Please make it a little lesser, Joisare?'

'What, Chinnayya, do you think that money will go to our father's house? It is the money that belongs to Sringeri Mutt[18].'

Now, no further negotiation was possible. Channigarayaru turned towards his wife and scolded her. 'Hey you slut, why did you need this headship? Why did you bring these damned people into our house? And now, will you push them out by their necks or not?'

Thangamma had stood inside the kitchen next to the door and was listening. Now she came out and asked, 'All these days you were like a trustworthy person to us. Now, why are you behaving in this manner Joisare? What harm have we done to you?'

'See, we are not unfriendly with you. *Dharmashastra* has prescribed thus. Knowing fully well the shaastras, if we keep quiet, will Sringeri Mutt leave us be?'

Until then Nanjamma had been standing silently; but now she spoke, 'It was Appannaiah who plucked the tali off his wife. Does he have any right or authority to pluck away his wife's mangalya, according to the shaastras? If you have to impose a fine, get it from him. Then, when their house was burnt to ashes and these women and children were literally thrown out on to the street, what should we have done instead

---

[18]A temple in Sringeri.

of taking them into our house? Is it written in your *Dharmashastra* that in such difficult times you should not help the victims?'

Both the guardians of dharma were baffled. Gangamma too felt as if she was slapped, looking at this scheming daughter-in-law, who now turned the panchayat against her son. The old Ayyashaastri was saying something like, 'The tali he tied, he...' By then, Annajois said, 'Uncle, you keep quiet. It is said she herself plucked out the tali, saying I don't want this tali tied by you. Is it not so Gangamma?'

'Yes, yes, that slut herself plucked it out and said I don't want this *tali.*'

Thangamma asked, 'Why do you speak so unjustly? Can all of you swear upon it?' Gangamma said, 'Hey you shrew, why should I swear, while this has been witnessed by the whole village itself?'

The dispute changed its course. If there was a man to speak strongly in favour of these people it would have been different. Nanjamma had understood this and said, 'See, Joisare, you don't have first-hand information about what happened. You wilfully create quarrels in others' houses, and enjoy the fun. This is not the way respectable people behave. Nobody had invited you to come here. Please get up and leave this place. Hereafter nobody should come to our house in the guise of the panchayat, justice, etc., all of a sudden, in this manner.'

'Look, Joisare, the arrogance of this slut', started Gangamma but before she finished her words, Saathu, who had stood near the door inside the kitchen, took the hanchi grass-stalk broom, came out, threw the broomstick on Gangamma's face and said, 'All this happened because of this home-wrecking widow!' For a minute, Gangamma was aghast. Appannaiah got furious and got up. Nanjamma panicked seeing the situation reaching this extremity. She pushed Saathu and Thangamma into the kitchen, closed the door and stood blocking it. In a cautioning tone, she finally asked, 'Will you people get up and leave our house or not?'

Both the Jois left. The two brahmins who had been sitting as if they had no responsibility in this, stood up and left the place. Meanwhile, Gangamma flared up. She took the wooden pestle kept in the corner and rushed towards the kitchen. Nanjamma obstructed her, stood in front of the door, and warned, 'See, our house means it is the office and residence of the Shanubhoga. If anything untoward happens here, I will inform the Shekdar and call the police.' Gangamma got really scared.

Appannaiah began to sweat. He seized and threw away the pestle from his mother's hand, saying, 'Come away Amma, let us not have anything to do with these sluts,' and got out of the house. Gangamma felt that it would be below her dignity if she left at once and for ten minutes continued her abuses while following her son out.

Though Nanjamma had cooked rice and sambar, Saathu and Thangamma did not eat. They were stunned and shocked by the incidents that had passed since that afternoon. Mother and daughter were very much worried about their future.

5

The mother and daughter were talking to each other the whole night. Thangamma woke up in the morning and told Nanjamma, 'For what pleasure or happiness should we stay in this village after this? We owned a house in our place. Six months ago we sold that house to come here. There are some villages of priesthood with us. Ramakrishna is already a boy of eight. If somehow his thread ceremony is performed and he is taught some rites as Punyaahavachana,[19] Navagrahadana[20] and such things, we will find a means of livelihood. We will build a hut in a place given by some good people and stay there.'

Nanjamma had no other solution for them. Moreover, mother and daughter were not accustomed either to work hard or to eat ragi balls and rotis. They had not tried to change their lifestyle. If they had tried, perhaps Appannaiah would not have behaved in this manner. If they return to their own place, their plight will not change for better. Thinking she could do nothing, Nanjamma consented to their plan. Their minds were burning eagerly to leave this village at the earliest. Saathu decided to sell her earrings. A woman living in the street of Nanjamma's house bought it for twenty-five rupees. That was enough for their travel expenses. The same day, Nanjamma prepared payasa, served them and put kumkum on the foreheads of Jayalakshmi and Saathu. The next day, she saw to it that a cart was harnessed and their luggage was packed and placed in the cart. She too went with them till the bus road. A little while before the Mudaliar bus to Tiptur came, wiping her

---

[19]Purification ceremony
[20]Donating grains in the name of nine planets.

S.L. BHYRAPPA

tears, Saathu said, 'Akka, both of us came to this house as daughters-in-law. You are somehow struggling. But my fate has turned like this.'

Nanjamma did not reply. Every incident, since she had come to this village after her marriage, flashed through her mind one by one. Questions were rising in her mind. 'Why were we born; why were we married off to such a house?' After the luggage was put on the top of the bus, they sat inside. When Saathu said, 'You must visit our place once', nobody among them believed they would meet again.

Nanjamma returned home, sitting in the now empty cart. In a little while, Soorappa master's wife Rukkamma came. After talking about some current topics concerning the village, Rukkamma said, 'I learnt that Annajois has written a letter to Sringeri, requesting the Mutt to excommunicate you.'

'What will they do by writing?'

'Ayyo, don't you know what it means? The Mutt would order that nobody should visit your house nor you should visit ours. We should not even help you by giving water or fire. If the people of your own caste keep aloof, how can you live?'

These words no doubt scared Nanjamma. But what benefit or help she was getting now from these caste people? She kept quiet, thinking it would be well and good if nobody came home.

After a fortnight, one day, Annajois and Ayyashastri came to Nanjamma's home and handed her a letter. It had the signature of the administrator of Sringeri Samsthana Mutt and had the emblem of the Mutt. The Mutt had ordered: 'Shanubhoga Channigaraya's family is excommunicated for taking into his house a woman who tore away her mangalya and said she did not want her husband. Until the family pays a fine of hundred rupees to the Srimutt and expiates by scorching their tongues with darba grass with the help of local priests, nobody should have any relation in terms of fire or water with that family. If someone does, they also should be excommunicated and the Mutt should be informed of that.'

After finishing reading the letter, Ayyashaastri asked, 'Now what are you going to do?'

Nanjamma answered, 'All these years, on the day of Rama Navami, somehow I was preparing Paanaka and Kosambari and offering all of you. Now I cannot do it.'

'Even if you prepare them, we will not come.'

'It is your wish.'

Both of them left, saying, 'See, you can lead life opposing the palace. But if it is the excommunication from the Mutt (Gurumane), it is not possible to live, understand this.' Nanjamma felt insulted by this but she was not afraid. The next day she wrote a letter to the Mutt explaining in detail what had really occurred here. She informed the Mutt, 'Obeying his mother, the husband himself tore away the tali off his wife's neck who had not committed any wrong. It was true we had given shelter to those helpless and shelterless women for a day and sent them away to their place. They had not committed any wrong in this context.' She told her husband to put his signature. When the postman arrived on Monday, she took an envelope from him and asked him to write the address on it and posted it. Much time passed but she did not receive a reply from the Mutt.

The death ceremony of Nanjamma's father-in-law would fall in the Pushya month. Till now it was performed in the house of Channigaraya, he being the eldest son. Appannaiah too would come here and without sharing the expenses, he would finish the rituals and leave. The eldest son Channigaraya had to change the sacred thread from his right shoulder to the left frequently while performing the ceremony. But the younger one's duty was to sit quietly donning a pavitra darba on his finger and prostrate whenever the Jois asked him to. For some years after they separated, Gangamma had not come here even to take prasada made in the name of her husband. Later, she had begun to come only on the day of the ceremony. Both the Jois had told earlier that they will not come either to officiate the shraaddha or to the ritual of first feeding of three Brahmins, as the family was excommunicated. Channigarayaru was much worried. Who was the cause for all this? Was it not his wife? He got angry and reproached her, 'Why did you take them into the house, you slut, you widow of an ass?' But the problem would not be solved by just abusing his wife.

The Jois decided to perform the shraaddha in the temple where Gangamma stayed and Appannaiah had to observe the main rite of changing the sacred thread from his left shoulder to right and vice-versa. To change the thread from left to right in a shraaddha meant he got the headship. He felt a sort of elation for he too was becoming an important person now. Besides, if shraaddha was performed at his own home, he could keep and eat vadas, rave laddoos and pooris, for at least a week. But he failed to take into account that the expenses of the ceremony would have to be borne by him.

Gangamma was not much worried about the expenses. She would somehow adjust fifteen to sixteen rupees. If she requests in the villages she goes around begging for grain in, saying, it was for her husband's shraaddha expenses, some good people would surely give cash of four annas, two annas, coconuts and pulses, and that would be enough to perform three shraaddhas. But Gangamma's thoughts ran on the lines of: 'When the eldest son is alive and he doesn't offer the *pinda* to his father and the younger son offers it, her husband who descends in the form of a crow, would not touch it. Just as the government, where the rule says, the post of Shanubhoga belongs to the eldest son, the pinda in shraaddha too should be offered by the eldest only, shouldn't it? Immediately she went to consult the Jois, and reasoned with him: 'Nobody has the strength to pay the fine of hundred rupees. Should her late husband Ramanna in the heaven starve without having food even once in a year, for the mistake these fools have committed? Moreover, it was her hypocrite witch of a daughter-in-law who had committed this mistake and not her son Chinnayya. Some solution should be found for this.'

Both the Jois agreed with her argument, and decided to take a little amount as fine and remove the condition of excommunication over Channigaraya and take him into the fold of the caste, but his wife should be kept excommunicated. But how could Channigarayaru pay the fine, as he had no money of his own! Both the Jois consulted each other and this is what they decided: Annajois had to pay the revenue tax of nine rupees and eight annas; Ayyashaastri had to pay six rupees, three annas and five paise. Channigarayaru wrote separate receipts mentioning the amounts; the revenue they had to remit to the government for the current year was collected. However, a way had to be found through which the total amount could be deducted from the annual salary of the Shanubhoga. Anyway, Shanubhoga Channigarayaru regained the religious authority to perform his father's shraaddha.

Annajois was invited for the ritual, first serving of food, and he had to fast from the morning. He did not have any other work to do. His wife was sifting and cutting vegetables in the kitchen. The Jois, perhaps as he was fasting, was remembering pooris—deep fried in ghee—which he had once eaten at his mother-in-law's. He told his wife: 'See, your mother once had served pooris deep fried in ghee. Oh how tasty it was! You have never prepared such pooris for me.'

'Bring that much quantity of butter. I will fry everything, whatever you want, in ghee.'

'Butter is four annas per seer. From where can I bring that?'

'If so, why do you crave for it? Then you keep quiet.'

Jois felt stupid. But the next moment an idea came to him. He challenged his wife, 'See, today I will eat sweetmeats deep fried only in ghee.'

She mocked him: 'Oh hoho, who is waiting to cook and serve you.'

'Wait and see,' the Jois said and ordered his son, 'Hey Narasimha, run immediately and bring Appannaiah.'

Appannaiah had donned a wet towel and was assisting his mother in cooking. He ran half naked to Annajois's house. The Jois said, 'See Appannaiah, I have a cold and am running a temperature. I cannot come to the ritual meal serving of the Brahmins.'

'If you say so at this hour, what can we do Joisare? Already the sun has come up as high as four men standing. At this moment who else can we search for?'

'You call your mother. I'll tell her.'

Gangamma too came running, hearing what the Jois said. She touched the ground at a distance and requested humbly, 'Please Joisare, don't make my husband starve.'

'Well, okay, when you are requesting in such a way, I cannot refuse. When we come to the ritual meal served first for the Brahmins, refusing or not eating the sweetmeats is not approved in the shaastras. So do one thing. Deep fry all the items in pure ghee. Then I will eat.'

'How and where will we get that amount of ghee now, Joisare?'

'Bring money, I'll go to the houses of gowdas and get you butter. Anyway, I have not yet taken my bath.'

Gangamma went home. It was not right to serve one Brahmin with sweetmeats fried in ghee and the other one, with those fried in oil. At least one and a half seers of ghee was needed to deep fry pooris, vade, aambode and chikkina undes, sufficient for two Brahmins officiating the ceremony. That means six to seven seers of butter. She hardly had a rupee or two at home. Gangamma still had a silver vessel given in her marriage, at home. She sent Appannaiah with that to Kashimbaddi Sahukar. He weighed it, gave two rupees for twelve tolas of silver at two paise interest per day.

Joisaru devoured the sweetmeats deep fried in ghee and asked for some for his children, packed it in a banana leaf and came home. He told his wife, 'Hey, you also eat,' but she said, 'How can we eat the ceremony sweetmeat from another's house?'

'Oh, no preta will possess you! Eat, and give some to the children also.'

'Look, I was born in an orthodox family. We are much afraid of shaastras and customs. But Joisaru is not afraid of anything, is he?' When his wife told him this and smiled, Joisaru felt proud of his courage.

6

After the ritual meals of the brahmins were over and all the rites of the ceremony were completed, Channigarayaru sat before the leaf on which food had been served as prasada, meant for God. He proceeded to consume this sumptuous prasada. Then he donned his shirt and went towards the tank bund. By then it was already half past four in the afternoon. He had not chewed tobacco since he had had his bath at noon, though tobacco was there in the Hanumantharaya temple. He did not have with him betel leaves and areca nuts, nor did he have even a single paisa to buy them. While returning from the tank bund towards the village through the groove of Amma, he came across Narasi's shop. The front square of the three square-tiled houses she had built, was her shop. She stored all her goods inside. It was said that she would cram the goods of the shop in the attic where her cooking provisions were kept.

When the Shanubhoga came, Narasi was present in the shop. She had an open bundle of betel leaves before her. Channigarayaru could not resist the craving for tobacco, went near the door of the shop and asked, 'Narasamma, will you give me a couple of betel leaves and areca nuts and some tobacco?'

Narasi was also chewing betel leaves. She had a broad face and wide eyes. Her mouth always looked red with betel leaves, nuts and lime, and the juice of tambula was so profuse that it seemed as if it would flow out of her lips. She seemed as though she had not endured much hardship in life and if she smiled, the brightness that danced in her eyes would winnow and toss the person standing before her. She asked, 'What is it, Shanubhogaare, you are asking me for leaves? Why? Did your wife refuse to give some to you?'

'No, there were no betel leaves at home. I had performed the shraaddha of my father, had gone towards the tank bund, and come this side.'

'Oh, come, surely I'll give. You are the Shanubhoga of this village. Is it possible to refuse you?' She flashed her eyes and smiled. He felt happy, thinking that at least she accepted his authority in the village and entered the shop. She invited him, 'Come, inside', got up and took him to the inner square hall. In the semi-darkness inside, he could not see all the things clearly. There were several sacks filled with provisions related to the business. A bed was spread on the cot placed in the corner of the wall. She said, 'Please sit here.' When he stumbled saying 'It is dark, Narasamma', she came near him, held his arms, pulled him and made him sit on the cot and herself sat beside him. Now Shanubhoga's eyes began to adjust to the surroundings. But without his control, his body and limbs began shivering, as if attacked by bouts of chill. Within a minute, the trembling reached an extreme and his teeth began clattering inside the jaws.

'Oh, Ayyanore, why are you shivering like this?'

'You...y-o-u, y-o-u. How could you touch me in this manner, Narasamma?' he asked, regaining his breath.

'Didn't you come and ask me for leaves?'

He did not understand what she meant and blabbered: 'I... I had no mo-mo-money, so I asked.'

'I am not asking you for money.'

'Why did you aaaagain tttouch mmme?'

She held his arms, raised him, brought him out and said, 'Now, go home quietly.'

Shaking with fear, he walked out hastily. When she called, 'Wait for a while', he stood with the same sort of fear.

'Come here please. I am not going to swallow you.'

He stood again before her shop. She put into his hands a pack of betel leaves, betel nuts and two long pieces of tobacco and said, 'Take it and go home. Ask Nanjavva to smear lime on the leaves, fold them and give them to you, and chew them. See, people like you should live obeying your wife at home. Do you understand?'

No doubt the Shanubhoga got a little angry. But he did not know how to call her names. Holding the pack of leaves, nuts and tobacco, he entered the village and directly went home. His wife, occupied with the account books, did not speak to him. He too did not say anything. He rolled on the mat that was spread near the pillar and began chewing tambula and tobacco.

CHAPTER TEN

1

Nanjamma felt more contempt than sorrow when she heard that her husband was allowed into the fold of the caste and she was not. She had developed her own opinion concerning dharma, karma, shaastra. Her father Kantijois was so well-versed in priesthood that none in that village or the surrounding places could excel him. If anyone had any doubts about auspicious or inauspicious rites, he or she would come to him and get them solved them. Such a person was not performing his father's shraaddha. If somebody asked, he would answer, 'I have gone to Gaya and offered pinda there already. Hence I need not perform shraadhha again.' He would recite a mantra to clarify, it was not necessary to perform the annual shraaddha after offering the pinda in Gaya. But no one could say whether he had really gone to Gaya and even if he had, if had offered pinda. Akkamma herself did not believe it. But who had the guts to speak before Kantijois?

Nanjamma pondered, 'If at all Appa was here, these Jois of the village would not have crossed their limits. Our lands too would not have been lost. If for once he had come and thundered, her husband and mother-in-law would have been scared and would have obeyed him. Where had he gone? He is not dead for sure. In the past too, when I was a baby, he had left the village and had not returned for four years. He travelled around Kashi, Rameshwara and other places. But nobody knows where he's gone now. Parvati was an eight or nine-month-old baby when he left. Now she is running nine. Either it must be his fate to wander in unknown places or our fate that he should go away from us in this manner!'

Nanjamma's mind became restless after her husband left for his mother's house on the day of the ceremony. If the rite was performed in her house, she had to fast, take a head-bath and cook. She reflected, *though she was excommunicated, could she eat something or not? She was the eldest daughter-in-law of the family; her husband would be performing the rituals, changing the sacred thread from left to right. How could she have food?* Such thoughts crowding her mind, she made roti and chutney for the children. *Even if the ceremony was performed, children would have had to have their breakfast.* She was doubtful whether those people would call and give the children prasada. So, she was undecided whether to cook for the children or not. Then she prepared another ten rotis. *If they called the children, the rotis would not go stale; the children can eat them later,* she decided.

The children went to school. Parvati and Ramanna were in the fourth, and Vishwanatha, in the second standard. Nanjamma was joining the flame of forest leaves. It was already noon, the time when the shraaddha rituals would start at her mother-in-law's house. At that time, Maadevayyanavaru came to Nanjamma's house. Though he used to come to her house now and then, he had never come at this hour. This was the hour he used to take his meal after completing his kantebhiksha. If he had gone around the village for bhiksha he would still be out of the village. It seemed Ayyanavaru had not yet taken his food. His face was very pale. Nanjamma thought, 'We are, after all people with families; we have to face many hardships and sorrows as soon as we get up in the morning. But he is a sanyasi. If his face has become so dull and pale, what might have happened?' and she spread a mat for him. She asked, 'It seems Ayyanavaru has not yet eaten food?'

'I have decided not to go for kantebhiksha in the houses of our caste people in this village, Avva!'

'What happened?'

'I go around villages and bring ragi. If the sadhus and sanyasis from other places visit our village, I give them provisions to cook in the temple. When I stay at the village, kantebhiksha is sufficient for my food. It seems that the people of Banajiga street in this village have talked among themselves about my bhiksha. I had been there now for bhiksha, and went to four or five houses. In every house they said, "Look, this Ayyanavaru wants the ragi of Karunya bhiksha in the morning and wants ragi balls and sambar of kantebhiksha in the afternoon." I felt distressed and weary and returned.'

Nanjamma was sad. Ayyanavaru never sold grains he collected from the villages and hoarded money. There was nothing in the world to call his own. He begged, enduring hardships only for feeding people who visited the village from other places.

'Ayyanore, will you not go and cook something for yourself?'

'No Avva, I am in an agitated mood. Even then, this belly feels hungry. If you serve me, I will eat.'

Nanjamma was not much surprised. This sanyasi until now, she remembered, had not even sipped a drop of water in her house. Now he himself was saying he would eat here. She said, 'Please wait for a little while, I will quickly cook a little rice and rasam.'

'No, no, all that is not needed. Serve me, Avva, whatever you have cooked,' he said.

Nanjamma went in, brought the rotis and chutney she had prepared in the morning on an aluminium plate with a cup full of curd, and placed it before him. He got up, washed his hands and began to tear the rotis. As she watched him eat, she recalled that her father-in-law's annual ceremony was being performed at her mother-in-law's house. By now, the ritual meal of the brahmins would have begun. She said, 'Ayyanore, today is my father-in-law's ceremony. They have not revoked my excommunication. Do you know that?'

'Yes, I know, I know. It seems these high-class brahmins asked for every dish to be prepared in ghee only. Else, they would not attend the meals offered to the ancestors. Appannaiah pledged a silver vessel, got two rupees at Kashimbaddi's shop and bought butter. At about nine or ten, I was sitting in front of the temple. On his way home, Appannaiah saw me and related to me all this. The jois had a running temperature it seems. He would eat sweetmeats prepared in ghee only, and he threatened them that he would not come if it is cooked in oil.'

There was no need of saying anything more, since, for sure, they would never get back the silver vessel paying up the interest. Nanjamma asked, 'Ayyanore, is there any truth in these ceremonies and other rituals? If it is only inviting and feeding these priests, it seems useless to me.'

'Who knows whether it is true or not. Perhaps it must be true. When Shanubhoga Ramanna was alive, not even for a single day did your mother-in-law cook and feed him at the right time. She didn't take care of him properly. Now she, who goes begging around villages, performs his ceremony.'

'Were you in this village when my father-in-law was alive?'

'I came here three years before Channayya was born.'

'Then which is your native place?'

'Is it important? Whatever the place may be? After Shiva brings us to life on this earth, we ought to stay in a place until our death.'

Maadevayyanavaru only told this much, but did not divulge the name of his place. Nobody knew about his place. It is said, he spoke the dialect of Hubballi, Dharwad or North Karnataka region, in the beginning, when he came here. Then people mistook him for a cattle buyer from the North, who came to the fairs of Boresante, Ramanathapura and other places. In the beginning, he did not know how to swallow ragi balls and used to eat only ragi rotis. But within a couple of years, he practised speaking like the people here and swallowed ragi balls. If anyone asked, 'Which is your native?', he would answer, 'Choleshwara temple of Ramasandra.' Now nobody asks him that question. For he was a respected elder familiar to the Ramasandra folk than the middle-aged like Channigarayaru. Nanjamma did not question him again about his native place.

Meanwhile, he finished eating the rotis. Children came home for lunch. They ate, without grumbling, the same roti and chutney their mother gave, drank water and went to school again. But Nanjamma did not eat, for nothing remained after serving the children. She didn't feel like preparing anything again. Ayyanoru was sitting outside. She came out and asked him a question that was pricking her mind, 'Ayyanore, I will ask you another question. If you feel like answering, all right, if not, let it be. Why did you come out in this way, leaving your house and family?'

'Where did I leave home, family or the Mutt, Avva? When did I have a family? I was born a sanyasi. I wandered through many places and came here. I felt like staying here, and I am here.' It seemed like he was evading an answer. To her, whether he had a home and family remained a mystery.

She sat reflecting upon the past life of Maadevayyanavaru. Had he married? Did he desert his family and come out? One day, her neighbour Puttavva had told Nanjamma that Ayyanoru was from the Bellari region; his wife, it seems, had deceived him; he was disgusted, left everything, deserted them and became an ascetic. Nanjamma had asked, 'How do you know this?' She had said, 'Some people used to speak among themselves when I was a girl. This Ayyanoru was much younger then.'

Puttavva's words were also not worth being trusted. Ayyanoru will never mouth these to anybody. Nanjamma thought: 'If he doesn't speak, well then, I too need not bother about it...who knows, what sorrow lies in his mind!'

Both of them sat for a while without speaking a word. Then Ayyanoru asked, 'What are you thinking, Avva?'

'Nothing.'

'All these days I was indebted to this village. I am thinking now of going elsewhere.'

'Ayyanore, after all you are a sanyasi. If ignorant people say something, should you feel distress or take it to your heart? Wherever you go, you have to face people of every type.'

'That's also true, Avva,' he said. Perhaps he was not in a mood to speak. After a while, he got up and left for the temple.

2

Maadevayyanavaru, who left for villages in the morning, did not return to Ramasandra even after two or three months. Nanjamma was agitated not knowing whether he had left the village forever. He was the only person in the village who could be called a good man. If he had gone away disgusted, who knew whether he would return! But his luggage remained in the temple. He used to lock the room where he stored two to three quintals of ragi, two sacks of horsegram, a bin full of chillies, some aluminium vessels and four or five mats. He had taken the key to the room. But Nanjamma had a premonition that he would return one day. The temple was bereft of his radiance once he left. Nanjamma never visited the temple. Now there was no attraction even for people like Channigarayaru to go there and while away time.

Parvati and Ramanna completed primary school. Ramanna was a very intelligent boy. His teacher Soorappa told Nanjamma that the boy stood first in the school. His handwriting was as beautiful as corals strung together. He would put rules in the account book of Shanubhoga without making mistakes. He could read anything in Kannada without faltering the short vowel, long vowel, unaspirated and aspirated letters. Nanjamma had taught her three children shlokas like 'Shaantaakaaram Bhujaga Shayanam' and 'Bhajagovindam moodhamate'. Parvati and Ramanna had learnt by rote, poems like 'Nalacharitre' and 'Lavakushara Kalaga'.

What other education was needed to manage the post of a Shanubhoga? Nanjamma had a different idea altogether. She thought, 'I don't want this post of Shanubhoga to go to my children. They should get educated, to at least get the post of a Shekdar.'

Master Soorappa said, 'Don't stop Ramanna's education. Send him to middle school.' Middle school was in Kambanakere, at a distance of five miles from Ramasandra. There were fifteen to twenty houses of brahmins in Kambanakere. *If someone could go there and fix* vaara *for the boy, he could stay and study there. He could come home on Saturdays and pack his food for Monday. It would be convenient if he got* vaara *for four days a week and once on Saturday afternoons. Shekdar may give one* vaara, *if we requested. But for another four days, whom should we ask? Perhaps Master Soorappa and Dyavarasayya may have some acquaintance there*, she thought.

But Ramanna did not agree to have his meals in others' houses. Whether it was shyness or fear, he said he would walk daily from Ramasandra to Kambanakere, and back, to Ramasandra.

Crossing the old mango tree that was beyond the temple dedicated to the village goddess, climbing down the Kabballi mound, Ramanna had to walk beside the mound, which was full of anthills. Nobody knew how many snakes dwelt inside them. It was frightening to look at the holes in the anthill which had grown like branched horns. Beyond that, there was Gowdanakoppalu. If you, then, walked across the lane filled with thorny cactus, you would reach Kambanakere. Ramanna was yet a boy of nine. He had to walk alone on this route. But without striving hard, how could he get an education?

He placed the primary school certificate Master Soorappa had given in front of the deity at home, prayed to it, pressed the certificate against his eyes and took it in his hand. Then Nanjamma packed rotis and chutney she had prepared for him. Of course, Channigarayaru had agreed to take his son to Kambanakere and admit him to school. But on the day fixed for admission he had to wake up at seven in the morning. So from under the blanket, he grumbled, 'Let us go tomorrow'. The date fixed after having looked at the almanac, though, could not be changed. Nanjamma herself accompanied her son. Ramanna prostrated before the God, his mother and his elder sister Parvati. One shouldn't prostrate before a person who is sleeping. His father did not get up, so the boy could not offer his respects to his father. The mother and son reached the school. In the place for the parent, the headmaster took the signature of the mother; with the admission fee of eight annas, he admitted Ramanna to school. Looking at the other boys there, Nanjamma felt she had to buy a lungi for his son. A black cap also was needed for his head. This was middle school. He could not attend classes in mere shorts.

He needed at least two lungis. If one was washed, there should be another to wear. Two lungis and one cap cost two rupees in all. He also needed pencils and exercise books. Besides, there should have been a coloured handbag to put all these in and the packet of roti and chutney. All these cost seven or eight rupees. But Nanjamma did not have that much of money at home. There were bundles of flame of forest leaf plates neatly joined. Villagers themselves had purchased the bundles from her home during the marriage season. The remaining bundles were kept in the attic. Nanjamma came home, climbed to the attic and counted the bundles. In total, there were hundred bundles left. At seven annas per bundle, it would be forty-four and a three quarter rupees. It should all be sold at once. But to harness the cart just for hundred bundles, would be a waste of rent. But where could she get money from?

She sent for Sarvakka. She had eighty bundles of leaf plates with her. If they jointly sent the bundles, they could share the rent of the cart. Sarvakka said, 'My husband goes to Tiptur to act as witness in the court. He goes alone in the cart which has an arched cover. Let us send the bundles with him.'

'Sarvakka, I agree. But you know the nature of your husband.'

'Yes, that's also true.'

Finally, an idea came to her. Sarvakka too should go with her husband in the cart with all the bundles. She should negotiate, sell the bundles and bring the money safely. Nanjamma consented to this. She gave a list of articles like lungis, a cap, books and a bag to be brought for Ramanna.

The following night, Sarvakka left in the cart with her husband. After the sale, she took the money from the shopkeeper. She purchased the articles Nanjamma had mentioned and returned in the cart the next night. On the way, she dozed off. When she reached the village and got down from the cart in front of her house, all the articles she had bought were intact. But the small bag containing money, which she had hung around her neck, had vanished. She asked her husband. He became ferocious and retorted, 'You were lying down like an ass and snoring. Who knows, where it fell down? You sisterfucking slut!' Nanjamma was at a loss to console Sarvakka, when she came running, shedding tears and narrated what happened. She had spent six and a half rupees for Nanjamma's articles. She had to give back thirty-eight-and-a-quarter rupee to Nanjamma. Sarvakka's thirty-five rupees also were in that bag.

'Nanjammare, I swear on this casket of Linga around my neck, please don't take me to be a thief.'

Nanjamma reflected patiently, asked Sarvakka many questions and said, 'Whatever you may say Sarvakka, the money has not been lost in any other way. When you were dozing, your husband himself has stolen it.'

Immediately, the truth flashed in front of Sarvakka too. She went home, asked her husband: 'It is only you who have taken the money. Come, give the money of Nanjammaru.' Revanashetty became like the *bhoota* that jumps about in the fair of *Veerabhadra*[21] and beat Sarvakka black and blue, almost breaking her bones. How could that gentleman, who gave witness in court, tolerate it if he was called guilty of being a thief?

Though Sarvakka was beaten hard, she decided to do something. The next day, she got up early in the morning, took her daughter with her and walked to her mother's place in Shivagere. Sarvakka had in her neck a golden casket of *Linga* given to her in her father's house. Either out of fear because it was God or simply because of the fact that the idea of stealing hadn't occurred to him, Revannashetty had not cast his eyes upon it; it had thus stayed intact. Sarvakka sold it to a goldsmith for a hundred and fifty rupees and ordered a silver casket of Linga for eight rupees. After two days, she returned and paid Nanjamma her dues. She entrusted the remaining money also to Nanjamma and said, 'When there is nothing to eat at home, I'll come and take a rupee or eight annas from you. Please keep it with you.'

'Oh, such a big amount, where shall I safeguard it, Sarvakka? By chance if something happens, what shall I do?'

---

[21]Veerabhadra was created from the wrath of Lord Shiva.

Sarvakka suggested: 'Put it in an earthen pot and keep that inside the string of the flame of forest leaves. Nobody would know.'

Nanjamma did so.

3

After Ramanna began attending middle school, Parvati stayed at home. Now, a new thought started to haunt Nanjamma's mind. Parvati was already a girl of twelve. She was like her mother, tall and well-built and looked older than her actual age. She should be married. But who would search for the bridegroom? All these years she had somehow simply managed her family. Now she had to provide for Ramanna's education, and was it a child's play to arrange a daughter's marriage? But it could not be simply left out or postponed.

Parvati had learnt songs and drew beautiful designs of rangoli her mother had taught her. Of late, Nanjamma used to make her daughter cook special dishes and had taught her traditional cooking for the festivals. After she left school, Parvati would join nearly two hundred leaves from morning till evening. She was growing and needed some milk, ghee and nutritious food. The cow Akkamma had brought while nursing Vishwa, had calved a female calf. But the cow had no one to care for. There was nobody to take her out for grazing in the fields. Such a good breed, now gave only three-fourths of a seer of milk. If three ladles of curds were not served with meals, her husband created a ruckus. From the curds that remained, how much could be shared between the children? The girl joined so many leaves that her body would get overheated. Was it not to her that the curds should have been served? Or to the boy who walked to school ten miles every day? Or to the younger one attending school in the same village? To what extent could Nanjamma act partially to her children? To whom to serve more and to whom less?

There were no rains that year although the Jyestha and Aashada months had passed. Someone said, there were no rains in Western Ghat region itself. There was no sprout of green on the earth which had dried up in summer. Without food, the cow began giving only a quarter seer of milk and soon stopped that also. There was not even a drop of buttermilk at home. Nobody had tilled the fields. The villagers were anxious about whether the crops this year would be completely lost or at least the monsoons from the north-east would pour and they could get the ragi crop. As usual, Nanjamma had asked her husband to write receipts for hundred rupees in the name of Patel Gundegowdaru and two other persons. But seeing how the rains had failed that year, Gowdaru said: 'Look Avva, the ragi that I have in my underground granary is sufficient for my family and my servants even if there's no rain for an entire year. But it seems that our in-laws in Jammenahalli, do not have even a grain of ragi. They had sent word and asked for at least four quintals of ragi. Neither can I give nor refuse; this is the situation. Take cash for your receipts. There is no ragi this year.'

Nanjamma would have been wise if she had purchased ragi by taking the money at an earlier date. But how could she have foreseen this? She had stored a little quantity of ragi at home. But it had gotten over two months ago. Yet there were no rains. Meanwhile, the price of ragi increased to one rupee for eight seers. Whereas a quintal used to be for three rupees, now it was available for twelve rupees. Her heart sank. When she went to Kurubarahalli one day to take money from Gundegowdaru, he said: 'I thought you had stored ragi. You did not come here at all. You buy however much is possible for you. In another couple of months, you won't get ragi even for sowing.'

'If so, please arrange it for me from somewhere, Gowdare.'

Chikkathammegowda of Nagenahalli, next to Kurubarahalli, had not yet opened his underground granary. When he did open it, Gundegowdaru purchased five quintals of ragi and sent it to Nanjamma. Now the rate of ragi was at a high. It was now sixteen rupees per quintal, which meant six seers per rupee and eighty rupees of Gundegowda's revenue tax was equated with that of the purchase of ragi. There was still twenty rupees remaining. Nanjamma needed money for other expenses, and got that amount in cash.

At least four seers of ragi were required every day for the five people at home. Besides, if there was more of milk, curds, vegetables, dal and pulses, need of ragi flour would have been less. But with the other items not within their reach, four seers of flour was required every day. If in the morning, they could stop making rotis, a seer of flour could be saved. But rotis had to be prepared to be packed for Ramanna who went to school. When the elder brother was given roti and pickles of gooseberry, the younger Vishwa would not keep quiet, and how could the girl Parvati be refused? She could somehow restrict her children's hunger. But to control and console her husband's hunger was not child's play. If roti was not ready the moment he woke up, he would stand in the street and begin loudly his mantra of 'whore, slut and widow', so as to be heard by the whole village like the Yakshagana dancers. She did not want the dignity and honour of the house auctioned thus. Besides, she tried as far as possible to prevent the use of this language in front of the children.

As such, if four seers of ragi were spent every day, then five quintals would be finished off within four months, and there would be no money to buy again. Whatever was to be earned had to be by joining and selling leaf plates. So, mother and daughter would join at least four hundred plates every day. That year she was not needed to write accounts. What accounts could be entered into the ledgers, when all the fields were parched due to no rains and all the wet fields and dry fields had become like burnt lands of ash. But account books had to be sewn, headings had to be written, transverse and lengthwise rules had to be put in red ink and pencil. In every column of the ledger, against survey number and khata number, the tax had to be marked as 'nil'. Government accounts must be accurate. But in case of gardens or coconut and mango groves, it could not be marked as nil. Nanjamma managed this task along with the work of making the leaf plates and household chores.

By the next Pushya and Megha months, the cattle too were struck with the calamity that people were afflicted with. There was neither water to drink nor grass to graze. When there were no crops at all, it was difficult to put grass in mangers for the cattle. Villagers who had extra grass transported it from hamlets to the lofts of their homes. If not, they would be stolen. They were trying to provide just enough to sustain the life of the cattle, similar to the lives of people, for which they gave them half the amount of fodder. The cattle were dying where there was no fodder. Nanjamma used to sell young bulls born in her house. Her two cows and a young calf were starving without grass. She thought of sending them away to Nagalapura. But there too, was the same famine. This drought had affected not only Ramasandra. This time, Tumkur, Hassan, Kolar and other flat provinces were drought-prone. The people who had lands irrigated by channels were fortunate. Many people went to Ganni and Sreenivasapura and brought paddy straw, giving fifty rupees per cart load. When they went the second time the price was raised to sixty-five rupees. Nanjamma did not know what to do. One day, she drove her two cows and a calf to Kurubarahalli and told Gundegowdaru: 'Gowdare, please take the cows and the calf as godaana—from me. Provide them with a bundle of grass every day and keep them alive. If they survive, your children and grandchildren may drink their milk. I cannot watch them die.'

'Avva, being born a farmer—a Vokkaliga, could I take any daana, that too Godaana?'

'If so give me three coins. I'll hold their rope and hand it to you and say they are sold. It is most important to save their lives.'

Gowdaru too had the scarcity of fodder-grass. It was true he was a well-off person. He would always stock provisions and grass for cattle in advance for the coming year. But, if rains play hide and seek in the coming year too, what would happen? Scared of the uncertainty of the coming year, how could he refuse the request of a woman like Nanjamma now, who was standing at his door? It was not the question of mere words of Shanubhoga's wife, but the question of three cows. So Gowdaru said, 'Well, I will keep them and care for them. No daana or sale is needed. You give me the female calf when this cow gives birth, later. This cow is fair and beautiful.'

Nanjamma was rid of her worry, and returned home. Many cattle died and the remaining had reached the state of dying in Ramasandra.

As the mother and daughter together made leaf plates, they had emptied all the leaves with them by the Marghashira month itself. By then, ragi also got over and the empty pot in which ragi balls was cooked was rattling. Nanjamma climbed to the attic and counted the bundles of leaf plates; there were more than twenty thousand of them. Perhaps the price of these plates also must have increased. While the price of everything had increased, shouldn't this too be raised? If calculated as eight annas per hundred, she would get one hundred rupees. Nanjamma hired two carts and went to Tiptur with Sarvakka and Ramanna. Sarvakka had six thousand leaf plates. Looking at the number of leaf plates they had, the trader Shetti said, 'Look Ammayyare, everywhere there is famine. When there is nothing to eat, who needs plates? As you have brought them, I'll buy them at the rate of four annas per hundred.'

Nanjamma asked, 'What's this Shettare, you speak this way? Is it dharma if you fix four annas per hundred for our labour of carrying the leaves on our head from the forest, stringing them, drying and then joining them?'

'It is not of dharma karma; you may inquire at other places if you want.'

Nanjamma and Sarvakka enquired elsewhere. They said they would give three annas. So, they sold all the bundles to the first one, and shared between them the rent of the cart. Sarvakka gave one and a half rupee and Nanjamma three and a half. Nanjamma bought two sarees for herself and two for her daughter at three rupees each, a shirt for Ramanna, and a shirt and shorts for Vishwa. Thirty-seven rupees remained after all these expenses. They returned home biting the dry roti they had taken with them. Now the price of ragi had become twenty rupees per quintal.

The epidemic plague Maramma struck everywhere during this very time. This time Gudemaramma too did not come and foretell its arrival. Nobody was aware or got any hint of its coming. The epidemic suddenly struck and began swallowing lives in every village. In all the surrounding villages, rats fell. In some villages, people fell dead much before rats. In Ramasandra, some had tumours. Without any delay, villagers vacated their houses. People who owned lands, built sheds in their gardens or in dry fields. People like Nanjamma, Gangamma and Sarvakka who had lost their lands, built theirs behind the shrine of the village Goddess.

In the new year too, there were no rains and the flame of forest trees did not sprout well and there was no yield of good leaves. The old leaves had become hard as hide. Even if they were plucked and carried home, it would not be possible to join them. What could be done sitting in the shed without work? Ragi bought with the money by selling leaf plates, was about to finish. In another three days, the stove in the kitchen would not be lit at all. Some men broke into the gardens of others, plucked half ripe coconuts and stuffed their bellies. If the owners of the gardens kept watch at nights and hindered them, they would be pelted with stones. They gave up patrolling out of fear for their lives. As there was no other way, gold and silver of the villagers started accumulating in Kashimbaddi Sahukara's shop. Then the brass and copper vessels too gradually followed and his shop was filled with these articles.

When ragi in Nanjamma's house was completely finished, Ramanna walked to school stubbornly on an empty stomach. As the Kambanakere school was two furlongs away from the village and was situated on high ground, there was no need to vacate it. Ramanna was extremely interested in studies. He had already studied the lessons in his book, which were to be taught. Looking at the examples given in the text he would do the sums in the next chapter. He had learnt by rote the first English reader. He did not like missing school even for a day. Walking five miles on an empty stomach, he sat pale and dull in school. In the lunch break at one thirty in the afternoon, at the stroke of the bell, students from Kambanakere returned to their sheds for meals. Students from other villages walked towards the tank behind the school to eat rotis. Now, some wells that could be reachable were dug deep for water in the dry area of the village tank. Ramanna sat dejected under a tree behind the school.

Nanjamma was worrying at home for her son, who had gone to school on an empty stomach. While Parvati sat with a pale face, Vishwa was crying and shouting that he was hungry, and pulling the edge of his mother's saree. One can fast for a day or two. But, for how many days is it possible to live in this manner? Until now, Nanjamma had not pledged any utensils to the moneylender, Kashimbaddi Sahukara. He would give two rupees for the vessel and when getting it back, one would have to pay twenty-five rupees. The rate of ragi was now one rupee for two seers. If four seers of ragi was brought for two rupees it would suffice for one or a day and a half. Then again another vessel had to be pledged. This problem of fasting would not be solved even after losing all the vessels of her home within fifteen to twenty days. Times would not be the same. A time would come again when you could get ragi. But it would not be possible to buy the vessels once lost. Besides, these vessels had been given to her by Akkamma.

Nanjamma's mind was brooding and calculating. But the distance between the belly and the brain was long. Parvati lay down. Vishwa cried and after a tantrum, beat his mother and rolled down in a corner without speaking with her. Nanjamma too felt her stomach burning. Her husband had left in the afternoon. He might have gone to his mother's shed and had got something to eat. Gangamma had some ragi left with her. As they were only two, mother and son, she had sufficient stock of grains. Besides, both of them had gone a begging twice in three months to lands irrigated by channels and had brought sacks of rice. Ramanna had not yet returned from school today. It had grown dark hours before. The boy had gone on an empty stomach. Did he fall down somewhere without having enough strength to walk? She thought of going on foot to Kambanakere and look for him. But how could she go alone in the darkness? Parvati was lying down, weak and unable to get up. Besides, if she took Parvati with her, how would little Vishwa stay alone in the shed? Moreover, it was risky to lock the shed and go. Someone might break in and carry away whatever he would get. During the time of drought and hunger, anything and everything was stolen.

Nanjamma told Parvati and Vishwa: 'Be careful. I will just go towards the tank and return,' and came out of the shed. There was an old mango tree, if you walked three furlongs towards Kambanakere. That ancient tree was full of hollows, and owls dwelt in them. Their hoots were heard by the people in the sheds during nights. Its cries heard as 'Guu-Guu, bring the spade' was considered a bad omen. If it cried 'Guu, bring the spade' perching on anybody's house, either a child or a small boy would die in that house. It was customary to cremate the elders and bury the children in case of death. Non-brahmins buried whosoever died. So, if the owl hooted while being perched on a Brahmin's house, only children would die. But if it hooted while being perched on the house of people belonging to other castes, it was a bad omen as any member in that house could die. Nanjamma was scared by the time she neared that tree. She thought of returning. But Ramanna would have had to walk back from under that tree too. How could the ten-year-old boy bravely cross that tree?

She could neither return nor stay there. She walked another two furlongs. There was a rock near the road. She climbed the rock and stood staring in the direction from where Ramanna had to come. Half an hour passed but there was no hint of her son. She felt scared. The story of Harishchandra came to her mind. Chandramati was waiting for Rohitashwa the same way. But Rohitashwa was killed by a snakebite. This came to be known to Chandramati, from the boys who had gone with him. Oh! How loudly Chandramati must have sobbed! Nanjamma too felt like crying. There were anthills in the road to Kambanakere also. The road passed beside the mound of anthill beyond the Kabballi mound. The horns of the anthills stood erect on the whole mound. It is said that the snakes that came to catch frogs in the pits and streams would go into these anthills.

'Oh, while walking on the road, the boy, unaware, might have trodden on a snake or he must have pelted a stone mischievously on a snake which was heading to the anthill. Oh God, I wish that things do not unfold like that. Ramanna is a clever boy. He does not commit such mischiefs. It is Vishwa who indulges in all such mischiefs,' she brooded.

She stood there for a little while more, and thought of returning to the shed and sending some men to look around for the boy and she too would go with them. But the father who sired the son did not have any such worry. Since the afternoon he had not shown his face. About to turn around to return, she stood again to wait a little more. Her eyes were fixed towards the direction from where Ramanna would come. Even the place she stood at was not considered safe. Three years back, Patel Siddegowda of Channenahalli was murdered beside the rock she was standing on. It is said that he was placed on the rock and his head was smashed with a stone. It was believed that Channegowda had become a ghost and roamed near this rock on dark nights. People who came by cart had reported to have heard his loud cry.

Nanjamma was afraid. For a minute, her body and limbs shuddered. Again she felt like returning. But her son had not yet returned home. She stood there waiting, and thought: 'If being a grown-up woman, she herself was frightened, how could that boy come alone?' In the darkness, she could not see anything even at a little distance.

It was believed that ghosts do not remain in one place and that they would be wandering around. Another thought gripped her mind. What if the ghost travelled towards Kambanakere and caught Ramanna? After all, he was coming on his own. But at once, her mind comforted itself: 'All these ghosts and devils are completely false. Doesn't my father and Kalleshannayya walk miles and miles in pitch darkness alone? If there are really ghosts, why don't they do them any harm?' But reminded of the fact that Ramanna was still a small boy, anxiety and fear again occupied her mind.

Meanwhile, she felt someone nearing her. Yes, really, it was a man. But there was a bundle on his head. How could there be a bundle on the head of the boy who went to school? No, he was not Ramanna; might be some other person. The figure seemed to turn left on the road and walked towards the garden. It walked rapidly as if frightened on having seen something. Then she herself took heart and asked, 'Who is it?' He did not speak. She asked again, 'Who is it going that way?' He stopped there. When he asked,

'Oh, who is it? Amma?' she knew it was Ramanna.

'It is me, dear! Why are you going there towards thorns and stones?'

Ramanna came near her. There were three big unripe jackfruits on his head, tied by toddy palm leaves. Ramanna had coiled his lungi, put it on his head and placed the bundle on it.

Mother asked, 'Why were you walking to that side, my child?'

'Oh, something appeared dark from that distance. Was it not near this rock that Channenahalli Siddegowda was murdered? Weren't people saying he had become a ghost? Thinking that it must be his ghost, I was running to that side. How on earth could I guess it was you?'

'From where did you bring these? Give me, I'll carry it,' she told him, and transferred the load on to her head.

'On the way home, near Gowdanakoppalu, in one of its gardens, I spotted a tree bearing jackfruits. So, on purpose, I started after darkness. Slowly I squeezed through the fence and plucked these unripe fruits. I had brought with me toddy palm leaves' rope from Kambanakere itself, removed from the trees there, and had kept it in my bag. If we cut the fruits and make curry and eat, our bellies will be full. Will that not be great, Amma?'

She did not know how to react to her son's adventure and cleverness. She had taught her children that it was a sin to steal or to tell lies. Ramanna was studying in middle school. He was aware of these ideas of paap and punya. Now she did not advise her son. Both walked fast. Children were lying empty stomach, completely exhausted. They were also hungry. If she cut unripe jackfruits and prepared curry, it would sustain them for now.

By the time she reached their shed, her husband had returned, spread his bed and was snoring. She knew by experience, that without a full stomach he would not sleep and snore. Ramanna too knew about it. But none of them spoke to him or woke him up. Parvati and Vishwa were rolled up and sleeping. Nanjamma took the wooden plank with a knife attached to it, cut the three fruits quickly, removed the skin and the hard parts from inside the fruits, left out the seeds that were a little ripe to be cooked, and put a fistful of sambar powder into it.

While it was cooking, Ramanna asked softly, 'Amma, is it a sin to eat roti in the house of other castes, the Vokkaligas?'

'Why, child?'

'This afternoon I was sitting under the tree, starving. There is one student, Narasegowda of Kengalapura. He had extra rotis with him. He asked: "Why didn't you eat roti?" I did not reply. He said: "Hey, eat this, nothing will happen. I won't tell anybody" and handed me a roti and jinjili powder. The roti was as thick as a palm and I ate it. He has sworn, touching my palm, that he won't tell this to anybody.'

Nanjamma did not say anything. Ramanna asked again, 'Oh tell me Amma, is it a sin? Will God punish me?'

Nanjamma answered, 'Was not Vishwa eating off the plate of Madevayyanavaru?'

'He was a little boy then. Am I not a grown up boy now?'

She could not answer her son's question. These notions of *paap* and *punya* that children do not have, from where and how do grown-ups get stained by them? Nanjamma was pondering. After the jackfruits were cooked, she woke Parvati and Vishwa. She asked her husband, 'Do you eat jackfruit curry?' He answered sleepily, 'I don't want it' and started snoring again.

Oh! How tasty that curry was! The children ate to their heart's content. Besides, it was sufficient for the mother also. After going to bed, she told Ramanna. 'Hereafter, don't go to that garden. If they realize there was a theft, they will be watching.'

5

With the increase in the outcry for food, the efforts for its search also increased. The village tank had dried up, the black earth on its surface was parched and cracked. The fisherman, Maata, found out that if one dug into the silt, one could find roots or tubers of plants that could be cooked and eaten. So the whole village rushed there. Each person dug at different places. They got roots of sweet potatoes which were as thick as thumbs here and there. By searching in the silt from dawn to dusk, one could get roots that could suffice for four people. Nanjamma and Parvati got to this task with a pickaxe and a basket. Instead of making leaf plates, now they had this work. Even though they had covered their heads with the pallu of their sarees, the burning sun was scorching their faces and bodies. The smell of the tubers, even after being thoroughly washed with well water and cooked with salt and chillies, would not allow them to eat it. But the stomach did not mind the smell. The cooked roots were consumed. The mother and daughter decided to go very early next morning, before the sun became hot.

The next day when they started, Sarvakka too accompanied them. When the three of them were digging the silt, Nanjamma said: 'See Sarvakka, Maadevayyanavaru left, and this village is now facing these calamities. That's why it is said, the curse of sadhus and virtuous people is not good. See, the whole village has to bear the brunt because of some vicious person's words. It is said it was the people from your caste group who spoke thus.'

'Oh Nanjammare, you still don't know the real matter. It was my husband who instigated them to speak so. Is it not he alone who knows all these legal points?'

'Perhaps he will come again, Sarvakka. He has left some of his vessels, ragi, pulses and chillies in his room in the temple. The key is with him.'

For more than a week, Sarvakka came with them to dig roots. One day, she brought five seers of ragi and one seer of rice secretly to Nanjamma's shed and said, 'Nanjammare, please don't disclose this to anyone. My husband had gone to Tiptur for some court work; he brought two sacks of ragi, twenty-five seers of rice and coffee seeds.'

If this ragi was hidden and used frugally, she could prepare rotis for eight days in the mornings to send with Ramanna who walks to school and could give some to little Vishwa too. The stomach was burning from having eaten the roots. At least for a day Nanjamma could cook rice and eat with tamarind rasam. She felt happy at Sarvakka's well-meaning gestures towards her. She thought whatever vices Revannashetty might have, he uses his mind at the right time. He must have caught a gullible client in the court and offered some lip service and coaxed him. Otherwise, how could he have gotten the money for two sacks of ragi and twenty-five seers of rice? But all his earnings were through evil means, she thought. Nanjamma started grinding ragi.

Within a week, a quarrel started between the Banajigas, Nonabagowdas and other castes among the villagers who knew that Maadevayyanavaru had stored ragi and pulses in his room at the temple. What Nanjamma had casually mentioned to Sarvakka, she informed her husband. She too desired that those grains reach her house. Revannashetty was very shrewd in such matters. He thought of going to the temple, breaking the lock of the room and embezzling the grains. But he was afraid to go alone into the village that was deserted. It was believed, Sunkalamma would be moving around in the village. He had to do this work only during the night. He should

S.L. BHYRAPPA

enter the inner hall of the Eshwara temple and break the lock. Is not Sunkalamma, Parvati herself, the divine consort of Eshwara? If he enters into her shrine, she would not leave him alive; she would make him vomit blood and he would fall dead. At the same time, he could not let go of the desire of ragi and pulses. He thought two men were better than one and conveyed his scheme to his cousin Puttannashetty. He whispered this in the ears of his wife. As such this 'secret' was known to all the Banajigas. It reached this point: 'Maadevayyanavaru belongs to our caste. Let all of us divide it among us.' This information spread to ones belonging to the Nonabagowda caste also, and then to those of the Vokkaliga, Kuruba, Magga, Besta and all other castes, and it spread through the whole village. Everyone in the village was obstinate: 'Ayyanoru did not get bhiksha only from Banajiga houses. We also have given bhiksha. So, we too should get a share.' This bull-headedness turned into a quarrel and there was fighting too. Finally, Patel Shivegowda gave the verdict that everyone should get a share of the grain. So, everyone had to accept. Each group would get two seers of ragi from that stock.

One afternoon, all the villagers gathered—one man per house—and entered the village. They got into the temple and saw that the Maadevayya's room's lock was missing. There were neither sacks of ragi nor the bin of pulses. The pot of chillies too was empty. Only some aluminium vessels remained.

Everybody said, 'Some bastard has cheated us', but how to find who that bastard was, they did not know. All returned, disappointed.

The roots in the tank also got exhausted. There was not an inch of place in the whole area of the tank, which was spared by the people. Meanwhile, someone had cut the nodes of cactus, cooked them and eaten. When it was known that too tasted like the roots in the tank, the villagers' attention centred on destroying the cactus plants. The roots of the silt had to be dug out, washed and searched. As cactus was thick, they need not have worked so hard. So, everybody had their bellies full.

Two days after eating them, the villagers suffered from diarrhoea. Not having enough to eat, their stomachs had already become mere skin. And now, after loose motions, it seemed like they had crumbled and were collapsing. Fifteen in the village died of it. The rest understood the reason behind the diarrhoea and gave up eating cactus.

One day when Nanjamma, Parvati and Sarvakka had gone to the tank in search of tubers, Parvati had a severe headache. Though she covered her head with the pallu of her saree, it did not prevent the sun. Sarvakka said, 'You return to the shed, child. Nanjavvaru and I will pluck as much as possible.' When Nanjamma also insisted, Parvati left for home.

Treading on the earth, which had developed cracks owing to the rays of hot sun, Parvati climbed on the tank bund near the temple and walked towards the shed. She met Narasi at the end of the tank bund. She asked Parvati, 'Did you finish plucking the tubers, child?'

'No, not yet. My head is aching and I came back.'

'Just come to my shop. I'll give a little fried channa. You may eat some.'

Parvati did not say anything. When she reached the spot where she had to take a turn, she walked on. Then Narasi called her, 'Come, don't feel shy, come Avva. Nothing happens by eating channa prepared by one from our caste.' While she was speaking thus, Vishwa, who playing near the shed, saw his sister and came near her. When he heard Narasi speak again about fried channa, he insisted, 'Come, Akkayya, let us get the channa.'

Both went to the shop. Narasi gave them both two handfuls of fried channa and pieces of jaggery. Vishwa began swallowing hurriedly his share of channa. Parvati put a fistful into her mouth. At once her eyes were filled with tears. When Narasi asked, 'Why are you crying, child?', her tears increased and she began sobbing. When Narasi came near her, stroked her back and asked again, then Parvati said, 'Our Ramanna has left for Kambanakere on an empty stomach.'

Narasi felt sad. She poured two more handfuls of channa and a piece of jaggery into the end of Parvati's saree and said, 'Give this to him after he returns.' Parvati's sobs and tears stopped. 'Now, we will move to the shed, Narasamma.' She took leave of Narasi and went to their shed with Vishwa, opened the lock, spread a mat and lay down; then she started thinking. She had not spoken with Narasamma ever until today. People said she was an evil woman. Now she herself had called her and given her channa and jaggery. Perhaps she shouldn't have eaten it. If mother comes to know, she may scold her. She decided not to speak about this when her mother returned. But she remembered the share of channa meant for Ramanna that she had with her. After he came home, he would ask, 'From where did you get it?' What would she say? This Vishwa would tell mother as soon as she comes. What could be done? She reflected on this for half an hour. At last, an idea came to her. She untied the edge of her saree, gave Vishwa the channa and jaggery she had kept for Ramanna and said, 'You eat this also.'

'Ramanna?'

'By the time he comes, mother would have cooked the flour. Moreover, he doesn't like channa and jaggery. You eat it.'

Though Vishwa said 'A little for you and a little for me', she made him eat everything. When he poured out water from the jug and drank it, she called him close to her and said, 'See Vishwa, if mother comes to know that we ate what Narasamma gave us, she will beat us. You should not speak of this to anybody.'

'Why would she beat us?'

'Who knows why? Don't you know, villagers speak among themselves that Narasamma is a bad woman? You should not tell this to anyone.'

'Yes.'

'Then, swear it.'

Vishwa struck with his palm on Parvati's, pinched once and promised. But she did not feel entirely confident by only this. She took him to the shrine of the village goddess Kaalamma, made him touch the threshold of the shrine that was locked, made him swear and threatened him, 'See, now you have sworn in the name of Goddess Kaalamma. If at all you speak of this to mother, the goblin living in the shrine will come and swallow you.'

'Hey, I won't tell. Don't I understand?' Vishwa retorted angrily. Then she became quiet.

Mother came home in the evening, washed the tubers and was cooking. After sunset, Ramanna returned. Channigarayaru came back. When they sat to eat the tubers, Vishwa ate a little and left it. Mother asked, 'Why? What did you eat?' Parvati felt like her breath was stuck.

But Vishwa said, 'No, today it is not good as usual. There is some smell' and did not disclose anything. After everybody finished eating, Vishwa took her sister out of the shed and asked, 'See that? Didn't I tell you?'

'No, you are really a clever boy,' she appreciated him and went back inside the shed.

As the plague subsided in all surrounding areas, people from all these villages left their sheds and returned to their houses. The Ramasandra villagers too came back. There was not much difference between coming into the village and staying out. They had food neither here, nor there.

Nanjamma thought of an idea. It was in Gundegowdaru's backyard that Appannaiah had built his hut and then burnt it. The government had cancelled the revenue tax collection in all these villages that year, except in channel irrigated lands, as no crops had grown anywhere due to drought. Her husband had not visited Kurubarahalli that year for collection. What would happen to the hundred rupees Gundegowdaru had given to be adjusted in the annual salary of the Shanubhoga?

Channigarayaru had not been in the village for the past eight days. Nobody knew where he had gone. Nanjamma went to Kurubarahalli and asked: 'Gowdare, there is no revenue at all this year. I will adjust your money in the coming year.'

'Well, do so Avva. Even if I asked you for the money to be returned, where will you get it from?'

'There is another matter I would like to speak to you about. Is not your backyard empty? I'll fence it and grow some greens and vegetables there.'

'Oh! By all means. What do I have to lose?'

Gowdaru gave her a coconut and a seer of ragi flour, as a muttaide had graced the house. While returning home, blessing him and his progeny, Nanjamma's mind was filled with another thought. The government had cancelled the revenue tax for that year. But the annual salary of the Shanubhoga would surely come. If her husband got his hands on that annual salary, he would not return from the Tiptur hotel until all the money was spent. Her aim was to prevent him from laying his hands on that money. Whose help should she seek? She decided to go to Kambanakere and request the Shekdar with folded hands as no other person was competent to help her in this matter.

Her husband had not been in the village for the past eight days. Gangamma and Appannaiah too could not be seen. They had gone to beg for paddy in the channel irrigated areas about twenty miles away. They had access to good food every day. As such, her husband too might have joined his mother and brother. Nanjamma reckoned as much.

The following day she left for Kambanakere with Ramanna. When the mother and son stood before the Shekdar pleading, he said, 'What is it that has made you come? There is neither collection nor assessments of crops this year. Who knows what may happen in the coming year!'

Nanjamma informed him about her husband and explained to the Shekdar that every year she got the revenue tax of Kurubarahalli Patel Gundegowdaru and two others and would cancel it in the annual salary of the Shanubhoga. But this year, there was this remission of the revenue tax. Nanjamma explained the problem at hand.

He said, 'Look Amma, I too know the story of Channigarayaru. There is no Shanubhoga in this hobali who does not ridicule him. But as per the rules, I can do nothing. I will speak about this to the higher officer.'

'Please, do anything but somehow find a means for these children's food.'

Shekdar's wife told her husband: 'Today, anyway, you are going to Tiptur. You take her too, introduce her to your Saheb and inform him everything. Let the Saheb also know this Shanubhoga's irresponsible behaviour.'

Shekdar asked Nanjamma to go with him by the Mudaliar[22] bus service at eleven. When she said, shrinking with shyness, that she did not have money for the bus fare, he said: 'It doesn't matter. It would be four annas for you; I will ask him to take half the fare for the boy. I will give six annas, come with me.'

The mother and son had a breakfast of uppittu and coffee in the Shekdar's house. By noon, they reached Tiptur, and went to the Taluk Office. Immediately, the Shekdar asked the Hobali clerk. He said, 'Sir, it has already been eight days that the annual salary of Ramasandra region was disbursed.'

Nanjamma's heart sank. The Shekdar asked, 'What shall we do now?'

'Then, he must still be staying in this town, Sir. He will not have spent all the money. If you use your authority and threaten him, he will shell out the remaining amount.'

The Hobali clerk said, 'He stays at Madhavabhatta's hotel, sir. You go now. He will be relishing his meals inside.'

---

[22]Name of the bus company.

All three went to the hotel near the peepal tree which had a platform. Nanjamma and Ramanna stayed outside. The Shekdar went towards the dining hall door and peeped inside. What the clerk said was correct. Channigarayaru was seated on a wooden seat. In front of him, there was a broad plantain leaf with its forepart. He was raising the morsel from the heap of rice mixed with the sambar of potato, brinjal and onion in front of him. Around the heap of rice, were heaped curry, gojju, pickles and papads. The Shekdar did not disturb him in the middle of his meal, came out and sat on a chair. Nanjamma and Ramanna outside, and the Shekdar inside, had to wait for half an hour. After finishing his meal, the Shanubhoga came out and looking at the Shekdar, immediately folded his hands and said, 'I fold my hands, Sir.'

'Why have you come here Shanubhogaare?'

'Hhhhere...I had some wwwork sir,' he faltered.

'I have to speak with you. First pay for the meals.'

Channigarayaru gave ten annas and came out. Oh! There stood his wife and son! Shekdar said, 'Look Shanubhoga, there is a police warrant on you. Amaldar Saheb has ordered your arrest.'

Channigarayaru shuddered. Shekdar said, 'You have taken the tax from the farmers telling them it will be debited from your annual allowance. Now you have taken the amount and spent it on yourself. Is it not a crime?'

'Oh, I have wronged sir. This, slu...,' he said and at once controlled his tongue and asked,

'Did she say this, Sir?'

'It may be anybody. Come to Saheb's office.'

'I fffall on yyyour feet! Ppplease don't let the police arrest me sir. I am a respectable man.'

'Well, how much money do you have now? Take it out, and hand it over to me. Yes, this very minute. Yes quick!'

'I will hand it over, Sir. I have kept it inside.'

'It doesn't matter! You must hand it over here, now.' Channigarayaru raised his shirt, squeezed his hand inside his crossed dhoti, took out a small bundle tied to, and hanging from, his loincloth. There were six notes of ten and one of five. After counting the money, the Shekdar asked, 'What happened to the rest?'

'I spent it, Sir.'

S.L. BHYRAPPA

'Hey, don't you feel ashamed to stuff yourself like a pig when your wife and children are starving at home? Even if you throw a piece of roti to a hungry dog it carries it and feeds it to its puppy!' The Shekdar reprimanded him, handed the money to Nanjamma and told Channigarayaru, 'I know, you don't know how to write the accounts and it is this lady who writes it. Listen carefully—from now on, if you take your annual salary and gobble it up without the knowledge of your wife and children, you WILL be arrested. If I am transferred from here, I will instruct the next Shekdar about this and inform the Saheb also.'

Channigarayaru stooped on the road itself and held the shod feet of the Shekdar and implored him, 'Please sir, don't say anything to the Saheb, Sir. I am a poor man.' Then the Shekdar told Nanjamma, 'Amma, there is a bus at four. If you have to purchase anything, finish that task. I have to visit the Taluk Office. I'll also come in the same bus.' He left. Channigarayaru squatted on the platform in front of the peepal tree putting his head between the knees as if he had been defamed. Ramanna asked, 'Amma, I have never dined in a hotel. Today, will you let me?'

'See dear, Akkayya and Vishwa are hungry at home. They had only one roti each in the morning.'

He did not reply, but his face became pale. The mother's heart felt pricked. She took her son inside the hotel and asked how much a meal cost. It was six annas. When she told the hotel people to serve the boy, Ramanna said, 'No, Amma, if you do not eat, I too won't'. Then, she too sat. It was ten annas for elders. The food was tasty and smelt good. She finished her food, telling her son, 'If we have provisions, we too can cook like this. When you grow up and get a salary, I'll cook tastily and serve you.' It cost a total of one rupee for their meals. She bought four annas each of kharashev and parched rice and eight annas of Mysore pak for children at home. She enquired in a big nearby shop about the rate of ragi. It was only thirty rupees per quintal. In Ramasandra, it cost fifty rupees. She bought two quintals for sixty rupees and requested the man at the shop to put the sacks on top of the bus. As the Shekdar too boarded the same bus, he instructed that the ragi sacks not be charged. Nobody knew where Channigarayaru had vanished.

The bus moved on, unloading the ragi sacks on the road, a mile away from the village. Ramanna walked to the village, told the village-servant to harness a cart and returned. Till then, Nanjamma stayed by the roadside guarding the sacks.

Channigarayaru came to the village on foot the next day. Nanjamma did not utter a word to him. When Ramanna spoke to his father tauntingly, she advised her son, 'Look son, whatever he may do, he is your father, who sired you. You are a clever boy. You shouldn't say such words to him' and quietened him.

Everyone at home was elated looking at the two quintals of ragi, as though the wish-fulfiling Kaamadhenu from the heavens had descended onto their home. Nanjamma had become like a dried up cotton plant without proper food. Parvati and Ramanna, who were growing healthy and plump, were like scorched, emaciated apes. Vishwa was always sturdy and well-built. Now, he too had become bony. This was not the plight of only this family. The condition of three-fourths of the population of the village was like that, the other quarter well-maintained. In Nanjamma's family, Channigarayaru, although his body thinned, was sufficiently better than the others.

If everyone at home ate heartily, these two quintals of ragi would finish within two months. So Nanjamma decided not to spend more than two seers per day. This year too, there had been no rains yet; the future looked bleak. She instructed Parvati, 'See, you prepare seven rotis in the morning. All rotis must be equal in size and thickness. One roti for each. Ramanna will carry one to school. In the afternoon, you and Vishwa eat half a roti each. Nothing until night. Grind one seer of ragi for the night and make five balls of equal size. Only this much should suffice, even if somebody wants more.'

Somehow the children would feel that their stomachs were full by this system. Nanjamma was prepared to bear hunger. It was Channigarayaru who felt it hard to tolerate hunger. When he got angry, scolded his wife, Ramanna and Parvati revolted. Besides, the younger Vishwa too asked, 'Are you not our father? Bring rice, I want to eat rice.'

Channigarayaru headed towards the tank bund abusing his son: 'Tut tut, f... his mother!'

Nanjamma left the cooking and all other domestic chores to Parvati and engaged herself in cultivating Gundegowda's backyard. Only the soot-blackened walls of the hut that Appannaiah had burnt, stood there. Nanjamma pulled the burnt hut down with a crowbar and drew water from the well, wet the whole backyard, morning and evening. Each cubit of the earth which had not tasted water for a year sucked pots and pots of water. After the earth was softened, she began to till from one side. She gave two rupees to the untouchable Belura and asked him to bring a cartload of bamboo thorns. She planted rows of cactus, she tied two lines of bamboo thorns with toddy palm leaves, and strengthened the fence with babul tree thorns. She made a door, a wicket gate and arranged to lock it. She planted greens like dantu and keere in some basins. She went to the Kambanakere fair and bought the seeds of beans and brinjal. She sowed brinjal closely together and planted bean seeds in the pits she had dug. Her idea was to grow greens and vegetables and eat them, if there was nothing else to eat. They could eat at least greens twice a day. She drew water morning and evening from the well and drenched the earth. She felt, though the rains had cheated them, Gangammathaayi existed in the well for her support.

Meanwhile, Sarvakka's daughter Rudrani fell ill and started vomitting and was overtaken by diarrhoea. Within two days, the girl became weak and died. Nanjamma had not known about Rudrani's sickness; nobody had known about it. The moment she came to be aware of it, Nanjamma rushed to Sarvakka's house. Four people were already about to carry away the corpse, having placed it on a sheet and holding its four corners. Revannashetty was walking with his head bowed behind his daughter's corpse. As was customary in their caste, an individual was throwing fists full of parched rice while following the corpse on foot. Sarvakka was hitting her head on the threshold of her house, shedding tears but was not crying loudly.

Rudrani was four years elder than Parvati. If married, by now, she would have been a mother of two. She was well built like Sarvakka and had had long thick hair. It was difficult to identify who was the mother and who the daughter, if you saw them from behind. Nanjamma sat beside Sarvakka, took her hand though she was in defilement of death, and consoled, 'What difference will it make if you break your head? Don't do that. What happened to the child?' The mother, who had lost her daughter, at once burst out, 'What? Her father's disease struck her,' but at once she bit her tongue even in that grief.

Nanjamma sat there until Revannashetty buried the corpse and returned home. But when he returned, at once all the women left for their houses, like birds would take flight instinctively when a stone is hurled at them; only the menfolk remained. Nanjamma too came back to her home. Sarvakka's house was near the backyard where Nanjamma grew greens and vegetables. The next day onwards, Nanjamma would take Sarvakka there, make her sit nearby and comfort her telling her all the philosophy she knew. She would say to Sarvakka,'See sister, all these relations are maaya. We give birth to our daughters. Our parents beget us. All this is maaya, an illusion. 'This is how Nanjamma tried to console Sarvakka. But Sarvakka could not come out of her grief. Yet, she would on her own come to Nanjamma's backyard. She would not speak a single word. Nanjamma would draw water from the well in her house, carry a water-filled pot against one side of her waist and take another in the right hand and water the basins of green and pits of brinjal. Meanwhile, even if she spoke, Sarvakka wouldn't respond. One evening, after Nanjamma watered the basins of greens, Sarvakka said, 'What does fate do Nanjammare, if the father who begot the daughter, himself kills his daughter?'

'What does that mean, Sarvakka?'

'Oh! let us leave it.'

'Please tell, what is it? I won't disclose it to anyone. I swear on you.'

'Didn't I once bring a little quantity of ragi to you, told you that my husband has brought two quintals of ragi, twenty-five seers of rice and other things, by giving witness in the court?'

'Yes, I remember.'

'That ragi was received as a result of being a witness in the court. But that blackguard Kashimbaddi is there, you know. His wife and children live in Malayala. My husband, it seems, had taken a loan from him.'

'What if he took money as loan?'

'You and I were going to the village tank to pluck those tubers, didn't we? During that time, my husband himself used to bring that Kashimbaddi to our shed. Rudrani became pregnant.'

It was difficult for Nanjamma to fathom exactly what Sarvakka was saying. She had heard that during the drought this time, many women had abandoned their honour and chastity and earned food to fill their stomachs. She could not at once believe that a father himself would disgrace his daughter so.

'Do I tell lies about my own husband? But how could *she* agree to this even if that bastard, her father, asked her to? People from Shivagere had come for an alliance. Oh, how much did I compel him to marry her off. It was my husband who said, "Wait, there is no money for food, let us marry her off later".

'What happened then?'

'Oh, Nanjammare, I didn't know all this. Only after three months did I come to know about it. My husband beat his daughter and blamed her—"you slut, it is your own mistake." But Rudrani swore. "No, no Avva. Father himself brought Kashimbaddi, sent him into the shed, said, "Nothing happens, don't be afraid, it doesn't matter", and closed this side door." What else could be done? My husband himself brought medicine from that Narasi and administered it for three days. She started bleeding which did not stop at all and my child died.'

Nanjamma sat dumbstruck. Sarvakka once again cried loudly, then wiped her tears. Nanjamma started to think about Parvati. She was about to complete twelve. But for this drought and with adequate, nutritious food, she would've attained puberty by now. Nanjamma was anxious: If by chance Parvati attains puberty before marriage? What will happen? How could she arrange for marriage when there was such a famine? However frugally one performed the wedding, a minimum of seven to eight hundred rupees was needed. They had to search for a family capable enough to provide shelter and food, and marry off the girl. From where would she bring eight hundred rupees now under circumstances when it was hard to even get a stomachful twice a day? Sarvakka said, 'Nanjammare, you must not share this with anybody.'

'No, I swear on God, I won't, Sarvakka. Your honour and my honour are not separate. You need not worry.'

'Oh, I feel like deserting him and returning to my parent's home, tut, tut, I hate this man's company. But if I go there, I must live under my sister-in-law's reign. At least you tell me, Nanjammare, why are we still alive?'

Nanjamma had herself asked this same question many times which Sarvakka asked now. Yes, what was there in her life? Was there husband's love? Mother-in-law's affection? The happiness that comes from a parents' house? Yet she lived, did not wish to die. She has children. Now when she searches for an answer to the question 'Why am I still living?', her children come before her mind. Watering vegetable saplings in the backyard, preventing her husband from stealing and swallowing the annual salary of the Shanubhoga, making plates from the flame of forest leaves from dawn till dusk, serving children half a roti or a ragi ball, and if that too is not available, a fistful of boiled greens, in an aluminium plate with holes that are covered with torn rags—for this, only for this much, should she live? She brooded—yes only this much. What else was there in her life?

8

After the plague completely vanished, many people were struck with *Naagaru*—a skin disease like scabies that was accompanied by itching and boils. Everyone, whether standing or seated, would scratch and scratch. People who had boils on their legs and thighs would limp. Until the boils burst after fomentation, their suffering was indescribable. Those who suffered from scabies—their bodies, hands and the slits of fingers were smeared with pus.

In Nanjamma's house, first Ramanna got infected. Then Parvati and Vishwa got it and finally Nanjamma too was affected. The only remedy they were taking recourse to was sitting in the morning sun to feel the heat on the body or kindling the stove and holding the parts of the body that were affected with scabies against the fire, to get some comfort from the heat. Some days, by early morning there would be boils resembling small white wild berries on the forearms. Children would not leave them be. Somehow they would prick them open to draw out the pus. They made it their job to pierce the boils with the thorns of the babul tree and bring out the pus. Then the pus would touch other places and the boils would spread. First, the insane urge to itch. And then the compulsive scratching of the itch, being unable to bear it. Unable to bear the burning sensation after scratching the itches, Vishwa would cry aloud. Ramanna and Parvati too could not hold back their tears. Parvati was looking after the domestic chores until now. Now that she was infected on both her hands, she could neither wash dishes nor could she grind ragi holding the peg. In the same way, Nanjamma too could not hold the rope and draw water for the plants in the backyard. The greens and vegetables that were grown with so much hard work for several days were now withering.

The villagers made a vow to the snake god Nagappa.[23] For eight days continuously, Nanjamma too took cold baths, also bathing the children in cold water, poured half a cup of milk she brought from Thammegowda's house into the anthills, and made the children prostrate before them. But God Nagappa was not placated. The scabies and itching increased.

A month after these people started suffering from the scabies, Channigarayaru also got affected. He danced wildly at the sight of the first boil itself. Though the whole village suffered from scabies, the Patel and some other well-to-do people were not affected. Gangamma and Appannaiah too were free from it. Pus was oozing from the boils on Channigarayaru's fingers when he went to his mother's house. She said, 'There is an excommunication by the Swamiji of Sringeri. That slut did not undergo any expiation. She does not observe the custom during her periods, or any norms of purity and impurity. Won't Nagappa strike if she touches the basins of green and waters them while having periods? You too got this because of that slut. Look Channayya, unless you give her up, you will never be cured of this.'

Channigarayaru was well aware that his wife wouldn't be scared if he said he would leave her. Moreover, what should he do for his food after leaving her? If she complained to the Shekdar? So he did not take to mind his mother's advice. But something had to be done about the infection. Mother and son went to Annajois's house. While he was suggesting something, Ayyashastri arrived. Ayyashastri was an elderly person and knew what customs and traditions were prevalent in which houses in the village. He said, 'Gangamma, don't you remember you had performed Naagaru rites when your husband was alive? Have you performed it at least once after his death? What else could you expect except troubles from the Snake God?'

Yes, Gangamma remembered. It was a rite to be performed with great faith and devotion. On Shasti or the sixth day of the fortnight all the members of the family must go to the garden and dine there. The preceding day, men had to go and dig a small well in the garden. On the day of the ritual, vade, obbattu, payasa, rice, sambar, rasam and other dishes required must be prepared in the water from the newly dug well. Two priests and their wives, a widow and widower and a celibate

---

[23]It was believed that skin diseases were caused owing to the curse of the Snake God.

must be invited for dinner as guests. Wheat flour and rice flour must be mixed in water, kneaded, and an idol of the Snake God, with its raised hood, must be made from it and everyone should worship that image. A sumptuous feast should be served to the invitees as generously as on the day of shraaddha, and a dakshina of one silver rupee must be given to each of the guests. Dhoti to the men invited, saree and blouse pieces to the women, and a single dhoti and single sacred thread and dakshina to the celibate should be offered. Then the members of the family must eat what remains as prasada and perform mahamangalaaarati to the Snake God. Following that, they must take the rice, pulses, flour and whatever was left over, along with the image of the Snake God and drop all of it into the well and cover its mouth. Without turning back and looking at that direction, they should return to the village by dusk. 'See, if you do this, much of the scabies and itches run away on their own. Did you ever suffer like this while your husband lived? You gave up the rituals you were doing and all this is happening.' Ayyashastri said this while scratching his own hand that was affected with scabies, and Gangamma decided to perform the rite of the Snake God at any cost.

Annajois said, 'You need not worry about other things Gangamma. Myself and my wife, Ayyachikkappa and his wife will come as invited Brahmins. Our Narasimha would be the celibate, I will call my sister from Kondenahalli as the widow and for the place of the widower, I will send for my wife's brother from Rangapura. You arrange for other requirements.'

Gangamma said she would perform the religious rites of the family very soon, and came home. She sent word to Nanjamma through Channigarayaru.

'Chinnayya, tell your wife to pay half of the expenses.' Nanjamma heard her husband's description and calculated. In all, it would come to at least one hundred rupees. Half of it meant fifty rupees. Besides, the Jois would raise the question of excommunication and demand money for expiation. How to bring money for all this when there was none for buying food to fill the belly? She decided not to be bothered with this Snake God ritual. Nonetheless, she was scared a bit, for the same god Nagappa was believed to be the cause of scabies and itches if he got angry and would take someone as sacrifice.

Gangamma was haunted by the worry: 'Anything may happen to her daughter-in-law and grandchildren, but what if herself and Appannaiah were affected by scabies?' So, she took Channigarayaru with her and headed towards Akkihebbal to beg. If they visited houses in villages and requested, 'Please donate for observing the Snake God ritual,' they might not get money, but might get two seers of paddy from each house. If the householder refused paddy, he too would be a sinner. The mother and the sons started to collect paddy, sold it and earned hundred rupees that month, and returned to their village. They decided that all three of them would perform the rites for Lord Nagappa in a garden.

Ramanna did not stop attending classes even though he was suffering from scabies. Now he was in English second standard. There were many boys in his school who had been infected. This skin disease had spread just like the plague epidemic. The Master would tell the students infected with scabies to sit separately. One day, the Headmaster, who became disgusted at seeing this, informed the doctor at the Government hospital. The chairman of the village panchayat and the doctor wrote to their higher authorities and ordered for milk-injection tubes. For two days, the doctor administered injections to all the boys and gave them an ointment. Although they didn't apply the sulphur ointment, the injections did their work. The scabies dried up and within a few days, their skin became normal.

Ramanna told his mother: 'Look Amma, it pains when the injection is pricked. But look at my body, now it is cured. All of you come one day and take that injection in the hospital.'

One day, Nanjamma went to Kambanakere with Parvati and Vishwa. When she narrated her plight to the doctor, he gave them injections without taking any money. After four days, they went to take another injection. The scabies on their bodies began to dry. One day, Ramanna said, 'See Amma what our headmaster said: There were no rains and crops in the last year. Nobody ate or drank neither milk nor curds. As there was nothing to eat, people devoured tubers, roots and whatever they could get their hands on; the blood had become impure. That's why scabies and itches affected the people. This Nagaru-pagaru—all this is a lie, a stunt. If all the villagers take these injections, they will be cured.'

Meanwhile, Gangamma, Appannaiah and Channigarayaru came back after performing Nagaru rites, handing out dhotis, sarees, dakshinas to brahmins and serving them sumptuous meals with utter faith and devotion. When Gangamma learnt that Nanjamma had gone to the hospital with her children and taken medicines, she prophesied, 'When the Snake God has appeared, this slut has taken medicines. What does she think of Lord Nagappa? You will see, her body will rot and she will die of it.'

When Nanjamma and her children were cured and there was not a mark on their body or their hands to be seen, many villagers, seeing this, went to Kambanakere one by one. For five rupees per injection, they were all cured.

9

Jyestha and Ashaadha months passed but there was not a drop of rain. It was certain, the drought would continue this year too. The well-to-do who had stocks of grains from last year were feeling anxious this year. Clouds would collect in the sky but from somewhere, winds would rise and scatter them. It was prophesied in the almanac itself that there would be three measures of rains and nine measures of winds that year. No doubt the winds were capricious, but not even one per cent of rain poured from the clouds. Nanjamma would work in the backyard from morning till evening after her scabies got cured. Nowadays, the entire family had to satiate its hunger with only one seer of ragi flour every day. She would boil greens, brinjals and beans and serve. It was only her family that had found this means to have a stomach full of food. She knew it was quite natural that there would be theft in her backyard. So she would wake up four times during the night, take the children with her and watch the backyard. Even the coconut trees were pale, as there were no rains in the past year. The owner of gardens would pull down tender, unripe coconuts, carry them in carts and sell. As such, coconut thieves were deprived of that too.

One midnight, all of a sudden it began to rain. As hailstones fell, big drops of rain poured down. Monsoon had passed long ago, the North-East monsoon too was about to end, but now suddenly there were torrents of rain that surpassed the rain during monsoons. All the villagers woke up, came out of their houses and looked up. There was no wind; just rain. The sky was frozen dark. It seemed it had no other work except to pour water cascading down on to the earth's surface. From where and when had these water clouds, which were absent all these days, gathered and collected in the sky? Yes, it must be the grace of the village deity Choleshwara. If not, how could there these unseasonal rains come now? Within half an hour, the streets of the village were filled with water and slush was flowing. Nanjamma felt anxious at the thought of the rains flooding away the vegetables in her backyard. At the same time, she was happy. If there were rains and bountiful crops in the village, her family too would have enough food. She could sow seeds again and grow vegetables. If there were good crops, that would be enough.

When there were no rains, no one could think of fixing the tiles of their roofs properly. Besides, the tiles had been displaced at the beginning of the year thanks to excessive winds. Still, everybody had only one thought now: Let the houses leak, let the walls sink in, it doesn't matter. Thank God, we have rains at last!

The rains stopped by dawn. Everybody walked towards their wet fields and dry fields in the morning. The village tank was half full in one night. That meant even the villages along the catchment had received rains. Nanjamma was walking towards her backyard. There she saw Maadevayyanavaru coming. She had come to believe that Ayyanavaru had left this village for good.

She asked, 'Ayyanore, how is it that you had left all of us and gone away for so many days?'

'I had been to Kashi, Avva. All these days I stayed there; somehow, I felt like coming here and I returned.'

She took Ayyanavaru to her home. Channigarayaru had woken up and gone out. Nanjamma asked, 'When did you come back?'

'It was late in the night. I thought of coming and waking you up. But the rain started.'

By the time he finished his words, Sarvakka came there. 'Oh, Ayyanavaru has come back, and so have the rains.' How long was it since he left this place? Immediately it flashed in her mind, 'Our Banajiga caste people had refused him kantebhiksha. Ayyanavaru felt dejected, perhaps got angry and left the village. Since then the rains had stopped. Yesterday he returned and the rains too have started. What have our people thought about saadhus and sharanas?' Sarvakka came near and prostrated at the feet of Maadevayya.

Nanjamma asked, 'Ayyanore, why did you despair and leave the village?'

'I desired to go somewhere, Nanjavva. I had good company. I went to Kashi, to the feet of the Vishwanatha. There is a Mutt called Jangamavadi. Any Jangama of our side may stay there without any worry or problem. There also I was singing the bhajans as I used to here. After all, it was not our place and our people are not living there. People at the Mutt were no doubt our people. Yet I felt like coming back and so I returned.'

Sarvakka asked, 'Ayyanore, did you check? Your ragi and cowpeas have been stolen?'

'Yes, I struck the matches and saw at night, nothing is left there. There is famine around here. Maybe some hungry people have taken them. Whoever eats it, it would become mud, won't it?'

Sarvakka had come for a loan of one seer of ragi flour. She took it and left, as she had guests at home. After Sarvakka went, Ayyanavaru said, 'I saw your Appaji.'

Nanjamma asked excitedly, 'Where?' It had been twelve years since her father Kantijois had vanished suddenly. It was said, if twelve years were completed without seeing each other, such people should be considered permanently estranged. She had reflected several times whether her father was alive.

'Yes Avva, he is in Kashi. A month back one morning I went to the river bank. That place is called Hanuman Ghat. Perhaps there were some Brahmins from our side who were performing ceremonies. And it's not just from here; people from all over India visit Kashi. Your father was chanting the mantras loudly. I spoke to him. After two days, he came to Jangamavadi Mutt. He enquired scarily, "Is there still the police order to arrest me?" I asked him what that was. He said, "The one about the death of Shanubhoga Shamanna of our village." I didn't know all those details and spoke of whatever I knew, "Well, it was said you won the case in the court. After winning the case, why did you leave your village?" He did not reply, but said, "It has been nearly twelve years since I left my place. I shall return to it in the near future."' Then I did not meet him. He did not show me the place of his stay.

Now, everything was clear to Nanjamma. After Shamanna came home following the case in the court, he had said, 'Let that bastard be caught, the judge himself will hang him.' Perhaps her father was scared of that and had left the village out of that fear. It was said such cases would be barred by limitation after twelve years, and after that period, the government would burn those papers. Nanjamma thought deeply if it was her father's fate to leave home and hearth and wander like a mendicant. By then Channigarayaru came home. He felt very happy seeing Ayyanavaru. Now the Shanubhoga was killing time easily by listening to the bhajans, the philosophical verses, and the lavanis that Ayyanavaru sang. Channigarayaru enquired where Ayyanavaru had stayed all these days and how he had lived all this while. As soon as he heard the word Kashi, Channigarayaru felt like asking a question, for he had heard so many things from several people about Kashi. Until now he had not met anyone who had stayed in Kashi for a year and a half like Maadevayyanavaru. So he asked: 'Ayyanore, I have heard people say, there are rajas there who arrange for samaaraadhana daily—hold community meals and serve laddoos and give one rupee in dakshina to everyone. Is it true?'

'There are many dharmashaalas of different Maharajas. In each dharmashaala, pilgrims—travellers—are offered free meals for three days. On festival days too, meals are offered. Sometimes one rupee dakshina is given for every extra laddu you eat.'

'If so, I should go and stay there only, Ayyanavare.'

'Oh, Shanubhogaare, do you think there are no beggars in Kashi? Won't there be a number of people who have a desire like yours, to go and stay there? And which Raja can offer free food daily for you all?

'Tut tut, let me strike the worthlessness out of that Raja's mother with my chappal! What sort of Maharaja is he to have such fate?'

Ayyanavaru neither answered nor commented on his words. Channigarayaru sat for a while and then got up. Nanjamma said, 'Everything that was in your shrine has been stolen. I'll give you a little ragi flour, pulses and sambhar powder. If not, will you have your food in our house today?' Maadevayyanavaru reflected for a minute and said, 'I came to stay in this village. I will go for bhiksha in the surrounding villages with the square cloth hanging from my shoulder. There is no obligation of my caste people any more. I'll come here for my food,' he said and left.

Not even half an hour had passed since he had entered the shrine, that all the men from the Banajiga community came one by one and gathered. Revannashetty, Shettappa, Marulappashetty, Lingadevaru all came together and prostrated before Ayyanavaru. Revannashetty said,

'Ayyanore, you are a religious person, a saint. You were angry and left us. There has been no rainfall and crops in the village. Yesterday night you came back and it rained. We committed a sin by denouncing you. You must forget everything and forgive us please; come to our houses daily for kantebhiksha.'

Ayyanavaru had really forgotten about that incident. Now these people were reminding him about it. He began ruminating; was there no rainfall here because he had left this place? No, there were no rains not only in Ramasandra. The whole region was hit by drought. Even in Tamilu and Telugu countries he had seen while coming on the train, there had been no rains. What was the relation between his returning here the previous day and the rainfall? Even in the upper region of the villages, it had rained. Maadevayyanavaru said, 'No, I am not any saint—Mahaantha. Rains and drought, crops and famine are the will of Shiva. He gives all these according to the paapa and punya of the people. I will cook ragi balls myself.'

But those people did not budge. Again they folded their hands and requested, that Ayyanavaru should take kantebhiksha in their houses and bless them. Ayyanavaru did not refuse. He had heard that it was becoming hard to get a square meal every day in most of the houses in the village. Yet he brought kantebhiksha to the shrine and ate it. He told Nanjamma, he would come to her house for dinner. Her son Vishwa had half-forgotten Ayyanavaru. Now he was going to school. He could not be with Ayyanavaru when he dined as it was school-time.

The news spread around the village that there were no rains and crops in the village for Maadevayyanavaru had left the village and there was rainfall because he returned. The Kurubas, Kumbaras, Badagis and Chammaras—all visited the shrine, folded their hands in front of Maadevayyanavaru. Only people like Patel Shivegowda did not believe in this. That night, Ayyanavaru slept alone in the shrine. By midnight, someone called 'Ayyare, Ayyare' and woke him up. Ayyanavaru got up, struck the matches and saw it was Gorava, the bonded labourer of Patel Shivegowda. He touched the feet of Ayyanavaru and said, 'Yappa, please don't curse me. I have not committed any wrong.'

'Get up, why, what happened?'

'Our Gowdaru came into this deserted village in the night, ordered me to carry your ragi, cowpeas and chillies. He himself broke the lock.

I carried all that to his shed. I did not take any of that into my house.'

'Well, forget it. You have not committed any wrong.'

'Appa, don't tell anybody what I have informed you now.'

'No, I won't,' Ayyanavaru promised. Gorava left.

It was not unknown to Ayyanavaru what sort of a person Patel Shivegowda was. He had rightly guessed that without the support of some such person, no hungry thief would enter the deserted village, break the lock of the room in the temple and steal ragi.

The next morning an unusual incident occurred. There was some sound as if a hundred lions were roaring in unison. Everyone working in the mud of wet and dry fields raised their necks and saw a huge aquila was flying in the sky. It was not flapping its wings nor did it have a beak, but its end portion appeared like a tail. Something was spread on both the sides like wings. When it reached above the village, something fell from it. They were chits of paper which scattered in the village everywhere on the ground like dry leaves winnowed by a storm. Many villagers, though they had not seen such a thing in the past, imagined it was an aeroplane. Nanjamma took a pamphlet from the ground and read.

The government of His Highness Sri Maharaja, who was reigning the Mysore State, had printed it: The war was on, Germans were advancing in Europe. The Japanese were proceeding to conquer India. Bombs might be dropped on Mysore also. When the aeroplanes fly in the sky, people should not come out, stand and look at them. They must lie on their stomachs. Everyone must contribute to the war fund to drive away the enemies. In the end of the pamphlet was written, 'Victory'.

A week following the incident, the Shekdar came to Ramasandra. The government had ordered to collect money for the war fund. The same government had dismissed the revenue tax as there was no rainfall and no crops. But now it was not possible for the Emperor of England to win the war without people's support. People must give as much as possible in support of the Government. When the Shekdar had himself come, what could be done? Shivegowda, Kashimbaddi and others had to shell out as much as the Shekdar asked. Even Narasi, who ran her provision stores outside the village, gave five rupees. A total of hundred rupees got collected in Ramasandra. 'The honour of your village is saved,' the Shekdar said and left.

The next day when Ramanna came from school, he had pinned on his shirt a coloured paper with a 'V' printed on it. He came home and said, 'Mother, this was put on the shirts of all students and a procession was conducted. Look at this—had I not taught you the letter "V" of English. "V" means victory. Our Headmaster has asked all the students to bring two annas each. There must be victory for us in the war,' the boy explained. But the mother was thinking how she could get two annas for the boy.

CHAPTER ELEVEN

1

Even after so many years, Kamalu had not conceived. Akkamma was worried, for the lineage would not continue from her grandson, who she had reared. It would not have even mattered much if she did not bear children, but Kamalu failed to even keep her husband and grandmother happy.

In Nagalapura also, drought prevailed and there were no crops just like in Ramasandra. But Kallesha ran his family intelligently. He used to stock grains sufficiently for more than a year. Last year, when he got the hint that there would be no rain, he sowed haraka, a coarse grain, in his dry fields, and got three quintals. There was ragi at home. But to get paddy was difficult. However, this stock of grains was enough. Even cooked "millet" would be tasty. But Kallesha could not eat it, for it would increase his rheumatism. If he ate it, his paralysed left hand would begin to shake. So, if one quintal of paddy that was in the house was pounded now and then, at least fifty seers of rice could be obtained. Thus, Akkamma decided to cook only half of a quarter seer of rice for Kallesha, and along with ragi balls she, and Kamalu ate cooked millet only. Though she was aged, eating millet did not affect Akkamma.

Kamalu was enraged when she saw Akkamma prepare two kinds of rice and serve her grandson and his wife differently. Her question was in what way was he special and she, ordinary. She had not got rid of the feeling that she belonged to the town of Hassan, though it was twelve years since she had come to Nagalapura. Therefore, as if out of obstinacy, she had not touched the ragi balls with her hand. And now, how could this cooked millet get through her gullet?

One day, Akkamma finished cooking, went to the backyard and was sitting under the papaya tree. Kallesha was pricking the beds of vegetables with a hand pickaxe. Irrespective of whether it was a period of plenty, or one of famine where ragi, rice and other grains were scarce, he would always grow vegetables in his backyard. It was not in his nature to sit quietly and laze out. He took out the mud he pricked, filled the beds with red soil and dung manure, covered them with old soil, made the bed, drew two pots of water and watered the plants. Looking at the backyard, he decided on the plants that needed to be tended to and said, 'Get up, Akkamma, come and serve me some food.'

Kallesha drew another pot of water, stood on the stone slab and washed his hands and feet. Akkamma went in and was stunned by what she saw. Kamalu had placed a silver plate in front of her and was eating. The rice prepared for her husband was on her plate. The small vessel in which the rice had been cooked was empty. Kamalu had poured as much ghee as she wanted on the rice, poured in the rasam made of mixed pulses and was devouring it all, enjoying the taste. Akkamma stood speechless, but Kamalu was least bothered and continued her meal. Meanwhile, Kallesha too entered the kitchen. As soon as he looked at Kamalu, he understood what had happened. Straightaway, he neared the oven, took a piece of firewood and began beating Kamalu repeatedly on her back, hands and thighs.

'Let her eat, don't beat her so,' Akkamma said and tried to pull away Kamalu. But he pushed her with his left hand, and to that force, the old woman fell on the ground near the wall.

Kamalu retorted rudely, 'Hey, what, how dare you beat me? Do you beat me for eating rice in your house? Unable to provide a little rice to your wife, do you tell me to eat that bloody millet' rice she cooks? Don't you feel ashamed? Ha ha...he comes to beat me!'

Kallesha was enraged. When he began beating her left and right, the piece of firewood broke away. A splinter pierced his palm and blood oozed out. Kamalu's body and hands were swollen and blood was trickling from the wounds. Kallesha threw away the broken firewood, came out, put on his shirt and left without having food. This was not the first time that he had left his house in this manner. Nobody could say precisely where he would go, but Akkamma knew. Kamalu too almost knew it—either to the house of Devi, the prostitute whose name resembled that of God, to Putty of Nagalapura, or to the third wife of Mammy saabi, the police constable of the same village. He would have his food there. No matter where he went though, he would return by the midnight. If he would go to any other place, he would not stay there for more than a day.

As soon as he left, Kamalu turned to Akkamma and cursed her, 'Hey, you old widow, you carry tales about me and make your grandson beat me so hard! I wish your belly never gets any food. Let your corpse be eaten by street dogs.'

Akkamma did not utter a single word. It was never certain in this house whether one could have lunch on time, no matter how tastefully one cooked. Either Kallesha would get angry without reason, or his wife would enrage him in this manner. Something of this sort would occur daily. But today it was a little too much. Akkamma came out and again sat under the papaya tree.

Even as he rained blows upon his wife, the choicest abuses emanated loudly from Kallesha's mouth. If the sound of the beating was heard only by some three or four surrounding houses, the loud abuses reached twenty houses. After Kallesha put on his shirt and left the house, Shanubhoga Shamanna's daughter-in-law came. She was more or less of Kamalu's age. Since five or six years, they had become very good friends. Both of them would go to the village tank together. Many times, Kamalu would visit her house. Two years back, Shamanna's wife died, and the daughter-in-law Puttagowri the mistress became of the house. Her husband would obey whatever she said. As such, she was Kamalu's counsellor. Kallesha would certainly not oppose her coming to this house. Akkamma too had warned that Puttagowri not come to their house. But as if stubbornly, she would come, speak with Kamalu and take her to her house. Akkamma guessed that Shanubhoga Shamanna was purposely sending his daughter-in-law to their house to spoil Kamalu's mind, make her quarrel with her husband always and enjoy the fun. Kallesha too knew that Akkamma's guess was correct. Yet, of late, he was not opposing Puttagowri's coming to this house. Akkamma did not know the reason. She believed, if Puttagowri would give up, Kamalu would be sufficiently reformed.

After Kallesha left, Puttagowri came. Kamalu went to her bedroom, lay down on the mat and covered herself with a blanket. Puttagowri applied salt fomentation to the swellings and bruises on her friend and consoled her. Besides, she had brought along from her house rice and sambar mixed in a basin and made Kamalu eat it, almost putting it into her mouth. Should there be more insult than this to the house of Kantijois? Puttagowri showed the basin to a few houses, making it clear. 'See, there is no rice in Kalleshajois's house to feed his wife. I took some and gave her, look here,' so saying, she went home.

Kallesha came back the next morning. By then, his wife had already woken up, had washed her face, made coffee, drank it and was again lying in her chamber, indignant. She then realized that to the force of yesterday's beating, her earrings had broken and had fallen. Kamalu questioned Akkamma whether she had swept the pieces unknowingly or had hidden them to send to her granddaughter.

Akkamma argued, 'I am not a thief.'

Kamalu said vehemently, 'They were given to me in my marriage. Now they are lost. If they are not given to me now, I will write to my father.'

By the time Kallesha returned home, his anger too had subsided. He stirred the garbage where Akkamma had thrown the sweepings. He did not find anything. He did not believe that Akkamma had stolen the pieces and concealed them like his wife was accusing. Anyway, he repented; he should have struck his wife on only her back and not touched her ears.

For two months, Kamalu walked around the village without earrings. Thinking it as an insult—his wife roaming without earrings—Kallesha somehow adjusted seventy rupees and bought a new pair of earrings with white stones on them and gave them to her.

2

Nearly a year had passed. As there was no rainfall, the village faced the problem of drinking water. Normally half of the village used to bring sweet water from the tank, which was, half a mile away from their houses. After the tank dried up, four small wells were dug in the centre of the tank. It was quite a long distance that the people had to cross earlier; now people had to walk still further to get water. One afternoon, Kamalu went to the tank to bring water. As it was ekaadashi, Akkamma had gone to the Keshava temple in the outskirts of the village. Puttagowri came to Kallesha's house with a pot on her waist, and another on her head, called 'Kamalamma' and went inside. But nobody was there. She went to the backyard. No one could be found there too. When she came into the house, the front door was shut. She was surprised and turned towards the backyard and found that that too was closed. All alone in the darkness, Puttagowri was scared. Even before she could shout 'Ayyayyo' full-throatedly, she felt someone cover her mouth tightly.

When she returned home, her heart was thumping. She had heard villagers talking about the character of Kalleshajois on several occasions. *Let him do what he wants outside the village...oh! But he closed my mouth even before I could yell loudly...locked me in his house. Me, a Brahmin lady who had gone there to call his wife to accompany me to fetch water!*

Puttagowri's limbs were still trembling. Her whole body was burning with disgust.

She had not yet reached her house. A few neighbours around Kallesha's house came and asked her, 'What happened? You shouted so loudly.'

'Oh nothing, the cat in their house fell on me.'

'We rushed here. But the front door was locked from inside.'

She knew not what to say, but said, 'Yes, Kamalamma was in the backyard.' At the same time, Kamalamma passed in front of that house; she was carrying water from the tank and was returning home. Shamanna got suspicious, went inside and questioned his daughter-in-law, 'Tell me the truth. If anyone has misbehaved with you, I will have him hanged. Tell me, don't be scared.'

'I went into the backyard to see if Kamalamma was there. But nobody was there. I was going to return when suddenly Kalleshajoisaru came and asked, "Why did you come to our house?" I was scared and shouted, then ran from the backyard and came out from the door through which the cattle enter. Could he speak with me in such a manner?'

Shamanna's reasoning warned him. If he suspected his daughter-in-law's words to be false and raised clamour, the honour of his family would be at stake. To save that was more important than the veracity of his daughter-in-law's words. His son Nanjundayya understood nothing, but strictly ordered his wife, 'Did that bastard speak so to you? Don't go to that house hereafter.'

When Shamanna came to Kallesha's house, Kamalamma was there. Akkamma had not yet returned. Meanwhile, Kallesha had gone somewhere. Shamanna said to Kamalamma, 'When my daughter-in-law came to call you to accompany her to the tank, it seems your husband spoke to her disgracefully. I could have filed a case against him and could have him punished. Somehow, I have given up that idea. Hereafter don't come to our house. My daughter-in-law also need not visit your house.' He then left.

For two days, Kallesha did not come home. The third night, at ten, when he did, Akkamma cooked rice and tamarind rasam and served him. He asked whether Shamanna had caused any commotion against him. Akkamma whispered so that Kamalu should not hear. 'It appears that you spoke in an insulting way to his daughter-in-law and asked why she had come here. So, Shamanna had come and enquired how Kallesha could have spoken thus to his daughter-in-law and warned that hereafter both Puttagowri and Kamalu need not visit each other; he had left thereafter. Well, thank God, it is a great relief. If only you had spoken these words four years ago, that woman's frequent visits here and making this ape drunk, could have been avoided. This shrew could have been a little straight.'

Kallesha was satisfied to know that Shamanna had not created any uproar. It was like two birds had been killed with one shot. His deed was known neither to Akkamma nor to his wife.

Contact between Puttagowri and Kamalu was completely cut off. One day, they saw each other near the well in the tank. Though Kamalu spoke to her, Puttagowri turned her face away and left. Within eight days, it was clear to Kamalu that their friendship had broken forever. Along with losing an intimate friend, Kamalu had another reason to be anxious. But she could neither say that to anyone nor keep it to herself.

For eight days, she struggled alone within. One morning, as soon as she got up, she went to Shamanna's house. She was well aware that neither Shamannan or Nanjundayya would be at home at this hour. She went straightaway to Puttagowri, stood before her and said, 'My husband might have said one or two words. But should our friendship be ruined for that?'

Puttagowri did not know what to say immediately. Yet she spoke, 'Ahaha, was it one or two words? Enough enough. I don't want your friendship; I don't need to visit your house. If my father-in-law comes to know that you have come here, he'll chop your legs off. Now get out!'

'I'll go. Give me my earrings and money.'

'Which earrings? What money?' she asked as if she knew nothing.

'Oh what is it Puttagowri, you are speaking in this manner? A year ago, on the day my husband beat me, had I not removed my earrings and given them to you? When I was coming to fetch water, did I not bring you rice and coffee seeds, filling copper pots with them? Should you not give me a full fifteen rupees for all that?'

'Hey Kamalamma, if you tell lies, worms will pour down your tongue! Out! Go out! Don't stand in our house even for a minute. See, my father-in-law will come now!'

Kamalu's body began burning with anger and her lips trembled. She could not speak again. Such sturdy earrings of those past days! It would cost at least eighty rupees now and another fifteen rupees. This slut has planned to swallow both. *Yes, that's why she has concocted the lie that my husband spoke to her in this manner and that and stopped talking with me. If I am going to let this slut have my money, I am not a woman from Hassan town!* While deciding thus, she turned her eyes around. She saw the big large copper cauldron in the bathroom. She did not know what she was doing, nor could she be aware of its consequences. She rushed into the bathroom, pushed the vessel, toppled it, poured out the water, held it in her hands, said, 'Give back my money and take your vessel,' and walked away. Could Puttagowri, keep quiet and allow the vessel to be taken away?

'Ayyo, you thieving slut, entering my house, you carry away our copper cauldron?' she shouted, rushed forward and tried to prevent Kamalu. But Kamalu was stronger than Puttagowri. She threw her down and without bothering about the soot at the bottom of the pot, placed it on her head and came running to her home.

Several people in the street saw Kallesha's wife carrying a big copper vessel. They did not see any significance in it. When Kamalu came home, her husband was not there. She kept the pot inside the kitchen and closed the front door of the house. Akkamma could not understand anything. When she asked, 'Hey, what's that, who does that belong to?' She did not answer. Akkamma listened to what Kamalu was grumbling to herself: 'Ahaha, that thieving slut had schemed to embezzle my money. Doesn't she know the angry nature of my husband? Yes, he might have asked, "Why did you come here?" Should that much be the pretext to swallow my money? Let her come to my door for the cauldron. I will show that cheating slut widow, what sort of a woman I am!' Akkamma, however, could make out nothing.

In a short while, there was noise in the street. Shamanna's voice could be heard. He was shouting. 'Hey, you thief, have you stolen and brought our copper vessel?' He was on his way to Kallesha's house. There was noise from a crowd of about twenty to thirty-people-strong. Shamanna knocked on the front door. Kamalu was saying, 'No, don't open the door until my husband comes home', but not knowing what the matter was, Akkamma opened the door. Gathered in front of the house was a crowd like that of a fair. Shamanna said, 'See Akkamma, your daughter-in-law has stolen and brought here our copper pot. Give it back!'

Kamalu shouted from within. 'No, until my money is returned, I won't.'

As she did not understand anything, Akkamma said, 'Kallesha has gone towards the tank bund. Someone among you, go and fetch him. Until the master of the house comes, we don't know what to do.'

Two people ran. In a little while, Kallesha came back with those two people who had gone to summon him, and they had reported to him about his wife's deeds. He came in quietly and asked his wife, 'Hey, what's this?'

'That thieving slut has swallowed my money.'

Shamanna asked, 'Which was that money? Where did she get it from? You ask her Kallesha.'

'She has to return a pair of my earrings and fifteen rupees.'

'What sort of earrings? Whose father had given them?'

'They were my earrings. They were broken. Your daughter-in-law said she would get them repaired and took it from me.'

'If your earrings were broken, you should have given them to your husband and had them repaired. Then what about that fifteen rupees?'

'She had taken coffee seeds and rice from me.'

Shamanna now asked the people gathered in the street to give their opinion and said, 'Did you all hear this? Can anyone believe it!'

Kamalu retorted, 'Who should consent, who should believe? She stopped speaking to me with the purpose of swallowing my money and concocted "your husband called me this and that". Call her here. Ask her what did my husband say. Let her swear and tell, holding her children.'

Shamanna asked tauntingly: 'Oh you barren woman, whom do you hold and swear?'

Kallesha understood in which direction the matter was going. He was afraid that when there was a question of swearing and oath-taking, Puttagowri might blurt out the truth without hesitating. So, he turned to Akkamma and asked, 'Where is that copper pot?'

'She has kept it in the kitchen.'

Kallesha went inside, brought the pot out and placed it before Shamanna. He raised his leg, kicked his wife who stood in his way, saying: 'No, you should not give it back until my money and earrings are returned.'

Shamanna rebuked, 'Tut-tut, this thieving slut should be slapped on her head with chappals until all her hair falls down' and said to the village servant who stood there, 'Hey, carry that vessel to my house.'

The crowd slowly scattered from the front of the house. But people wouldn't go away so easily, given the extraordinarily juicy incident that had occurred in the village. They crossed the turning beyond Kallesha's house, gathered there as a group and began speaking jokingly about the incident. One by one, those who were not witness to the earlier incident joined the crowd.

Kallesha closed the door of the house, took a rope that was kept for tying cattle, joined and held it. As the police lash the thieves to confess about their crimes, he brandished the rope and whipped his wife on her body, hands and legs repeatedly. Akkamma quietly went into the backyard and sat in the cowshed, for she knew, if she tried to pull or save Kamalu from him, he would whip her also. When he whipped her fifteen or twenty times and asked, 'Why had you given her your earrings? What for? Open your mouth, you harlot!

Only then did she open her mouth, 'I had kept them to give it to Rangamani.' Rangamani was Kamalu's sister, about to be married.

'How did you pass on the rice and coffee seeds?'

She did not answer. After suffering a dozen or more beatings, she said, 'I used to put them in the pot when I went to fetch water.'

Kallesha threw away the rope. He went into the kitchen and brought a staff of firewood. Looking at it, Kamalu screamed with terror, 'Ayyayyappa, he will kill me, oh, I am dead.' The crowd that had gathered at the bend beyond Kallesha's house, rushed noiselessly to the front of the house. Sounds of beating with the staff, Kamalu's screams and curses, in between Kallesha's 'fuck your mother, fuck your sister' were falling on the ears of everyone gathered there. One or two from distant houses rushed forward to knock the door and rescue the woman. But people from nearby houses who knew it was usual and there was nothing special in it, stopped them, signalling by their hands.

Whether the staff of firewood broke away or he himself felt it was enough, Kallesha stopped beating. Blood was flowing from Kamalu's back, shoulders and arms and she had fallen down, deprived of the strength to even cry. Kallesha removed from her ears the pair of earrings he had given her last year, climbed on to the attic, kept them in his box, locked it and tied the key to the string around his waist. He opened the front door and came out. Looking at the crowd that stood in front of the door, he got enraged and asked, 'Hey, was a bear dancing inside? Why are you all standing?' Owing to the force of the manner in which he asked them these questions, they all got scared and dispersed.

Kamalu wailed for two hours. After cursing that her husband's hands shrink, that his legs are broken and he be sent to the gallows, her mind began reflecting on what had happened since the morning. She realized that she should not have gone and brought that copper vessel from Puttagowri's house, even though that thieving slut had guzzled the earrings and fifteen rupees. *What had occurred through the previous year became known to all because I brought home that damn copper and this pauper son of a widow beat me as if to kill me.* But she decided he must be taught a lesson for beating her. If she remained quiet, he would beat her more another day. Oh! that terrible, son of a slut!

3

Kallesha stayed at Devi's house in Maruvanahalli the whole day and started for his village the next morning. When he was walking through the cactus lane, four or five stones came and hit him. When he raised his neck and looked to see who it was, another stone hit him from behind. He at once shouted, 'Hey, who the hell is it, fuck your mother' and the stones stopped. He was a little scared to rush to that side on his own. What if there were many and they all attacked him at once? But if he walked quietly, it would not be known who it was and why they were behaving in that fashion. As it was broad daylight, Kallesha took courage and squeezed in through the cactus lane. He spotted the faces of men who sat hiding in the cover of the fence. When they knew that Kallesha had seen and recognized them, they squeezed amidst the cactus lane and ran away.

All of them were Shamanna's henchmen. Then there were the village watchmen and men who distributed water on the fields. None of them had any enmity with him so as to cause them to pelt stones at him. Kallesha understood that it was the mischief of Shamanna. Mischief was rooted in this Shanubhoga's very nature and mentality. He did not have enough courage to rush forward and do anything openly. He would always cause things to be done behind one's back. Kallesha knew that when his father was there, this Shamanna had sent his men to pelt stones on their house in the night. His father had gone to Shamanna's house in broad daylight and broken the tiles of his house. But Kallesha didn't have the courage of his father. But why did Shamanna do this? *The reason might not be that Kamalu had brought the copper vessel from his house. I myself had returned it. Perhaps he had realized what had happened to his daughter-in-law? If he opened his mouth and picked up a quarrel, his family would be defamed. That's why the bastard had started to take his revenge in this manner.* Kallesha decided not to deal cunningly with him; he needed to hatch a plot. He need not have bothered about that Puttagowri. After all, what beauty was she? Yet, he had desired her for many days and was satisfied. Thinking thus, Kallesha returned. By the time he came home, another problem awaited him. Akkamma asked, 'Where were you the whole of yesterday? Kamalu threatened, "I'll drown myself in the well, and send you and your grandson to the gallows." I didn't have a wink of sleep in the night. I sent for the tenant Honna and asked him to stay with us.'

Kamalu remained in the chamber of wrath. Kallesha asked, 'What's it now, you whore?' She answered arrogantly, 'I'll certainly send you to the gallows.' His mind at once thought of taking a staff of firewood, but he remembered that she did not budge even though he beat her right and left the previous day and gave up that thought. He remembered that in the past, she had once fallen into the well. A plan emerged in his mind and he asked, 'Hey, do you want to fall into the well?'

'Yes,' she addressed him scornfully.

'If so, come.' He held her arm and pulled her rudely and rapidly towards the well in the backyard. Akkamma prevented him saying, 'No, Kallesha, if something untoward happens, we will have to bear the consequences.' But Kallesha pushed Akkamma away, took the rope near the well, widened the noose, put it around her armpit and tightened. While she was still gabbling something, Kallesha supported his legs on the wall of the well, picked her up and slowly lowered her into the well through the new pulley. She was crying and shouting 'Ayyayyappo' while he was lowering the rope. As she came closer to the surface of the water and her feet, knees, thighs and waist slowly drowned in the water, she was shouting 'Ayyayyo', and Kallesha loosened the rope from above, drowned her head once inside the water and raised her above, up to her arms. Inside the well, Kamalu was both sweating and trembling. He shouted from above, 'Hey, you, will you fall into the well?'

'No... Nooo....'

'How dare you talk back like that?'

'No, no, no, I would request you please pull me up.'

He supported his legs on the wall of the well and tried to pull her up. But he felt he could not manage to pull up that weight all by himself. Some strong man should be called from outside. But if someone from outside was called, there might be an uproar. Meanwhile, there was a knock on the front door. While he was telling Akkamma, 'wait, don't open the door', the person who was knocking said: 'Akkamma, Kallesha, open the door!' Akkamma recognized the voice of her son Kantijois. She got up, opened the door, and when he came in, she closed the door again. The long bag was full and heavy and was swinging back and forth on his left shoulder. He let it hang there and placed the bag in his other hand down on the floor as he inquired about the welfare of his son. Akkamma said, 'Come here, just don't talk now.' Then, the father and son duo pulled the daughter-in-law out of the well. She went inside her room in her wet saree. She neither spoke again nor yelled nor created any uproar.

There were enquiries about mutual welfare. Kantijois now sported a beard like a sanyasi. He said he was in Kashi all these days. But he did not answer the question about why he had gone to Kashi. He had entered the village after enquiring in the nearby villages whether Shamanna was alive.

The mother asked, 'Why have you grown the beard? Have you been initiated into sanyaasa?'

'Nothing of that sort. Hey, Kallesha send for the barber.'

The barber came, shaved the beard and the top of the head, leaving a tuft enough on the head to make a knot. He had not withered nor emaciated a bit, since the last twelve years. Even now he had a healthy and well-built body. After bathing, he performed his *sandhayavandana* and did some *japa*. He had perhaps learnt to perform a japa in Kashi. While serving dinner, Akkamma asked, 'See Kanti, twelve years have passed since you left home. Relationships had as if been abandoned. However, we should have seen each other first in a temple.'

'See, I have brought Gangajal from Kashi. When that is with us, no need of all that custom and shaastras, you know. Ganga Samaaraadhana should be arranged.'

Kallesha said, 'It is very difficult to arrange samaaraadhana in these times. There was no rainfall and crops last year. Last year, we suffered drought. There is no stock of grains at home.'

'I have money with me. After all, how much will be spent?'

Many people in the village visited Kantijois and spoke to him. Staying for twelve years in Kashi, he had become a more learned scholar than he had been previously. Several people who had desired to go on pilgrimage to Kashi and but had never been able to fulfil that desire, came and touched his feet. Jois gave a thread of Kaalabhairava to such persons. Within two days of Kantijois's arrival, the Ganga samaaraadhana was held in a grand way. Though everyone came to the samaaraadhana, Shamanna and his family did not participate.

Meanwhile, Jois went around the village, met his old friends and learnt about the matters in the village. In the moonlit night after the Ganga samaaraadhana, he sat near the well and asked his son, 'Kallesha, your wife had stolen her own earrings and given it to her sister. That Shamanna's daughter-in-law has also joined in this?'

'Yes.'

'It seems you insulted her.'

'Yes, I told her not to come to our house.'

'See Kallesha, I am a Kashi-returned man; besides I am the father who begot you. Tell me the truth. Did you simply say to her: "Don't come to our house" or any untoward incident happened?'

'Who told you what? What did they say?'

'The whole village speaks in a different manner. It seems to me that Shamanna himself feels that it's disgraceful to open his mouth and speak the truth about what happened.'

Kallesha lowered his head and said, 'Yes, that Shamanna was sending his daughter-in-law here, to spoil Kamalu's mind. What else should be done to such people?'

'See Kallesha, a man can win through any kind of brave and valorous deed, but he must be strict in this one. If virility becomes unbridled, such a person can't be victorious in any other deed. What you did was wrong.'

Kallesha was ashamed. But to defend himself he said, 'I was coming back from Maruvanahalli, the previous day, the day—you returned home. Shamanna sent his servants and they pelted stones at me. How could he do so?'

'Damn that bastard! He had to face all this for pelting stones at my house. Did he think Kantijois is dead? You leave that to me; I will take care of him.' He decided on what was to be done, but he did not let out what the plan was.

Two days later, it was a Friday, the day of the fair in Nagalapura. There was no one who did not visit the fair where people of surrounding villages gathered. By three in the afternoon, Shanubhoga Shamanna left his house and was going towards the fair. He had donned a white dhoti, a shirt and an upper cloth and had put a black mark of Saadu on his forehead. He was walking with bearing the haughtiness of a Shanubhoga, when out of nowhere, Kantijois appeared before Shamanna. He wore a dhoti in crossed style, and an ochre-coloured shirt, three lines of vibhuti on his forehead and a rosary around his neck. He held in his hands a big earthen pot. The stench coming out of it made the people around cover their noses. 'Hey, you bastard, did you scheme to pelt stones at my son?' saying which Kantijois raised the pot that was in his hand, on top of Shamanna's head, and poured what was in it down on his head as if he was performing abhisheka. From the stench and colour of what was poured on Shamanna's head, people around knew it was human excreta. Only Kashi Vishweshwara, whom he had worshipped for twelve years, knew from where and how he had collected such an amount of it and how he had mixed it in the right proportion and brought it here. After all of it was poured down, the ingredients from the pot flowed through and smeared Shamanna's white shirt all over. Finally, placing the pot upside down on his enemy's head, Kantijois vanished into the crowd.

S.L. BHYRAPPA

Kantijois was not to be seen in Nagalapura for the next one month. Nobody knew where he was staying. However, they noticed that once every three or four days, Kallesha would go off to an unknown place. People inferred that he was meeting his father and informing him about the happenings here. As Kallesha used to go out during nights, no one dared to follow him. While returning, he would come early in the morning. What was the use of that? Who needed it? In his absence, in the last twelve years, Kantijois had become a legendary person, a Purana Purusha. Now, returning home, he had performed the Ganga samaaraadhana and three days after that, he had indulged in a great adventure that no one in the surrounding areas had before. Shamanna ran into the house the very moment the excreta was poured on him, rushed to the bathroom, put shikakai powder and with coconut coir rubbed hard his head and body, and washed himself thoroughly. Not more than ten to twenty people had witnessed the act. Only a few people had been able to recognize him while he was running home. But all the villagers were now describing the incident by adding colour to it as if they had been witness to Kantijois's pouring the pot down on Shamanna's head, and how some of the excreta had gone into his mouth too, and how it had drenched his body and limbs, like during Muharram they painted an individual's body to look like a tiger's.

Shamanna considered if it would be possible to file a suit against Kantijois. But he could not remember clearly any person who was there when the deed happened. Moreover, he was ashamed to have to proclaim that the fellow had insulted him in this manner. Besides, no one talked about this in front of him. He reasoned, it would not be wise to publicize this by raking it up. He remembered how he had filed a suit against this same Kantijois and had to shuttle to Narasipura. He recalled how Kantijois had thrashed him even after the acquittal. He pondered, 'I thought this bloody widow's son was dead. If I had kept that Kallesha's wife aloof, all this would never have happened. Wonder what sort of troubles I will have to face in this old age.' While these thoughts clouded his mind, another aspect was worrying him: 'This Kallesha, Kantijois's son, is a rascal like his father. In times of trouble, he uses skill and is a schemer. He is courageous too. But my son Nanjunda, is an utter coward! My time of raking up quarrels has ended.'

Kantijois returned home after a month. None questioned him directly about this matter. He too did not speak. If he set out on the street, rosary around his neck, three lines of vibhuti on his forehead, people looked at him with reverence and walked at a distance from him.

S.L. BHYRAPPA

CHAPTER TWELVE

1

Though there was delayed rainfall that year, the ragi harvest was good. A terrible war was being fought in Europe between the English and Germans. There was a war even in Burma, a country adjoining India. The Indian government was going to ration foodgrains. One day, the Shekdar came to Ramasandra and explained to Nanjamma what that meant and taught her the method of estimating the cost of crop yields while writing the accounts the next time. If there were six quintals of ragi crop per acre in a dry field, it would be sixteen annas. If it were four quintals, twelve annas, and for three quintals, eight annas. In this manner, the cost of ragi, paddy, horsegrams, cowpeas and all other crops had to be estimated. According to that estimate, the government would be deciding the quantity of the crops for every farmer and as per the census of population and the livestock, and debiting his home expenses and leaving some for the seeds, they would buy the remaining foodgrains at government rate. That meant a new authority for the Shanubhoga.

Nanjamma went to Kurubarahalli one day and explained about this new calculation to Gundegowdaru. He asked, 'What? Should we give to those fellows what we have grown with our hard labour?'

'Yes, the government has made it a rule. Else, the police will come to our doorstep.'

It was Nanjamma's wish that there should be no damage to or trouble for Kurubarahalli, no matter which village in it would come to be involved in this food rationing issue. If that village was hurt, it would be dishonourable for Patel Gundegowdaru. How could she tolerate if the village which nurtured her family got into trouble? But many of the villagers had flocks of sheep. Every year, they let the sheep into the dry fields. The excreta of sheep would provide good manure and the farmers grew more than six quintals per acre. She had to write a lesser estimate. But the Shekdar had said that the Amaldar himself would come and personally inspect the fields.

247

Nanjamma and Gundegowdaru discussed the matter and arrived at a decision: she had to write in the account book the estimate of eight annas and nine annas crop in general. A total of one hundred rupees had to be collected from the village and handed over to the Shekdar and the higher officials. This would keep them in the government's good books. When the government came to buy the grains, twelve quintals would be given as the government's share of the crop.

That year it went on according to their plan. The people of Kurubarahalli somehow got over the trouble by giving hundred rupees in cash and twelve quintals of ragi at a price fixed by the government. Earlier also, people of that village were giving ink charges to the Shanubhoga. Now they started to collect ten seers of ragi per house to the Shanubhoga. But Ramasandra and Lingapura villages were hit hard from this method of controlled rationing of food. Neither the Patel Shivegowda of Ramasandra nor others could understand what was meant by crop estimation. Nanjamma had accurately written down the accounts of these villages. One day, after the harvest season was over, the Shekdar, his two peons and two police constables visited Ramasandra. Under the Shekdar's directions, the peons barged into all the houses. They searched the attics, corn bins, granaries, underground granaries, earthen pots and other bins. They pushed deep into the bottoms of the bins and granaries their long bamboo staves. This was their way of calculating the length and width of the bins and granaries based on which, they estimated the quantity of grain in a particular house and measured them arbitrarily. Then they filled the grain into sacks and heaped the grains before Maadevayya's temple. Then, on the spot, the peon would demand twenty, forty or fifty rupees from the house owner and tell the Shekdar, 'There were only two quintals, sir.' After that, he would share some of this booty with the Shekdar and would pocket the rest. On his part, the Shekdar would give the police some share of what he had taken.

Anyway, the Shekdar collected four hundred quintals of ragi from Ramasandra, hundred quintals from Lingapura and left the village. The farmers had to present the receipt the officers had given them before the Patel and Shanubhoga, provide some honorarium for concerned officers and get their money. Those servants in their 'skilful' method of measuring would lift away seven to eight seers per quintal.

One day, after fifteen days, Patel Shivegowda sent the village servant Kulavadi to bring Nanjamma. Whether the Shanubhoga should present himself, when the Patel sent for him or the Patel should come when the Shanubhoga asks for, solely depended on their property and pride. Till now it was the practice that Shivegowda would send for and Channigaraya would go. But today he had asked Nanjamma to come. Nanjamma got enraged. However, without losing her patience she told the servant, 'If there is some work, tell him to come here.'

In a short while, the Patel himself came. The village servant following him stood near the door. Shivegowda sat on the toddy palm leaf mat that was spread near the pillar. He was struggling for five minutes, not knowing how to start the conversation. Then he said, 'It is said the officials took twelve quintals from Kurubarahalli. How is it they took away four hundred quintals from our village?'

'How should I know that Patelare?'

'You should tell me how, and what you know. Are you not writing the accounts?'

'Look Patelare, I have not come to your door begging. Speak with a little respect,' said Nanjamma and went into the kitchen.

'I know Channigaraya from his birth.'

'If so, you ask him yourself. You sent word with the village servant asking me to come to your house. Do you think your post of Patel means exercising authority?'

Shivegowda felt as if he had been slapped on the face. He had never spoken to this woman directly. His whole body burned seeing the pride of this woman who had lost her house and property, made plates by joining leaves and sold them, grown vegetables and eaten them and one who wrote the accounts for her husband.

'Well, why didn't you prepare a lower estimate while writing the accounts of our village?'

'Who are you to question that?' Nanjamma asked from inside.

'I will ask the government itself whether a woman can write the accounts,' Shivegowda said, got up and left. He, who was flaunting like a king before the whole village, today experienced great defeat. That too before the village servant, whom he had been treating with arrogance all these days; this woman had ridiculed him in this manner. He took his brother-in-law Shivalinga with him, directly went to Kambanakere and asked the Shekdar whether a woman could write the government accounts. The Shekdar knew in detail why this question was being raised. Though it was only six months since he had come to that hobali, his predecessor had informed the newcomer the intricate details of each subdivision region. He spoke skillfully and made Shivegowda come out with the basis for his objection. However calculated, if the estimation was more in the account of the Shanubhoga, it would be profitable to Shekdar also; even otherwise, if it was less, then too he would gain. So why would the Shekdar let down the Shanubhoga? He said, 'Look Shivegowda, even the deputy Commissioner Saheb is aware that she writes the accounts. He himself has said in his Jamaabandi that in the whole of Tumkur district there is no one who writes the accounts as well as this lady. There is no government rule that women should not write accounts.'

Shivegowda returned with a beaten face to the village, with his brother-in-law. On the way, Shivegowda asked his brother-in-law, 'When that son of a whore Shekdar comes here, this harlot prepares him uppittu and coffee. So did you see, brother, how he has favoured her?'

'Hey, leave it uncle, will he favour and take her side only for uppittu and coffee? Whenever he comes, she spreads her bed beside him and sleeps.'

'Tut-tut, whore of a widow, the bitch,' said Shivegowda and consoled his mind. But he or his brother-in-law did not have enough courage to speak the same in front of anybody, once they returned to the village.

Nanjamma was contemptuous of Shivegowda for his haughtiness and arrogance. It was not the arrogance that came off of the mere Patel's post. Now all the villagers knew that the moneylending and borrowing business of Kashimbaddi ran with Shivegowda's money. Kashimbaddi, being a man from another country, did not want to build a home or buy lands in this village. He would calculate his part of the interest and send the money to his country Malayala. In the beginning, the business of interest of these two ran on mortgage and the pledge of gold, silver, copper and brass. The villagers who lost these metals from their houses would pledge their pieces of land and take loans on calculation of interest by paise and the mortgage papers would be written in Shivegowda's name. They would cut off the paise interest of three months and give the villagers money. That meant, if the mortgage was written for a thousand rupees, only five hundred would be given to them. If they would go to court also, they would get twelve per cent interest for one thousand. During the drought, that too when there were no rains and crops for two years, Shivegowda had become very powerful. It was not possible for anyone in the village to subdue him. Nanjamma was well aware of it. But when he tried to impose his authority on her, she had given him an apt reply and sent him back. After the food control, the Shekdar had to visit the village frequently. When Nanjamma came to know that Shivegowda had gone to meet the Shekdar, she knew, he would have received a nice dressing down.

2

There were good crops after the rainfall, but the prices of grains did not drop. War still continued. Alongside the usual accounts of the Shanubhoga's post, were added the responsibility of accounts of food control of crops and grain stocks. The government started giving a separate allowance to Shanubhogas besides their annual salary. Nanjamma's earlier annual salary of the post of Shanubhoga was a hundred and twenty, and now she got an extra hundred rupees as allowance. She could not get the time to make leaf plates, as writing these extra accounts consumed time. Parvati looked after domestic chores and watered the vegetables that were grown in the backyard. She took care of the cows brought back from Gundegowda's house. Ramanna was in the third year of middle school. He stood first in his class. He would put rules on the new account books, and would do arithmetical calculations of quintals without any errors. Sometimes, he would find errors in his mother's entries and would show her. Once the Shekdar himself sent for him and asked him to copy his account book. Nanjamma felt elated about how intelligent her son had become. But she did not like the idea of Ramanna becoming a Shanubhoga in the future. He should at least complete high school and become a Shekdar. She brooded: 'Why wouldn't it happen, if there was enough of God's grace? Ramanna has so much intelligence.'

Vishwa was in the third year of primary school. In the whole village, no one was as mischievous as he. But he was also very brave. He would swim for approximately seventy yards in the village tank like the adults. He would go alone near the burial grounds, search for beehives, open them, squeeze honey from them into the bark of areca nut plants and bring it home. He was like his grandfather Kantijois in courage, speech and pride. More affection than earlier had developed now between him and Maadevayyanavaru. If Maadevayyanavaru sang tatvapadas, Vishwa would strum the ektaari and play the drum. He had again continued sharing food brought through Maadevayya's kantebhiksha.

Nanjamma's family had no problem with food now. Her earnings too had increased, as of other Shanubhogas and Patels, after the food control accounts came to existence. Everyone at home now had a pair of clothes. She had bought four blankets from Kurubarahalli for the winter season. But one thought was haunting her. Parvati was almost completing thirteen. If there was no drought in the last two years and she was provided with nutritious food, by now, she would have attained puberty. She had become like a stick without food and only now could she have two meals and was taking breakfast of roti and curds. Her marriage was not yet fixed. Nanjamma was deeply distressed with this thought—what if Parvati attains puberty before marriage?

Was it child's play to perform a marriage? At least seven to eight hundred rupees were needed, however niggardly your estimate of the expenditure. Moreover, a responsible man—preferably a father—ought to have been there to search for a bridegroom and to take care of all other matters. She knew what sort of a person her husband was. All twenty-four hours of a day, her mind would be tormented by this.

Someone said there was a groom in Thirumagondanahalli near Tiptur. She sent her husband and the school teacher Venkateshayya, who had recently come to the village school, to inquire about the groom, visit their house and fix the marriage. The next day, the teacher came back and said, 'See, Nanjammanavare, if this Shanubhoga is taken along, can the groom be finalized? We went to their house and asked for the horoscope of the boy. They asked us to give the girl's horoscope first. I gave it. They asked us to have lunch. I said, "We have come here to give our girl to your house. You know—the custom—that if Gods will, until the Kanyadaana is completed, we should not have even a glass of water in your house." But this Shanubhoga did not heed my word at all. Though I told him not to take meals there, he removed his shirt, washed his hands and legs and sat for lunch. But I didn't eat. After Shanubhoga finished his meals, the brother of the boy's father came out and said, "See the bride's father himself took meals in our house. Now the marriage proposal should not be continued. I think you know the custom."

Hearing Venkateshayya's words, Nanjamma felt anguish and anger simultaneously. She asked her husband, who was resting on the mat, 'Why did you have lunch there, when the teacher asked you not to?' Shrinking on the mat, he said, 'I didn't know what else I could do, when my belly was burning with hunger.' Nanjamma remembered the proverb 'Don't throw stones on shit and cause it to splatter on your face', and did not speak to him again. But she thought to herself, who else was there to take responsibility of this girl's marriage and make it happen.

To her misfortune, Parvati attained puberty that night itself. Though it was not unexpected—the time of its arrival—Nanjamma lost her heart. Who was going to marry a girl who had attained puberty? She had heard that nowadays, in big towns like Tiptur, such girls too are married in well-to-do people's houses. But that was the case in wealthy families. Nanjamma's family, however, was poor; besides, they were villagers. If the girl attained puberty before marriage, they would not survive the ignominy. Already the village Jois had excommunicated her and her children. In case, somehow, she arranged for the money and a bridegroom, they would not officiate in the marriage rituals without asking to shell out the fine. And now, if this too was known, there would be a huge uproar. If people had an inkling of this, they would whisper in the ears of the would-be groom's people and avert the marriage. Nanjamma sat as if enveloped by gloom for more than an hour. Channigarayaru was sleeping comfortably. To tell him anything was the same as whispering in the mouth of a bugle—they would have the same effect.

Nanjamma came to a decision. She strictly instructed Parvati not to mouth to anyone that her periods had started and asked her to stay indoors. She did not allow Parvati to do any domestic chores, told her to sleep in a corner and say that she was suffering from stomach ache. She informed the matter to Ramanna. He was intelligent enough not to share it with anyone.

But Vishwa was a little boy and did not understand these things. So Nanjamma did not inform either Vishwa or her husband. Channigarayaru would never inquire about the children whether they were healthy or were suffering from illness. But Vishwa touched his Akkayya's stomach and asked how she felt and did she still have pain. He directly came into the kitchen. After Parvati started to take care of the domestic chores, Nanjamma observed the three days of periods sitting separately in a corner, not doing any household chores or touching anything in the house. Besides, now she had kept a Saaligrama along with the photo of God. For the Saaligrama's sake, Nanjamma was observing purity. Today Vishwa had touched his sister who was menstruating and come into the kitchen. Nanjamma wore a madi saree, took the Saaligrama, put it in a clean copper pot and placed it on the beam of the roof. She was not that scared of other means of pollution. But she had to be careful regarding the Saaligrama.

Ramanna, however, went to Kambanakere daily. Nanjamma asked him to bring jinjali seeds. She herself went to Kurubarahalli one day, requested in four or five houses, asked for copras, saying there was some religious ritual and bought twenty copras. Every day, she fed Parvati fried jinjali seed, jaggery, copra and fenugreek seed flour, making her sit in the kitchen and eat heartily. Now butter cost ten annas per seer. Ramanna brought that secretly from Kambanakere and Nanjamma fed her daughter ghee too. Her attaining puberty could be hidden. But Nanjamma was always concerned of her daughter's health. If care was not taken and nutritious food was not given during this time, what would happen to the strength and health of the girl in future.

Five months passed thus, without anyone getting even a small hint. But the changes occurring to Parvati's physical body and face made everybody aware that she had attained puberty. She was a girl of tall build, broad shoulders and a face resembling that of her mother. Although the care Nanjamma took was not enough, sufficient amounts of jinjali, copra and fenugreek were being fed to the girl. Once a week, she gave her daughter an oil bath. Parvati now did not water the greens and vegetables in the hot sun and so even her complexion and face turned fairer. How could her beauty be concealed? If the care she took was stopped, the girl would not get enough strength and survive. It was a dilemma for Nanjamma. For a moment, she would feel happy looking at the healthy body of her daughter, but at the same time she would become aware of the present condition and her mind would become burdened with the thought: 'Oh! God, will she get married at all? Let our honour be saved!'

Parvati was a sensitive girl. She was completely aware of the problem that afflicted her mother's mind. That was the problem of her daughter's life. Parvati knew her marriage had to happen by now. She knew that in this region, if girls attained puberty before marriage, they would be blindfolded and left in the forest. But somehow, her mother would perform the marriage. But what sort of groom would she get? Would he be like her father, her uncle, her maternal uncle Kalleshajois, Revannashetty, or Shivegowda? Her mind would reject every one in this village, not wanting to have such a husband. She could tell her mother, she wanted this or that type of a human being and only that. But her mind was always aware of the fact that her family did not have the strength and means to search for a groom to her liking and perform her marriage. She felt it would have been better if she were not born. Even now if she died, it would be well. But dying meant going away from Amma, Ramanna and Vishwa. When she realized that, the thought of death vanished from her mind. She determined that no matter what sort of a husband she got, she would live with him and run the family as her mother was doing. If her fortune was good, she might get a good husband. School teacher Venkateshayya never beat his wife, and he had no bad habits like chewing tobacco or smoking beedis. No bad word came out of his mouth. It would be enough if she could get such a person—such thoughts and desires hammered inside her mind.

One evening, Channigarayaru came home and asked his wife: 'Hey what? Has Parvati attained puberty?'

When her father enquired, Parvati too was there. Nanjamma got angry and said, 'What? Are you out of your wits? Who told you so?'

'Annajois asked me: "Why does your daughter not come to the backyard to water the greens?" Has she attained puberty or something?'

'What did you say?'

'I don't know, I will ask my wife.'

'What would have happened if you had said "no"?'

He spoke angrily, showing his ire. 'How do I know these things?'

Nanjamma told him skillfully to tell whoever asked him: 'No, not yet. Now she is busy at home making leaf plates.' Then Parvati's father became quiet.

This meant that the Brahmins in the village had already got suspicious. These matters were difficult to be kept secret for a long time, however much careful one was. When the jasmine bud blooms in the creeper, however strongly you cover it, it comes to be known to everybody. It is the same with a girl who attains puberty and experiences good care and nutrition. It will be known to everybody.

3

After this incident, the next afternoon, a cart covered with an arch stood in front of their house. Even before the yoke was lowered from the neck of the oxen tied with a chain of bells, a person, tall and well-built, descended. Parvati had not seen him earlier. He had smeared three lines of vibhuti on his forehead and had a rudrakshimala around his neck. After the yoke was lowered, Akkamma got down. It had already been four years since Akkamma had visited. Her body was bent. Parvati shouted: 'Amma, Akkamma has come!' Soon Nanjamma got up and rushed out. There stood her father in front of her.

He asked, 'Nanja, you have become thinner than before. Is this the girl who was born in Nagalapura?'

Parvati and Nanjamma's other children had heard about their grandfather. Now they had a chance to see him in real. Akkamma had brought deep-fried snacks like kodubale and chakkuli. Grandpa had brought a saree for his granddaughter, and shirts and shorts for the boys. Besides, there was a sealed copper pot filled with holy water from the Ganga in Kashi. Vishwa came back from school and was much excited.

Nanjamma asked, 'Appa, it's been thirteen years since you left this place, isn't it? Shouldn't you have come first to the temple and sent for us?

'No, people who have been on the Kashi pilgrimage need not observe these customs. Besides I have brought Gangajal with me.'

To her a question arose why all of a sudden he had left and gone to Kashi for so many years. Kantijois did not answer it satisfactorily and said instead: 'I somehow felt like going to Kashi and live near God Vishweshwara. So, I left. Does it matter to me where I stay?'

Akkamma herself mentioned the reason for their coming together now. 'There would be no children in the womb of that barren slut. It is already sixteen years. We have decided to bring another girl for Kallesha. If the lineage ceases, who will do the ceremonies and put pinda for us?'

'Has my brother agreed to this?'

'Yes, why wouldn't he agree? It was he who hired the bullocks and cart and sent us here.'

'What can I say to that? Moreover, what do I know?'

'Give Parvati as bride to our home. In a single day, let us complete the Kanyadaana.' When Akkamma said this, Parvati was present. She could understand nothing. Even Nanjamma was stunned by this unexpected proposal. It was unimaginable. Akkamma continued, 'See, Kanti has brought three thousand rupees, twenty gold rings and many other things. All that would belong to our girl. She will live like a queen.'

Nanjamma said, 'Akkamma, what is Parvati's age and what is Annayya's? Besides, he is the maternal uncle and Parvati, maternal daughter-in-law. If he had a son, she should have been married to that boy.'

'If there were a son, why would he have decided to marry a second time? How many girls have not married maternal uncles? After all, what is Kallesha's age? It must be thirty-six or thirty-seven. He is still strong and sturdy like a prince.'

'Will sister-in-law allow this and keep quiet?'

'What else will she do except keeping quiet? Let our girl give birth to a child. If she wants, she may stay here serving Parvati. If not, she can go back to her father's house, wearing an old saree.'

Nanjamma could not decide at once what to say. Confusion reigned in her mind. Akkamma said, 'You have seen, there is no scarcity of food in our place. Kallesha looks after the lands, works hard, and the house is very good and spacious. Kanti has brought three thousand rupees. If you want, he will buy gold for all that money and put it on her. She will be the granddaughter on the one hand and his daughter-in-law on the other. If I die without Kallesha getting a child, how will I attain salvation? Two of you survived born of your mother's womb, I brought you up. Now I myself am requesting, give your daughter, he is not a stranger.'

Nanjamma's heart melted, but her mind did not accept the proposal. She said nothing. That night after dinner, when Kantijois explained the matter to his daughter, Channigarayaru also was present. From the very beginning, he was scared of his father-in-law. It was he who had caused the post of Shanubhoga to be transferred from Shivalinga to him. Kantijois now explained everything. Akkamma had told her granddaughter and great granddaughter, and turned to his son-in-law and asked, 'What do you say, Chinnayya? There is so much land, a house; besides, three thousand rupees too will be your daughter's. Now where will you search for a groom and marry her? Simply say yes.'

Why would Channigarayaru say 'no'? 'Yes, it is all right. This sis..', he had started, but controlled his tongue and said instead, 'You tell hhher. I have nnno objection.'

'See, your husband too has consented. What do you say Nanja?'

Even now, Nanjamma did not know what to say. She said, 'Let it be so. Let us think and speak tomorrow.'

But Kantijois communicated his decision, 'What is there to think? When all of us have consented, it is as good as fixed. After returning to my place, I will arrange for everything. Within another week, I will finish off the marriage.'

Nanjamma said, 'Are you not going to stay here for a few days. Let us talk over the matter.'

'No, no we have no time to stay here now. We must return and make necessary preparations for the marriage. You don't spend even a single pie,' Akkamma said.

After Akkamma had uppittu and others finished dinner, all of them went to bed. Akkamma and Kantijois were soon asleep. Channigarayaru was snoring. But Nanju, who lay down near Akkamma, could not manage even a wink. They had already decided on the matter even before she had expressed her acceptance or non-acceptance of an offer that had come all of a sudden. It was true, as they said, there would no trouble with or hardship over food. They would never eat without ghee, curds and milk. They grew paddy and ragi sufficient for more than a year. And three thousand rupees would be Parvati's. And that was not a small amount. They had not even touched that much money. What happiness had the girl experienced since her birth in this house? For a little while, Nanjamma thought, yes here, if there was a stomachful of food, there was no proper clothing; if there was clothing, there was no food. But the question hovered in her mind. While there is that great termagant, Mahamaari-like first wife living, could she give Parvati, that too to her brother? Nanju's brother was seven years older to her. That means there would be a difference of twenty-two years between Parvati and her brother. She had known people who had married a second and even a third time with a difference of thirty years between them. It was not rare bringing a second wife while the first one lived and had borne no children. But why did Annayya not beget children? Was it because of womanizing? Or was her sister-in-law barren? She is of a savage nature, agreed. But if I give him my daughter, would my child be happy?

She thought she must give a convincing reply to her father and Akkamma. In such a situation, with whom could she relate her hardships or happiness? As soon as her father mentioned abundant grains in the house and three thousand rupees in cash, this *Appa*—Channigarayaru—opened his mouth. Both the parents should discuss and think about the children's marriage. But why should she pine uselessly for the fortune she did not have? Suddenly, she remembered Maadevayyanavaru. She reflected that it would be wise to consult him and then decide about the marriage. She got up, went out in the darkness and when she was closing the door noiselessly, Parvati too followed her. Nanjamma was not much surprised to see her. She warned her daughter not to make any sound, closed the door quietly and walked on. Parvati followed.

She came to the shrine and awoke Ayyanavaru. When he lit the lamp, they saw tears flowing from Parvati's eyes. Ayyanavaru asked, 'What Parvatavva, are you crying to say I don't want to marry my maternal uncle?'

Nanjamma asked, 'How did you come to know all this, Ayyanavare?'

'Your father had come here, in the evening. He told me everything. What have you thought about this?'

'I came here as I could not come to a conclusion.'

Meanwhile, Ramanna arrived there and joined them. His mother asked, 'Why did you come here leaving the house?'

'I have locked it from outside and come here. I too could not sleep. I knew you two would be here,' he said and showed the key.

Ayyanavaru asked him, 'What do you say about your Akkayya's marriage, Ramanna?'

'No Ayyanavare, it should not happen. Kallesha uncle goes to Narasi's house...,' he stopped, for he felt he should not utter such words before elders. Then he said, 'No, Akkayya should not be given in marriage to him.'

Ayyanavaru said, 'Look Nanjavva, I too will say what is in your mind. Don't give your daughter, considering that he is your elder brother. If you ask me, don't marry her to anyone from the surroundings. Who is wise and reasonable in these surroundings? Good grooms are those who are in government jobs. Whatever hardships you have to suffer, give your daughter to a school teacher. They will live respectfully. All others are scoundrels.'

Ayyanavaru had mouthed what was in Parvati's mind. Nanjamma too felt it was right. 'But,' she lowered her volume and said, 'We have to look at the age of the girl. If she attains puberty, what will happen?'

'All such customs are not observed in towns. Search for a groom there and marry your daughter off. Now, you have with you the accounts of government grains. If you raise the subscription in the villages under your post of Shanubhoga, five or six hundred is not a big amount.'

'Oh, Ayyanavare, it is said they demand large amounts in dowry in big towns. I fear about whether I will be able to perform my daughter's marriage successfully at all.'

Ramanna expressed his idea. 'Amma, I am studying in the higher class. I'll teach Akkayya. If she too appears for a lower secondary examination in private and comes to possess a certificate, she can become a school teacher. Even if there is no marriage, who cares for it!'

'Let us think about that later. If possible, you ask Venkateshayya's opinion. Answer your father later,' Maadevayyanavaru said.

Ramanna left to fetch Venkateshayya. Nanjamma warned him, 'See that no one is awakened. None should know about this.' In a little while, the teacher came. Parvati got up and sat behind the pillar. Nanjamma explained everything in detail and the teacher said, 'See Nanjammanavare, in small villages of Arsikere and Banavara side, girls attain puberty before marriage. But nobody openly announces it. You need not be scared about that. I'll try and look for a suitable groom and fix the marriage. If he is a teacher in primary school, the salary will be low. We can get such alliances. You arrange for the money. Five or six hundred rupees is enough.'

'See Sir, the character and conduct of the groom should be good. He should not be foolish or indiscrete. If the salary is less, my daughter is proficient in making leaf plates. She can earn fifteen rupees per month sitting at home.'

'Don't I know? Any man must be fortunate enough to marry Parvathamma.'

S.L. BHYRAPPA

It was resolved not to marry off Parvati to Kallesha. The teacher suggested an idea. 'Let she herself stubbornly say "I don't want this marriage", and you add, "The girl is so obstinate, what shall I do?" and smoothly get out of this. But don't say rudely "I won't give my daughter to your house".

All three came home, opened the door without making any noise and went to bed.

Kantijois woke up in the morning and was in a hurry to leave. He asked Nanjamma, 'See, Nanja, there is a lagna on the eighth day from today. Where shall we have the marriage? Should it be here in your house or in Nagalapura?'

'Appa, please wait a little. Let us ask Parvati's opinion and then decide. If we speak among ourselves, it won't be fair.'

'Why should we ask her? Had I asked you when I fixed your marriage? Hey! Girl, come here,' Kantijois called his granddaughter and asked, 'What do you say regarding this?'

Parvati did not speak at once. When he asked her again, she answered, 'No, I don't want it.'

'Why not?'

'I don't like it; no, grandpa,' she said and then left for the kitchen.

'Hey Nanja, what's this, this slip of a girl says no?'

'If she doesn't like, it is not right to go against her liking. Leave it father.'

Kantijois was enraged. He too entered the kitchen, stood before Parvati and asked again, 'Why don't you want this marriage?'

'I don't like this arrangement. You should not compel me. 'When she uttered these words, Kantijois slapped Parvati on her cheek. Nanjamma had not beaten her daughter even once. As soon as she heard the sound of the slap, Nanjamma came in and said, 'Why do you beat the girl, Appa? You are so stubborn. Whatever idea enters into your head that should at once be carried out! Did you ever enquire before you married me off? Were you prudent enough in performing Annayya's marriage? To have children is destiny. But if you had enquired about the nature and conduct of the girl, he could have gotten a better wife at least.'

'What is lacking in your life now?'

'What else should happen? Your son-in-law and in-laws joined hands, lost all their lands and brought the family to this distraught condition. If I had not laboured hard, the children would have died of hunger.'

'That's why I said, give your daughter to Kallesha, there is no dearth of food there.'

'No, whatever you may say, I won't give my daughter away when she herself has refused. If you are so particular of performing his marriage, you go, search for another girl in some other place.'

'Listen to what I say, if that is to be so, you are neither my daughter, nor I your father, you sister-fucking slut,' saying thus, Kantijois came out, called his mother: 'Come out, Akkamma, we should not drink even a drop of water in this pariah woman's house.' He then gathered his clothes and sat in the cart that stood before the house. Akkamma too was angry for her wish had not been fulfiled. She too bundled her sarees, came out and got into the cart. Before the servant raised the yoke, Nanjamma came out and said: 'There is no *runaanubandha* between us and so it isn't destined to happen. Why are you so angry and leaving in this manner? Can't you stay here today at least?'

Akkamma retorted, 'Oho ho, you have honoured me in a very good manner for rearing you, nursing you and your children.'

Kantijois spoke as if it was final 'Hey! Did I not tell you that neither are you my daughter nor I, your father? Don't speak to me.'

Nanjamma did not speak again.

4

Eight days passed. On a late afternoon, Nanjamma and Parvati were grinding ragi, holding the same peg. There was no one else at home. They felt someone, come inside. Nanjamma turned and saw that it was Narasi. Till now, Narasi had never come to their house. Nanjamma did not talk to her on her own while crossing her shop. Narasi would ask, 'Are you going to Kurubarahalli Avvavre?' and Nanjamma would answer 'Yes', and that was all. Now she herself had come and it was not good manners to not speak with her while she had come to the house. Moreover, she had no tiff with Narasi, though her conduct was not such as to develop into a friendship.

Nanjamma said, 'Be seated, Narasamma' and Narasi sat leaning against the pillar. Parvati got up and went into the kitchen. Nanjamma thought there must be something, otherwise, she would not come to their house, and asked, 'What's the matter, you have come this far?'

'Avva, I wanted to tell you something. Is it true you are marrying Parvathavva to your Annayya?

'Who told you?'

'I have relatives in Shingenahalli and their relatives stay in Nagalapura. They said the people in Nagalapura were saying so.'

Nanjamma did not like sharing her household secrets with her. So she said, 'No, Narasamma, all that is false.'

'Your father and grandmother had come. I thought they must have come with that sole purpose. By God's grace, let it be a lie. Avva, please don't tell that I said so to anybody. Do I feel jealous if you, brother and sister are happy? No. But don't give your daughter to that man.'

'Does my brother come to you even now?'

'No, four years back I kicked him away. That fellow does not have loyalty even while he visits a prostitute.'

Nanjamma did not reply. Her grown-up daughter was in the kitchen. Such words should not be heard by her. But how could Narasi have such sensitivity?

'Leave it Narasamma. Let us not speak about that.'

'No Avva, I am not telling you this out of anger against that fellow. Hundreds come, hundreds go. I don't nurse my anger against anybody or remember them. Parvathavva is like my own daughter. You please marry her off to a worthy person. See, should that fellow lift away money from the shop and pocket it in the midnight after sleeping with me?'

Even now, Nanjamma did not speak. As if the work for which she had come was over, Narasi got up and left, saying, 'I'll move, Avva. My heart could not bear it, so I thought of informing you and came here.'

After she left, Parvati came out and again held the peg of the grinding stone. The minds of mother and daughter, who were holding the same peg and grinding on the same stone, were thinking about the same thing. Though both of them thought that it was for the better that they did not accept this marriage proposal and sent the family away, none said anything openly.

5

Nanjamma determined that she would fix and finish off her daughter's marriage at any cost that year. But she was anxious about the fact that if by chance the groom was fixed and she had no money to perform the marriage, she would be disgraced. It was important to arrange for the money first. After the work on the food account was completed, getting ragi from Kurubarahalli against writing advanced revenue tax had stopped. Besides, the government was paying hundred rupees per year separately for preparing this extra account. She was certain of getting two hundred and twenty rupees. But one thought worried her—what if her husband, without knowledge of anybody, went to Tiptur at the end of the year and swallowed the annual salary of the Shanubhoga and the extra salary from the food accounts? One day, when Gundegowdaru came to Nanjamma with the revenue tax receipts of six persons from Kurubarahalli and asked her husband to put his signature on them, he said: 'No, I won't sign.'

Nanjamma explained to Gowdaru, 'Gowdare, we should marry off our daughter. Please keep this money with you and you ask him to put his signature.' Then Gowdaru said in a threatening voice: 'Hey Chinnayya, are you going to put your signature here or do you need bludgeoning?'

'Oh, why do you team with her and make me a pauper without a paisa? Am I not the Shanubhoga at all? No, what will you do if I say I won't put the signature?'

'See, I will bludgeon you; wait, I will do it when you step into our village,' Gowdaru said, standing up and taking his walking stick into his hand. Channigarayaru shuddered with fear and put his signature on all the receipts. But his anger did not diminish. 'Fie this slut, begotten of a pariah', he said as he left home abusing his wife.

Nanjamma said, 'See Gowdare, now there is this two hundred rupees. The marriage needs at least six to seven hundred rupees. I don't know what I should do. You must guide me.'

'Your daughter is as beautiful as Goddess Lakshmi. If she was born in our caste, they would have selected the girl, putting all the jewels like a choker, head jewellery like nagaru, earrings and other things. Yours is a bad caste, Nanjavva.'

'Whichever caste we are born in, we have to live according to the custom, haven't we?'

'Don't worry for coconuts, pulses and grains. You fix the groom. I will raise the subscription by ten and five rupees per house in our village. There are forty houses there. By that, can we not raise three hundred rupees? Are you not protecting our village in the food accounts? In all, you will have five hundred rupees. Somehow, finish the marriage frugally.'

Nanjamma felt her mind freed from the burden by his assurance. She decided to search for a groom, hereafter. Leaving for his village, Gundegowdaru called Parvati to come out, and blessed her, 'Oh you are a very beautiful girl, my child. You will get a strong and handsome boy, don't worry.'

Nanjamma had thought of requesting her brother's assistance to look for a groom. But, given that her father and grandmother had come with the offer of her brother as the bridegroom, and had to leave angry and disappointed, she would now have to take help from others. He should be a trustworthy person, else there was no hope of getting a deserving or worthy groom. Nanjamma entrusted Venkateshayya master with the whole responsibility and said, 'Sir, you will earn the punya of Kanyadaana. You must show the way.'

Venkateshayya master visited four or five places, but was unsuccessful. There was a big landlord in a village near Arasikere. He had sent word that he would take this girl for his second son. But Venkateshayya master said, 'Look, Nanjammanore, I did not assure them anything. I feel that there must be some defect in the boy, if such a wealthy landlord is ready to bring a girl from a poor family to his house. Perhaps it is so. Is there not an adage that there should be parity in any marriage? But no, let us not give our girl to such a wealthy family.' Nanjamma agreed with Venkateshayya master's opinion.

After about four months of intense search, there was a proposal. It was from Dyavarasayya of Thimmlapura. The bridegroom was a distant relative of Dyavarasayya's wife. His name was Sooryanarayana. He had passed S.S.L.C and was working as a teacher in middle school. He was twenty-seven. His first wife had died four months back, leaving a girl aged three years. Sooryanarayana had lost his parents. As such, he himself was taking care of the child. He took the little girl with him to school. He was handsome, got a salary of sixty rupees, had suffered a lot and was as virtuous as gold. Dyavarasayya had sent word with his son to Nanjamma, 'You need not hesitate or have any doubts. You give him your daughter. He is very prudent. Your daughter will be happy. Your daughter should just care for his child with love and not treat her like a stepdaughter.' Now, Dyavarasayya was incapable of walking this far.

Nobody had to tell Nanjamma. She knew Dyavarasayya was a wise man. If she did not trust his words, whose should she? She asked his son, 'Have you seen the boy?'

'We do not know exactly. He is a distant relative from my mother's village. Now he is a teacher in a Middle School in Baalekere in Gubbi Taluk. If you send word, he will come to see the girl.'

Nanjamma asked Venkateshayya master. He himself went to Timmalapura with Dyavarasayya's son, enquired about the groom, returned and said, 'Nanjammanavare, I know him. While I was working in Kadaba, Gubbi Taluk, we have met several times. I have seen him on payment day and spoken with him many times in the Taluk office. He's a very good man. I did not know he had lost his wife. Forget it is a second marriage; it is difficult to get such a groom.'

Nanjamma asked Parvati's opinion. She said, 'Amma, it is enough if you agree, don't ask me anything.' Nanjamma wrote a letter in her husband's name and sent it with the village servant to Timmalapura.

After fifteen days, Dyavarasayya came with his wife, his son and Sooryanarayana in a cart to see the girl. By seeing his face, it was evident the groom was not more than twenty-seven. He had a dignified nature and was a man of few words. His three-year-old daughter would not leave her father even for a moment. Then Venkateshayya master came. He was much older than Sooryanarayana. Conversation ensued between them. By the time Nanjamma cooked payasa and other dishes and served them in the afternoon, Sooryanarayana's daughter Ratna had adjusted to Nanjamma well. She was walking with the child on her waist; she sat for some time on Parvati's lap and then holding Vishwa's hand, went out to play in the street. Sooryanarayana said, 'She has never taken to anybody in this manner. Within half an hour she was with Parvati, she has become very familiar with her.'

The interview was over. Sooryanarayana told Nanjamma, 'Amma, I have brought my horoscope. If you want, you may have both the horoscopes scrutinized by anyone. But I have lost belief in it. The first time, two or three Jois had said they had not found such a great match pair. But within four years of marriage, look what happened. Dyavarasayya uncle has explained everything about me. He has also told me about you. If you want, enquire from another four or five people. If all of you are satisfied, give away your daughter on an auspicious day.

It is enough if you prepare rice and tamarind rasam. But your daughter must take care of my daughter without discrimination. Regarding this, I am strict.'

Venkateshayya master knew a little about checking horoscopes. Dyavarasayya too knew a little. Both of them examined the horoscopes. The Griha maithri koota, Yoni koota and Naadi koota[24] matched. In all, twenty-three points matched. Usually, there could not have been a better match than this. Venkateshayya master took Sooryanarayana to his home. Then Dyavarasayya asked Channigarayaru, 'What do you say, Shanubhogaare?'

'What should I say? Does she consult me when she does anything?'

'You are the master. Though she manages all the work, is not the place of the master yours?'

'She is hopping and jumping about so much. Ask her how will she manage the money?'

'Why don't you yourself ask your wife about how she will arrange the money?'

He turned to his wife, asked, 'Hey what will you do for money, you sl...,' he started, but was ashamed at his own words. He started from the beginning and asked, 'How will you arrange for the money?'

'The annual salary of Shanubhoga for this year is with Gundegowdaru. Besides he has assured me, he would raise some money in Kurubarahalli.'

Channigarayaru remembered how Gundegowdaru had forced him to sign the receipts and said, 'He is a family-ruining bastard.' Nanjamma did not reply. Dyavarasayya too kept quiet as he knew this Shanubhoga's nature.

Venkateshayya master also invited Maadevayyanavaru to his house and introduced the groom. From there, all three came to Nanjamma's house. The marriage was fixed. Sooryanarayana said, 'Shaastra of Lagnapatrike can be done on the day of the Kanyadaana itself, and the marriage should be performed within a month from then. Besides,' he said of his own accord, 'You don't spend much for anything. Whatever I have to, I will bring for the bride. A pair of mill dhoti, a copper glass and copper spoon are enough to gift the bridegroom.' Before leaving the house, he prostrated in front of Nanjamma and Channigaraayaru,

---

[24]Aspects part of horoscopes which, based on calculations, are scrutinized.

brought in the child who was playing outside with Vishwa and made her bow too, then carried her in his arms and left. Though the oxen were harnessed, Dyavarasayya and his son walked till the outskirts of the village. Venkateshayya master and Maadevayyanavaru went a little beyond the village, took their leave, and returned.

6

The marriage was decided. To fix the *muhurtha* and officiate the marriage, the assistance of purohits were needed. The local purohits had excommunicated Nanjamma. She could have asked her father for help but he had gone away offended. These local purohits might cause trouble today or tomorrow, if she did not keep herself in their good books and kept them in her control. They might inform the bridegroom that the girl and her mother were excommunicated. They may create tales, scandals and cause discord. Though the bridegroom is good-natured and has practical knowledge, one cannot say how one's mind reacts in these matters.

It was not difficult for Nanjamma to bring down these two purohits. After food accounts prevailed, many of the villagers used to come to her house and grumble before her, so that she should write a lower estimate for their crops. These jois had not come personally. They had sent word in a roundabout way through the tenants who worked in their lands. It was not unknown to them that Nanjamma was the de-facto female Shanubhoga of the village, who wrote all the accounts. The whole afternoon, she reflected on whether she herself should go to their houses, and by the evening, sent for the village servant, saying: 'Go, tell Annajois and Ayyashastrigalu that I have sent for them and bring them with you.'

What Nanjamma did was a courageous act. It was the custom that poor people go to their doorstep and stand and prostrate before them by touching the ground, for they were the representatives of Sri Sringeri Mutt. She doubted whether they would come with the village servant. She was also, worried thinking what she should do if they did not come. But that did not happen. In ten minutes, Ayyashastri, and five minutes later, Annajois, came with the village servant.

Nanjamma said in an authoritative voice to the village servant: 'Mayiga, you sit and wait on the platform outside the house and spread a mat for both the Jois'. They enquired about each other's welfare and said, 'We learnt your daughter's marriage is fixed. We are very happy.'

'See, that's why I had to send for you. Horoscopes are to be scrutinized, the lagna is to be decided and then the marriage has to be officiated by you. You are also aware that now my father has returned from Kashi. If only I say, "you stay here until the marriage is over and look after all the rituals of the marriage," he will come riding on his horse. But, when there are local purohits like you, I thought I should not send for him, and I gave up that idea. I'll do as you advise.'

'No, no, no, why should you? When we are here, why should you send for him? It is our duty to officiate the marriage that takes place in our village. Come, give here the horoscope of the bridegroom,' Ayyashastri said. The change in their behaviour was only on account of the food account being in Nanjamma's hands. It would be a troublesome situation for both of them if her father came and stayed in this village. They knew that man was not only an expert priest, but he was such a strong and hefty man that if he got angry, he would hold anybody and thrash them. They had heard that he who was absent since twelve years had appeared all of a sudden. They asked for the almanac, calculated and said the horoscopes matched. They said that on the twenty-sixth day from then, there was an auspicious lagna and assured her: 'Don't have any worry about the marriage. If the purohit from the groom's side fails to come, we two will perform everything.'

'See, Joisare, in the same context, I am thinking finishing off Ramanna's thread ceremony also. Can we have it on the day of Kanyadaana?'

Again they calculated and said, 'No, you fix it on the previous day.'

Nanjamma had not thought that all this would be resolved so smoothly. Now she had a lot of work, like arranging for the money and preparing the required things for the marriage. The next day she left for Kurubarahalli. Gundegowdaru sent for all the houses and asked for subscription. According to Nanjamma's list, there was the account of two hundred and seventy rupees. Gundegowdaru said he would offer thirty rupees and instructed Nanjamma, 'See Avva, you take with you today the two hundred rupees from the revenue tax receipts. I will raise this three hundred rupees within eight days and bring it to you personally. I will ask the owners of coconut trees to give five or ten coconuts each. Is it not enough if there are hundred to hundred and fifty coconuts?'

'That should be enough, Gowdare.'

'You must go to Tiptur to get the provisions and other things. You send word to me and I will send our bullock cart. Purchase jaggery in excess.'

Nanjamma returned. The list of provisions and other articles required had to be prepared. How many people from the groom's side might come was not known. It seemed he did not have many relatives. From her side, except people from Nagalapura, there were none. There were seven Brahmin families in the village. On the night of the Kanyadaana, at least one person from each house should be invited.

Hence Nanjamma estimated a little more of provisions and then calculated money for clothes, gold, silver and other essentials. She took Venkateshayya master and Ramanna with her and went to Tiptur by cart. She purchased a pair of laced dhoti, silk shirt, cotton coat, laced turban and a silver glass and spoon for the bridegroom. For the bride, she bought two sarees—one costing thirty-five rupees and the other for twenty-five. Ramanna and Vishwa did not have decent clothes. She took for them two shirts each. Also shorts for Vishwa and two lungis for Ramanna. Along with these, she purchased a small silver cup to be used as bhikshapatre in the Upanayana. Then she bought a pair of white dhoti and shirt to give her husband for eight rupees. She had her marriage saree with her, and so decided not to buy anything for herself. The master said, 'Nanjammanavare, you must have been left with around hundred and fifty rupees in cash with you. You should spend money very strictly and prudently.'

Then Nanjamma wrote a note and sent it with the village servant to Nagalapura at dawn. The servant returned in the night and said, 'It seems like nobody will come.'

'Who said so?'

'Your Ayya himself.'

'What else did he say?'

'He said, "When I requested her, she said—'I won't give my daughter.' Now when she marries off her daughter to another person, she will never prosper".'

She knew well her father's nature. Everything and everybody must always be controlled with his anger and obstinacy. There was nothing more valuable before that—feelings like that of a mother, a daughter, affection or pity.

'What did my grandmother say?'

'She did not speak to me at all.'

Nanjamma felt very sad. She was familiar with her father's nature, but how could she bear if her grandmother, who had reared her, nursed her at childbirth and afterwards, would not attend this marriage? Her heart could not tolerate this. She thought of going to Nagalapura and inviting them personally. But it would take two days, one day for going and one day for returning and there were only thirteen days left for the marriage. A lot of work was pending. No arrangements had yet been made for firewood. Flours for chakkuli, tengolalu and other snacks had not been prepared. Rice flakes and parched paddy had to be prepared. Artists that played the nadaswaram had to be hired.

She decided to write another letter and send it with the village servant after three or four days, and warned him: 'See, after two or three days, you must go there again. You should not speak of this to anyone here, about your going there and what they have to say in their reply, that they would not come.'

The village servant went again to Nagalapura, in vain. Kantijois scolded him. Nanjamma warned him again not to inform the matter to anyone. She feared that if the discord between herself and her father was leaked, these local purohits might become impertinent.

There were no relatives from her side. Until now, she had not invited her mother-in-law, and she too had not come on her own. But Gangamma gathered information from her son Chinnayya about the goings-on and the provisions Nanjamma had brought. At last, Nanjamma herself went to her mother-in-law's house, two days before the marriage ceremony and invited them. 'Amma, yourself and Appannaiah—please come. It is you who have to guide and help the function go on without a hitch.'

'Ahaha, you pretentious shrew! Did you call me all these days either to bring the provisions or to fix the bridegroom? Why did you agree to give the girl to the widower as if there was no one else in the world?'

'Amma, there may be thousands of grooms in this world. But I am incapable of maintaining their status. Please, you and Appannaiah come.' Without entangling herself in further argument, Nanjamma quietly went away.

Channigaraayaru was also angry at his wife. She had ruined the chances of any help his father-in-law could have provided by being stubborn that she would not give her daughter to Kallesha. And now, after the marriage was decided, she did not consult him for anything. Nanjamma had learnt from experience that he would only be an impediment. He was thinking of a way to take revenge against her, for neglecting him.

Appannaiah came the same day. As per the instructions of his sister-in-law, he took the responsibility of digging big stoves in the kitchen, stalking firewood and supervised the construction of the pandal the village servant had to set up. He visited Kurubarahalli twice and loaded the carts with coconuts and other articles they had collected and brought them to Ramasandra. Gangamma came on the day of Upanayana. Either she did not know any work or it was out of a sense of proud reserve that she sat quietly in the kitchen.

There were not many from the groom's side either. Dyavarasayya and his wife from Timmalapura did the duty of receiving the bride in the Kanyadaana ceremony. Only Dyavarasayya's son, daughter-in-law, three grandchildren, two colleagues of the bridegroom and a purohit, had come. There was no further obstacle to the marriage. Everything went smoothly. Before bringing the bride and the bridegroom to the dais, rituals had to be performed first by the parents of the bride on the dais. The Jois called: 'Channigaraya, you come quickly on to the decorated plank.' But this man sat indignantly. Nanjamma went and pleaded, 'It is already getting late. Please get ready quickly.'

He said adamantly, 'It is your daughter's marriage. If you want, you yourself perform it. I won't come to the dais.' She was shocked.

The master who was there, enquired, 'Why Shanubhogare, what happened? Please tell me.'

'See sir, she herself acts as the head of the house. Had she consulted me for bringing the articles or provisions?'

'Oh, you are the head of the family. Is not everything being performed in your name only? Come on, get up, it is already late.'

'Look here, what sort of dhoti she has bought for me. Shouldn't she have brought a pair of laced dhoti? I won't come to the Kanyadaana mantap wearing this dhoti', he said and was unshakeable. Besides, he had also another point to make. It was a practice to store all sweet and hot snacks like unde, chakkuli, tengolalu and other things in the dark room, lock it and hand over the key to a responsible woman for supervision. Nanjamma had handed over the key to the wife of the master. What had been prepared was very little. Some part of the snacks had to be given to the in-laws, when they would be leaving for home. Some had to be distributed to the women in the village and among those who had helped and laboured for the function too. Nanjamma had placed the responsibility of distribution of unde and chakkuli to the master's wife. Now Channigarayaru questioned, 'Why has she not given the key of that snacks room to me?'

Now Nanjamma spoke, 'Distributing all that is a woman's job. What will you do with the key?'

Though Nanjamma protested, the master took the key from his wife's neck and handed it to the Shanubhoga. Channigarayaru opened the door of the room, filled unde, chakkuli and other snacks in a big bamboo basket, carried it in front of everybody and put it inside the big box where Shanubhoga's account books were kept and locked it. Ayyashastri asked, 'Why did you bring it and keep it here, Chinnayya?'

Channigaraayaru answered, 'I want to eat once the marriage is over.' He then went in again and insisted on his first point, 'Why did you not bring a laced dhoti for me?'

Nanjamma explained, 'See, so much of money is already being spent. I have not purchased a new saree for myself. How can I buy such a costly dhoti for you?'

'If it is so, I won't come on the dais.'

The purohit from the bridegroom's side sent word as to why the bride's people had not yet come to invite the bridegroom, for the fixed lagna-muhurtha was nearing. The bridegroom's people had been accommodated in the master's house. Here, the father of the bride sat unwavering. Unless the shaastras here are completed, how could they go and invite the groom for Kanyadaana? The master's mediation failed. Maadevayyanavaru came. He too could not convince the Shanubhoga. Although the purohit did say one or two words, he was enjoying the fun. Dyavarasayya came and tried to drive home some wisdom into Shanubhoga's head. It was of no use. The Shanubhoga had become stubborn. Gundegowdaru, who sat near the door, had almost taken his staff into his hand. But Nanjamma requested Gowdaru to be calm, for her husband might become even more stubborn. Appannaiah, who had kept silent till then, said: 'Hey, Chinnayya, will you get up and quietly move towards the dais or do you need to be thrashed?' Now, Channigarayaru added another condition: 'Should this bastard speak to me in this manner? The elder brother is equal to the father. He must hold my feet and apologize.'

Nanjamma consoled Appannaiah and asked him to be calm. But Gangamma intervened, 'He is the master of the house. How can he perform Kanyadaana without a laced dhoti on him? Don't you know even this much? Even now you can ask someone to fetch it quickly.'

Channigarayaru became firm when he knew there was one person to support him. 'Yes, even now you can send someone to Tiptur and ask him to bring me a laced dhoti. Till then I will be sitting here.'

Gangamma challenged. 'Ahahaha, take out the money which you have kept locked in the box whose key is tied to your waist.' Channigaraayaru was aware that this was spoken in his favour.

If she got angry, the whole thing would be spoiled. But no plan, no idea was working. Nanjamma swore on God and said, 'I'll surely bring you the laced dhoti from Tiptur as soon as the marriage is over.' But her husband wouldn't budge. He was obstinate. 'I want the dhoti now.'

Nanjamma did not know what to do. She went to a corner and stood there wiping her tears. Maadevayya, who had sat in the pandal, knew what was going on. He got up, went to the shrine, came back, asked the Shanubhoga to come out and said: 'Look Chinnayya, here is twenty rupees. Keep it with you; you can buy the dhoti after the marriage.'

The Shanubhoga said, 'Oh no, I don't want money. I only want the dhoti.'

At last, Dyavarasayya called Nanjamma separately and suggested, 'Amma, do one thing, give him the laced dhoti you have brought for the groom. We have brought a pair of Raja mill dhoti to gift the groom. I'll give it to you and you give that to the boy. He will not ask you why you have brought this. He is not such a boy.'

'But look at his nature, Maavayya. No doubt we can do as you suggest. But shouldn't we have some respect? What if some other day they comment before our girl that your people gifted only a white dhoti to the bridegroom and performed Kanyadaana? Won't the girl feel ashamed?'

'Nanjamma, he is not of that nature. By chance if he makes such a comment, what can be done? It would have to be tolerated. I have told him everything about your husband. There are different kinds of strange people in the world. Now, this is the only way left. You do as I say.'

Nanjamma brought the dhoti to be given to the groom, placed it before her husband and said, 'Now, get up and wear this.'

'Is it single or is it a pair?'

'Don't fear, it is a pair.'

Channigarayaru was now satisfied. He got up, wore one and sported another on the shoulder. Now he had got three birds at one shot. He had taken revenge from his wife and had got a laced dhoti to wear. Whether Nanjamma would have saved snacks for him at the end of the marriage or not, now he had a basket full of them. He came on the dais with a victorious feeling.

The Kanyadaana was celebrated without any other obstacle. The bride's father had worn a laced dhoti and the bridegroom had donned a simple white dhoti. The Shekdar arrived in time for the Kanyadaana ceremony. He asked Dyavarasayya about the dhotis the bridegroom and his father-in-law wore for the ceremony. Not revealing the exact reason, Dyavarasayya said, 'It is the old dhoti of Channigaraya's marriage.'

At the very moment the Kanyadaana was being performed, an arched cart came and stood before the house. Akkamma got down. Seeing her, Ramanna rushed in and informed his mother. Nanjamma, who had until now suffered a dumb pain, got a small reprieve. Akkamma directly came inside and said, 'Kanti and Kallesha prevented me and said I should not go at any cost, but I insisted. "I ought to go and I will go. It is my great-granddaughter's marriage." Oh already the Kanyadaana is being performed. Take this, this is my gift for Parvati.'

So saying, she untied the edge of her saree, took out a gold chrysanthemum flower and gave it to Nanjamma. It was a jewel Akkamma used to wear when her husband was alive. She had somehow saved it. She went in, changed to a red saree of fibre cloth and sat. Gangamma wore the same kind of saree. She did not speak with Nanjamma's in-law and Akkamma too kept quiet. She watched the marriage ceremony sitting near the door. When Nanju came to her side for some work, she whispered to her, 'Nanju, you have done a good thing in selecting this boy. He is like a prince. Is it a small thing to be a teacher in an English school? He seems to be still young. What does it matter, if there is a stepchild?'

The Kanyadaana was over. Sooryanarayana's daughter Ratna was playing with Vishwa. Ratna now would be the daughter of Vishwa's own sister. Master Venkateshayya said, 'Let us also marry these two off now.' Vishwa felt shy and left the company of the child. Sooryanarayana too laughed and said, 'Perform it today. I will leave my daughter here.'

The next day, there was the shaastra of Naagoli to be completed. 'In the evening, after Kanyadaana, the master and his wife called Nanjamma separately and asked, 'Nanjammanavare, please don't misunderstand us. The bridegroom's people have come to know that the girl has already attained puberty.'

Nanjamma was scared hearing this. But the master said, 'You need not be scared. Sooryanarayana had stayed in towns like Tiptur and Tumkur and had gone to Mysore for training and stayed there for one year. In those places, marriages are performed after sixteen or seventeen years only. The day after Naagoli, they will arrange for the consecrating the nuptials and then send the bride. It is said that in one day, the rituals of erecting the pandal, the betrothal, Naagoli and nuptials are all performed in Bangalore. Sooryanarayana himself told me. However, tomorrow, after the Naagoli shaastra, if you finish the shaastra of the nuptials also, he can take the girl with him. Moreover, you have to adjust money and arrange for the feast if it is performed later, which will be an additional cost for you. I think, it would be better if you finish it now. If the need arises, I will go to Kambanakere and bring a pair of bed and blanket.'

Nanjamma's heart was saddened, as her daughter would leave her and go to her husband's place. More than that, there was another fear in her mind. Until now she had not revealed to anybody that her daughter had attained puberty. Annajois or others in the village would have informed about this to the groom's side. Luckily, Sooryanarayana had not made it an issue and quarrelled. If she agreed to arrange for the nuptials, it would be as good as accepting that her girl had attained puberty before marriage. Everybody would know that all these days she had hidden this fact. What would happen now? But even now she did not want this matter to be revealed. She feared the consequences if she suddenly changed her position on it now. Her heart said, two or three months after the marriage, when Parvati would have her monthly periods, it should be announced that she has attained puberty, she should be made to sit out as per custom, then arati and other rituals be performed, some auspicious women be invited, nuptials celebrated on the sixteenth day and then she should be sent to her husband's house. At the moment, she should not alter her stand, she felt. Nanjamma told the Master, 'Look sir, it is true the girl has attained puberty. But it would create a problem for us if we do what the people of big towns do. You know about the Jois of this village and you know my husband's nature too; he may also behave madly. I have not told him. Let us perform the nuptials after three months.'

'If so, you may do so. Sooryanarayana will not unduly persist. His thought is, why you should bear additional expenses and therefore he gave this suggestion. Besides, it will be difficult for him to cook, take care of the child and attend to school work for the next three months.'

'You ask him to leave the child here with us.'

When the master explained the suggestion, Sooryanarayana gladly agreed. However, although he was well aware of the situation that prevailed in the villages, he was unwilling to leave the child here, just after the marriage. He also felt it was not a practical idea.

The next day, while the bride was being given away after Naagoli, Ramanna was crying along with Nanjamma and Akkamma. The brother and sister had grown up together and had developed much mutual affection and intimacy. Though he knew everything, he went to his mother and asked, 'Amma, will Parvati go from here?'

'Yes, is she not a daughter, child?' mother consoled him.

All of a sudden, Appannaiah too felt like crying. He had not visited this house frequently or spoken much with Parvati. When she was watering the beds of greens, for a few days he used to ask her, 'Can you give me some greens?'

'You take as much as you want, Uncle,' she would say.

Beyond this, there were no further exchanges between the uncle and niece. Now, somehow he came on his own and helped in her marriage. He was the only one except Nanjamma who had worked hard, day and night, not bothering about food and sleep. His sister-in-law, master's wife, Akkamma, and even the Jois would entrust him with tasks. He had laboured more than a hired servant—from draining starch from big rice pots, to removing the leftover plantain leaves after meals, to washing and cleaning the floor with cow dung and filling the copper pots with water in the bridegroom's house. When Parvati came and prostrated before him, after the ceremony of giving away the bride was over, tears trickled from his eyes and fell on her head.

The next day, while sending the in-laws, the bride and the bridegroom were made to hold each other's hands and walk till the shrine of the village deity in the outskirts of the village. The Nagaswaram players were in front. Nanjamma was walking behind with all the others, carrying Ratna. Once the worship of the village deity was over, they prostrated before the idol. After going towards the bullock cart and before leaving his wife's hand, Sooryanarayana softly squeezed her hand and whispered: 'I'll come and take you with me in three months.' Parvati stood with her head lowered breathing heavily and trembling; she could not respond. Sooryanarayana too did not expect a reply.

He prostrated in front of his parents-in-law, the Jois, Venkateshayya master and Maadevayyanavaru. A little intimacy between him and Maadevayya had already blossomed. Parvati stretched head downwards in front of Dyavarasayya, who was the eldest from both the sides, and other relatives of her husband, and all of them got into the cart. Sooryanarayana had to go to Timmalapura, perform the shaastra of shaking the pandal and leave for Balekere.

CHAPTER THIRTEEN

1

Nanjamma was extremely happy for the marriage was accomplished without any impediments. She remembered everyone who had contributed to its success. Since there were fewer people from the bridegroom's side, the sufficient amounts of provisions like rice, dal and chilli powder that had been bought still remained. If they were spotted by her husband, he would pester her to cook rice and sambar daily. But there was the nuptial ceremony to be arranged in three months. So, she hid them all. She covered half a tin of oil with a lid and put it where it could not be found. For the nuptial ceremony, it would be enough to purchase provisions worth about twenty rupees. Fifty rupees were needed for the beds and blankets. What should she do for the vessels to give to her daughter, while sending her to her husband's house? There were a lot of utensils with her mother-in-law. Even the vessels given to Nanjamma during her marriage were there. But Gangamma would never part with them. There was no money for purchasing new ones. So she decided to give some that were here, and later, when possible, to buy more for her daughter. Moreover, Sooryanarayana was not that sort of a husband who would badger his wife for not bringing along vessels, etc.

Now, Parvati put on black glass bangles on her hands. There was a chain of black beads around her neck. Big white stone earrings shone in her ears. On the day of Naagoli, her nose was pierced. A weighty white stone nose ring adorned her nose. Until Parvati put on earrings and a nose ring, Nanjamma herself had not known that she had such a broad face. There were toe rings on her feet.

Sarvakka came one day and warned Nanjamma, 'Oh! how beautiful Parvathamma looks. Nanjammare, don't send her alone near the village tank and other places. She is newly married.'

Ramanna said, 'Wearing earrings and the nose ring, Akkayya looks very beautiful. If she puts on golden bangles like the Shekdar's wife, she will look more beautiful. Won't she, Amma?' His mother said, 'When

279

you become a Shekdar, we will give her that too, child.'

Even Parvati felt that. When she looked at her reflection in the mirror, she found something new in it. In another three months, she would have to leave her mother's house. When she would remember this, she would become gloomy. One day her mother said, 'See child, your husband is a very good man. If not, who else would have been considerate and adjusted so much, and married you? You are well versed in cooking and in doing domestic chores. But look after that child without any discrimination. Your husband will be happy. If that motherless child sheds tears, that sin will haunt us also.'

'Will I ever do so, Amma?' the daughter assured.

Ramanna asked, 'That little girl is very beautiful. Later we may marry her to our Vishwa. Is it not possible, Amma?'

His Amma said, 'He is so mischievous. If he does not study properly and fails to complete the high school, will Parvati's husband give his daughter?'

'No Amma, our Headmaster says mischievous children are very clever.'

Akkayya said, 'Then though you are soft and serious, how do you always stand first in school?'

Her brother answered, 'If I was mischievous, perhaps, I would have scored more marks.'

While they were conversing thus, Vishwa was busy searching Maadevayyanavaru's jaggery pot.

It was already one month since the marriage. Sooryanarayana had written a letter informing of his welfare to his father-in-law. Nanjamma remembered that she had a vow to offer jaggery-rice and curd-rice to the village deity, if Parvati's marriage were to go through without any hitches. She was aware that there should not be any delay in fulfiling a vow made to the village deity Kalamma. She decided to carry it out at the earliest. Besides, she need not have to spend extra money. Rice, jaggery, coconut and curds, were all at home. There was a blouse piece also, to offer to the Goddess. The day after tomorrow was Friday. She asked Ramanna to take leave from his school. When she told Channigarayaru: 'We have to go to the shrine of the village deity; be ready', he readily agreed.

Gangamma and Appannaiah had gone to the villages near Gandasi and Duddha.

Nanjamma had sent word to Kala, the priest, that she would visit the shrine on Friday. She woke up early in the morning, boiled water, bathed and entered the kitchen. Then Parvati bathed Vishwa, and took bath. After Ramanna washed himself, Channigarayaru entered the bathroom. Then all of them got ready. Nanjamma cooked three seers of rice, put half of it into the jaggery syrup, and mixed cardamom, copra scrapes and groundnut seeds into it. She seasoned the other half with mustard seeds, coconut scrapes, curry leaves and mixed it with curds. Then she filled it into separate vessels and covered them with towels. She arranged the tray of arisina, kumkum and oleander flowers and instructed Parvati to wear the saree worth eighty rupees that her husband had brought for the marriage. When Parvati walked in the street, holding the arisina and the kumkum tray in her left hand; her cheeks smeared with turmeric; kumkum put in a transverse line on her forehead; with loosely combed hair and a flower set in it wearing earrings, a nose ring and toe rings and adorned in such an elegant and costly saree, everyone stared at her. Nanjamma, who was walking with her, was worried that her daughter might fall prey to some evil eye.

Ramanna had put Gopichandana paste on his forehead, held both the vessels of rice and had worn nice and clean clothes. Vishwa held coconuts. Channigarayaru walked behind.

The priest, Kala, was waiting for them. Nanjamma took her daughter into the sanctum sanatorium and told Parvati to worship the feet of the Goddess. Ramanna climbed the tree in front of the shrine and plucked red flowers. Along with arisina, kumkum, and oleander flowers, when the red flowers adorned the Mother Goddess who sat cross-legged, her statue filling the whole square, it seemed as though she was the Chandi who would swallow any person. When these people spread the blouse piece on the lap of the Goddess, the priest Kala lit the thick wick soaked in ghee and performed mangalarati. After completing the mangalarati, everyone prostrated before the Goddess. Nanjamma gave dakshine to Kala and also a sumptuous amount of prasada on a plantain leaf and came out of the shrine. Meanwhile, many people had gathered there for prasada. She gave them all a handful each. Then, the family went near the pond behind the shrine. They sat on the edge of the pond. Nanjamma distributed prasada to everyone on the plantain leaf. It was sufficient for all, including Channigarayaru. Nanjamma too ate, and only a little remained to take back home. Mother and children again went to the shrine, sat for a while on the platform, had another darshan of the goddess through the hole in the door, prostrated before her and set out for home. Even while returning, men, women and children looked at Parvati to their heart's content. Some women asked Nanjamma, 'What's this Avva, she is newly married, why did you let her wear such a grand saree and made her walk in the village? Won't she be affected by evil eye?' Nanjamma too agreed; she feared it would be true.

Food had not been cooked in the afternoon. By three, everyone ate a little of the remaining prasada they had brought from the shrine. Parvati changed and wore the usual saree with a border. Kumkum on her forehead, the earrings and the flower in her hair remained. She felt drowsy, spread a mat and slept. Ramanna was writing his English lessons. Vishwa had gone to school. Channigarayaru slept on the platform of Maadevayya's temple. Sarvakka was visiting Nanjamma to talk to her. Looking at Parvati sleeping on the mat, she remembered her daughter Rudrani. She felt sad; if only her husband was not so greedy, Rudrani would have been married by now and been a mother of a child.

After a while, Parvati woke up. Her eyes had become a little red. She said, 'Amma, I am feeling very chilly. I feel like warming myself sitting in front of the oven.'

It was nearing summer. What sort of a chill could she feel now? Nanjamma came to her daughter and touched her forehead. She was running a temperature. Yes, it was a fever with chill. Immediately, Sarvakka said, 'Nanjammare, why did you take the newly married girl in the morning? Besides, she wore that grand saree too. People's glare will not be the same. You light broomsticks and wave it before her to ward off the effect of the evil eyes.'

Nanjamma lit half the sticks of the broom, waved them before her daughter, threw them into the corner where they burnt to ashes, making a crackling sound. She defended her argument: 'Oh! did you see? It is really the result of evil eye. How loudly it crackled had gone?'

Parvati sat quietly. By evening, Sarvakka home and Nanjamma went into the kitchen to cook. Parvati, unable to sit, removed the blanket and lay down on it. Ramanna sat near the bed and helped her to be cheerful. By night, her cold and fever increased. After cooking was over, Nanjamma prepared a decoction of cumin seeds, pepper, cloves and basil leaves, administered it to her daughter and let her sleep cozily. She was thinking: 'It was my mistake to let her wear that grand saree. Everyone's glare won't be benevolent.'

The whole night Parvati ran a high temperature. Now and then she was saying she had terrible body pain. Her face seemed to have become stiff, with bloodshot eyes. Nanjamma again administered the herbal decoction. Parvati felt drowsy by dawn and her mother too slept. When Nanjamma woke up, the sun had already risen. Though Parvati's temperature had come down a little, it was not normal. She was moving from side to side and saying, 'It is very painful, Amma. I feel as if my body is being sliced.'

'Because of the severe heat of the fever, you feel so. Now the temperature is coming down. You sleep. I will warm up some water. Then you may wake up and wash your face,' Nanjamma said and turned to the left. Ramanna was still sleeping. Usually he would wake up at the crowing of the cock, light the kerosene lamp and studying. But today he was still sleeping. Nanjamma asked, 'Why have you not woken up yet, child?' He answered from under the blanket, 'I have cold and fever Amma.' Nanjamma panicked, raised the blanket and saw that his face too had become like that of Parvati's. It was stiff and the eyes burnt like live coal. She began to heat the copper pot filled with water for the bathroom, pondering why it would have happened so. Both the children are affected with cold and fever on the same day? She washed their face in warm water and placed their beds side by side. Before that, she cooked the gruel of broken rice and made them drink, though they did not want to. She then boiled the decoction of ginger and pepper again. She reflected, this cold and fever comes and will get cured. But Ramanna's examination was coming close. It may be said, Parvati was affected by the evil eye. But why did Ramanna catch fever? He too had come to the shrine wearing a clean lungi and covering his shoulders with a towel. He too had been newly initiated into Upanayana. But what sort of evil eye would affect the boys? He had worked so hard during the marriage. Besides, he shuttled to school in the hot sun daily. If the examination was over in another month, then he would get summer holidays and he could be free for a month and a half.

By the evening, Parvati's temperature rose again. Her eyes were like the burning eyes of the village Goddess Kalamma. The sparkling earrings in both the ears and the shining ring on the nose made her appear frightening if you looked at her face. Nanjamma removed the earrings and nose ring and kept them inside a box. Parvati said at night, 'Amma, it seems there is a tumour-like swelling in the joint of my right thigh.'

Parvati had not worked much after her marriage. She had not walked that much too. Nanjamma wondered if she had the pain in the leg because of having walked to the temple. But the temple was right in front of the village. Moreover, Parvati was not a weakling, she would not get tired even if she walked ten miles. How could there be a tumour-like swelling only from walking that much? Anyway, she heated salt, fomented the joint of the thigh, again gave her the decoction and the gruel, and helped both Parvati and Ramanna to lie down warmly. Ramanna's temperature too had not come down. He had been lying silently, not even moaning a little. Channigarayaru came at eight in the night after listening to the bhajans in Maadevayya's shrine. Vishwa had arrived earlier. Nanjamma served them the food she had cooked earlier and did not feel like eating. Besides she felt sleepy as she had not slept the previous night also. She touched her children's forehead again, covered them properly and lay down near their heads. For a while, she did not get sleep; afterwards though, she was in deep sleep.

Sometime during the night, Nanjamma had a dream. The scene of their visit to the shrine of the village goddess the day before appeared in the dream. The face of Amma—the Mother Goddess—was stiff and swollen like Parvati's. Both the earrings in her ears were burning and the eyes had become like fire. She sat cross-legged, spreading herself on the square of the shrine. Ramanna and Parvati were lying down nude on each of her two laps, as newly born twins. Nanjamma was trying to cover the children with a blanket, but she could not cross the threshold and enter into the sanctum sanatorium. But the door was not closed; no obstacle could be seen before her. Something, however, was preventing her from entering inside. But she was trying and trying. Then there was a sound of someone moaning 'Ayyo...' The dream was interrupted and she woke up. Ramanna was moaning. She raised the wick of the burning lamp, put her hand on his head and asked, 'Why, child? What do you want?'

'Amma, in both the joints of my thighs, there are tumour-like swellings. It is paining very much, Amma.'

At once, her heart shuddered. Then what Parvati had was not any usual swelling. Was it the tumour of plague? But there was no hint of it in the surrounding areas.

In the village too, rats had not fallen. She pushed aside the blanket and put her hand on Ramanna's thighs. Though he felt shy and embarrassed, he lay quietly in the drowsiness of the fever. In the joints of both the thighs, the tumours had swollen to the size of jackfruit seeds. When her hand touched them, Ramanna cried out 'Haaa'. She felt lost and sat quietly for about five minutes. Then she came near her husband, shook his shoulders and said, 'Look here, Ramanna and Parvati have got tumour-like swellings. Maybe it is the plague, or some other thing. Get up and see.' When she shook him thrice and called him, he said: 'Hey, leave it, let me see it tomorrow morning. Now I am feeling sleepy.' Then he covered himself with the blanket. She thought of bringing Maadevayyanavaru. But she felt scared to go alone. She was never afraid of darkness. But today she was feeling terrified. She woke up Vishwa, said: 'Come with me, child. We must bring Ayyanavaru. Come, let us go.' He at once jumped, stood up with sleepy eyes and said, 'I will go and bring him.' He rushed to the door, opened the bolt and ran out even before Nanjamma could say: 'It is pitch dark outside, wait, I will also come.' It was past midnight. The whole village was sleeping as though dead.

In a little while, Ayyanavaru came holding Vishwa's hand. Nanjamma explained the illness of both the children and said, 'I couldn't know whether it is plague. I am afraid; you look and tell me.' Ayyanavaru touched the hands of both the children. He put his hand on the tumours of Ramanna, felt them and said, 'The Shanubhoga had come in the evening. He did not say anything about children's illness.'

'What does he care about all these things! Please tell me what has happened to the children.'

'Yesterday evening itself Guruvanna of Horakeri and Puttayya of Kurubarahalli were saying that rats had been falling in their places since two days.'

Nanjamma felt her life had fled away, her heartbeat stilled. For two minutes, she sat baffled as if in a delusion and then suddenly started sobbing violently. Ayyanavaru consoled her: 'Avva console yourself, if you begin to cry, who is there to look after the children?' But her sobs did not stop. 'Ayyanore, who will survive the attack of this damned, slut plague?' she said and cried loudly. Ramanna heard it and said, 'Amma, will it not be cured if we take medicines? Why do you cry? Don't be upset.' She felt a little courageous. Parvati did not have the strength even to say that much.

Ayyanavaru said, 'Even after the attack of plague, many people have survived. Once they survive, it will not attack again.'

Nanjamma felt comforted. *Yes. Her brother Kallesha had also been struck by plague. Did he not survive*? This memory alleviated her anxiety a little more. Silence reigned in the house except the snoring of Channigarayaru. Vishwa sat quietly on his bed. Ayyanavaru told him, 'Why are you sitting, child? Go to bed.' He then went to sleep. In a short while, Ramanna too started sleeping. At the moment, Ayyanavaru could not return to his shrine. None of them knew what to say, sitting there. But he knew, even if he sat there silently it would be a comfort to this woman and it would give her courage. So he did not get up. After a while, Nanjamma said, 'Ayyanavare, I had a dream in the night. In that dream, Ramanna and Parvati were lying naked on the lap of the Mother Goddess. When I tried to enter the shrine to cover them with a blanket, I could not enter it. There was no wall in front of me, no stone. I felt something was obstructing me. What is the meaning of this?'

'If both the children were lying on her lap, doesn't that mean Her grace is bountiful and she is kind? And she is also the source of this disease. Yet the meaning is that she will protect them from it.' Nanjamma's mind got a little succour. 'But why was I not allowed inside?' she asked.

Ayyanavaru did not know the answer to this. Though an answer, 'What authority do men have to go near the children protected by the God' flashed in his head, he did not mouth it. Nanjamma also started thinking about that. Although her mind felt a hint of something ominous, her heart could not accept it and she tried to understand things in a different way. She asked, 'Ayyanavare, doesn't it mean, "what authority do you have to touch the children lying down on my lap? Till they are with me they will be safe".'

'Yes, yes, that is correct.'

'Then, Ayyanavare, shouldn't we bring any medicine and administer to the children?'

'How is that possible?'

'What if the Mother Goddess gets angry if medicine is administered to the children lying on her lap?'

Yes, that was also a problem. For some time the question of whether to administer medicine to them or not, haunted them. At last, Ayyanavaru said, 'Look Avva, when there was scabies, it was not cured simply by worshipping the snake God. Did you not go and get injections? Now too, do the same. Tomorrow itself you should call the doctor. If not, we should go to Kambanakere, harnessing a cart.'

Nanjamma decided that that was the right thing to do. She asked Ayyanavaru whether she should call the village servant immediately and send him to hire a cart. But Ayyanavaru said, 'It will not be proper to carry children having such a high temperature in the cart; we should try to bring the doctor here. You tell him to harness the cart. I'll go in the cart.'

Ayyanavaru sat quietly until the cock crowed, then he went off and brought along with him the village servant. He hired a cart for one and a half rupees. Even before sunrise, Ayyanavaru sat in it and reached Kambanakere.

By the morning, the temperature of the children had increased further. Along with the tumour in Parvati's thighs, both her armpits began aching. Her face seemed as if flecked and had taken on the appearance of Maari, the Goddess of epidemics herself; it was terrifying. Her mind had become dull as though in the state of semi-consciousness, half awake, half asleep. When Nanjamma brought warm gruel for her and shook her, Parvati woke with difficulty and said, 'My limbs feel tired.' It is because of the fever, child. You drink some gruel, it will be all right.'

'No, I don't want...'

'You won't get any strength in your body if you don't drink this. Please drink a little, my dear.'

Without contradicting her mother, she swallowed the gruel put into her mouth and closed her eyes. When she woke up, Ramanna, was completely conscious and asked: 'Amma, when will the doctor come?'

'By nine perhaps, child.'

'I don't know whether he will come. The doctor is scared to visit the plague-stricken village. This doctor is a new one.'

'Wait, let us see.'

As his mother said this, he drank the gruel and lay down. Both his tumours were aching more now. Unable to bear the pain, at intervals he would utter 'Ha, ha, ayyo, amma!' Channigarayaru, who had gone behind the tank bund, had not yet returned. Vishwa, not knowing what to do, was shuttling from the kitchen to the hall, behind his mother. Meanwhile, the announcer Belura was beating a drum and announcing something. Nanjamma went outside and stood near the platform. Belura came from the distance, beating the drum 'damma, dakka, damma dakka' and stood in the corner of the street near Nanjamma's house. Then he stopped beating the drum and proclaimed loudly: 'Plague Amma has come to the village, Panchayati has decided that everybody must vacate the house, put sheds and leave the village. Within the coming Friday, everyone must vacate the village...' he shouted, and again started beating 'damma dakka, damma dakka' and proceeded.

Nanjamma was not aware till midnight that the village was struck with plague. She guessed, perhaps it had first struck her house. She had taken Parvati to the shrine of the village deity to fulfil the vow. The newly married girl was so beautiful, that the Mother Goddess's eyes had fallen first on Parvati. *But, were not village Goddess Kalamma and Sunkalamma of plague, different deities? Didn't the village Goddess exist to prevent plague Maari Sunkalamma from striking the village? Why was Parvati attacked by plague before anyone else in the village? Following her, Ramanna, her brother, was affected by it. Who knows whether all these things were true or false? Why did this damned plague visit once in two or three years? Oh was there no medicine to cure it?* Along with this last question she would take heart by the decision: *But yes, certainly there is medicine. If the doctor comes immediately, he will cure them. We must quickly put a shed and vacate the village.*

By eleven, Ayyanavaru returned with the cart. But the doctor was not with him. He said, 'In Kambanakere also, it is said that rats are falling. The doctor is busy in giving inoculations there. He said, he can't come now, and asked me to bring the patients there.'

'How can we take the children running such high temperatures, Ayyanore?'

'This cart has an arch. Let us spread paddy straw and on that, place the beds and take them. What else can we do?'

Nanjamma did not delay. The cartman brought the straw and spread it evenly. She placed the beds on it. She prepared gruel again and coaxed them into drinking it. The cartman and Ayyanavaru together took the children one by one, laid them in the cart, and covered them with the blanket. Channigarayaru hesitated for a while about whether he too should go with them and finally decided to go. Nanjamma told Vishwa to stay in the house of the master and sat in the cart near the heads of both the sick children. Ayyannavaru and Channigarayaru walked behind the cart.

Swaying on the uneven road, climbing up and down the Kabballi mound, going around the Gowdanakoppalu and through the cactus lane, the cart reached Kambanakere by one in the afternoon. By then, the doctor had left for home. They parked the cart before the hospital and instructed Channigarayaru to take care of the children. Nanjamma went to the doctor's home, with Ayyanavaru. The doctor was resting after lunch, and felt a little annoyed at first, but then took the key and went to the hospital. He examined the patients on the cart itself and said: 'Why did you keep quiet until the disease advanced to this extent?'

'We didn't know at all, Sir. The tumour appeared only last night. We thought it was mere cold and fever.'

'Now inoculation should not be given. I'll give medicines. Take it and return to your village. Have you brought the bottle?'

'No Sir, we didn't know anything.'

The doctor asked angrily, 'What should be done if you come without a bottle while coming to the hospital?' But he opened the door of the hospital, put the medicine into an empty bottle and said, 'Now administer this to both, thrice a day. This will be enough for today and tomorrow. Day after tomorrow, come again.'

He did not say anything else and these people did not know what else to ask. The cart was harnessed, and they started towards their village. Swaying on the uneven road, by the time they reached home, it was half past four in the afternoon. Vishwa had not gone to the master's house. The door of the house was open and he was lying down on a mat. Except a piece of roti baked on live coal in the morning, he had not eaten anything. He too felt severe body ache and the temperature too was rising. Looking at his eyes and face, Nanjamma came running and touched his head—*oh, he too was struck with the disease*. She drew his face close to her bosom and began crying loudly: 'Oh Ayyanavare this damned Maari has come to take away all my children! Look here, Vishwa too has fever.'

Parvati and Ramanna were still in the cart. They were tired of having travelled ten miles on the rough road by cart and had lost more than half of their consciousness. Ayyanavaru and Nanjamma together carried the children inside and laid them on the beds. Then Ayyanavaru said, 'Avva, you take care of these two. The bullocks are tired. I will hire another cart, take Vishwanna with me and again go to Kambanakere. The disease has not yet taken a fuller grasp on him. We must go at once.'

She did not have any other idea to suggest. Ayyanavaru went to the shrine, took all the money from his box, came back, gave ten rupees to Nanjamma for any emergency, and put the remaining money—nearly twenty rupees—into his pocket. By then, the same cartman had gone home, eaten ragi balls, taken another pair of bullocks from someone and returned. Then they put a different bed inside the same cart, laid Vishwa on it, Ayyanavaru too sat with him and they started.

It was already very dark by the time they reached Kambanakere. He told the cartman to drive the cart to the doctor's home, went in and called the doctor. He asked, 'Why did you bring the patients stricken with plague into the town?'

'You were not in the hospital, Sir.'

'What do you think? Do you expect me to be there the whole day and night? Hey Kariya, you go and open the door of the hospital. There on the table, there is a big bottle, the second one from the right. Give this man three ounces from that,' he instructed the peon and went in.

Kariya accompanied Maadevayyanavaru to the hospital. Perhaps he must have felt a certain devotion seeing the ochre clothes of Ayyanavaru. He said, 'Ayyare, the disease is not cured with this medicine. You may get a medicine called Hemadi Syrup in Tiptur. Three rupees per bottle. You may get it at the shop of Venkataachala Shetty. His shop is in front of his house in the market street. You administer that to the boy. The disease has not spiralled yet. He will be cured.'

'But the doctor said so, brother...'

'Let him say whatever. You do what I say. If you want, I'll give this liquid too. But it won't help cure the malady.'

Ayyanavaru decided to leave for Tiptur at once. The cartman hesitated. Ayyanavaru persuaded him, 'Hey, look, you shouldn't hesitate when a life is in jeopardy. Remember, you too have children at home.' Then out of fear, a sense of obligation and good-heartedness, the cartman agreed. There was a direct road from Kambanakere to Tiptur. There is bus service too. It was a distance of ten to eleven miles. Ayyanavaru bought a packet of biscuits, thinking the boy might feel hungry on the way. He told the cartman to harness the cart and started immediately.

It was past midnight, by the time the cart reached Tiptur. Ayyanavaru knew the shop of Venkataachala Shetty. He remembered that Shetty's residence and his shop were the same. Ayyanavaru asked the cartman to lower the yoke and got down. He knocked on the door. Shetty woke up, came out and after hearing what Ayyanavaru had to said, 'This Hemadi Syrup is the only medicine in Ayurveda. We buy it directly from Venkatacharlu Company in Madras. It is better if given before the disease increases; it will be cured. After it shoots up, it may or may not abate. How many bottles do you need?'

'How much should be administered to one who is sick?'

'Four spoons at a time and four times per day. One bottle will last for three days. Three rupees per bottle.'

Ayyanavaru had only twenty rupees with him. Shetty took eighteen rupees, gave six bottles of medicine and said, 'Administer four spoons to the boy right now. It will be as sweet as honey. But you should not take the boy into the plague-stricken village. And you should not enter into the house where there is plague. You must keep him somewhere outside the village.

Saying this, Shetty went in, closed the door and went to bed. The bullocks were too tired to be harnessed at once. Besides, the cartman and Ayyanavaru were also much fatigued. If they could get something to eat at that hour, it was only at the railway station hotel. They drove the cart there. Ayyanavaru took a cup from the hotel. First, he administered the medicine to Vishwa and then gave him a cup of coffee. Except vadas and pakodas, there was nothing else to eat. He bought some for eight annas. The cartman and he ate it. After that, the cartman, as if remembering something, said, 'Ayyare, we too have to vacate the village and put a shed. The bullocks are a bit tired but not completely exhausted. Let us drive them slowly.'

'Yes, that will be fine.'

So, they raised the yoke and harnessed the cart. Though Vishwa was running a temperature, he had not lost consciousness. Ayyanavaru would frequently touch the joints of his thighs and armpits and ask 'Does it ache, child?' He would answer "no". It was the only one hope for him. With the assurance that his sickness might be eliminated at the root itself, as the medicine was given before the appearance of the tumours, he too began dozing, leaning against the frame of the cart. The tired bullocks were moving slowly. As there was a motor road until Kambanakere, the cartman also supported his back against the inner frame of the cart, and was clicking his tongue now and then, his eyes closed.

By the time the sun rose, they had already covered half the distance. They stopped near a pond beside the road. Ayyanavaru told Vishwa to rinse his mouth and fed him the medicine from the bottle itself. Vishwa still had fever but no tumour had appeared. Ayyanavaru became more hopeful. He gave two biscuits to the boy. The cartman and Ayyanavaru walked till the bank of the pond, returned and harnessed the cart. While on their way, an idea came to him: *Everybody was leaving the village. So, at any cost he should not take Vishwa into the village. When the village was vacated, the shrine on the tank bund was his. So, he should take the cart there and lay Vishwa in the shrine itself. Then he could go into the village and bring his own mat, blanket and pillow.*

He did as he had planned. By eleven in the morning, the cart reached the shrine on the tank bund. He lowered down Vishwa there, gave him the medicine again from the bottle itself and instructed the cartman to be there until he returned. He went into the village with four bottles of medicine.

2

People in each house were going out of the village with loads of bamboo and areca plant strips to put out the sheds. Some people carried provisions and vessels of their houses even before the sheds were completed. By the time Ayyanavaru returned, Parvati and Ramanna seemed to have become almost unconscious. But Parvati was crying in a feeble voice, 'Ayyayyamma', because of the pain the tumour caused. Nanjamma panicked seeing Ayyanavaru alone. Having noticed her, Ayyanavaru said, 'Don't be scared, Avva. I took the cart to Tiptur. Vishwa has fever but tumours have not appeared. I have brought good medication. I have made him lie down in the shrine on the tank bund. They told me not to take the boy into the plague-stricken village. Take this medicine. Administer this to these two, four times per day.'

She opened the lid of the bottle, poured the required quantity of syrup into the small cup with a spout and administered it to her children. They did not have either the strength or consciousness to drink from a cup. 'This is the only medicine. If Shiva saves these children, he must with the help of this only,' Ayyanavaru said. He then asked her, 'You must leave the village as early as possible. Haven't you made any arrangements?'

'I am staying at home. In such circumstances, who comes to enquire about us?'

'Where is Chinnayya?'

'I don't know. He left home at eight in the morning and hasn't yet returned.'

'I'll go to my shrine, take the blanket, mat and other things and keep them in the shrine on the tank bund. You don't worry about Vishwa. Take care of these children. Vishwa should not enter this village at all. I'll call the village servant or someone, and tell them to put a shed for you,' he said, gave her the bottles of medicine, and took half a seer of broken rice to prepare the gruel for Vishwa. Nanjamma had lost hope of Parvati and Ramanna's life. It would only be God's grace if they survived. Tumours in both the thighs and armpits of the children were swollen and ripe. The temperature was rising intermittently. Now and then, Parvati would open her eyes and try to see but her sight was not in this world. It was frightening to look at her stiff, swollen face. Ramanna was lying down quietly without any movement. His tumours had grown as big as sweet potatoes. None of them had uttered a single word since morning. Maybe the medicine Ayyanavaru had brought was very effective. It had been brought from Tiptur. *What did the Kambanakere doctor say*? Ayyanavaru himself had said not to worry about Vishwa. Nanjamma wanted to see Vishwa at least once. But if she went there, who was to look after these children?

At the same time, the master's wife came. She had a vessel in her hands. The master had visited Nanjamma's house in the morning. Master's wife said, 'See, it seems that it is a shaastra that the food cooked in one house should not be taken to others' homes separately.

So, I have brought along mixed rice and sambar. I will put it inside. My husband is packing, and I must leave. How are the children now?'

'There's been no change. They have not spoken a word since the morning.'

'You send your village servant and some other people with him. My husband will put a shed for you also. You come there with your children. We will pack the luggage and bring them there. Where is the Shanubhoga?'

'Who knows where he has gone?'

Master's wife left hastily. Bamboo and strips to erect the shed were stored in the loft of Nanjamma's house. Only coconut leaves were needed. As the leaves were now needed for all the villagers, it was a little difficult to get them. She could send a cart and bring a pile from Kurubarahalli. She did not know whether that village also was being vacated. But who was going to take responsibility? Nanjamma got up and once again fed the children the Hemadi Syrup. She asked if they wanted some gruel but the children seemed not to comprehend her question. She thought, *it had been only recently that the medicine had entered their systems. Let half an hour pass.* She was patient. Meanwhile, Channigarayaru came home. He was carrying on his head, two washed dhotis and a shirt. The towel he wore was half wet. Looking at the vibhuti on his head, she understood that he had gone for bathing and washing clothes either to the well in the garden or the outlet of the tank. The vibhuti on his forehead indicated he had finished sandhyavandana. Usually, when he started sandhyavandana, he would never get up without chanting the Gayatri mantra hundred and eight times or one thousand eight times as though he was swallowing it—'Oom tatsavitatatatata oom tatsavitatatatata'. From the time he had spent outside, it was certain he had completed thousand and eight Gayatri Japas.

Nanjamma said, 'Children are dying at home. The whole village is being vacated. Why the hell did you want to wash your clothes today itself?'

'For how many days can I wear the soiled dhoti? It's been four days since you washed my clothes. You too are wearing the same saree. Were you not born a Brahmin?'

She became silent, realizing how pointless it was to argue with him. As soon as the husband entered the kitchen, he spotted the vessel from the master's house. He removed the lid, served the food onto the aluminium plate that was close by, filled a glass with water, put some water into the palm of the right hand and performed parishseshana, and put chitrahuti five times. Chanting 'Chitraaya namaha, Chitraguptaya namaha, Yamaaya namaha, Yamadharmaya namaha, Sarvabhootebhyoo namaha', he started his meal formally, and completed eating in no time. But how could the wife of the master know Channigarayaru's hunger? The food was not enough for him. However, by the time he finished the meal, took aapooshana and came out of the kitchen, Maadevayyanavaru came back. By then Parvati was panting. Not knowing what else to do, Nanjamma put her hand on Parvati's shoulder and sat. Ayyanavaru said, 'Chinnayya, go directly to the shrine on the tank bund and stay there. In the central square, Vishwa has been laid down. Horakeri Nanja's son was grazing sheep, I have left him to stay there. You go and just sit there; you need not do anything.'

'Would I not feel bored to stay there all on my own?'

Ayyanavaru got enraged and burst out, 'Hey are you a man or a beast? Why don't you listen to what is being told?' Ayyanavaru had never got angry at anybody. The Shanubhoga was stunned hearing Ayyanavaru's words. He said, 'Yes, yes I will go, give me a little tobacco if you have some with you. If I do not chew it after meals, I feel at a loss.'

'Oh, you have finished eating too? Who had cooked?'

'Don't know, perhaps this wife of mine must have.'

Nanjamma said, 'The master's wife had brought some.'

'I have carried all my things into that shrine. My bag of betel leaves and betel nuts is also there. You chew as many as you want and even areca nuts,' Ayyanavaru said. Then the Shanubhoga took out the dhoti which had been spread out to be dried, put it on his head and left for the shrine.

Ayyanavaru asked, 'Avva, what did you arrange for the shed?'

'Oh, let the shed be damned! Parvati is breathing in this manner. Please come and see.'

Ayyanavaru neared Parvati and put his fingers near her nostrils. Her breathing was not in order. 'When did you give her the gruel?'

'She won't drink at all.'.

'She is suffering because of an empty stomach. Get up, and cook some gruel first. Meanwhile, I will send someone to Kurubarahalli for coconut leaves for your shed,' he said and went out. Venkateshayya master had a son. He was two years older to Vishwa and was very smart. Ayyanavaru went to the master's house and asked him, 'Can you go on your own to Kurubarahalli and come back, child?'

'Oh yes, I'll go running and come back.'

'See, you go to the house of Gundegowdaru and tell him: "All the three children of the Shanubhoga's house have been struck by plague. They have no coconut leaves to spread on the shed. Bamboos and other things are there. You must please send a cartload of leaves along with two servants. Nanjammaru sits weeping." Can you tell him all this?'

'Oh yes, I will remember everything and tell him.'

The master also asked his son to go quickly. Maadevayyanavaru came back to Nanjamma's house. The gruel was boiling on the stove. Ayyanavaru was quite confident about Gundegowdaru sending coconut leaves and servants immediately. He thought it would be helpful if the bamboos and strips were taken out of the loft and put out by the time the servants came. If the shed was erected that night itself, the house could be vacated within the next morning. Without leaving the village, the children would not be cured. So, he himself climbed on the loft made of bamboos. The bamboo piled in the corner of the attic was covered with dust, for it had not been used at all. Ayyanavaru told Nanjamma, who brought gruel for Parvati, 'Avva, cover the heads of the children with the blanket. Dust will fall. I will bring the bamboos down.' He then slowly brought them down without making a sound. He climbed down the ladder and quickly took out the bamboos. Till then, Nanjamma had kept the gruel in the kitchen, lest the dust fell on it. Now she went in, poured the gruel from the vessel into a glass and removed the blanket from Parvati's face. Her breathing had become slower. Though the spout of the cup went inside the side of her mouth, Parvati did not gulp the gruel. Nanjamma shouted, 'Oh, Ayyanore, come quick, let the bamboo remain there!' Hearing this, he came closer, sat down and looked at Parvati's face. He became suspicious. 'You feel and test the state of the tumours. I'll wash my hands and come.' He then went to the washroom.

Nanjamma placed her hands on the tumours and saw that the tumour of the right thigh joint had burst and pus had spread around. She shouted, 'Ayyanore, the tumour on the right side has burst! Come and have a look.'

S.L. BHYRAPPA

He came, pushed aside the blanket and saw that the tumour which was swollen had burst and white pus was oozing out of it; a substance that looked like blood was seeping out too. It was as if a carbuncle had opened, blood and pus all mixed and oozing. He pushed aside Parvati's saree and examined the tumour on the other side also. That was also about to burst. He realized the situation. He straightened the saree, covering her till the chest. Possessed by gloom, Nanjamma asked, 'What is it, Ayyanore?'

'We must wait and see, Avva, what is Shiva's will.' She, too, understood that dark gloom. Parvati began breathing a little faster. Till now, Nanjamma had not seen death. She could not comprehend the sign of the extremely feeble breathing now becoming stronger. Her mind and attention failed to grasp this and she saw that her daughter's eyes had lost their lustre. Ayyanavaru knew everything. But he sat silently, not knowing what to say and what not to. At last, as if arriving at a decision, he asked: 'When your father returned from Kashi, he gave you a thali of Gangajal. Is that at home?'

'Why?' Now the meaning dawned on Nanjamma.

'You shouldn't panic now. Only Gangamma thayi can help her survive. Go in, bring it Avva.'

Nanjamma rushed in, brought the thali, Maadevayyanavaru scraped the lac on it with a sickle, pierced a hole in the lid and said: 'Put your daughter's head on your lap, Avva. You sit in the right position, I will place her head on your lap.' Then he slowly raised Parvati's head and placed it on Nanjamma's lap. He wiped away the gruel from the spouted cup, poured Kashi Ganga into it, handed it to Nanjamma and said: 'Pour it slowly into her mouth. Wait, I will hold the lips and widen the mouth.'

Nanjamma's hand was shaking. The Gangajal was spilling out from the spouted cup. Ayyanavaru held Nanjamma's hand, skillfully inserted the spout of the cup through Parvati's teeth into her mouth and the Gangajal went through the gullet. Though her eyes were half open, they were unseeing of the mother's face bent down towards the daughter. She had lost the sense that her head was on her mother's lap. Her breathing became still slower. It reached its slowest pace, and then exhaling only once, Parvati did not breathe in again. As if to push out everything that was inside of her in one stretch, the half-opened mouth did not close again.

Nanjamma, sobbing with broken breath, cried out 'A..yya...no...re'; she put her head on her daughter's bosom. Ayyanavaru knew, there was no use consoling Nanjamma now. He remembered the tasks to be carried out further, got up and walked to the house of the master in a running stride. The master, who was loading the last instalment of the luggage into the cart, was shocked at hearing of Parvati's death. Ayyanavaru said, 'See, this is not the time to stand still. It is already evening. Firewood must be collected; you and the people from her caste gather, first finish the required rites and cremate the corpse.'

The master came running; his wife followed. Nanjamma was still sobbing, with her head on her daughter's chest. Ayyanavaru came near her and said, 'Avva, this is a corpse. Leave it. Now look after Ramanna. You have not given him gruel. Get up, turn to that side.'

'Ayyanore... Parvati...'

'Parvathamma has reached Shiva's feet. Now, take care of Ramanna,' he said and lowered Parvati's head from the mother's lap. The master folded the hands and legs of the corpse, lest they should become stiff. All of a sudden, Nanjamma stopped crying. Her mouth ceased to speak. She got up, went into the kitchen, warmed the gruel, put it into the spouted cup, raised Rammanna's head and placed his head on her lap. She did not know to what extent he was conscious. The liquid part of the gruel went in. She felt a little hopeful. She poured the Hemadi Syrup to the same cup, administered it and covered him warmly with the blanket. She put her hand in the joints of Ramanna's thighs, tested the armpits. The tumours had not burst. She did not have any clear knowledge about what would happen if the tumours opened, what would happen if they did not or if the patient would die if the tumours burst, or survive if they did not. In fact, nobody there had any knowledge. But after the tumour burst, Parvati had died. Ramanna's tumour had not opened. His breathing, too, was regular. So, Nanjamma felt a sort of hope and courage. Now, she left the body of her daughter, which was devoid of life and could never be alive again, held the head of the son still living and sat like a dumb woman.

Ayyanavaru had brought down the bamboos from the loft and placed them before the house. Now, it would be used for the bier. The master informed the two Jois. The news was conveyed to three other Brahmins of the village. Everyone was in a hurry to vacate the village.

But if the corpse was not cremated quickly, it would be night and one would have to wait till morning. The people from Nanjamma's caste rushed. Now, Channigarayaru too must come. Vishwa would remain alone in the shrine. Who would be with him? Ayyanavaru decided that he should remain there only. He thought of assigning the responsibility of Vishwa's care to anyone he would meet and started towards the shrine. But he could see no one who would be suitable for the work. Narasi was sitting in her shop outside the village. She asked Ayyanavaru, 'Is it true Parvatavva of Shanubhoga's house passed away?'

Ayyanavaru requested her help. He explained everything and said, 'See, you need not vacate your house as it is outside the village. Close your shop and come. You must take care of the child until I come back.'

Narasi locked the door and followed him. Channigarayaru had opened the lime box of Ayyanavaru and was smearing the betel leaves with lime the sixth time when Ayyanavaru entered the sanctum sanctorum, brought out the lamp for God, placed it near the child and said to Narasi, 'If it gets dark, light this lamp. Look at this bottle; feed the boy the medicine that's in the bottle once in three hours, four spoons at a time. If the boy says he is hungry, there is broken rice. Cook gruel and give him.'

'I will do everything. Now you leave.'

Vishwa was lying down silently. Ayyanavaru told Channigarayaru, 'Parvathamma passed away. Now you leave, other rites have to be performed.'

'Ayyo, why did she pass away Ayyanore?'

'First, you come; you may ask her,' Ayyanavaru held the Shanubhoga's hand and set out.

By the time they reached home, the bier was ready in front of the house. Annajois himself had taken responsibility and was directing everything. Ayyashastri was always scared of corpses. He was speaking from outside the street. Nanjamma sat, as if struck by an evil spirit, staring at Ramanna's face, with the pervasive feeling that her daughter had not died at all and she had nothing to do with the funeral preparations going on in the house.

Annajois said, 'Real responsibility of this falls on her husband. Should funeral be performed without informing him?'

Venkateshayya master answered, 'How can we inform him now?

That, too, it is a corpse that died of plague. If we leave it, the body will turn black. I will take that responsibility. It was I who mediated the marriage. I'll write a letter to him later. Now, don't delay.'

Master's wife put arisina and kumkum on Parvati's lifeless body and covered it with a new blouse piece that was at home. Nanjamma gave the only five rupees that was in the house, the money that Ayyanavaru had given to her the previous day. When the corpse was tied to the bier and carried, the master's wife was shedding tears. But Nanjamma did not cry. Channigarayaru, too, was wiping his eyes saying, 'Why did this poor girl die?'

By the time they left, firewood had been collected in the grove behind the tank bund. As Parvati was a married girl, the cremation had to be done according to the prescribed funeral rites. Annajois was well-versed in both auspicious and inauspicious rites. Though Ayyashastri followed the corpse, he stood behind, before getting down at the tank bund. He stood there and waited even after seeing the fire rising twelve feet high following the cremation. The bier-carriers bathed in the well of the crematorium. When all of them returned together, he stopped them and asked, 'Did the skull split quickly?'

'Yes.'

'Chinnayya, how much dakshina did you give to the corpse-bearers?'

'Eight annas each.'

'See, I too should have come with the corpse. I have walked such a distance. But if I had gone there, I would have had to take a dip in the cold water in the evening. That wouldn't suit the condition of my body. So I did not go. Now, give me my share of the dakshina.'

Hearing this, the master felt his whole body burning. But Annajois immediately said, 'Yes, give him, give him.' Channigarayaru took a coin of eight annas from the money he had put in his waist and gave it to the old shastri and the old man felt very happy.

He asked, 'Are you performing the shraaddha in this village itself?'

The master answered, 'Is not performing shraaddha the duty of her husband?'

'Oh, well, I had forgotten,' he said and he too returned with the five others.

After Parvati's body was carried away, only Ayyanavaru stayed with Nanjamma at home. The luggage of the master's house was in the shed outside the village. Yet, some articles had remained in the house. Master told his wife, that he would take it and come back. After five minutes, he left, and his son returned from Kurubarahalli to inform: 'Two men would come with two carts loaded with coconut leaves tomorrow morning, two hours following sunrise. Somebody should wait near the shrine of Mother Goddess and show them where to build the shed.'

Ramanna was breathing very feebly. Ayyanavaru asked, 'Did you administer the medicine again?' Though Nayamma had given two spouted cups of medicine a little after Parvati's death, she again took the cup, poured medicine in it and tried to make Ramanna drink it. He did not open his mouth. She opened the jaws forcibly, pushed the spout of the cup into his mouth and poured the medicine. It did not go in. She said, 'Ayyanore, he is not gulping the medicine. See, it seems the temperature is going down.'

He came closer and first touched Ramanna's forehead. The rise and fall in temperature was a common symptom of the plague. But now it seemed that the temperature had completely come down. Perhaps, the temperature coming back to a normal range was a sign that Ramanna had been cured of the disease? Ayyanavaru said, 'Avva, the plague had affected two at home; it took one as sacrifice. It seems like Ramanna will survive. Fever, too, is coming down.' Hearing this, Nanjamma was consoled and felt as though dead Parvati had come alive. She said, 'If that much happens, I will gift a new saree to Goddess Kalamma and take her in procession.' The warmth of the patient's body was going down minute by minute. For nearly five minutes, Ayyanavaru too thought it was a good sign. Then he became suspicious, put his hand under Ramanna's blanket and touched his legs. They were getting cooler. He asked, 'Some ash is needed, where is it?'

'In the oven, in the kitchen.'

He ran to the kitchen, took a fistful of ash and began rubbing it on both of Ramanna's legs. Even after rubbing for five minutes, there was no warmth. He did not say anything openly. He pushed aside the blanket and saw that the tumours in the thighs and the armpits were still swollen. None of them had burst though. Again, he covered Ramanna with the blanket and felt his pulse with his right hand. It was very feeble, uneven and he could not gauge it correctly. Kashi Gangajal must be administered to him also. But he did not have the heart or the strength to communicate this to the mother. But if he kept quiet knowingly, the boy would die without the holy water in his mouth. The question arose in Ayyanavaru's mind, 'While the life itself is passing away, how does it matter if drops of water are poured into one's mouth or not. Were not all these our delusions?' Yet he thought, the mother should not lament afterwards that she could not even put a drop of water into the mouth of her child. He took the thali of Kashi Gange, threw out the medicine that was in the spouted cup, filled it with Gangajal, placed it in Nanjamma's hand, opened the lips of the boy and said, 'Avva, pour it into his mouth.' Nanjamma understood.

'Oh, Ayyo, will Ramanna too pass away Ayyanavare?' While she was in the middle of asking this question, Ayyanavaru made her touch the cup and he himself poured the Gangajal. It was not known how much of it went inside and how much spilt out. Ayyanavaru put his left hand near the nose of the boy, held his pulse with the right hand and sat looking at the patient's face. Nanjamma sat as if possessed by a ghost, fixing her glare on the face of her second child. Though both of them were looking at the boy so vigilantly, none of them came to know when the life breath finally escaped. The pulse too which was descending and vanishing from the touch of the fingers of Ayyanavaru, and finally went down to an abyss never to come up.

Now at least Ayyanavaru ought to speak. He should convey the facts to the mother, and fold the hands and legs of the corpse. The hands and feet would stiffen if more time was allowed to pass and would no longer be limp enough to be folded. But how could he speak? Not that Nanjamma had not understood the fact. But the meaning known to the consciousness could not enter deep inside. She was not crying now as when Parvati had died. She neither put her face on Ramanna's chest nor did she did hold his hands. But his head still lay on her lap.

Ayyanavaru thought, by now Parvati's cremation must have finished and they might have started coming back. This news must be conveyed to them at once. Again firewood had to be arranged. It was already dark. He didn't know whether they would carry the corpse there alone and cremate it or want to wait until daybreak. Anyway, the hands and legs had to be folded. He said, 'Avva, when the life has reached the feet of Shiva, what is there in this skeleton? I will fold the hands and legs.'

'You do your work, Ayyanavare', said the mother, slowly lowering her son's head from her lap, and moved to a distance. Ayyanavaru completed his work and covered the body with the blanket. By then, the master and Channigarayaru had come back.

'Oh master, Ramanna too has breathed his last. You make further arrangements for his funeral,' said Ayyanavaru.

'Alas, oh God!'

'Yes, he went to God's place. Now there is no use talking much. Call the Jois.'

The master ran to Annajois's shed, for, by then Annajois's family had vacated the house and transported the luggage to the shed. Channigarayaru knew nothing of what to do. He squatted before the corpse of Ramanna, shedding tears.

The master came back with Annajois. Ayyanavaru asked the jois, 'Swami, could further rites be performed tonight itself or the corpse should be kept until daybreak?'

'How will it be possible tonight?'

Master intervened, 'Do you remember? Once that big epidemic had struck, you know, that benki jwara[25]? Then, whenever there was a dead body, they immediately carried it and cremated it. Sometimes, unable to provide firewood to cremate each corpse separately, two or three corpses were burnt together. When the maari devil enters the village, we cannot observe any shaastra or tradition strictly. Let us finish the funeral rites now itself.'

The jois too agreed, and left to call the bier-carriers who had come earlier. Anyway, bamboo staffs and strips were scattered in front of the house. Master started making the bier. Ayyanavaru went to collect firewood and sent it to the crematorium.

Ramanna was a boy who had been introduced to the Gayatri mantra. His Upanayana too had been completed. So, as with his married sister, the funeral rites should have been as per the shaastras. The bier-carriers came. In a little while, Ayyanavaru returned and said, 'There are plenty

---

[25]A form of severe fever

of logs, coconut shells and husks in Sooregowdana Koppalu. Load them and take them along. Anyway, we are vacating the village. Ayyanavaru offered his own cart also. His son, a few servants and himself are loading the cart. They will drive the cart directly to the crematorium. Now you move.'

Everything was over. The only task that remained was that the corpse had to be brought out, laid out on the bier, be tied to it and rice grains be put in its mouth.

But Ayyanavaru did not see Nanjamma. She was nowhere to be seen. He asked, 'Where is Nanjavva?' No one knew as they had not noticed her in all their hurry. The Jois at once warned, 'Oh, search at once either in a well or in the tank...'

The Master guessed, 'No, no, she must have gone somewhere hereabouts...'

To Ayyanavaru however, that did not seem to be the case. 'You search anywhere you want. I will look for her in my shrine on the tank bund,' he said and went to the shrine in the middle of the tank bund, with quick strides, at times running in between. When he entered the door, he saw that his surmise was true. Vishwa was lying with his head on Narasi's lap. Nanjamma sat at about a five-yard distance near the pillar and was looking at her child. There were no tears in her eyes, but her sight appeared to have been struck by the devil.

Narasi told Ayyanavaru, 'Nanjavvaru came running in the darkness. I was giving gruel to the child. She came and placed her son's head on her lap. Then I don't know what she thought but she called me near her and said, "Narasamma, this child is not mine. If I say he is mine, that sinning bastard God will take him away. I will give him away to you. You have no children. You bring him up. Come and sit near me. I will put him on your lap and say there is no relation between him and me; he is neither my son nor am I his mother", and put the child on my lap. Since then, she has been sitting at a distance. Look there.'

'You do that, Narasamma. Ramanna also died. We have to go perform other rites. You take care of these two. Shall I send some men to be with you?'

'When I am here, what is there to be afraid of? No one is needed.'

'What is the temperature like?' Ayyanavaru touched the child's forehead and asked, 'Does he complain of pain in the joints of his thighs?'

'A short while back, he talked. I myself squeezed the joint of the thigh and asked him. There was no pain. But the temperature seems to be boiling high.'

'Whatever it may be, keep administering the medicine once in two or three hours. Don't miss doing that,' he said to Narasi. Then to Nanjamma, he said, 'Nanjamma, don't be scared. No tumour has appeared as of now. The medicine is suiting the boy.' He tried to console Nanjamma and then hurried towards the village.

The master had gone towards the bushes in front of the village where women from the village go to relieve themselves, shouted 'Nanjammore' and returned. Other people were talking about the disaster that had come upon this family. Ayyanavaru came and said at once, 'Nanjavva is in the shrine, you carry on with performing the other rites.' Four people raised the bier. Channigarayaru accompanied them. Ayyanavaru took two bottles of Hemadi Syrup that was near Ramanna's bed, two blankets, locked the house and went towards the shrine. In the meantime, the new corpse was carried to the cemetery and placed on the earth. Through the slit amidst the leaves of the coconut trees, the flames of the earlier corpse could be seen. In that darkness, Ayyanavaru saw the old priest Ayyashastri standing alone with his back bent in the same place down at the tank bund.

4

By eight in the morning, two servants came with two carts loaded with coconut leaves from Kurubarahalli. They did not enter this vacated village. The village servant of Ramasandra stacked the cart with the bamboo staffs that were in front of the Shanubhoga's house. By afternoon, a shed was built in the field near the grove behind the shrine of the village Goddess. The master came to the shrine on the tank bund, took the key of Nanjamma's house, took from there the items needed to the best of his knowledge and put them into the cart and sent them to the shed. By that evening, the whole village had vacated.

Although Vishwa's fever was constant, tumours had not appeared so far. Tumours had appeared on Ramanna and Parvati within twenty-four hours of their coming down with fever. It was already two days since Vishwa had been running a fever. Yet, there was no tumour. Perhaps it was the result of the medicine Ayyanavaru was administering him or the result of having given this new medicine to him as soon as the fever had started. Anyway, nothing bad had happened as of yet. Nobody could say for certain if death would stop in a house where this Maari had entered. Ayyanavaru said, 'Nanjavva, this is the shrine of God Eeshwara. How can the Maari enter here? That's why Vishwanna does not have a tumour.' Nanjamma did not reply. She had been sitting like a piece of stone at a distance, quietly looking at Vishwa until daybreak; she had not blinked even once. Ayyanavaru was completely exhausted by the morning. Since the last two days, he had not eaten anything. Except for a short nap while travelling by cart the night before the previous day, he had not had a wink of sleep. Nobody in that village knew his right age. No doubt he had crossed seventy-five. His body had toiled continuously for two days. He had sat leaning against the pillar and unknowingly he had gone off to sleep. Narasi spoke, 'Avva, God did not grace my life with children. I used to worry for I did not have children. But it is worrying even if one has children.'

Nanjamma sat quietly. Meanwhile, the master came and took the key to Nanjamma's house that was near Ayyanavaru. Still, Nanjamma sat silently. Narasi too did not know what else to say. But she was giving the medicine to the child without fail. The child's head was on her lap. In a short while, the master's wife came. She shed tears but Nanjamma did not cry. She said, 'Get up, please. Let us go to our shed. You take a bath. I have stirred some uppittu. You have not eaten anything since the whole of yesterday.'

Nanjamma shook her head, indicating she would not come. The master's wife returned and brought some uppittu in a vessel. But Nanjamma did not get up even for washing her face. Narasi asked, 'Where is Chinnayyaru?'

'After coming back from the crematorium, he lay down outside our shed, spreading a gunny bag. Just now, I gave him uppittu and came here.'

'Doesn't he know the child is here?'

'Yes, he knows. My husband informed him. Perhaps he may come now.'

'Ammare, please don't say this Narasi speaks bad words. If a whore like me had children, no one would have come to take care of them when they were suffering. Since no one would have known by whom they were begotten, why would anyone come and care for them? But this

S.L. BHYRAPPA

Chinnayya eats uppittu and does not come to see the child he begot!'

Nanjamma, gesturing with her hand, asked Narasi not to speak like that. The master's wife said, 'See, Nanjammore, these village deities— Maaramma, Sunkalamma—all these are not benevolent deities. They only ruin, not protect. But Sharadammanoru of Shringeri will ward off any sort of hardships and extremities. You observe a vow that you will go to that temple and perform kumkumrchana during the Navaratri, if Vishwa gets well. He will surely be cured. Given the deaths of Parvati and Ramanna, you are undergoing the period where you cannot indulge in anything auspicious. You don't do anything. I will go home, wear a madi saree and tie, in a cloth, a coin of four annas and place it in front of God in your name?'

Nanjamma shook her head in the negative.

'Why do you say so?'

'No god will do anything. God and all that is a lie. If the child is fated to live, he will; if not, no.'

Narasi said, 'Nanjavvare, don't speak like that in your anger. Say it was a mistake, beg forgiveness, tell her you will observe the vow.'

But Nanjamma bluntly refused, 'It is no mistake or anything. I don't want to make a vow to any God.' Again both of them forced Nanjamma to which she finally said, 'As you feel best.'

The master's wife left. Meanwhile, several villagers started coming one by one near the shrine. Everyone had to arrange and organize his or her shed. Yet, everyone who came to console Nanjamma felt sorry for her. They praised Parvati's beauty, the many good qualities she had and also Ramanna's intelligence. He was so clever that if he had lived, he would have reigned as an Amaldar. Perhaps Shiva pulled them away, thinking such good and intelligent children should not live in this world but they should always be only near him? Anyway, Nanjamma should not have taken the newly married Parvatamma, wearing such a grand saree to the temple. It seemed like the eyes of the village Goddess had fallen first on that girl. The villagers said, until then, the plague had attacked eight people. Since last night and until four this morning, two people had died. Neither Nanjamma nor Narasi, who was staying in the shrine outside the village, knew about it. All except Sarvakka, left one by one.

Nanjamma and Sarvakka were intimate friends who had shared

their hardships. Sarvakka too had lost her daughter who had attained puberty. With the memory of her daughter's death, she would remember Narasi. The same Narasi is sitting here and Nanjamma's child is on her lap. Nanjamma was sitting at a distance as though it was not her child. Sarvakka's whole body would burn hearing Narasi's name. If the circumstances were different, Sarvakka would have slapped Narasi with her chappals. But now she sat quietly, unable to understand anything. She did not want to leave Nanjamma and go away. But she did not know what to say either.

Meanwhile, the child began breathing loudly. It seemed that the fever had increased. Narasi said, 'Avvare, my thighs are burning because of the rise in Vishwa's temperature. The child is breathing loudly. I feel scared! Please come take a look.'

Nanjamma opened her mouth, 'No, I won't touch him with my hand. Sarvakka, you go and see.'

Sarvakka neared the boy, put her hand inside the blanket and saw that the child was sweating. Her palm became wet. She did not know what was happening. Under normal circumstances, perhaps Nanjamma would have understood. But now she was incapable of comprehending anything. Narasi called Ayyanavaru. He was fast asleep. Sarvakka shook his shoulder and he got up. For a minute, he rubbed his eyes and looked around; then he understood what Sarvakka was saying. He put his hand on the chest of the child and assured: 'The child is sweating. Before the temperature comes down, this is what happens. Thank God there is no tumour! Nanjavva, Vishwanna is saved, his life is saved!'

Nanjamma sat looking at the child like a dumb woman. Sarvakka exclaimed, 'Luckily Shiva has cast a benevolent eye.' The child was still sweating and the fever was coming down. By then Revannashetty had arrived there. Till now, Nanjamma had not spoken with him even once. He, too, had not directly spoken to her. He heard that the child was sweating, touched the child and said, 'Thank God the child is saved.' To Nanjamma, he said: 'Nanjammore, you have the wisdom to advise this whole village. Who can console you?' He said whatever came to him and then, turning to his wife he said, 'It seems Ayyanavaru has had no food since the last two days. Go home, cook ragi balls and bring here.' He left for home with his wife. Ayyanavaru forced Nanjamma to get up and wash her face. The uppittu the master's wife had brought was in the vessel. Ayyanavaru said, 'See Nanjavva, hereafter you must take care of Vishwanna. If there is no strength in you, how will it be possible to look after him? You have your food Avva.' But she did not heed these words. At last, Ayyanavaru admonished her and compelled her to eat. Narasi too forced her. Nanjamma took a mouthful, could not swallow it, spat it out and pushed away the vessel. Then Ayyanavaru searched for a small box from his luggage, took two pinches of black powder from it and said to her, 'Swallow this.'

'What's this Ayyanavare?'

'It is the prasada of Shiva. I had brought it from Kashi; only a little remains. You put it now into your mouth. All your misfortunes will be averted. Vishwa is sweating and the fever has reduced.'

Nanjamma quietly swallowed it. It tasted a little bitter and caustic, but sweet. She again leaned against the pillar and sat looking at the child. Meanwhile, Channigarayaru came.

Narasi asked him, 'What were you doing for such a long time Shanubhogaare?'

'I was on my way but several people stopped me to offer their condolences. So I sat there.' 'Wah wah, what a man to beget children!' On Narasi's saying this, Channigarayaru simply blinked and looked at her.

Ayyanavaru said, 'Narasavva, don't say anything more.'

Within ten minutes, Nanjamma was dozing off. She, who sat leaning against the pillar, put her head on the knees. Ayyanavaru spread the bed he had carried the previous night, held her by her shoulders, put her on the bed and covered her with an old blanket. In another two minutes, she was fast asleep.

Narasi asked, 'Ayyare, what was it you gave Nanjamma?'

'It is a medicine that helps get some sleep. They have it in Kashi. I had brought it while coming back from there; only a little was left.'

Channigarayaru asked, 'If so, give me some too Ayyanore.'

'Men should not take that medicine. Nanjavva will not wake up tonight and until tomorrow. You stay here. I will send word to the wife of the master to bring food for you,' he assured Channigarayaru and then said to Narasi, 'Narasavva, now there is no room for fear or anxiety. You lay down the child, go home and prepare some food for yourself. The whole night you did not sleep a wink. Go home and sleep for a while.'

'Ayyare, it is enough for me if the child survives. I can remain like this for two more days.'

'Go home, finish your meals, sleep and come back.'

Ayyanavaru folded a small blanket and gave it to Narasi. She placed the head of the child on it and left for her home. But Nanjamma did not wake up. By the afternoon, Gundegowdaru of Kurubarahalli and several people came near the shrine. As Ayyannavaru told them not to speak loudly and make a noise, they called Channigarayaru to come out and offered their condolences. When Channigarayaru said, 'We did whatever we could Gowdare, but the poor fellows did not survive,' his eyes filled with tears.

Venkateshayya master conveyed this bad news to Sooryanarayana on a card he sent him through post, putting black colour in the place of writing 'safe'.

5

It had been six days since both the children had died. Nanjamma had returned to her shed. Only Channigarayaru and herself were living in the shed. Vishwa was completely cured and free from fever. Maadevayyanavaru said, 'Let him not come home until the ten days of defilement by death are over. I will keep him in this shrine.' So, Nanjamma had left Vishwa in the shrine. Moreover, she was scared to bring him to her shed. During mornings and afternoons, she went to the shrine. But remembering that she was in defilement of death, she wouldn't enter the shrine. Though Vishwa too was under defilement, he was only a boy. He had gained strength to get up and sit, but Ayyanavaru always made him lie down. Nanjamma sat at the door of the shrine, looking at her son, and returned to her shed not speaking to even Ayyanavaru. Though Vishwa had no fever, Ayyanavaru was still administering him the Hemadi Syrup brought for Ramanna and Parvati.

A question always haunted Nanjamma. *Why do children die before the eyes of their mothers*? However much she reflected, no answer came to her. One day she put this question to Ayyanavaru. Then he answered, 'Avva, this is God's maaya. It is said, when Krishna was a little child, he used to test his mother in many different ways. If he fasted, she too would fast. Until he drank milk, she would not drink even water. He wanted to test this affection of love. One day he asked, "Avva, if I die what will you do?"

S.L. BHYRAPPA

She said, "Oh my child, can I live without you? I will follow you and die."

"Is that true?"

"Perfectly true. I swear by you, my child," she promised.

One day, little Krishna slipped and fell down into a deep whirlpool nearby. He drowned, feigning as if to reach the surface. He shouted: "Avva, pull me up, oh you too come inside the water. I am drowning, dying! Come save my life!" Water was filling the child's mouth. Gopamma stood on the bank and screamed, "Oh, somebody please come, pull my child to the bank!" But no one came. Then she untied the saree she wore, held one edge and threw another edge of the saree towards her son. But he couldn't catch it. Screaming loudly "Avva, Avva", he drowned in the water and died. Gopamma, then, wore her saree, sat on the bank and cried and cried for a long time. Then she got up, stood on the bank thinking she too should jump into the water and end her life. But somehow she felt scared to die. She did not jump into the whirlpool. She abused the mother Ganga who had swallowed her son. She repeatedly hit on her own mouth crying, "ayyo, alas", and sat on the bank, but didn't fall into the water. One day passed, two days were over—Gopamma would come near the whirlpool daily, sit on the bank and cry. But she did not jump into the water. The third day, Krishna himself came out of the water and cursed her, "What Avva, is your love only this deep? Even when I died, you did not die. Hereafter, let the children die before the mothers who bore them!" It is said, that is why it happens so.'

Hearing this, Nanjamma got extremely angry with Gopamma. *If only she had jumped into the whirlpool with firm resolve, the children in this world would have never died before the eyes of mothers. But after all, Gopi was only a human being; Sree Krishna was God. He wanted to test the love of the human mother and acted accordingly. If she would have been a divine mother, perhaps she would have followed suit. If Gopi was a divine mother, she would have followed suit and died; then her son too would be alive. Then this story would not have happened.*

Even after coming back to the shed, Nanjamma was pondering over this. The question regarding whether the story was true or mere fiction arose in her mind; *perhaps, it was a story.* Again another question came to her mind: *Even then, why did she not die after the deaths of Parvati and Ramanna*? She was startled to come across that question. Besides, the firm decision that she too must die formed in her mind. By then, it was eight in the night. Channigarayaru sat chewing tobacco on the stone slab before the shed. Nanjamma spread the bed inside and lay down but did not get any sleep. The resolution took root in her firmly: *She must die that day and follow Parvati and Ramanna. If only she died with an unflinching intent, would God save her and also send back her children?* This hope too arose in her mind. *It happened in the plays of Yakshagana, in the songs she had learnt, and in the stories of the Puranas she had heard. So, why shouldn't this happen to her also?* But her belief in Gods and the Puranas was destroyed the very moment both her children had passed away and that too on the same day. It did not matter to her whether Gopi had hesitated to die for Krishna or not. Now that her children were dead, she had suffered hell for six days without them. *No, she wanted no more of this hell. She too must die.*

Meanwhile, her husband had come inside and slept off. His snores could be heard clearly. Nanjamma got up. It was already ten or eleven in the night. She closed the door of the shed and came out. Without clearly deciding on where to go and how to die, her mind directed her to climb down the tank bund and took her to the crematorium where her children had turned to ashes. She had not gone there when the corpses of her children were burnt. Going to the cemetery was a taboo for a Brahmin woman. Now she directly went there. She had no fear, hesitation or anxiety. The thought of ghosts, demons or devils did not hover in her mind. Even in the darkness, she could see the spots where the two corpses had been burnt. Except for her two children, at present no Brahmin had died. So the spots that lay with traces of burning firewood were surely the places her children had been in. But she could not know which was Ramanna's and which was Parvati's. What was the use of such knowledge anyway? The rites of collecting bones on the third day were over. Yet she bent down, took a fistful of ash from both places, and kept it in the tied edge of her saree. There was a pond near the crematorium. After the corpses were burnt, the corpse-bearers and performers of rites would take a bath in that pond. Nobody would use that pond at other times. *As such a the water would be a little dirty. She must jump into that pond; she should stand on the cornerstone stretched out on the opposite side and jump.* She closed her eyes. The dim darkness became dense. She lost control for two seconds and felt each nerve of her body swelling. Her hands, legs and body were out of control and trembling. The water in the pond appeared as if to stir and dashed against all the corners. But gradually the nerves became peaceful and the trembling stopped. The mind became a vacuum as if all its activities were dead and there were no thoughts and feelings. Did death mean only that much? No one was there. Parvati, Ramanna and she—no one and nothing. There was only one thing that remained—to take half a step forward and jump into the water. That was the step to take easily, without the least effort and hardship.

Before taking that step, the memory of those that had survived in this village floated before her mind—one was the husband. *He would suffer his own fate. Vishwa?* But Vishwa? Her mind wavered as soon as she remembered Vishwa. *He did not die of the plague; he had survived. Who would bring him up?* Her mind said, *only Ayyanavaru was his refuge.* She was assured. *Ayyanavaru would never forsake Vishwa, knowing well that Nanjamma had ended her life unable to bear the grief of her children's death. But Vishwa would be an orphan without her. Whatever would Ayyanavaru do? Would having him around be equal to having a mother? When Parvati and Ramanna were struck by plague, why didn't she get it too? Perhaps God saved her with the purpose that she had to bring up Vishwa, and saved Vishwa so that she should mother him.* Vishwa's face came before her. He was the combination of Parvati's broad face and Ramanna's sharp intelligence. *He had survived on behalf of those two. Now, if she lost her life, what would be the meaning?*

Reflecting thus, Nanjamma squatted on that corner step. The panorama of her life moved before her mind: her marriage, stepping into this village, birth of these children, the hardships and joys during intervals of their coming into this world, the drought without rainfall and without crops. *Oh how peacefully Ramanna and Parvati used to bear hunger! Perhaps God took them away because of their goodness.* Vishwa would beat his mother, unable to bear the hunger. It was his nature. Courage, valour, anger and rashness—it would have to be always he to get to eat the meals first. But he did not have the mean greediness like that of his father. Even when he plucked berries from garbage dumps, he would never eat them without sharing them with his Akkayya and Annayya. *Oh, what fortune would I earn by making him an orphan and dying? If I die now and enter the world of the dead, and there Parvati and Ramanna question me, 'Amma, you left Vishwa there and came. What will be his fate? Didn't you have at least that much of sense?'— what would I say?*

Without being aware, she stepped back from the cornerstone. Careful of thorns and stones, she took the same path back and reached the crematorium. She stood for a while at the place Parvati and Ramanna had been burnt. From there, she walked through the garden path and climbed the tank bund. But without turning right to go to the shed, her steps turned left towards the shrine. Even in the darkness, the road on the tank bund was clear. The tank bund was so wide that bullock carts could negotiate on it. When she neared the shrine she could hear Ayyanavaru singing. A castor oil lamp was lit in the central square of the temple. Vishwa was asleep on the bed. Covering him with a blanket, Ayyanavaru sat on the side of the same bed and was strumming the ektaari and singing:

> Near the stream the creeper got cooled
> And the berries got mellowed,
> Did the fruit, before falling on the earth
> bid farewell to its creeper?

Ayyanavaru noticed the figure standing near the door and turned towards it. He recognized her and said, 'It was just this evening that you had come. Now again you have come. What for, Avva? You don't worry. Vishwanna is now as strong as a rock. Hereafter, you don't call him Vishwanna, call him "Gundanna". He will grow strong like a rock.'

She determined in her mind. Yes, the blessings of Ayyanavaru are pure. He is right. Hereafter, I must call him 'Gundanna' only. She said, 'No, nothing, I'll make a move.'

'Why did you come now?'

'Just like that.'

'If you want, stay here. But Avva, people's tongue will not always be decent. It is better you go home.'

She agreed and said, 'I will leave', and left.

'Just wait, Avva, I will come with you till a certain distance.'

'No, no. The child is sleeping alone,' she said and walked hastily towards the tank bund. By the time she reached the shed, she

S.L. BHYRAPPA

remembered the ash she had tied in the edge of her saree, got down on the left side of the tank bund, untied the knot, stirred the ash into the water and whispered: 'Oh mother Gangamma, let this reach your womb.' Nanjamma then climbed the bund, came to the shed and went to bed.

6

On the seventh day following the death of Parvati and Ramanna, Nanjamma was sitting in her shed after having visited Vishwa in the shrine. Ramanna's obsequies had to be started from that day. What were these shaastras, what worthless rubbish were they—she had not thought much about them, nor had anyone reminded her of them. The responsibility of performing Parvati's rites was her husband's.

It was noon. Nanjamma sat in the shed, her head on her knees. Channigarayaru had gone somewhere. She felt as if someone wearing white clothes had entered the shed. She raised her neck and saw that it was Sooryanarayana, Parvati's husband. He held his daughter Ratna's hand in his left hand. A big bag was hanging by his shoulder. There was a heavy bamboo basket in his right hand. Nanjamma did not greet him or invite the guest to sit down, nor did she go inside with modesty because her son-in-law had come. Sooryanarayana himself said to Ratna, 'Go to grandmother, child.'

The child had not forgotten this grandmother. She went to Nanjamma right away and touched her shoulder. Nanjamma held the child's hand and made her sit on her lap. Sooryanarayana opened the lid of the basket and said, 'Please keep these inside. These will wither in the hot sun.' He took out the things one by one from the basket—a packet of fragrant jasmine flowers, tender betel leaves, oranges and bananas and packets of snacks from the hotel. Seeing all these things, Nanjamma could not contain herself. She hugged Ratna and sobbed once. Sooryanarayana was bewildered, raised his neck and looked at Nanjamma. Nanjamma left the child, got up and went into the area meant as a kitchen. He could not understand anything, but could hear the violent sobbing from inside. He asked, 'Amma, what happened? Why are you crying?' Nanjamma did not answer. He was embarrassed to enter the kitchen portion and ask her. He sat silently, not knowing what to do. But a sort of unknown fear and suspicion arose in his mind.

Half an hour was spent in this manner. At last, Sooryanarayana asked, 'Why, Amma, aren't you speaking to me openly?'

Nanjamma did not speak. She went out of her shed, called a boy who stood near another shed and told him: 'Look, child, go to the shed of the master and tell him I sent for him. Bring him here at once.' The boy ran and within five minutes the master came and asked, 'Why did you send for me?' She said, 'Go to our shed and see,' she said, walked towards the tank bund and went to the shrine.

The master came into the shed and saw Sooryanarayana sitting baffled. Before him were the packets of fruits, flowers, betel leaves and snacks.

Ratna stood holding the shoulder of her father. The master asked, 'Did you not receive my letter?'

'Which letter? No. I didn't.'

'I wrote to you five days back.'

'We get the post once in a week in our village.'

The master did not say anything else. Sooryanarayana asked: 'Venkateshayyanavare, I don't follow. Please say something, what is it?'

'Oh, how can I bring myself to say it?'

'No, you please tell.' When Sooryanarayana said this, he was acutely anxious.

'Both Parvatamma and Ramanna passed away. It is the seventh day today.'

'What!' Sooryanarayana's mouth remained agape.

'Plague. The epidemic that struck the village, first attacked their house. The sister and brother died the same day, one following the other. Vishwa is recovering,' the master explained everything in detail.

Sooryanarayana sat like a person unable to speak and heard everything. He could not control himself when the master said, 'It's all ill luck. Who can avert fate?' Though he suppressed the cry that sprang from inside, he sobbed continuously and breathed haltingly. Looking at her father crying, Ratna too started crying, though she could not understand anything that was going on.

'Venkateshayyanavare, I am an unfortunate person,' he said. He pulled the child near him, hugged her and hid his face on her back.

The master too failed to say anything further. For ten minutes he sat silently and then said, 'Please get up. Let's go to our house.'

S.L. BHYRAPPA

'No, I want nothing now. I will go back to my place.'

'You may go back. But come, at least the child should have some food,' the master forced him, closed the door of the shed, took the lock put on the grinding stone, locked the shed and started. After reaching his shed, the master's wife served Ratna, putting in front of her a leaf plate. Sooryanarayana did not take even a cup of coffee. After Ratna's meal was over, he removed the leaf, cleaned the floor with cow dung and said, 'Now, guide me to the shrine. Let me see Vishwa.' They walked towards the tank bund. Sooryanarayana carried Ratna.

By the time they went to the shrine, Nanjamma had returned to her shed. She sent a boy to the master's house and fetched the key. Till then, she was eating whatever the master's wife would bring for her into the shed. She would eat a morsel of that food, and put out the remaining for the dogs. Now when she opened the door, the flowers, fruits and snacks Sooryanarayana had brought along were still there. Unable to look at them, she turned her face and went inside. Inside the big box in which the account books of the Shanubhoga were stored, she had tied in a white towel the marriage sarees of Parvati and the earrings, nose ring and silver bangles that Sooryanarayana had brought. She took out the bundle and kept it ready.

It was nearly one in the afternoon, when they returned from the shrine. Sooryanarayana stood silently. The master said, 'Nanjammanore, he wants to leave. He has to arrange everything and has to begin the rites at least from the ninth day, that is, the day after tomorrow.'

Nanjamma did not say anything. She brought the bundle she had kept ready, placed it before Sooryanarayana and said, 'Here are her sarees and jewels. These belong to you, please put them in your bag.'

Looking at the bundle, his eyes filled with tears. He said, 'Amma, the most important thing I adored is no more. What shall I do taking these? I don't want them.'

'As soon as we gave her in Kanyadaana, she became yours. What will I do keeping her sarees and jewels with me? If I look at them, I cannot control myself.'

When the master too compelled Sooryanarayana, he took the bundle and put it inside his bag. He prostrated to his mother-in-law from where he stood and made his child do the same. Then, holding the bag in one hand and the hand of the child in the other, he left, walking slowly.

Master followed him till the motor road.

Now, three buses were moving on this route. Along with a Mudaliar bus service, two from the C.P.C. Company were also running. If they could reach the road within ten minutes, Sooryanarayana could catch a bus to Tiptur. By the time the master returned, Nanjamma had come into the master's shed. Master told her, 'He will start Parvatamma's rites from day after tomorrow and finish it as quickly as possible. Ramanna had got his Upanayana. Some shaastras and rites ought to be performed. If we are caught with these jois, they will clean-shave us. They will not consider our plight. Leave to me all the responsibilities. I will complete everything in twenty-five rupees. No matter what we do here, or how much we spend here, it will not help the dead person. We perform these rites only to be freed from our karmas.'

'Now it would be hard to get money. Please visit Kurubarahalli. Gundegowdaru will never say no at a time like this. We may debit it in the revenue tax of the coming year.'

The master at once set out for Kurubarahalli. Nanjamma went back to her shed.

7

The same evening, Akkamma and Kallesha came by cart. While getting down from the cart itself, it was visible that Akkamma had been constantly crying. Kallesha's face was gloomy too. Coming into the shed, Akkamma said tearfully, 'What Nanja, were we all dead for you? It seems seven days are already over. Shouldn't you have sent word to us?'

Seeing Akkamma, Nanjamma too felt like crying. But she controlled herself and said, 'What happy news was it to send you word about at all?'

Kallesha said, 'Shouldn't we care for and share in your hardships and happiness? Have we become so distant to you? Now get up. Stay with us for a couple of months at our place. You need to forget all this a little.'

But it was not possible for Nanjamma to start at once for her parents' home. Vishwa was still recovering. Ramanna's obsequies were yet to be completed, although that would be a brief process. Besides, she was not much in favour of the idea of visiting her parents' home. Years had passed since she had gone there. But Kallesha forced her. He and Akkamma went to the shrine and enquired about Vishwa's health. Akkamma hugged her great-grandson, the only one surviving, and shed tears.

They stayed there until the period accompanying the defilement of death was over. As Akkamma and Kallesha were purified of the defilement on the third day itself, Akkamma started cooking in this shed. In the meantime, Kallesha went in search of Revannashetty.

Akkamma told Nanju, 'See, even Kanti will not stay in the village now. You remember he had a horse earlier? That one died four years after he went to Kashi. Now he has bought another one, and will be wandering wheresoever possible. It is being said that he has learnt many new mantras and tantras. People from Hasana, Channarayapatna, Shantigrama and Arakalagudu consult him for averting or performing witchcraft, black magic, preparing medicines, etc. It has been twenty days since he left the village.'

Later, Akkamma said, 'The daughter of Ningegowda of Kurubarahalli has been given in marriage to the brother of Koli Chikkanna of our village. This Ningegowda visited our village yesterday. This morning Chikkanna himself came and said: "Both your granddaughter's children are dead. Everyone has vacated the village. Won't you go there?" I doubted whether it was true. Then he said that his in-laws themselves had informed him of the situation. Kallesha at once told Honna to harness the cart and we started.'

'Didn't you search for a bride for Annayya anywhere?'

'Kanti had fixed one from Alanahalli near Anekere. This witch had an inkling of it. She stealthily wrote a letter to her father. Her father came, held Kallesha's hand, shedding tears and requested: "I have served you in your hard times, thinking of you as my son. God did not grace you with children. I beseech you, don't get into a second marriage." Till then Kallesha had agreed to marry again but then he changed his mind. He refused to marry. Kanti and myself forced him, but he did not budge.'

Under the supervision of the master, Ramanna's rites were completed within twenty-five rupees. After the period of defilement was over, Nanjamma carried Vishwa home. Now he could get up and walk slowly. The boy who had grown chubby and was strong as a bull, was now emaciated like a thin, bony calf. Kallesha had sent away the cart the day after they had arrived here. Now Kallesha again asked, 'Nanja, I will hire a cart with an arch. Come, let us go to our village.'

She did not support the idea in her mind, but she should not be rude. Sister-in-law might be bad, but her brother had not treated her badly. They had asked her for the girl and she had refused; that is why they were angry and had not attended the marriage. Now they had come of their own and were asking her to go with them. Why shouldn't she go? But it was the season of collecting revenue tax. All these days she had not seen to that work. If she left for her parents', her husband would not stay alone, nor would he do the government work. So she said, 'Let Akkamma stay here. After the collection of revenue arrears of this year, I will come with Akkamma. Afterwards, I will stay for ten or fifteen days, and by the time the collection of revenue arrears starts, I will come back.'

Kallesha walked alone to his village.

CHAPTER FOURTEEN

1

Gangamma and Appannaiah had gone begging towards the villages of Gandasi and Dudda this time, and returned after a month and a half. Still ten miles away from Ramasandra, they heard that the whole village had been vacated. If they came back to the village, they would have to adjust bamboo strips, staffs and coconut leaves and put up the shed. All the vessels and other items of domestic needs were in the room of the temple of the village that had been vacated too. They doubted whether they could open the room and bring the items out. To avoid any such problems, they again started towards the west. They wandered around the places they had not visited before and went round the Habbanaghatta and Haranahalli regions. Three months had passed by the time they reached the village. The village had received good rains twice and all had left the sheds to return to the village.

Gangamma became furious upon hearing that both her grandchildren had died on the same day and wanted to abuse her daughter-in-law. But now, she had developed a sort of fear and was scared to even open her mouth in her presence.

When she went to her daughter-in-law's house, without realizing why, she felt like crying. She expressed her grief. 'Could that child had survived had given if you her to that widower? Did you at least consult me before fixing her marriage?' There was not much contact between her and her grandchildren when they were alive. Now and then, she used to go out of the village and even when she stayed, she would not frequent their house. The children, too, would not go to her house. On some days, when she would meet Parvati either near the bed of greens or near the tank, she would ask, 'Your mother had gone to collect revenue from Kurubarahalli. How much of ink charge did she get?' Parvati would answer, 'How do I know, grandma?' There itself the affectionate words between grandmother and granddaughter would end. Sometimes, she would ask Ramanna. 'They say, you study English and will become a Shekdar...When you become a Shekdar, will you bring me a red saree?' Ramanna would answer, 'Yes grandma, I will.' And the conversation would end. But now the memory of these two somehow began haunting her. For three or four days, she remembered her grandchildren and she gave her sorrow an outlet by abusing her daughter-in-law, that she did not take care of the children and therefore they were dead.

But it was Appannaiah who suffered more sorrow. He had laboured hard in Parvati's marriage. It was perhaps owing to that that he had developed a great affection for her. When he had heard that Ramanna had come first in class, he had felt proud of the boy. Oh, he was a boy who wrote accounts for the Shekdar himself! He may learn English and become a Shekdar in future. Though he did not speak much with the children, somehow the feeling that they were his own children had developed in him. Now Appannaiah stood before his sister-in-law, shed tears and said, 'We are sinning bastards. We were not fated to save the children.'

There were good rains and crops that year. Writing the revenue accounts for the village had also been completed. One day, the master's wife came and said to Nanjamma, 'See Nanjamma, I had observed a vow in your Vishwa's name that I will come and pay a darshan to Sringeri Sharadammanavaru and pray Kumkumarchana to be performed. The coin that I had had towards that prayer and tied on to the edge of my saree, is still on the niche of the deity in our home. Navarathri will start in another eight days. You take the child with you and fulfil the vow. His temperature came down the very day I made the vow. Any vow made in the name of God should not be postponed.'

Nanjamma decided to go on pilgrimage to Sringeri. She thought, 'We don't know what powers the Gods have. If we forget them, any calamity may occur in future. I have only one child, Vishwa. I must go there.' The master told her, the route: 'Boarding the train in Tiptur, you have to get down in Tarikere. In between, change the train at Birur. Spending the night at the Tarikere station, you should reach Narasimharajapura in a narrow gauge train. From there, a bus goes to Sringeri via Koppa. Fifteen annas per passenger from Tiptur to Tarikere, and from there to Narasimharajapura—seven rupees less than a quarter anna and two rupees for the bus. There is a choultry in Sringeri for the pilgrims. Free boarding is available twice a day in the Mutt.'

Nanjamma was to leave with Vishwa. But she thought it would be good to be in the company of someone with travel experience and that too in trains. But it was difficult to adjust money for another person. She had to offer five rupees for the kumkumarchane. Appannaiah came on his own and said secretly, 'Don't disclose this to anybody. I have twenty rupees. I'll give it to you now. You may pay me back when I need it. Now, I too will come with you.'

Both mother and son used to sell the ragi they would get. Sometimes, Appannaiah sold some without his mother's knowledge and collect the money for betel leaves and tobacco.

Twenty rupees would not be enough to cover all the expenses. Nanjamma had spent everything she had for her daughter's marriage and all other inevitable rituals that followed. How many times could she ask Kurubarahalli Gundegowdaru? Appannaiah suggested, 'We may walk from here to Tiptur. Then, till Narasimharajapura, we may travel by train. Again, we may walk the bus route. Twenty rupees would be enough.'

Yes, that would be enough. It was decided that Nanjamma, Vishwa and Appannaiah would start off. But would Channigarayaru keep quiet? He was stubborn that he too would come. How could Nanjamma arrange money again for him? Moreover, there was no hope that he would walk like the others. He said, 'Somehow I'll bring money; you need not worry about it.' She put a condition, 'You should not write a receipt for the revenue tax and bring money.' Channigaraya agreed he wouldn't do so. Anyway, he did manage to arrange for the money. His expenses would be separate and the expenses of these three were separate. Nanjamma ground five seers of parched ragi flour. Appannaiah brought eight seers of paddy from his mendicancy, without his mother knowing. Nanjamma prepared rice flakes from it and packed that too. Gangamma too had desired to go for the pilgrimage, but did not want to go with this daughter-in-law. She asked her son also not to go. But Appannaiah said, while his sister-in-law shouldered the expenses, why should he miss this opportunity?

Nanjamma had nourished Vishwa after his recovery from the plague, by giving him enough milk and ghee. Moreover, he was a strong boy from the beginning. One day before dawn, from even before she went off to pluck the leaves of the flame of forest trees, Nanjamma, Vishwa and Appannaiah packed rotis and chutney and started on foot. Channigarayaru said he would come by bus as he knew someone in the Tiptur bus route and would join the rest of the family later. The bundle of parched rice, parched flour, jaggery, tamarind, four dehusked coconuts, two seers of rice, two vessels and a couple of clothes were put in a small gunny bag. Appannaiah carried it on his head and set out. Nanjamma packed a couple of her sarees and blouses, Vishwa's clothes, two blankets and a carpet, carried the small bundle on her waist, held Vishwa's hand and walked. By daybreak, they had walked about three miles. Vishwa would leave his mother's hand and run faster than his uncle. He would challenge, 'Look, mother, am I not stronger than you?' After they crossed six miles, all three sat near a small pool and ate roti and chutney. After having walked another two or three miles, Vishwa's pace was becoming slow. He again held his mother's hand and began walking slowly. It was beneath him to say that his legs ached. Meanwhile, a bus passed in front of them making a loud sound.

Appannaiah asked, 'Did you see him, sister-in-law, sitting in the back seat?'

'No.'

'Amma, the bus people take Appa without a ticket. Why don't they take me also free of cost?'

'Oho! Do they take him without a ticket? Really? What you've heard is all lies, all bloody bogus...thoo, thoo, fuck his mother!' said Appannaiah. Although Nanjamma tried to restrain him from speaking further but he continued: 'Whatever you say, our Chinnayya is a wretched bastard. He is like that since his boyhood. Himself and his belly, that's all. Such fellows should be slapped with chappals, tut-tut, fuck his mother...'

'Appannaiah, we are going on a pilgrimage. Why should there be bad words in our mouths? Leave it...' Nanjamma calmed him and told Vishwa, 'Vishwa, I had taught you that shloka "Bhaja Govindam, Bhaja Govindam"? Recite it. Are we not going to Sringeri now? That shloka was composed by Sri Shankaracharya who founded that Mutt.'

Vishwa began chanting it slowly and melodiously. His mother corrected him wherever he committed a mistake. Appannaiah took out betel leaves from his pocket and smeared half a leaf with lime. He then put it into his mouth with areca nuts and then rubbed a piece of tobacco on his palm, filling his mouth with it too. Within a little time, his mouth was filled with the juice of the betel leaf with lime and tobacco. He walked spitting the juice.

The scheduled time for the train's arrival to Tiptur was one in the afternoon. Though they stopped once to take rest, as they chose the nearby rural path to reach the station, they reached it at twelve itself. Once again, they ate the roti with chutney. By then, Channigarayaru had come there, finishing his lunch at Madhavabhatta's hotel. Appannaiah bought two and a half tickets. Channigarayaru took his.

These three drank water from the tap at the Tarikere railway station and ate roti and chutney again in the night. Channigarayaru said he would like to take a look at the town and left. Appannaiah asked, 'Do you know where he went now?' Nanjamma said, 'Let him go wherever he wants. We don't want that; you also don't worry about it.' Spreading a carpet in a corner of the station, Vishwa and she slept. Appannaiah spread a sackcloth, covered himself with the sheet, made the bundle his pillow and slept in the side, near Nanjamma's and Vishwa's heads. At once, all of them were asleep. Channigarayaru finished his meals, came back, spread a dhoti beside his brother and lay down.

By the next morning, there were still ten rotis remaining in their pack. As they had been baked two days earlier, they had become hard. But they could be soaked in water and eaten. The chutney had become stale. Meanwhile, Channigarayaru washed his face and entered the hotel. Vishwa desired snacks from the hotel. Nanjamma said to Appannaiah,' Bring sambar for one anna, one idli and two plain dosas for Vishwa.' In all, that would come to three annas.

As soon as the narrow gauge train of Narasimharajapura started, Vishwa felt elated. Oh, how many trees there were out of the window! Oh! So many in a row, it was impossible to count them. Green creepers spread around them. Just then, the monsoon was over and in the month of Ashvayuja, plants were a shining and luxuriant green everywhere. Vishwa saw a big animal rushing past. From the memory of the picture he had seen in his book, he recognized it to be an elephant. He asked his mother, 'Amma, is this what a forest is like?' His mother too understood. 'Yes, it is'. But she too had never seen such dense trees.

Appannaiah said, 'It is so in this region. If you go beyond Shivamogga, the forests are even thicker.'

'When did you go to Shivamogga?'

Appannaiah remembered something and was silent. Nanjamma too remembered that at once, and she felt she should not have asked him. He became gloomy as he remembered how, with his leg, he had kicked the same sister-in-law and how, out of the fear of being arrested by the police, he had wandered in these regions. Now he sat looking out of the window. Channigarayaru was rubbing tobacco.

By twelve in the noon, the mini train reached Narasimharajapura. The agents of the surrounding buses shouted, 'Sringeri Sringeri, urgent Sringeri!'

Channigarayaru asked, 'Did you people come by bus or on foot?'

Appannaiah said, 'Where did we have the money to come by bus?'

'I have sprained my leg and I will go by bus. I will reserve some place for you in the choultry by going early. You may come later,' he said and walked away. Appannaiah shouted, 'Chinnayya, wait a little, you take sister-in-law and Vishwa with you. It costs only three rupees. They charge only half the ticket price for Vishwa. If you request the conductor that you are four people, we will make the boy sit on our lap and tell him not to take his charges, they will allow him to travel without a ticket. I will come on foot.'

'No, I don't have the money. If she has, let her come in the bus,' he said and walked further. Hundreds of travellers getting down by the train were running in crowds and filling in the buses. Channigarayaru too boarded one and secured a seat.

These three soaked the dried hard rotis in water and ate. Despite eating the rotis, their stomachs didn't feel full. Nanjamma melted jaggery in tamarind juice, mixed parched ragi flour in it and gave Vishwa and Appannaiah; she too had it. Then she filled Vishwa's pocket with a piece of jaggery and rice flakes; Appannaiah also put his sister-in-law's bundle in his bag and set out. Nanjamma walked holding Vishwa's hand.

Nanjamma had never seen such a dense forest. She always loved greenery and felt an unusual attraction for plants and trees. When she used to visit Cholanagudda to bring the flame of forest leaves, she would stand still, looking around the green fields full of crops. Here, wherever you saw, there was the forest with big, huge trees. An inexpressible joy swelled in her mind and stirred her heart. The same flora that gladdened the mind brought to her the poignant memory of her two children. Oh how broad are these leaves of teak! Could meals be served and eaten on only one leaf? If the leaves of the forest of flame trees were as broad as this, there would be no problem of joining them at all. When they used to go to bring the leaves, if he spotted big leaves, Ramanna would run, shouting: 'Oh Amma, look there, what big leaves!' and pluck them. But big leaves were not suitable for joining; if joined, they would become too broad. Ramanna's shirt was full of stains from the sprinkling of the juice of the tree. He had reserved a separate torn shirt for that work.

While Parvati would accompany her mother for plucking the flame of forest leaves, she would always be humming a song. Oh! How much she liked singing and drawing designs in rangoli! She had learnt everything her mother had known. By the time she had completed twelve, she had released her mother from the job of grinding ragi. It was so lovely to hear her sing melodiously while grinding ragi early in the morning. The master had said: 'Parvati's husband loved music very much. If he sang the poems of the *Mahabharata* melodiously with the shruti of harmonium, the listeners' eyes would be full of tears. Besides, he knew many shlokas and devaranamas[26] also. Daily he used to read *Bharata* at home. Such a good-natured person, one without anger or jealousy. With what care he used to look after his daughter Ratna! A husband should be like that. Our Parvati was not destined to live with such a person.' Nanjamma's mind would compare Sooryanarayana with Channigarayaru. Then feeling utter disgust, her mind would turn to other things, thinking that all this was the result of one's previous birth.

Vishwa felt extreme joy looking at the forest. He exclaimed, 'Oh Amma, look there, that is taller and bigger than the sour mango tree of the grove in our village!' Then he would turn his eyes towards another tree and say: 'Oh, see the tree beside that, it touches the sky!' Again he would ask, 'Oh look at that monkey. Why is its face of that shape? The monkey in our village is lovelier than this one. Isn't it?'

His mother would answer, 'This is a forest monkey, child.'

'If so, what sort of monkey is in our village?'

'That's a village monkey.'

'If so, it won't stay in the village at all. That is a garden monkey,' he himself would answer.

---

[26]Hymns

Walking through the forest, they found a couple of snakes also. They were not strangers to creatures like snakes, as snakes were there in Ramasandra also. But as it was a dense forest, they had to walk carefully. It was learnt that there were pythons in the forests of Malenadu. They would swallow an entire man and would be lying like a log.

. Vishwa felt bored having to walk continuously holding his mother's hand; so he shook off her hand and walked on his own. Sometimes, he would run for about twenty-five metres ahead of her and sometimes remain ten steps behind her. At one point, his mother's mind was immersed in some thought. Appannaiah, as usual, was walking ten or twelve metres further from the two. All of a sudden, Nanjamma felt something and turned around. Vishwa was nowhere. She was shocked and her heart skipped a beat. For the first time, she remembered there were tigers, lions and hyenas in the forest, and there was the danger of snakes also. She called Appannaiah and said, 'I don't see Vishwa anywhere. Please look for him!' Both of them retraced their steps. A furlong behind, Vishwa had climbed a small teak tree beside the road and was mimicking the monkeys on the opposite tree shouting 'kee kee kala kee kee kala'. His mother asked, 'Why did you do this without asking me?' He answered, 'See, that monkey mocked and aped me, that's why...'

From then onwards, Nanjamma did not leave Vishwa behind, but made him walk in front of her.

Appannaiah could not take to or enjoy the beauty of the forest. He preferred the plain country. In Malenadu, there was only paddy and there was no ragi. He wondered how they could acquire strength without eating ragi balls. He had heard that the people of Malenadu were not as strong as people from the plain country. More than all this, Appannaiah reminisced about the incidents of his past life. His daughter Jayalakshmi must be Parvati's age. The second one Ramakrishna was much younger to her. He did not know about the third one. He ruminated: Really, it was I who begot Ramakrishna. But my mother had said I had not. Wasn't it me who had gone there now? I don't know whether he has been admitted to school. It seems like these people had said they would make him learn mantras and train him to become a jois. Perhaps the child must be going around the village on his own, bringing gifts, donations. Don't know how she is now, whether she remembers me or not. Anyway, I too should not have forcibly taken away the tali and sent her away. That slut of an ass, if she too had joined leaves and adjusted the expenses of some provisions like chillies, salt and other things, they could have lived happily. Why should they want coffee as soon as they woke up in the morning? How was it possible that they ate Tovar dal sambar and coffee daily? Did his father give them heaps of money? Yet that slut should not have left him. When he thought of these things deeply, Appannaiah felt an acute loneliness. A sort of weariness, a feeling that there was no happiness in life, would seize him. He asked his sister-in-law walking behind him: 'Did you hear?'

'What did you say?'

'Would they have performed the marriage of that girl too by now?'

'Who are you talking about?'

He was embarrassed to say precisely the name of the girl and became silent. His sister-in-law asked again, 'Which girl?'

He said, 'Oh let it go, I don't know why I remembered Rudrani, Revannashetty's daughter'.

'Alas, it is two years since Rudrani died. How is it that you speak of her now?' Nanjamma's mind was tangled in its own worries and so, she couldn't quite comprehend the basis of his words. They started walking in silence once again. Appannaiah walked around twelve metres ahead. Vishwa would sometimes walk a little ahead of his uncle or would walk between the two. If he felt bored, he would hold his mother's hand...

They rested for a while and by seven at night, reached Koppa, having covered a distance of fourteen miles. Nanjamma thought of soaking rice flakes in a vessel, putting jaggery to it and mixing parched flour in another, or setting three stones beneath a tree she could cook rice and bring sambar for two annas from a hotel. Appannaiah suggested: 'Malenadu Sahukars feed any number of guests in their houses. Let's go and have our meals in one such house.' His sister-in-law said, 'No, let's not go to anybody's house for food.'

'If so, Vishwa and I will go and have our food. I will set stones for you to cook and bring sambar from the hotel.'

'No, let none of us go. Let's eat what we have brought.'

It was decided that they would do as Nanjamma said. Appannaiah gathered a few stones, brought along some dry twigs and set a stone oven. Nanjamma cooked rice. They got more than half of the vessel of sambar in the hotel, and the three of them had a stomach full of food.

They slept on the platform of a shop, woke up at daybreak, mixed parched flour and soaked rice flakes. Appannaiah went to the hotel and scraped half of the coconut he had broken. They mixed jaggery and scrapes of coconut to rice flakes and had their breakfast, packed the remaining soaked rice flakes for Vishwa and walked further. It was sixteen miles of walk, day before yesterday from Ramasandra to Tiptur. Yesterday, they had covered fourteen miles from Narasimharajapura to Koppa, continuously. Both of Vishwa's thighs were aching. His mother also was feeling the pain in her feet. But there were no other means to reach the site of the pilgrimage except by walking. The mother asked, 'Do your legs ache much, child?' He answered heroically, 'No, boys don't feel any ache,' and ran. Hariharapura was six miles away from there. There also was Sringeri Mutt. They walked slowly and reached Hariharapura by ten in the morning. After bathing in the river and completing the darshana of the God, they had their food in the Mutt. Nanjamma did not feel any embarrassment as hundreds of Brahmins and muttaides were gathered there for meals. After their meals, Vishwa started dozing. Sringeri was another twelve miles away. The pain in Nanjamma's feet and legs had increased. So they decided to halt during the night and start again at the daybreak. Vishwa was laid down in a choultry; Appannaiah too lay beside him. Nanjamma desired to sit beside the river flowing in front of them. She walked on the sand, reached the river, and sat on a stone there, dipping her feet in the water. She felt it to be very soothing. But her mind was completely seized by the memory of Ramanna and Parvati. If only she could have come here when they were alive, how happy they would have been! They could have walked chatting with each other. She wiped her eyes, thinking that she was a cursed soul. She sat there quietly until Vishwa and Appannaiah came there in the evening and called her.

2

Channigarayaru had become familiar with Sringeri by the time these three reached. He had gathered information about the Mutt, the pantry, the kitchen, the number of halls where meals were served, the number of people who can be accommodated in each hall, the halls in which meals were served first, etc. Besides, he had visited the Narasimhavana on the other side of the river, the Kala Bhairava hillock and other places as soon as he had arrived. Now, during the Navarathri season, when thousands and thousands of pilgrims visited Sringeri, it was difficult even for VIPs to get separate rooms. So how could Channigarayaru get one? When he begged and beseeched the manager though, he got a place beneath the steps of the upper storey. Though there would be the 'thud, thud' sound of people climbing up and climbing down, at least he could get that much space. Besides, he could have put his bundle there without any fear as the watchman of the choultry would be nearby.

Nanjamma and party reached Sringeri at nine in the morning, and she soon saw her husband. They also kept their luggage with that of Channigarayaru's in the choultry and went near the Mutt. Nanjamma bathed in the river, washed the clothes, dried them in the sun and visited all the temples. As it was late for Kumkumarchana, she decided to get it done the next morning. After lunch at noon, all three set out for Narasimhavana in a boat. Channigarayaru too joined them. Vishwa browbeat his father: 'You came alone on a bus, leaving us to walk. You don't come with us anywhere in future.' Appannaiah too joined Vishwa and said the same thing; Nanjamma chastised them: 'No, none of you will speak even a single word. See, Vishwa, you won't be called a clever boy if you speak like this.'

Oh, how many roses were there in Narasimhavana! Till now she had not even imagined such abundance of roses. It was learnt that devotees pluck them and offer the roses to Goddess Sharadammanavaru. Anybody could pluck them and take them to the temple. Vishwa ran, plucked two flowers, not minding the thorn that pierced his fingers, and said, 'Amma, you put these in your hair.' She took them and said, 'No, child, it is for the goddess. We should not put them in our hair.' At once, she remembered her daughter. Parvati had thick, long hair. If combed and braided, it used to be so thick that it would be affected by the evil eye. During the season of Suragi flowers, Ramanna would go before daybreak and bring a bag full of those blossoming buds. Parvati would weave them into a thick garland. After she attained puberty, one day when Nanjamma braided her hair, she set the garland of Suragi flowers on it and how beautiful the girl had looked! One day, Ramanna had brought two roses from his school compound. Parvati had looked lovely when she had stuck them in her hair. The brother and sister had heartfelt love for each other.

Though Nanjamma's heart withered looking at the roses, she walked with Vishwa and the others to all the places. Channigarayaru explained about the cave where the senior Swamiji was performing tapasya, the Bhairava Hillock and all the other places. While returning, Nanjamma plucked roses, put them into a wet towel and offered them at the shrine of Sharadammanavaru.

The next morning, they started a little earlier for Kumkumarchane. Until the poojas were over, Vishwa also had to keep a fast. It was already half past seven in the morning. Channigarayaru returned to the choultry. tied to the edge of his dhoti, he had brought fifteen to twenty bittergourds. Appannaiah asked, 'Hey, why did you bring those here?'

'They are fine. They gave this much only for one and half annas. Hey, you prepare curry of this!' he ordered his wife.

'Are you kidding? We need to start for the temple now.'

'Then, cook it after you return. I have a tiffin carrier with me. I will take the curry in it and eat with the community meal. The rasam and sambar they serve are unpalatable and tasteless without salt and chillies.'

'What do you say? Won't people make fun of you if you take this dish and put it on your leaf, while thousands of people are dining?'

'Hey, who is there to laugh, f... his mother!'

Nanjamma said, 'You have come to a sacred place. Why do you utter such foul language?'

Appannaiah said, 'Where is the oven here? Where should the masala for it be ground and fried? What, brother, should you demand bitter gourd curry here in Shringeri?'

'There is an oven and mortar here. We can also set three bricks for the oven. If we ask the watchman, he will give firewood.'

Vishwa intervened, 'Amma! Don't do it Amma.'

'Hey you born of a slut, how dare you instigate your mother not to do it, you f... your mother...!'

The watchman of the choultry heard this. He warned, 'You should not use such obscene language here. If the manager comes to know about this, he will throw you out of here.' The watchman also said that they should not light an oven there and make the place dirty. Channigarayaru was greatly disappointed. He liked bittergourd curry very much. In Ramasandra, such good bittergourds were not available. Though they were available here, it was useless. He abused, 'Tut-tut, damn that manager' and kept quiet.

Nanjamma felt at peace while the Kumkukarchana was being performed. Till now, she had seen the Goddess Sharadammanavaru only in a photo. She had come here in the afternoon too, but then the idol had not been decorated. Now, so many devotees had observed the vow for Kumkumarchana to be performed. Oh, Ammanavaru shone with great lustre—what dignity on the face! By looking at the face of Kalamma of Ramasandra, one used to get scared. But looking at the face of this Sharadamma, all fear vanished. Vishwa was saved only by the grace of Ammanavaru. She decided to vow to this goddess only, whenever there were hardships, sorrows, diseases and any other troubles. Hereafter, she should not seek the help of any other god. She told Vishwa to prostrate three times. She too circumambulated and prostrated, put the coin of four anna that she had vowed, into the hundi, and took the prasada of kumkum. Appannaiah too circumambulated the deity and prostrated with devotion before Her.

The next day, they finished their morning routine. It was seven in the morning, and they had to go to the river to bathe. *Perhaps Vishwa was outside the choultry?* But he was not there. Channigarayaru said he would go towards the river but it was not known when he would come back, and so, there was no need to wait for him. While Nanjamma and Appannaiah were worrying about the boy vanishing amidst such a big crowd, Vishwa came crying and pulling the edge of his mother's saree, and said, 'Come, get me dosas too.'

'Wait, child, I'll bathe and afterwards give you parched flour and jaggery.'

'No, Appa is eating dosa! Get me dosa also,' he insisted.

Appannaiah asked Vishwa, 'Where had you been?'

'Appa was going alone to the hotel. He sat and ordered two dosas. Then he looked at me, asked, "Why did you come here?" I said, "If you don't get me a dosa, I won't keep quiet."

He said, "No, I don't have money. Go and get parched flour and jaggery from your mother and eat it." I asked the waiter of the hotel, "Give me dosa too." Then Appa told the waiter, "See, I don't know this boy. He is asking for dosa; you don't ask me for money afterwards!" Then the hotel people scolded me and sent me away.'

Appannaiah said, 'See, he comes here to eat a share of rice flakes and parched flour also. Then stealthily eats in the hotel. Do you see the greed of that son of a thieving slut?'

'Let him do whatever he wants, but you don't say a word. Take the child and get him dosas for an anna.'

The mother gave an anna and the uncle got a dosa for the boy. Then all three went to the river for bathing. Vishwa was desirous of bathing where there were fish. Neither his mother nor he had seen such big fishes. Appannaiah said he had seen such big fishes in Ramanathapura. Vishwa was not satisfied looking at the shoal of fish rushing to the surface if one threw some snacks like parched rice or rice flakes. He threw all the rice flakes in his pocket towards the shoal of the fish.

Nanjamma went a little further up from the bathing ghat near the trees, bathed herself and washed the clothes. Then Appannaiah got down into the river with Vishwa. But Vishwa, as if by magic, had hoodwinked both of them, and was swimming in the river. Within two minutes, however, caught by the current, he was going down. As he knew swimming, he was not getting drowned. Nanjamma shouted as if choking on her own breath, 'Oh my child is drowning! Someone save him!' The next moment, Appannaiah plunged into the river and rushed towards the child. But by then, Vishwa had gone too far. Appannaiah constantly hurried with his strokes and went further; Vishwa too was beating his hands on the water. Appannaiah held him and they reached the bank. Nanjamma felt as if she had got back her life. She ran on the bank and reached the place where they were coming out of the water. By then, several people had gathered around.

After reaching the river bank, Vishwa said, 'Amma, if it is a tank, we can swim how much ever we wish. But in the river, it pulls us away somewhere else from here.'

Nanjamma got extremely angry. She held Vishwa and thrashed him. But Vishwa defended himself, 'I felt like swimming and plunged into the river.'

Someone nearby said: 'If you had gone lower still, you would have been caught in the whirlpool.'

They stayed for six days in Sringeri. Every day, they would witness the kumkumarchana rituals in the morning till Mahaswamiji ascended the throne in the night. The day after Chandihoma,[27] they started for their home. Appannaiah told his sister-in-law, 'Calculate the money that remains. If there is enough for the train fare to Tiptur, you and Vishwa may go by bus day after tomorrow. I'll start today itself and go to Narasimharajapura on foot.' They could have done so. However, if three rupees were spent for the bus fare, there would be nothing left if Vishwa asked for anything on the way. Besides, Nanjamma wondered if she would ever get to see such a dense forest again! She had become deeply attached to that forest. Though his legs ached, Vishwa was not a boy scared of walking. So all three set out walking. Appannaiah carried the bundle. Nanjamma rolled the three copies of Sharadammanavara's photo and held it in her hand.

On the way back, Nanjamma's felt pleased. She often felt that perhaps it was God's will that both her children should die. Who could avert the will of God? Vishwa was pulled away by the river, but was saved. It seemed he was destined for a peril, but it was averted. She thought, after reaching home, she must send for her father, give him Vishwa's horoscope and ask him to predict his future correctly. Appannaiah was very morose. Even in Sringeri, he had been dull and silent, as if he was immersed in some thought. He had never stayed in the company of his sister-in-law continuously. He was used to being with his mother, wandering off to different places and begging. Nanjamma too kept quiet, thinking that he was quiet out of shyness.

They reached Narasimharajapura, cooked rice, brought sambar from the hotel and finished lunch. By then, it was one in the afternoon and it had been two days since they had left Sringeri. The food that remained was kept tied in the vessel. Meanwhile, Channigarayaru got down from the bus. Vishwa burst out as soon as he saw his Appa's face: 'Amma, you should not give this food to him. Why did he eat dosas alone, without giving to me?' Nanjamma was anxious lest anybody hear those words. There was still time for the train. Channigarayaru did not ask for food from these people. There would be food at the station hotel.

All the four slept at Tarikere station in the night. The next morning, Nanjamma cooked rice at nine, before the train arrived. Appannaiah brought sambar. Channigarayaru did not eat with them even now.

---

[27]A fire ritual in the name of Goddess Chandi.

Appannaiah was even more dull that morning. Even after boarding the train, he sat gloomily. He did not chew tobacco though his brother offered some to him. After they changed in Birur, some kind of worry was written all over his face. Nanjamma wanted to speak with him and know the reason. But she kept quiet, thinking she should not ask him in front of her husband. Other passengers said the train would stop for a long time in Kadur station to fill up water. Channigarayaru got down in search of vadas and bondas. Appannaiah asked his sister-in-law, 'Do you have enough bus fare for you and Vishwa to travel from Tiptur?'

'Why?'

'You go. I will go to Nuggikere and then return home.'

Though unexpected, Nanjamma felt happy with what he said. So many years had passed since he had beaten his wife brutally and taken away her mangalya. If he goes now, would she speak to him? Appannaiah had behaved like that upon his mother's suggestion.

It was when Nanjamma was thinking that it would be good if the family unite at least now, that Appannaiah said, 'I feel like seeing the children.'

Nanjamma counted the money. There were two rupees and two and half annas. Twelve annas were enough to cover the bus fare of both Vishwa and herself. She gave a rupee to Appannaiah and said, 'Go and meet them. Jayalakshmi is now of marriageable age. Being a father, if you don't care for the children, who will look after them? Please go and find whether Ramakrishna is attending school or making rounds for donations in the villages.'

Appannaiah untied the gunny bag and was taking out his shirt and dhotis. In the meantime, Channigarayaru returned and asked him, 'Where are you going?' Without a second thought, Appannaiah blurted out, 'To Nuggikere.' Immediately Channigaraya asked, 'Hey, you spoiled Rama[28], will you set out to see that deserted wife of yours?' By then the train had started. Appannaiah did not respond and quickly got down from the train.

By three in the afternoon, they reached Tiptur; by six in the evening,

---

[28]'Spoiled Rama' is a form of ridicule that people in rural areas used to describe people who went in search of their wives who had left them. This is in reference to Lord Rama of Ramayana, who fought with Ravana to bring back Sita.

they were back home. There was a little rice for the night and Nanjamma did not cook again. She went directly to the master's house to give Sharadammanavaru's prasada and her photo.

It was difficult for Nanjamma to maintain the peace of mind that she had experienced in Sringeri. Gangamma came to know from Channigarayaru about Appannaiah's decision to go to his wife's place. The next afternoon, she came to Nanjamma's house, stood in the street, showered the choicest of abuses for two hours: 'Are you a *madam!*[29] Did you send him off to arrange their nuptials again?' Nanjamma did not open her mouth. When Vishwa set out to give his grandmother an earful, she pulled him inside and made him sit quietly. Having completed her sahasranama[30], one question kept haunting her mind, following her mother-in-law's departure: '*We live on our own without troubling anybody. Yet why does God make these things happen? Though I don't want to, why does she come and quarrel?* She did not get an apt answer even from Madevayyanavaru. He uttered faithfully, 'Shiva does so, to test us.' *But what sort of a test was this? Why should Shiva put one to such tests?* Nanjamma questioned herself.

After four or five days, when Sarvakka came over, she asked, 'Nanjammare, your grandmother had given Parvatamma a golden chrysanthemum flower, didn't she? What did you do with it?'

Nanjamma did not remember it. She tried to recall if she might have put it with the jewels of Parvati given to Sooryanarayana when he had come. But, as far as she could remember, she had not put it with those jewels. Now she would have to search at home. But she neither wanted to search for it nor see anything related to her daughter. She had also given away Ramanna's clothes to the son of Mariya, an outcast.

'I don't know…Why do you ask, Sarvakka?'

'See, before you left for Sringeri, your husband sold it to Kashimbaddi for fifty rupees.'

'Who told you?'

'Shivegowda's daughter. She said, "It is antique, and of pure gold," and now she is wearing it.'

Nanjamma remembered her husband's pilgrimage to Sringeri. Her

---

[29]Here, Gangamma refers to her daughter-in-law as a female pimp.
[30]Chanting one thousand names of the Lord.

mind boiled with anger. But within two minutes, she reassured herself. She thought what had happened had already happened. What use was there by abusing him now? Nobody could rectify his nature. 'Forget it, Sarvakka. Let me not think about it. If it had been at home, I could not have glanced at it without sorrow,' Nanjamma said and closed the topic.

3

Appannaiah's mind was filled with all sorts of thoughts while going to Nuggikere, which was nine miles from Kadur. *How would the children look now? Would she speak to me? If she says, A man must be there to support the running of a house; you also stay here so that you too can bring gifts and donations from villages; what should he do? She was pregnant when she had left Ramasandra. Would she have given birth to a boy or a girl?* Along with these thoughts, a sort of fear also engulfed his mind. *If she says, 'Why did you come here, get out,' what should he do?* He thought, *Shall I go back now itself?* Nevertheless, he decided that now that he had come here, he must go and see them. By the time he reached Nuggikere, it was six in the evening. When he enquired about them, he came to know that it had been more than three or four years since they had left that place. They were staying in Kadur, as it was difficult to earn a livelihood in Nuggikere. Their house was behind Gangadharappa's shop in the market street.

'What do they do for a livelihood there?' he asked.

'How do we know? How are you related to them?' the person laughed and asked.

Appannaiah would not have liked to disclose his identity: So, without questioning further, he started from there for Vaddarahalli, which that was on the other side of the tank bund. He said he was a stranger, begged for millet flour, made rotis, ate that, spent the night sleeping there, ate the remaining rotis in the morning and headed towards Kadur.

Kadur was not unknown to him. He had visited that town earlier. About ten in the morning, he reached there and enquired at the shop of Gangadharappa on the market street. Beside the shop, there was a small lane. If you went inside that lane, there was a small Mangalore-tiled house behind the shop. Appannaiah stood doubting whether this house, with the festoon of glass beads, was really the house of his people. Then a girl came out of that house—a girl of about fourteen or fifteen years. She had books in her hand and was wearing a glittering saree. As soon as he saw her with a powdered face, he recognized her in a minute: she was Jayalakshmi, his eldest daughter.

'Hey, is this your house?' When he asked her, the girl seemed not to recognize him and questioned, 'Who are you?'

'Oh, didn't you recognize me at all? Am I not your Appa?'

'Of which place?' she said and went inside.

He thought: '*Huh, tut-tut her mother...*' and entered the house. *Oh! What splendour inside!* Chairs with cushions, photos on walls and a radio on the table as would be seen in hotels. His wife sat in a chair wearing a silk saree, with braided hair and a powdered face. Oh, how beautiful she was! There was a girl of around two years on her lap. In a big chair nearby, there sat comfortably a dignified man who was smoking a cigarette. Oh, shining rings on his fingers, a gold chain around the neck, a gold watch...

Appannaiah asked: 'Is this the house? I went over to Nuggikere and came here.'

For a moment, Saathu, as if bewildered, became colourless seeing him. But before he could open his mouth to speak, she said: 'Who are you? Why have you come here?'

'Hey, you, do you ask me "who are you"?'

'Send him out of the house,' she said and went away to the room beside.

'Hey you, who are you?' the very manner in which that man questioned him, Appannaiah got scared. Without stopping there, he returned at once, running fast as if dogs were chasing him. He ran and ran without bothering in which direction he was running, got tired and began walking, taking long strides. After a while, at a distance, he saw a town. He asked someone which town or village it was. They answered, 'Birur.' He walked speedily and reached there. Somebody told him that the train for Tiptur would be arriving shortly. He reached the station, took a ticket and boarded the train. *Oh! Should that damned train come again to Kadur and halt there*? He was afraid of those Kadur people who might come in search of him, and sat curled up, closing the window to his side. Until he reached Tiptur, he felt scared. He got down at the station, ate dosas for the five annas he had with him and then he started wondering—'Who might that fellow be?' The answer came to him without much difficulty. *Yes, this slut of an ass has kept that bastard.* His mind became eager to go back and beat her with a broom. But he felt afraid even to turn his step back towards that direction.

He did not stop anywhere, reached home—the Hanumantharaya temple—at ten in the night and knocked on the door. He said, 'It is me.' His mother opened the door. After the kerosene bottle lamp was lit, he entered the house and sat. She enquired, 'Tut-tut, ah, had you gone again in search of that whore? Did she say she won't allow you into her bedroom?'

Appannaiah did not say anything. His mother continued her tirade— 'You shameless bastard, don't you feel ashamed? Telling lies about the pilgrimage to Sringeri; had you gone to commit adultery with her? And now you have come and are sitting in God's temple. I'll send for Annajois in the morning and tell him to excommunicate you. Fie, you spoilt Rama who went to join his leftout wife!'

Appannaiah got very angry and shouted, 'Will you shut your mouth or not, Amma?'

'Why should I shut my mouth, you shameless fellow? You went nosing around the reeking gutter of urine. You, born of a bitch...!'

Listening to his mother's abuse, Appannaiah got so angry that he felt his body burning. Again he screamed, 'Will you shut your mouth or not?' Gangamma began abusing even more loudly. Appannaiah saw a toddy palm broom before him; he got up, took it and thrashed his mother's face, shoulders, back, arms and body twenty or thirty times repeatedly with it.

'Ayyayyappo...he is killing me!' To her loud cry, seven or eight people woke up and arrived at the temple. Gangamma herself called Annajois. Ayyashaastri came too.

Ayyashaastri exclaimed, 'Ayyo, ayyo, is there a greater sin than thrashing the mother with a broom?'

Annajois gave his verdict, 'You should give a fine of one hundred rupees and go through the rites of atonement!'

Appannaiah shouted, 'Hey, you too get lost; you cannot pluck even a single hair from me!'

How could such a person be kept in the temple? That very moment, they excommunicated him and expelled him from the temple. Annajois argued, 'He must leave this village!' But Appannaiah was adamant and browbeat the Jois, 'Hey, Joisa, this is not a village gifted to your father as jagir and this land does not belong to him!' Till then, nobody had seen Appannaiah acquire such tremendous courage; everybody was stunned. He collected his clothes and left. His mother was cursing, 'Let worms pour out of his hands.'

Appannaiah felt like going to his sister-in-law's house. However, he did not go there, for what should he say if she enquired about Nuggikere? He walked noiselessly, reached the platform of Madevayyanavar's shrine and spent the night sleeping there. He was not in the village for a month.

Nanjamma came to know about the incident of the previous night. She got extremely angry at her husband who had broken the news of Appannaiah's visit to Nuggikere to his mother. But there was no use of asking her husband. And, that Gangamma was roaming around the village abusing to her heart's content, not only her son Appannaiah but Nanjamma also. But Nanjamma did not open her mouth. She instructed Vishwa not to talk back to his grandmother if he met her on the street and if she said anything.

A month passed. One day, Appannaiah came to his sister-in-law's house. Channigarayaru was not at home. Appannaiah said, 'What if I do not have this harlot slut's company? Can't I earn a livelihood? I have wandered the villages around Hiresave and piled up one and a half quintals of ragi, cowpeas, and chillies. You had taken from me twenty rupees. Please give it back. I will buy a few vessels.'

'Where will you stay?'

'Is there not a room on the platform of the cowshed of Kurubarahatti Beeregowda? I asked him. Beeregowda told me, "Oh by all means, you may stay like a king, cooking and eating there".'

Within three days, Nanjamma arranged for the money and handed him. Appannaiah went to the Kambanakere fair, bought an aluminium basin, plate, vessel, glass, a ladle, a pot for cooking ragi balls and a mat to sleep on. When he was in the village, he used to make ragi balls. Rarely would he prepare sambar. He would come to his sister-in-law's house, take sambar enough for both the times. Somedays, he used to have his full meals with his sister-in-law.

Gangamma told the Jois to excommunicate Nanjamma for she was admitting Appannaiah to her home. But she was the one who was writing the government food accounts. Besides, she had performed the pilgrimage of Sringeri. Both the Jois were now scared of her. Neither of them had even set foot towards Sringeri.

One day, Nanjamma asked Appannaiah, 'What did those people at Nuggikere say?'

'Fie, those sluts were not in that village!'

'Did not anyone tell you where they had gone?'

'What should they say! That slut of an outcast, pariah, has kept a Sahukara—a rich man—in Kadur,' Appannaiah said and explained in detail what he had seen and experienced.

Nanjamma's heart as if withered hearing that. Both the women had entered that family as daughters-in-law. Both these brothers did not treat their wives with discretion. How could they, who knew not how to live wisely, make their wives live like that? Anyway, the younger brother was better than the elder. If you spoke good words with affection, he listened to you. He worked hard. Nanjamma thought if Saathu had good sense, perhaps these things would not have happened. But everyone was not endowed with the same amount of strength to bear hardships. It was not possible to tolerate this sort of mother-in-law and the foul language of such a husband. Obeying the words of his mother, Appannaiah had set fire to the hut he himself had built, burnt it into ashes, and plucked away his wife's tali. Yet, the other daughter-in-law of this family should not have behaved like she did. She asked Appannaiah, 'Have you spoken about this to anybody?'

'No.'

'Please don't tell anyone. Our reputation will be destroyed.'

'Fie! If only I could speak about those sluts with my tongue, I would feel as disgusted as if I ate shit! No, I cannot speak of it.'

'No, not like that. Sometimes when you are angry, you blurt out things and will never remember what should or should not be said. Swear on God and assure me, you won't speak of this to anyone.'

'No, I won't speak of this to anybody. I swear on Sringeri Sharadammanavaru,' Appannaiah touched the photo of Sharadammanavaru on the wall and promised.

CHAPTER 15

1

In these eight years, the government had erected a new Primary School building outside the village. The rent that Shive Gowda used to get for the existing school building until now, stopped completely. There was a large playground attached to the new school and there were dry fields on three sides.

One day, Nanjamma was sewing the account book for the next year's receipts and payments when the master came home and said: 'Nanjammanore, do you know what your Vishwa has done?'

Vishwa must have committed a great mischief if the master has himself come to complain. Nanjamma asked anxiously. Then the master explained: 'There is a playground behind the school, beyond which there is an ant hill. Have you seen it? There was possibly a snake in the fence beside it. You know, before it casts off the slough, a snake is not active. Maybe it was warming itself in the sun. This boy took a stem of coconut leaf, went behind the snake and hit it.'

'Then?' Nanjamma questioned with fear.

'Luckily, the snake did not fall on him. It moved swiftly and rushed into the anthill. I too saw it squeezing itself into it. This boy was chasing the snake. I held him and thrashed him.'

'You should have beaten him and broken his hands!'

'There is no use beating him now. Snakes wait for twelve years to take revenge. Vishwa will attend the same school. What if it waits and takes its revenge someday?'

Nanjamma's heart began thumping. This boy was like this by nature. Courage, oh courage—tremendous courage. Such courage would cause grief to a mother's heart. She asked, 'What can we do now, master?'

'The snake must still be in the anthill. We should send for three or four labourers, dig the ant hill and kill that snake. Don't delay.'

Nanjamma at once got up, locked the house, and sent for the village servant. The village waterman also came with him. Nanjamma sent for Valmiki Sanjeevanayaka who was an expert in killing snakes, told him she would give a rupee to him, and sent him with those two. She too went with them. Vishwa was somersaulting alone in the field. His mother asked, 'Why did you hit the snake?'

He answered, 'Did not Sanjeevanayaka beat the snakes that day in the backyard of Thirumalayya's house? In the same way, I too hit it!'

Sanjeevanayaka held a bamboo staff and spear, and stood in front of the anthill. The village servant and waterman began digging the anthill. The opening at the mouth of the anthill spread to many places. Until the evening, they dug and searched, but they could not catch the snake.

Sanjeevanayaka said, 'Knowing, that we would come now to search the anthill, the snake has gone somewhere. It is not possible to search any more. But he would be waiting to plant his tooth on the boy.'

Nanjamma's anger was uncontrollable. She took the bamboo staff from Nayaka's hand and beat Vishwa four times on his back. He stood weeping. The master consoled her, 'What has happened, has happened. What's the use of beating him now?' Nanjamma held Vishwa's hand and went home. He was the only child she had after two of her children had died. Oh! In what adventurous deeds did he indulge! Swimming alone to the centre of the village tank, plunging into the river and swimming, climbing on to the roof of Maadevayyanavaru's temple and jumping from there, stealthily riding the pony belonging to other people, going alone to pluck the large beehive, and trying to kill a snake alone. Nanjamma would remember her father. Vishwa had been born with the qualities of his grandfather. By God's grace, it would be enough if he did not develop his grandpa's nature. But what could she do now for the danger he had created for himself? Snakes harboured revenge for twelve years. This boy would be attending the same school daily. Nanjamma did not send him to school that day and the next day too. The master came and said, 'It is ok. You are not sending him to school now. But for how long do you think you can keep the boy at home?

That was also a question to ponder upon. After primary school he had to attend the Kambanakere Middle School. Afterwards, he would have to go to Tiptur and study in the high school. If he finished that much, he might get the post of a Shekdar. Without education, he might become like his father or uncle. She did not know what to do. She consulted Maadevayyanavaru. He mulled over the matter the whole day and, then, coming over to Nanjamma's house, said, 'See Avva, now Vishwa is studying in the third standard. You take him to your Annayya's house. Let him finish fourth standard there. After that, he won't come to this primary school. Arrange, somehow, for food in Kambanakere and admit him to middle school. Even if he visits this place during his vacations, it will be sufficient enough reason for him not to go near that school. By that time the boy would be grown up. If for men themselves it will turn out to be difficult to recognize him, how will the snake recognize him?'

'You know, Ayyanore, what sort of a woman my sister-in-law is.'

'What does it matter what she is like? There is grandma in the house. There are no other children. And your Annayya will also take care of the boy.'

Nanjamma, too felt like this was the best course. But the sorrow of having to stay alone at home, separated from her only living child was causing her pain. If he was kept in the village, his death was certain. Her sorrow of being separated from her son was not as great as that fear. During holidays, he could be brought home. She could also go and see her son. Anyway, she decided it was best that Vishwa should stay there for one and a half years.

The next day she gave him an oil bath and ordered the tailor to stitch new shirts and shorts for the boy. She deep-fried snacks like kodubale and chakkuli. Vishwa began beseeching, 'Amma, I will never do such things from now on. Please don't send me anywhere.' Nanjamma wiped his tears and consoled him. She was also shedding tears. She said: 'Look, my child, it's only for one year... Then you may come to Kambanakere. I myself will come there and cook for you. Why did you not stay away; why hit that snake?' She told the cartman to put two sacks of ragi, twenty seers of cowpeas, a measure of castor oil and ten seers of soap-nut powder into the cart. She kept Vishwa's school certificate safely with her and then set out with him in the cart to Nagalapura. Channigarayaru did not accompany them.

Kallesha was really happy to keep his sister's son in his home. Akkamma was excited. She was not capable of drawing water from the well. Yet, she said that she would give oil baths to her great-grandson once a week. Only one person that was stiff was Kallesha's wife, Kamalu. But her behaviour was not unexpected for anybody.

Looking at the grocery Nanjamma had brought with her, Kallesha said: 'Why did you bring all this? Don't I have this much of food in my house? Carry all of it back.'

'No, Annayya, I did not bring this as the expense for his food. He is also like your son. I had these at home and brought them along. There are milch cows in your house. There would be no dearth of milk or ghee. You need not do anything. He is very mischievous. He had not the fear of a father in our place. Women cannot control such boys. Don't hesitate to punish him. Drive home some sense into him by giving him a spanking now and then, and keep him in fear. He is clever in his studies. I was coaching him at home. If possible, you teach him. If not, arrange for private tuition. I will send a rupee every month.'

Kallesha could not say anything else. He, along with Akkamma, insisted: 'Stay here for four or five days more.' But Nanjamma had her work of revenue accounts in her place. She started the next day by the same cart.

Vishwa was crying: 'Amma, I too will come with you.' The mother too felt like crying. Wiping her tears, she climbed the cart.

She could not meet her father, Kantijois. She learnt that it had been three months since he had left home.

2

Nanjamma found it hard to spend time after she left Vishwa in Nagalapura. No doubt, there were the usual domestic chores. But the house wore a deserted look. The memory of Parvati and Ramanna began haunting her. Both the children had fallen ill and died one by one in this same hall where she wrote the accounts, sifted through and ground ragi, and spoke with visitors. She did not feel like staying in that house. But where else could she go? At this juncture, she remembered: *it was more or less thirteen years since she had come to this house. This house of Gundegowdaru had become almost her own.* Gundegowdaru did not need it for his use. Yet, a desire of having her own house in this village arose in her mind.

Another thought too occurred: *Why should she need a new house?* She did not want Vishwa to be in this place when he grew up. He should become a Shekdar; if not, he should at least be a middle-school master. He should not stay here. She would go with her son, wherever he would stay. However, there must be a nest, a home in one's native place. There must be a place to come and stay for a few days during vacation. In that context, there was a site for sale. Cheluvashetty of the Ganiga caste got a good property in the village in which his wife lived. So, he had decided to part with his property in this village and shift to his wife's place. Nanjamma agreed that she would write all the sale deeds. That meant, she would prepare the content, while the handwriting would be Channigarayaru's. The buyers of the land need not give anything to her for writing the deed. But the area of the site must be included in the total purchase. Cheluvashetty had to write this portion off in Nanjamma's name. It was enough if she gave fifty rupees. Everything happened accordingly. As she was well aware of the law, Nanjamma made Cheluvashetty write the site off to only her. She arranged that fifty rupees to be given by the other purchasers of the land, by writing receipts of their revenue taxes. The site was convenient to have a platform of two squares, a hall of three squares inside, a kitchen of one square, another room for storing ragi and other grains, and a room for her son to be with his wife after his marriage. In the backyard, a small hut for two cows could also be managed. In the remaining area, she could grow vegetables. At least one and a half thousand rupees could be estimated to cover these requirements, with country tiles for roofing.

Even now, she had the accounts of grains. After the grain accounts, not only farmers of Kurubarahalli but also those of Ramasandra and Lingapura had started giving a fixed measure of ragi per house to the Shanubhoga. Nanjamma did not have expenses at home as before. If she cooked once, it would be sufficient for two times a day. She could sell the ragi collected. Now the cost of ragi was raised to ninety rupees per quintal. Besides, the annual salary of the Shanubhoga for two years would be five hundred rupees. Moreover, if she asked the Kurubarahalli people to pay next year's now itself, they would oblige.

During the same time, one day, the master came to her house and said: 'See, now the Government has appointed an Adult Education Committee. There is a government order that all men and women must become literate, persons who have crossed eighteen should be taught to read and write during the night, from seven to nine. These are called night schools. I have been appointed as a teacher to the Men's Night School in this village. Apart from my salary, I get twenty-five rupees per month. Our inspector asked me whether there was an educated lady in our village. I have put across your name.'

'Can I manage that, master?'

'Oh what's this, why do you speak like this? It is eight months' work. You should start one group after the other. It is enough if they learn 'A Aa, E Ee' and other letters and can read the second standard book. Thereafter, they should keep practising by reading newspapers and other kind of writings. You will get twenty-five rupees per month. Your class will be only for women.'

'Who would like to learn the alphabet or to read, that too in this village?'

'The Government supplies slates, books, pencils, even soft-stone pencils[31] to write on slates. Money for the lamp you burn will also be given. Along with these, a blackboard and pieces of chalk, too, will be supplied. You run the school in your house. If you collect seven or eight women first, others may come later. I will send my wife also.'

Nanjamma did not accept this. But the Shekdar himself visited her and asked her to do the same. She finally agreed. The headmaster of Kambanakere middle school was the supervisor of the programme. He harnessed a cart and loaded slates, books, a blackboard, a lantern and other things and handed those over to Nanjamma. The master's wife knew the Kannada alphabet and still the master admitted her to the night school. Nanjamma was surprised when Sarvakka came on her own and joined the school. Though her husband had stopped her, she had not heeded his objection. Four women from the Lingayat group, two from the weavers' group, two from the Shepherd's Street and other women came. There were fourteen of them in all. It was a new experience for Nanjamma to write 'A Aa, E Ee' on the blackboard and teach the women.

Some learnt, some did not. But Nanjamma had never known that Sarvakka was so clever. She learnt eight letters in one day. Within eight days, she learnt fifty-two alphabets and could read simple words by joining letters.

She said, 'Nanjammare, if you had taught this to me earlier, I would have learnt and could have written accounts like you.'

'Where do all such people get the post of Shanubhoga to write

---

[31]Thin chalk pieces made out of soapstones.

accounts, Sarvakka?'

'Yes, that's also true.'

Nanjamma had domestic chores and the task of writing accounts. Some days, during the late afternoons, Maadevayyanavaru would come and chat. Night classes ran until half past eight or nine in the night. Then when she would go to bed, she would be asleep in no time. That was one advantage of this hard, constant work. While she taught, she remembered Vishwa. *How would he be now?* Perhaps he cried remembering his mother. However, there was nothing to worry until Akkamma was there. She would never hurt him.

The night classes ran for two or three months. Six women left and only eight continued to attend the class. The master had told her: 'Even if they leave the classes you put "present" against everyone's names in the attendance register.' The master's school for men was better than this. Among twenty-five who had joined the school, twenty attended it without fail.

One day, Channigarayaru was not home and the master came and was informing Nanjamma about his night school: 'See, even though they are grown-ups, they do not remember the alphabet despite teaching them for four days. Their minds will be elsewhere. Though I object to their smoking beedi inside the school, they won't listen. God only knows how these people will become literate.'

'Master, I will tell Appannaiah, when he comes tomorrow to take sambar, that you will admit him, too, to your night school. You teach him something even during the day, when he stays in the village. If he had at least a little education, his condition would not have been so bad.'

'Oh, Appannaiah is attending a different night school,' the master said and laughed.

'What are you saying?'

'It seems now he and Narasi are friends.' Nanjamma could not believe this. What money did Appannaiah have? Or was he a dandy? He was a poor Brahmin who brought ragi by being a mendicant, cooking ragi balls for food. Moreover, he was not the kind to be looking at women.'

Nanjamma said what she felt, 'Perhaps this is false news, master.'

'No, it is real. Now, there is nobody to interfere in her life. She doesn't have any problem as far as money is concerned. Who is there to give company to Appannaiah? Wife? Children? Mother? He begs here and there, cooks and eats. God only knows how this relationship developed.'

Somehow, Nanjamma felt ashamed. After all, Appannaiah was part of her own family; he was her brother-in-law. It must be his fate to beg and get his livelihood. But after so many years, why should this prarabdha stick to him? She had been thinking since a few days: *Let him stay at my home, have food and not go a begging. If he could take care of the two cows at home, it would be enough.* But if she suggested this, her mother-in-law Gangamma would begin quarrelling. She may start spreading scandals too. Besides, Appannaiah's mind too was not always steady. If he did not go for mendicancy, he might get irritated. This was his fate perhaps, Nanjamma thought and kept quiet. But she could not control her unhappiness.

For four days, she pondered over the matter—whether she should advise Appannaiah regarding this matter. At last, she could not contain itself. One an afternoon when he came with a vessel for sambar, Channigararayaru was not at home. She asked him, 'Appannaiah, I will ask you about a thing. Don't get me wrong.'

'What is it? Ask me...'

'See, people have no control over their tongues. They gossip about all sorts of things if you go to Narasamma's shop just to buy tobacco. Can't you buy tobacco in any other shop? Why should you be the fodder to people's tongues without any basis?'

'Let his mother be f...! Who was the fellow that said it?'

'Be that anybody. Isn't it good if we are careful?'

Appannaiah did not speak again. He took the sambar and left. The next day, he did not come to take sambar. Nanjamma used to prepare more every day. For eight days, it was wasted. Then she started cooking less. She felt guilty: *Why did she have to ask Appannaiah about that? Perhaps he had not come out of anger against her or he might have been embarrassed. Anyway, he was alone and it was difficult for a man to cook sambar along with ragi balls!* She decided it was his karma. Just when she thought of letting him do whatever he wanted, she came to know that he was not in the village. He had not returned to his place for three months since he had left it.

It was learnt that he had gone alone to the region where lands were irrigated by channels. On his return, he brought a quintal of paddy for his sister-in-law. Thereafter, he started to take sambar daily.

S.L. BHYRAPPA

Another day, the master said: 'It seems like Appannaiah does not go to Narasi's shop anymore. After he returned from the irrigated regions, he doesn't even walk before her shop.'

3

Within himself, Vishwa was very scared of his maternal uncle. Kallesha did not neglect the boy. He would bring parched rice, kharashev and sweet candies from the weekly fairs for him and take the boy with him to the fields. The boy would sweat at the very manner his uncle would chastise him and roll his eyes. One day, Vishwa quarrelled with a boy in the school. When Kallesha came to know about this, he slapped him so hard on the cheek that he fell down half-swooning, and relieved himself in his shorts. Akkamma scolded Kallesha, raised the child, sat near him and consoled Vishwa.

Kamalu had the least amount of sympathy towards Vishwa. She would always find fault with him, whether he sat, stood or spoke. But she would not abuse him or beat him because of her fear of her husband and Akkamma. She would always be grumbling and abusing to herself: 'Tut-tut, this damned brat has come to devour grub in our house!'

Now, the boy was not as smart and lively as he had been before. Even in studies, he was not considered intelligent as he was in his previous school. Kallesha imposed extra discipline on him, thinking, *he has become a dullard because of lack of disciplining.*

Yet, day by day, Vishwa was actually becoming a dullard. When Kallesha sat to teach him, his eyes would be open like that of the goat on the butchery slab, and with the edge of his eyes, he would concentrate his attention on the hand of his uncle, anxious with fear, anticipating that that iron hand may fall on him any moment. Akkamma was illiterate. However, Kallesha had all the satisfaction of keeping his nephew under control.

The tank of Nagalapura was bigger than that of Ramasandra. In the village part of the tank, there were many rocks in the middle. Vishwa had an indomitable desire to plunge into the water, swim towards those rocks, sit on them until he was dried up, warming himself in the sun, and again plunge into the water. But his uncle had strictly ordered the boy not to step into the water. Vishwa would cry and shed tears remembering it. He could not pluck the beehive in this place and he was not allowed to climb the trees. Sometimes, he thought of running away to Ramasandra. But he was afraid that his mother would bring him back and assign him to the control of his uncle. He scolded his mother in his mind.

One morning, he was going to school, holding a slate and a book. Several boys and grown-ups were moving in groups in the direction of his school. The person in front of the group donned a white shirt and white cap. There was a flag in his hand. The man holding the flag would put something in his mouth and shout, 'Bolo Bharat Mata ki'. The people behind him would shout simultaneously, 'Jai'. That man would shout 'Mahatma Gandhi ki', and the people cried, 'Jai', just like one shouted 'Hara Hara Mahadeva' while the chariot of God was pulled at the festival. Vishwa thought it was so amusing. Hearing it four times, he learnt whatever the person in the front was saying loudly. As soon as the person in the front stopped, Vishwa shouted, 'Bolo Bharat Mata ki'. Everyone said, 'Jai.' He shouted the other 'Ki's also. People cried 'Jai' to every 'Ki'. The person in the front patted his back and said, 'You are a clever boy. Come, you yourself shout out these lines. Come, take this flag.' He put the flag in Vishwa's hand, and he held that 'something' before his mouth. *Oh, he was the leader of all. He felt merry! Oh! It was so joyous!*

The crowd moved near his school. Everybody sat in the field in front of the school. The man who had given the flag to Vishwa stood up. Another one held that 'something' before his mouth, took a wire from it, put the wide bugle-like-something on the nearby table. He began speaking: 'Brothers and sisters, now our country is in the hands of red monkeys. They are looting our gold and silver. All of us must be ready to free our mother. Now we are all soldiers prepared to fight...'

Oh! What he said came across in a loud volume. It was called a loudspeaker. Two or three more people spoke. At last, that person said: 'Today is Saturday. In the afternoon, the fair gathers in Channarayapatna. There will be a huge meeting. All of you must come there and display your patriotism.' Many people started with him. Vishwa, too, desired to go with them. He went near the person who had given him the flag and asked, 'May I too come with you, sir?'

He asked, 'Can you walk for eight miles, child?'

'Oh yes, I have walked to Sringeri itself.'

Well, the group started. He too set out with them. On the way, they came across a sand pit, toddy palm groves, banyan groves, spinney shrubs and many other places. Vishwa felt that there was no forest such as the one he had encountered on the way to Sringeri; yet, this one was very jolly. By one in the afternoon, they reached Channarayapatna. By then, Vishwa was hungry and tired. He asked the man, 'I feel hungry, sir.' He held Vishwa's hand and took him, saying, 'Everyone is given food; come.' Food was cooked on a large scale in big vessels, and was served as in the samaaradhana of Sringeri. Then, everyone went to the field where the fair was. There were people, people, people. Vishwa had not seen so many people in Sringeri or even in the 'Ammana jaatre' in Ramasandra. No, not even in the fair of Nagalapura. In the centre of the field, a platform as high as two men had been erected and a loudspeaker had been placed on it.

The person who had given Vishwa the flag and brought him here was a native of Holenarasipura. He asked Vishwa, 'Child, would you also like to give a speech?'

'What does that mean, sir?'

'Didn't I speak in Nagalapura, standing on that platform? That's what giving a speech means.'

'Oh, yes, I would like to.'

'Then I'll teach you what you need to say.'

'I remember everything that you said there. I'll repeat the same thing: "Those red monkeys have kept our Mother in jail."'

'Yes, right. I will teach you some other matter also, wait,' he said and then instructed Vishwa regarding what to say and how he should say it.

Before the meeting started, a person climbed on the platform, stood before the loudspeaker and said very effectively 'Vande Mataram'. Then he announced, 'Now, a young son of Bharat Mata will speak. We should all be inspired by his speech.' He stood aside. The Holenarasipura man hoisted Vishwa on to the platform. He too climbed on it and made Vishwa stand before the mike. Vishwa saw the people in front of him. They had thronged the field and were streaming out as if water from the tank was overflowing. He felt fear and his face reddened. The man who came with him told him in a low voice, 'Say, "Bolo Bharat Maata ki".' Vishwa shouted it. *Hah, oh, how loudly his voice was heard! How did they make this loudspeaker? What do they keep inside it? Yes, he too should keep such a thing with him.* While he was still thinking, the people assembled there shouted *'Jai.'* The sound was akin to a roar when it came out of the loudspeaker. Every *'Jai'* was preceded by a *'ki.'* And he knew many words having the *'ki.'* The man from Holenarasipura said, 'You can speak now.' He began immediately as if he had dived into a tank full of water.

'Brothers and sisters, you all know this: They have put handcuffs and shackles around the hands and legs of our Bharat Mata. They have chained her. Now we're all slaves. These red apes, these bastards, are looting our revenues in the form of taxes. None of you should pay them taxes. They encourage us to drink toddy.'

Vishwa spoke in a continuous barrage, liberally peppering his speech with 'bastards,' 'widow-sons,' and other choice obscenities that flashed to him on the spot. But he had been taught that it wasn't good manners to use obscenities like 'fuck your mother/father.' As soon as his speech was over, the man standing beside him put a garland of chrysanthemums around his neck and shouted, 'Bharat Mata ki,' and the crowd responded with 'Jai,' applauding non-stop. After Vishwa was brought down, another person climbed the platform and began speaking. He praised Vishwa profusely. He said some words which Vishwa couldn't follow even one bit.

'All of us must take inspiration from this brave boy. You must protest against these foreigners like how this boy has done, like a lion cub. None of you should pay tax this year. If the policemen come, just recall this boy and you will get courage...'

Meanwhile, people got up and began scattering. Several policemen clad in khaki uniforms arrived with lathis that looked like long bamboo staffs. They surrounded all those who wore white caps and seized the loudspeaker. There were some words between the police and them. At last, the police took away all of them in the van to the police station. Vishwa too was one among them. They crammed these people into a big room, shut the iron door and locked it. People inside the lockup were shouting 'Bharat Maata ki jai'. Some chattered about several things. Some others were speaking in English. Vishwa did not know anybody there. The man who had brought him and taught him how to speak, was not there. Vishwa began sobbing violently. People near him stroked his back and consoled, 'Hey, don't be frightened, child. Are we not here? You are a clever boy.' He stopped crying but remained scared.

However, whatever had happened since that morning was very thrilling and amusing. But why have they locked all of these people here without food? Is that what jail meant?

He asked: 'Is it what jail means?'

One of them answered: 'No child, this is the palace.'

'If so, where is the royal throne?'

'Oh, a tremendous boy!' all said among themselves. But nobody answered his question.

Meanwhile, the police came, held Vishwa's hand and called, 'Come out.'

The rest of them stood up: 'No, we won't allow him to go out with you. You will beat him.'

'Why would we beat such a small boy? His guardians have come,' they said, held Vishwa's hand, took him out and locked the rest of them. After he was taken to the office, a stout policeman, who sat on the chair questioned him, 'Where do you come from, boy?'

'Ramasandra.'

'Ramasandra? Where is it?' he asked the other policeman who stood there.

Then Vishwa himself answered, 'Ramasandra of Kambanakere Hobli, Tiptur Taluk, Tumkur District.'

'Oh good, you know everything. Which class are you in?'

'Third standard.'

'Whose son are you?'

'Son of Shanubhoga Channigarayaru.'

'Hey, how could you, being the son of a Shanubhoga, participate in such activities? Who brought you here?' When he was asking Vishwa these questions, the other policeman said: 'Ramasandra belongs to a different district Sir; he has not come from there,' and asked the boy directly: 'Where did you come from?'

'From Nagalapura.'

'Why did you go there?'

'I am attending school there.'

'Where are you staying?'

'In the house of Kallesha Jois.'

'How is he related to you?'

'He is the elder brother of my mother.'

The policeman who was seated, said, 'Oh, now I know, Sir. That Kallesha worked as a police constable with me. Do you know, Sir, there is a house called the ghost's house behind the mosque of this town? Is there not one Kantijois by name, who lives alone, and performs black magic, etc.? Kallesha is his son. Hey child, how did you come here?'

Vishwa narrated everything in detail—from leaving his home till his reaching Channarayapatna. The senior policeman said, 'Send the boy to Kantijois's place. Why do we need unnecessary headache?' He turned towards Vishwa, widened his eyes menacingly and admonished, 'If you shout "Jai" or some such slogan once again, and if you join these people, beware! I'll thrash you with this belt.' He ground his teeth and stamped his boot loudly on the floor.

'No, no,' said Vishwa, mortally scared. The policeman who was standing, took Vishwa's hand and went out into the night. He crossed the market street, reached the big house beyond the mosque and knocked at the door. 'Who is it?' came the voice from within.

'Open the door. It's your grandson,' said the policeman. The man, who lit the lamp and opened the door, had a broad face and tall stature. 'Your daughter's son has joined the Congress people. He's come here without understanding anything. Take him inside...'

Vishwa remembered seeing this grandfather. *Had he not come with Akkamma to Ramasandra much earlier than Akkayya's marriage*? But he could not remember correctly. He went in with his grandfather and felt scared at what he could see. Inside, a tiger skin was spread out. Human skulls and bones were kept there. Along with those, there were cowry shells, beads, copper foils, raw threads and many pairs of chappals. Vishwa said, 'I feel scared here.'

'Oh how courageously you spoke today. Why are you afraid? I did not know you were my daughter's son. Wah re wah, you are a rustum, boy. I feel proud that you are my daughter's son. Oh, it is rewarding,' he said, held Vishwa's hand and made him sit close by.

Kantijois's anger against his daughter had not decreased even after he heard about the death of his grandchildren. He could not forget her disobedience at overstepping his word, and refusing to give her daughter to his son. He sometimes felt that his daughter grieved because of the death of her children. Still, the vague affection rising within him towards his children was akin to a dumb feeling attributable to his paternal love towards his own daughter. Besides, there was anger. But now, this grandson had done a valiant deed. He had given a speech before fifteen to twenty thousand people, that too, unafraid of the police, and he had been garlanded. He himself had seen and heard the people speaking about the boy appreciatively. 'Oh, he is a lion's cub!' He was also listening when the boy gave his speech. Now, affection and pride sprung up in the grandfather's heart towards his grandson.

He asked Vishwa, 'Where did you come from?' Vishwa spoke about his stay in Nagalapura. Of late, Kantijois had not gone to his place at all. Nor was he staying in Channarayapatna. He stayed around Hassan, Koushika, Magge and Ramanathapura.

He asked, 'Are you hungry, child?'

'Yes.'

'See, there are bananas and sugar now. You eat that and sleep. At daybreak, you may have breakfast in the hotel.'

'Dosas?'

'Yes, whatever you ask for.'

Grandpa himself peeled the bananas and, dipping them in sugar, gave them to the boy, who ate a bellyful of them. He asked the boy to lie down on his own bed and covered him with half the shawl; he put off the light. The boy slept, but the grandfather did not get any sleep. He thought of visiting his daughter. It was about a year or so since her children had died. *How much she must have pined for them! I did not attend that girl's marriage also. Akkamma had said, Nanju had selected a good boy and married off her daughter. But Nanju's husband was a despicable sister-fucker. Where does that cur have the merit to marry the daughter of a person like me? Anyway, it doesn't matter. This lion cub was born out of her womb.* That is enough. Kantijois was immersed in these thoughts.

By then he felt someone knocking at the door and said the words, 'Open the door.' Kantijois recognized Kallesha's voice. He got up, lit the lamp and opened the door. Kallesha's anxiety diminished looking at Vishwa sleeping there. He had waited for the boy until afternoon, had searched the village tank and all the wells. By night-time, someone said, of course doubtfully—that Vishwa was seen in the group that went to Channarayapatna. At once, he started and came here. Everyone had slept as it was midnight. He got suspicious, went to the police station and enquired about the boy. His old colleague, Yallappa, now a Daffedar, spoke about Vishwa and informed him, 'Your father stays in that ghost's house. I myself took the boy and left him there.' He described the courage of the boy.

Kantijois too spoke of his grandson's valour. Then Kallesha explained in detail about Nanjamma's pilgrimage to Sringeri following the death of her children. Vishwa's adventure of swimming in the river, his beating the snake in his village and its escape, and, as a consequence, of that, Nanjamma's sending him to Nagalapura to pursue his studies.

When they woke up, it was late. When he awoke and turned, Vishwa saw his uncle sitting nearby. He became dull with fear. Finishing their morning routines, all three went to the hotel. When grandpa asked, 'Do you eat masala dosa, child?' Vishwa did not answer at all. When asked again, he bluntly said: 'No, I don't want anything.' Kantijois could not understand why the boy had such fear regarding Kallesha. However, he ordered masala dosas, Mysore pak and many tasty dishes for the boy. When Kallesha started, he said, 'Don't take the boy on foot. I have bought a new horse. I have tied it at the back. Harness it and take him on the horse.'

He untied the horse, brought it harnessed and hoisted Vishwa on to it. Oh, Vishwa was elated. In his village, he used to mount Patela's pony stealthily and ride it now and then. But he had never sat on such a big red horse with a shining harness. Although for a minute he was scared, he did not say he would get down. After Kallesha too mounted and sat behind, the boy's grandfather said, 'Look Kallesha, keep the horse for a fortnight there. By then, make him practice horse-riding. A boy should know horse-riding.'

Vishwa enjoyed horse-riding very much. He felt so light-hearted. His uncle did not scold him on the way; he did not speak a single word. Vishwa desired the horse to be ridden faster. But he was afraid to express it to his uncle. Sitting quietly, he was relishing the joy of riding a horse. He was recollecting the words of his speech the previous day. His imagination took wings: *Oh, how fine it would be if this horse were only mine! I should ask grandpa to give it to me. Riding this alone in the night, I will go to my home and wake up Amma. Hereafter I must stay in our village only. I should not live without Amma. And how can that snake bite me if I am always on the horse? I must again join the school* in our village. I should say to the master: 'You must teach me lessons while I'm seated on the horse.' After I finish primary school, I'll go to Kambanakere middle school daily, riding the horse. If this uncle was not with me now, I could have ridden the horse directly to my village. Fie, this one beats me! I wish uncle's hand shrinks.

After reaching home, the horse was halted in front of the house and Vishwa was taken off the horse. Akkamma came out, hugged him and said, 'Where did you go, my child?' Kallesha left his chappals outside and directly entered the kitchen. By then Kallesha had grabbed a piece of firewood that he could lay his hands on and immediately began thrashing the boy repeatedly on his back, raising it high and smacking it down. Akkamma screamed: 'Ayyo, ayyo, the child will die, surely! Curse be upon you, you diabolical bastard! You shouldn't hit the child like this!' She tried to yank Vishwa away, but a blow landed on her hand. She yelled, 'Ayyo!' and said, 'Heyyy! Who strikes a mere child like this? You...you are Yama himself!' Even as she went on screaming and cursing, he had delivered eight or ten more blows on Vishwa.

'This rascal has grown, without any restraint. He had joined some worthless fellows. And if something had happened to him, who'd be responsible? Who'd get a bad name?' Even as he said this, he looked at the boy. Blood was pouring from his back. The boy had fallen unconscious. He had urinated in his shorts and it was flowing to the floor.

'Ayyo, she sent her only surviving child here, for she was afraid that if he stayed there, he would die of snakebite. Now here, will you kill him by thrashing him? Ayyo...' The neighbours came rushing. Kallesha touched Vishwa and examined him. He was still breathing. He ran, brought a jug of cold water, sprinkled some water on his forehead and patted it. Vishwa regained consciousness. When the shirt was removed, there were many slits and openings of various shapes on his back and the blood oozing out of the wounds was congealing and turning black. Kallesha washed the wounds. When he was smearing the country sandalwood oil kept at home, the boy was crying: 'Oh ayyayyo... It burns, burns terribly.'

4

Meanwhile, the master was transferred from Ramasandra. It had been five years since he came to this village. He was trying to get transferred to Huliyar, his native place. Luckily, he got the same place, and he left Ramsandra. Nanjamma felt unhappy and wearied. He had been supporting her like an elder brother in all her hardships and joys. Nanjamma shared a certain intimacy with his wife and they adjusted well together. Nanjamma's night school had run for six months and had ended. The headmaster of Kambanakere came, inspected, wrote a report that, first, this night school had been run perfectly and recommended that a second one be started. He had taken from her a receipt for hundred and twenty rupees as the remuneration for running the first night school and said the government would send the money. Now, another person was appointed in master's place. Nanjamma did not know him. Maadevayyanavaru also felt bored after Venkateshayya master's transfer.

During this period, Nanjamma started work on her new house. She did not have any other tasks at present. She was constantly at it, for she had decided to put tiles on the roof before the rainy season. She did not have any experience in constructing a house. She had to shoulder the entire responsibility of the work and ensure that it was done as per the directions given by her. If not, it would become expensive. The money she had managed to gather was enough for wood and bamboo. Planks for the loft could be fixed anytime. Money had to be provided for tiles. Plastering of walls could wait. Maadevayyanavaru too was giving instructions to the workers, to the best of his knowledge and experience. Nanjamma did not have any other work at home. Without sitting idle, she began helping in the construction work. She would throw the lump of mud, kneaded well by male workers, on the roof. She would draw water in earthen pots to mix the mud. The workers would get embarrassed when this woman, who wrote the revenue accounts for the Shanubhoga, started working. But she thought, it was her home, she must work and build it. Why should she sit idle?

The walls had been raised nearly nine feet high already. The only thing that remained to be done was to arrange the money for the tiles. One evening, she was scraping mud from the spade glued on the ground where the mud had been kneaded, making balls out of it and giving them to the worker standing against the wall, when her father arrived there. There was a big bag on his shoulder. He wore a dhoti and covered himself with a shawl. He was not the Kantijois of the past the wearing boots, hat and riding a white horse. He had come on foot, without a horse. He said straight away, 'Nanja, you are building a house! It looks fine.'

She left the spade there, instructed the worker who stood against the wall about what should be done the next day and went home with her father. She washed her hands and legs, entered the kitchen and lit the oven. 'Nanja, don't cook anything special for me. Rice and tamarind rasam would be enough.' That said, he too came into the kitchen and, dragging the wooden seat propped against the wall near the oven, sat on it. He explained everything he had seen, 'Look Nanja, your son is a valiant boy. That's how a son should be. Twenty thousand people called him a lion's cub.' Nanjamma was elated when she heard this praise for her son. But she was worried, 'If this boy does something rash, does something without being cautious, and his skull is broken by the police, what will happen?' Kantijois continued, 'Look, it's been really long since I came this side. Yesterday, I saw your son. Didn't I tell you? The policeman brought him and left him with me. This morning, I put him on the horse and sent him and Kallesha to Nagalapura. I don't know why I felt like seeing you. Wondering if should delay it, I carried this shoulder bag and set out.'

Kantijois did not speak about her children's death; Nanjamma too did not. He asked, 'You are building a house. It is good. If I had known earlier, I would have given some money. You could have covered the roof with Mangalore tiles. A month back, I purchased a horse for eight hundred rupees. Now, take this—I have two hundred rupees with me.' He took out the packet of currency notes tied in a cloth from his inside pocket, placed it near her and said, 'Take it, and use it for your house.'

'You may need this for your expenses. Keep it with you. I have arranged money for the house.'

'No, I don't have a problem of money. You keep this.'

Even after going to bed, father and daughter spoke for a long time that night. Nanju asked, 'Appa, you have become old. No doubt, God has blessed you with strength. Why do you roam around places? You don't stay at home for even three months at a stretch. Sometimes, for six months even. Akkamma said no one knows your whereabouts. Why shouldn't you be at home, calm and peaceful, at least hereafter?'

'What shall I do staying at home?'

'Just simply sit still?'

'How can I just sit still? I have to do some work.' Nanjamma did not know the answer to this question. After a while, he said, 'You know what sort of a woman Kallesha's wife is. Nobody will be happy until that slut is kicked out of the house. He too beats her, thrashes her, but he won't push her out of the house. It is not such a big problem to murder her and bury in any field. If he is destined to struggle with her, why should I intervene? So, I kept quiet. Why do I need to? I can stay anywhere. You don't worry.'

Nanjamma did not speak. She had a mind to tell him 'Come Appa, stay here', but he would never stay at his daughter's house. Moreover, if he stayed here, her husband would go out of the house. Her father might get extremely angry at her husband's conduct and might thrash him also. So, she did not say anything. He went to sleep quickly, as he had walked twenty miles to Ramasandra.

Nanjamma tossed and turned for a while. She was worried about Vishwa being taken away to the police station. She dreamt of something similar. Two dark-coloured constables were following her even as she ran and ran, trying to escape from them. There was a small stream in front of her. After she crossed it and came far away, they stood there guffawing, and said: 'Oh oho, where will you go escaping from us?' At once, she was awake. *Some nightmare!* She lay down thinking, *what wrong did I commit, if the police were chasing me so?* For a long time, she could not get sleep.

Kantijois stayed for three days in his daughter's house. He inspected the construction of the new house and gave some suggestions. As he was to perform some charm to a house at Kattaya in Hassan taluk, he left without staying for more days.

When she was worrying about how to arrange money for the tiles, her father gave two hundred rupees and left. On the same day, she went to Sannenahalli, and said that, she had adjusted the money, that the tiles should be brought within two days and they would get the money as soon they supply the tiles to her. The walls that were raised must dry a little; they should put a pillar and beam. Rafters should be raised and bamboo splits must be tied. Everything was ready. Following the payment for the tiles, fifty rupees would be saved. In the same instance, the flooring and lime wash should be completed. If only the work on the house was completed, the expenses of Grihapravesha could somehow be adjusted. By that time, if she could get the remuneration on account of the night school, she could finish with the Grihapravesha shaastra within fifty rupees from that amount. She should send for her Appa only. The Jois of this place should not be called. Vishwa must be brought here for the Grihapravesha and Akkamma too should come. Kallesha will certainly be present. But there was no guarantee of his wife coming.

Clouds appeared in the sky, this time, before the summer started. If there were rains before the tiles were covered, the walls would become soft and fall apart. So the roof work must be accomplished soon. Nanjamma pressurized the carpenters and went to Sannenahalli again. Potter Shetty was not at home. She waited for him at his house. When he came home, she warned him for his delay in supplying the tiles and returned. The next day, the tiles arrived. The sun was burning constantly. Clouds in the sky were threatening. The tiles should be placed on the roof quickly. The work of putting on the tiles too started on both sides of the house; labourers, who knew the work, climbed the roof from its sloping side and sat on it. Female workers climbed the ladder and were passing the tiles on to those on the roof. It seemed that it would rain in the evening. Nanjamma was also raising the tiles and giving them to the workers constantly since the morning. None among the workers rested. By four in the afternoon, the work was completed. Finally, the inverted tiles at the centre of the roof were also covered. The workers got down and said, 'Avva, your work is over. You won.'

Maadevayyanavaru, who stood there, said: 'Nanjavva, Appannaiah had set fire to the sugar cane field. Was it not for that that you lost all your lands? That day, Appannaiah and Chinnayya together climbed on the roof and with the wooden pestle, broke the tiles. Wasn't I saying that it is easy to break the house but difficult to build one? Anyway, you have built your own house.'

When he said this, Channigarayaru, who was also present there, got angry and left the place.

Only thunder struck; that was all. There were no rains in the evening. By night, there was nothing, not even a bit of cloud in the sky. Nanjamma was extremely tired, having raised tiles constantly since the morning. Yet, something had to be cooked to appease the hunger. She lit the stove, cooked some rice and served it with buttermilk to her husband. She too ate the same and went to bed. Her mind was enveloped with the thought of her dead children. Sorrow. The fact that her children didn't live even a single day in their own home deeply hurt her. Then she thought of Vishwa. It had already been more than six months since Vishwa had left for Nagalapura. *It would be summer vacation in another fortnight. I should bring him home. It was enough if care was taken that he should not go near the school of this village. I myself should go by cart. I don't know how much he would be pining for his Amma. I must bring Akkamma also with him. He should not stay there for another year. And then he should go to Kambanakere. He shouldn't shuttle ten miles every day from here to Kambanakere, like Ramanna had done. We should rent a small house and stay there. The accounts can be written when we come back here.* She went to sleep long after she thought through these things.

When she woke up in the morning, she felt that her body was heavy and she also had a high temperature. Both her armpits were aching. The previous day, she had worked in the hot sun, raised so many tiles and supplied them to the workers. Working in the hot sun was not new to her. But yesterday, the sun was especially harsh. It was the cruel sun that could bring rain. Besides, the human body is not the same at all times. Perhaps, some swelling has formed in the armpits from raising so many tiles? She woke up with this thought. She washed her face and milked the cows. After she had sent Vishwa away, much of the milk and curds remained unspent. Appannaiah too had not been in the village for over a month. Much of the buttermilk remained unused. Though she was suffering from fever, she baked six rotis, ate only half of a roti and kept the remaining five and a half for her husband, spread the bed and lay down. By the evening, she was half awake. None came home. *The husband? Who knew where he was and when he would come?* She got up, prepared a decoction of ginger and pepper, drank it and lay down again. She was in the state of being half asleep. She was neither aware when night had approached, nor when her husband had come back home and slept.

At midnight, she was woken up by the sound of her husband's snoring. When she got up to relieve herself, both her thigh joints were paining. A doubt arose in her mind. *The pain in the armpits might be due to picking up so many tiles. But if there was pain in the thigh joints from climbing up and down the ladder, why didn't it show up in the morning itself? Then, was it plague?* She had not heard news of rats falling anywhere in the village. When Parvati and Ramanna were afflicted by the plague, it had attacked without any forewarning, noiselessly. Had it turned up furtively even now? She was scared. She thought of asking Maadevayyanavaru.

She called her husband, 'Look here, are you awake?' Her husband's snoring went on uninterrupted. She called him again and shook his shoulders, stretching her hand. He chastised her eyes heavy with sleep. 'Hey, lie down quietly! Fie didn't cook properly at night and now spoils my sleep!'

Nanjamma got angry. She felt like retorting with 'Are you a man or beast?' But he would scold her even more to his heart's content and she would feel even more harassed. So, she swallowed the words that were on her tongue, and said instead, 'I think I have been struck by plague. Go and get Maadevayyanavaru.'

Her husband did not speak. In a short while, he was snoring. Nanjamma could wait until daybreak, but she would need to take some medication as early as possible. She got up, covered herself with the blanket, opened the door and got out. She was staggering. Although the thigh joints ached while walking, it was nothing compared to the pain in her armpits. She somehow reached the door of the temple and called out, 'Ayyanavare!' Because it was summer, he had slept on the platform. As soon as he replied, 'Yes, who's it?', she said, 'I think I have been struck with the plague. Come to our home,' and walked back. By the time she tottered back home, Ayyanavaru, who had followed her, came from behind and opened the door. Nanjamma struck a matchstick from the matchbox by her pillow, lit the lamp and lay down on the bed. In the light from the lamp, Ayyanavaru noticed that her face was swollen and her eyes were looking like balls of live coal. Her face revealed that she was running a temperature.

'When did you get this fever, Avva?'

'Last night itself. Armpits were aching. I thought there were swellings because of raising so many tiles. Now, after I woke up, there was pain in the thigh joints also.'

Pausing to think for a minute, Ayyanavaru asked, 'You had been to Sannenahalli for the tiles. Did you enter the village or stay outside?'

'That Lakkayyashetty's house is in the centre of the village. Why?'

'Did you sit for some time in his house?'

'Yes. When I went there, he was not at home. I sat waiting for him in his house for two hours. Why?'

'See, in that village rats are falling since ten or twelve days. They are ignorant villagers. They are staying there without vacating the place. This morning I had been to that side for karunya bhiksha and came to know of this. I did not enter the village.'

'Then, is it plague I am suffering from?'

'I can't say for certain. Anyway, medicine should be taken as early as possible.'

She felt tired by the time she spoke that. For a while, she closed her eyes; then she said, 'There is fifty rupees at home. You send someone to bring the medicine. You are the only source of refuge now,' and closed her eyes. Ayyanavaru considered which medicine to administer to her. He remembered how he had taken Vishwa by cart to Kambanakere hospital, but that doctor would do nothing. The Hemadi syrup would be better. Nanjamma directed him to the place where she had kept the money. It might still be midnight. The stars appeared in the sky in the shape of a manchadakalu[32]. Who was there to go to Tiptur urgently on foot, buy the Hemadi syrup and return by the first bus they could get? Channigarayaru was not courageous enough to walk in the night. Everyone was familiar with his laziness. He would be likely to stay in Tiptur, eating masala dosas and Mysore paks with the money given to him for the medicine. Appannaiah was not in the village. Maadevayyanavaru sat brooding. He himself could have gone, but he did not have the strength to walk till Tiptur at a stretch. Besides, if he left this place, there would be no one to take care of the patient. During such hard times, Narasi would help anybody. She had the experience of bringing provisions for her shop from Tiptur. But she was a woman. How could she go in the darkness of night? Nevertheless, he decided to ask her; she might be able to send someone else. He reached her shop and knocked on the door. She woke up at once, lit the lamp and came out. She heard what he said and assured: 'Ayyanavare, you don't worry, don't be afraid. Sambanna of Lingapura is in my home now. If I request him, he will surely go and bring the medicine.' Narasi went inside and woke him up. Sambanna of Lingapura was known to Ayyanavaru. He was a Nonabagowda.

---

[32]Legs of a cot

S.L. BHYRAPPA

Ayyanavaru had taken food from his house. Now he stood with his head lowered in shame because he had to face Ayyanavaru under such circumstances. On a piece of paper, Ayyanavaru wrote, 'Tiptur Market Street, Venkatachala Shetty's shop, Hemadi syrup.' He handed him the paper and twenty rupees. Narasi ordered: 'See, you should at once go running and return by the bus.' He put on his chappals, wound the turban around his head and strode away into the night.

Narasi questioned Ayyanavaru, 'Ayyare, there is no woman in this village as chaste as Nanjamma. But no one has suffered such hardships as she has. Now again the plague has struck her. Now you tell me, why should we live righteously?'

Ayyanavaru did not know the answer. His mind had become numb. 'I will tell you about it another day. No one is there to take care of her now,' he said and started walking.

'Shall I come too?'

'No, not needed.' He moved ahead a few more steps.

'Just wait a little,' Narasi called, came near him and said, 'No, I won't come. Nanjavva was running the night school for women, you know. Then I had sent word that I too would like to join. But she did not want to admit me. Even now, that woman may not like it.'

'Why, Narasamma? Are you angry because she did not admit you?'

'No, Ayyare. If she had admitted me, other women would not have come,' she said.

He told her to send the medicine as soon as it was brought and went back. By then, Nanjamma had fallen asleep. The kerosene lamp was burning. He decided not to awaken the patient, sat leaning against the pillar and was quietly looking at her face. Once, he thought of waking up Channigarayaru. Then he reflected, *If he had woken up, why would this woman have to bring herself to the temple?*, and kept quiet. Maadevayyanavaru sat looking at Nanjamma's face. The incidents of her life, from the moment she came here after marriage until now—the crucial turning points of her life—everything came to his mind. In the beginning, when she came as a daughter-in-law to this village, she did not speak with anyone outside her home. The mother-in-law who did not let her live happily and peacefully; the husband who was devoid of love and affection towards anyone; of them losing the lands and her prudent efforts to save them; coming alone with her children and building her family; helping her son pursue education; arranging for her daughter's marriage and the death of her children. And now, it seemed like death had come to swallow her too. Maadevayyanavaru recalled the question Narasi had asked him: 'There is no woman as chaste as Nanjavva. But no one suffered such hardships as she has. Now again the plague has struck her. Now you tell me, why should we live righteously?' Ayyanavaru pondered. Shiva protects the virtuous; punishes the villains. But what wickedness had Nanjamma committed? She suffered because of her mother-in-law's wickedness and husband's baseness. But should this plague strike her house, her children, and finally her too? He had read in tatvapadas and lavanis that God had created diseases in the world to punish for dharma-karma. But his comprehension of that concept evaded him at this point.

At the same time, Nanjamma woke up crying 'Ayyayyao', as if alarmed. Ayyanavaru asked, 'Why, what happened, Avva?' For five minutes, she opened her eyes, but as if understanding nothing, she asked: 'Oh, is it you?'

'Yes, what happened?'

'Dream. Earlier too, I had this dream. Two policemen chasing me. I cross the stream. They said, "Where will you go, escaping from us?" Now, the same dream again. Both of them hold me and tie me with a black rope, before I could cross the stream. Then I woke up.'

'Just lie down, Avva. From the heat of the fever, you are getting such dreams.'

'No, Ayyanavare, it is not out of the fever. My death is certain. Would you please cook a cup of gruel for me? Don't be embarrassed thinking it is a Brahmin's kitchen. I had prepared broken rice for uppittu when my Appa had come. It is in a black box on the shelf. There is jaggery in a brass vessel. If you cannot get it, you make the gruel without jaggery and bring it.'

He got up, took the lamp and went in. Even in the darkness, flies were hovering over on the bits of roti left over from what Channigarayaru had eaten the previous night. He found the broken rice and jaggery at once. He lit a dry coconut leaf, cooked gruel in a vessel and brought it with a glass. He raised her by her shoulder and made her sit. She drank all of the gruel and lay down again. After five minutes, she spoke: 'I have gained strength after drinking the gruel. Afterwards, I may lose consciousness. I'll speak with you now alone.'

'You lie down quietly. You should not speak much in the heat of fever; be quiet, Avva.'

'Please listen to me. Only I will speak now. It was said that my mother died as soon as I was born. It was said that—and I was a one-year-old baby then—one day, I was crying, screaming continuously while lying in the cradle. Outside, it was raining heavily. Akkamma was in the cowshed and so she couldn't hear my cries. My father was memorizing some Sanskrit mantra. And my wailing was disturbing his concentration. He became uncontrollably furious and said, "This is a damned thing. It keeps wailing all the time!" He took the cradle together with the baby and placed it under the eaves of his house where the rain falls with an even greater force. Then he went in and went back to his memorization. After a while, when Akkamma came, she saw that there was no cradle. So, she asked him: "Hey, where's the child?" He replied, "Under the eaves." It is said that my face wasn't under the pouring water; only my legs were. My face was towards the street. Else, I would have died right then. Akkamma brought me inside, gave me some brandy and averted the chance of my catching a severe cold and made me live.'

Ayyanavaru, who knew Kantijois well, thought, that it was not unnatural for him to have done so. Nanjamma said, 'I should have died then itself. But why didn't I die? Living for so many years, married to such a husband, giving birth to such good children, losing them—have I to die now, suffering so much? Ayyanore, why did things pan out in this way?'

Ayyanavaru was ruminating on this question since the last hour. What Narasi had asked and what Nanjamma was asking now, were the same question. *Why did, such things happen? What might be the will of Shiva?* Ayyanavaru had not studied the Vedanta. The knowledge he had earned was from the tatvapadas and lavanis. When he visited Kashi, he was listening curiously to the logical discussions on such questions inside and outside the Mutt. But he did not find any answer to the question asked an hour back by Narasi and now by Nanjamma. Nanjamma was more intelligent and literate. She would recite easily the stanzas of the Mahabharata and tell meanings which he himself could not understand. But what was the answer to the question she was asking now? *Yes, why shouldn't she have died when she was a child? She was more intelligent than him; yet why had she asked him for an answer to this question.*

By then, Nanjamma had gone into a stupor. Ayyanavaru sat looking at her face. Many lines appeared and scattered, and then disappeared on her face because of the fever. After a little while, she opened her eyes and tried to speak. But words were not coming out because of tiredness and feebleness. She gathered all her strength with much effort and said, 'When Parvati and Ramanna died, you told me the story of Gopamma. She was scared to give up her life and stood on the bank of that whirlpool. The same night, I had gone to drown myself in the crematorium well. I would have courageously plunged into that well, but came back worried about Vishwa. Now, I myself am going to die. Who will take care of Vishwa? Akkamma will cook something. I don't trust my Annayya. Food for the boy is not that important. But shouldn't the boy become an intelligent, educated man?'

She closed her eyes and lay down, in pain, and weary. Following this state of stupor, it seemed like Nanjamma had drifted off to sleep. Ayyanavaru sat quietly. He could hear the sound of the cock crowing in the Fisherman Street. It was the hour during which he woke up every day and felt like going towards the tank. For a moment, he thought of awakening Channigarayaru. But what use would that be to the patient? He did not extinguish the lamp, closed the door and went out. By the time he returned from the tank bund, the crows were cawing. Meanwhile, people who were coming towards the tank bund were speaking among themselves. Rats were falling in surrounding villages. The village chiefs had gathered the previous night and had decided to vacate the village at once, before the rats began to die here. This morning, Belura would proclaim this by beating the drum in the village. It was heard that the Kambanakere government department had sent word that the officials would pay this village a visit today. Everyone, including women and children, should come near the shrine of the village deity and take inoculation. There was an order from the government that inoculation should be given in each village before the disease spreads.

Ayyanavaru recalled that the Kambanahalli doctor had said last year that the inoculation would not be given to those who had already been affected by the plague. Last year also, this menace of a plague had invaded Nanjamma's house. This time too, even before one could become aware of the disease, it had struck this woman. Brooding, Ayyannavaru walked towards Nanjamma's house.

Within two days, everyone vacated the village. Ayyanavaru transported the strips made from the bamboo staffs, that remained after Nanjamma's building work was completed and helped to put a shed. He had the shrine on the tank bund for his stay. What was extremely surprising to everyone was Gangamma's coming into the same shed and taking care of her daughter-in-law. Though Gangamma grumbled continuously, saying things like, 'What hell would have broken loose if she had not built the house? She went to Sannenahalli and was struck with the plague maari. If only she had obeyed the words of the elders, nothing would have happened to this poor fellow', she would administer gruel and the Hemadi syrup regularly, as per the instructions of Ayyanavaru. This, despite the fact that Nanjamma refused to have any of it.

Channigarayaru would be lying either in the shrine on the tank bund or on the platform of the village deity's temple, for his left arm was painful as the result of the inoculation. Ayyanavaru objected to having that inoculation and said, 'I am a sanyasi. Why should I need this jab? Who is there to cry if I die?' The medical staff, however, said, 'It is not important whether you die. But the disease may spread from you to others.' They gave a jab to him too. Only for a day his arm pained a little. The villagers put up sheds and transported their luggage while in pain. Gangamma, however, bluntly refused to get the inoculation.

Four people held the four corners of the bed Nanjamma had slept in, brought it out and placed it in the shed. Meanwhile, she had lost consciousness and did not gain it back for a day. She was slowly gulping down the medicine and the thin gruel her mother-in-law put into her mouth. When she regained consciousness in the morning, she tried to speak. Ayyanavaru, who sat nearby, brought his ears close to her face and asked, 'What do you want?'

'Vi...shwa...'

'Do you want to see him?'

Recognizing the affirmation on her face, he went out saying, 'I will send someone to bring him here.' But everyone was busy in building and organizing their sheds. Where could he get hold of someone now? Dwelling on who to get, he reached the shed of the village servant, and said, 'See, Nanjamma is on her deathbed. She wants to see her son.

Someone should go to Nagalapura and bring her son here.'

The village servant said, 'Ayyavre, you yourself see. I have put only one coconut leaf on my shed. Today, I must go to Gowda's garden and fetch some more leaves.

'See, brother, you can do this tomorrow also. Shouldn't the son pour water into the mouth of his dying mother?'

The village servant agreed. Maadevayyanavaru told him to start at once and returned to the shed. Meanwhile, Gangamma said, 'She said something that I could not follow. You ask her, Ayyanavare.'

He brought his face close to her face again and asked: 'What is it, Avva?' After five minutes, as if he had heard something, Ayyanavaru said, 'Couldn't hear, speak a little louder.' Though it could not be heard very clearly, of what she had whispered, this much could be understood: 'There is plague in the village. Don't send for the boy.' Ayyanavaru started again towards the shed to inform the village servant not to go.

He also decided that Vishwa need not come to the plague-stricken village. Nanjamma's death was certain. Her wish that her son be healthy, strong and alive was enough; he need not come here and put a spoonful of water into her mouth. However, Maadevayyanavaru thought that it was important to inform her brother and her grandmother, who had brought her up, of her condition and ran to the village servant's shed. Just then, he was ready to set out after eating ragi balls. Ayyanavaru told him not to bring the boy no matter what, but he must bring with him Nanjamma's grandmother and her brother.

The village servant galloped. However fast he ran holding his breath, it was already two in the afternoon when he reached Nagalapura, crossing Cholanagudda, the sand pit, the red soil pit, and the cactus lanes. There too, the village had been vacated. He enquired for Kalleshajois's shed and went there. Vishwa had gone to school. Kalleshajois had gone to Hassan and would return the next day. Akkamma was panic-stricken on hearing what the village servant said. She could not wait for Kallesha. She instructed Kamalu to send him the next day as soon as he returned. Not trusting her fully, however, she told the people in the two other sheds beside theirs, asked Honna, who looked after the lands, to harness his cart, after which Akkamma set out at once.

Fie, that damning plague had taken as sacrifice her two great grand-children just a year back. This year, it has struck her granddaughter.

It was said that Vishwa was cured because of the vow made to the Sringeri Sharadammanavaru. Akkamma did not know whether someone there had observed a vow in the name of that Goddess. On her way to Ramasandra, she came across a small pool on the way. She stopped the cart, got down, washed her hands and feet in the pool, took a silver coin from the money bag she had brought, tucked into her waist, and vowed that if her granddaughter got cured, she would send her again to Sringeri and perform kumkumarchana, and sat in the cart.

This time, villages were vacated everywhere. But in all the villages, the government people had given inoculations. In Nagalapura, Vishwa, Kallesha, Kamalu—all had taken it. But only Akkamma had refused one. After all, she was an old woman. All these years, she had not even put into her mouth the hospital water. Now, why should she allow that water from the syringe to enter her body?

Again and again, she was enquiring about the condition of her granddaughter. The village servant did not know anything clearly. Yet, he would tell her whatever he had heard. Akkamma, assuring herself in her mind that there was no danger to Nanju's life, was urging Honna to make the oxen move fast. However faster they moved, it was already dark when they reached Ramasandra.

6

When Akkamma entered the shed, she looked for her granddaughter; she was not there. In-law Gangamma was crying loudly, beating against her own mouth. Maadevayyanavaru informed: 'Nanjamma breathed her last in the afternoon itself. Her last words were "Don't call my son to this plague-stricken village"; she did not speak again. Before dying, no tumour was pierced. She panted for five minutes and then her vital breath vanished. Her mother-in-law Gangamma put water into her mouth.' They had waited till the evening, keeping the corpse for her grandmother and her brother. If they'd have had to wait till nightfall, they would have had to wait till tomorrow; but in that case, the corpse might have started to decay because of the plague. 'So it was sent for cremation just half an hour ago.'

Akkamma hit hard on her chest and sobbed. In the darkness itself, she set out towards the crematorium, saying: 'I did not see her face. I will go there and see.' Though Ayyanavaru tried to dissuade her and said, 'Women should not go there,' she did not heed him. He held her hand and set out with her, thinking that this very old woman of such a ripe age might stumble and fall in the darkness. Ayyashastri had stood with his bent back in the place where these two would have to climb down from the tank bund. Looking at them, he asked, 'Who is it?' Maadevayyanavaru replied, 'Nanjavva's grandmother.' They climbed down the tank bund and walked through the narrow lane of the garden. By that time, a part of the shaastras were already over, the corpse was placed on the pyre and just the clothes were being removed from the corpse. Akkamma saw her granddaughter in the same state as when she was born. Oh, how fair that child was then! Now, the body had turned black. Akkamma came running and hugged the corpse on the pyre. It was very difficult for the others to console Akkamma and separate her from the corpse. They stocked firewood on the corpse in front of Akkamma and lit the pyre. The fire eventually caught, spread and began rising up in flames. Akkamma was looking at this without a blink and suddenly shouted, 'Wait, I will teach you a lesson, you whore of a thief!'

Nobody could follow what she was saying. Akkamma went back in rapid steps. Ayyanavaru came behind her and held her hand lest she fell. But she escaped his hold and walked further. She did not hear Ayyashastri, who stood at the spot from where one had to climb the tank bund, calling her: 'Oh, why are you running away in that way, Amma?' She headed straight to the shed. As soon as she entered it, in one hand she took a toddy palm broom that was near the door, then coming near the cart outside, took one of Honna's chappals which he had left there, in another hand, and rushed towards the village. For a while, even Gangamma was baffled. Honna could make nothing of it. It seemed as if a solid darkness was all around, as in the days before the new moon. In the darkness, Akkamma located the street where Nanjamma's house had been and went into the village. She, then, stood before the door of her granddaughter's house and began thrashing it loudly: 'Hey, you slut of death and destruction! Why do you come only to this house again and again? You eyed her two children and swallowed them. Now, before I vowed to Sharadammanavaru, did you have to devour my granddaughter also? Tut-tut—you sinning slut; yes only these blows of chappal are what you deserve. If we are scared, you climb over and attack us. Hey, why are you sitting stealthily inside?

Get out of this house once; I will slap you with the slipper until you turn bald!'

Akkamma again hit on the door with the chappal and abused the plague maari to her heart's content. Soon, however, she was exhausted and sat on the platform. The toddy palm broom and the chappal were still in her hand. Within half an hour, her anger cooled. She had come to console her granddaughter in the same house when her two great grandchildren had died. Parvati was married off from the same house. Why should that plague maari come to find only that house? Now, Akkamma felt like crying. The cry, starting like sobs, finally flowed like a flood. After a while, she got up. Now, she did not want to hit the door with the broom or abuse the plague maari. Walking in the darkness, she went out of the village.

Meanwhile, Ayyanavaru came in front of her, recognized her and said, 'We searched for you everywhere. Why did you go inside the vacated village?'

'I had gone to hit that harlot plague with the chappal.'

Men who had burnt the corpse had returned. Channigarayaru sat crying, wiping his tears: 'What the hell would have happened if she had not built the house. That Plague Amma struck her because she built a new house.'

Akkamma wept the whole night. A discussion was on about whether Akkamma should return by cart following daybreak or stay there until Kallesha arrived. Ayyanavaru asked her to stay until Kallesha came. Honna, too, stayed along with the oxen and cart.

At noon, Akkamma was lying down in the shed. Gangamma sat with her hand on her head. Channigarayaru had been lying on the platform of the shrine of the village deity and sleeping, to forget his grief. Vishwa was walking towards the village with rapid strides. Narasi, who sat in her shop outside the village, saw him and came running. She asked, 'Where are you going, child?'

He asked, 'Is it true, my Amma is dead?' Narasi hugged him. He escaped from her and asked, 'Why do you hold me Narasamma? I'll go to my home, let me go.'

'What will you do there, child?'

'My Amma is alive. No, she is not dead!'

'Come here. I'll tell you,' she said and holding both his both hands,

Narasi dragged Vishwa to her shop, sat beside him and asked, 'Did you come alone, child?'

'Yes.'

'Who told you that your Amma was dead?'

'Nagammatte, of the shed next to ours.'

'Did you come running immediately after you heard this from her?'

'Yes.'

'Did you know the road?'

'Had I not seen it while going on the cart? Going on the tank bund, crossing cactus lanes and the oleander pit, again crossing Hoovinahalla, Cholanagudda and the pit of the flame of the forest trees, I came here.'

Narasi felt like crying. Again, she hugged him.

'Why do you cry, Narasamma? I'll go to my home,' he tried to get up and release himself. Narasamma said: 'Come, I will take you home.' She held his hand and took him to the shed. Looking at her great grandson, Akkamma got up, grabbed him lightly and wept loudly: 'Ayyoo, my child, you have become an orphan.'

Vishwa too felt like crying. 'Then, is Amma dead?' He asked only this then crying loudly, he swooned and fell down.

7

By the evening, Akkamma had fever. Going by the features—of excruciating body pain, as if it being cut; the eyes, red and distorted; and a puffed-up face—Ayyanavaru at once said it was the plague. He had a feeling that this old woman would not survive. He decided that Vishwa should not be left near the patient and brought him to Narasi, left him there and instructed her: 'See, Narasavva, don't allow him to go out of your house. Breakfast, lunch, whatever it is, you yourself make him eat. Caste is not affected by that. The plague has struck his great grandmother. He should not come in contact with her.'

Vishwa did not eat anything. He was crying and crying, remembering his Amma. Narasi made him sit near her and did not let him move anywhere.

The Hemadi syrup brought for Nanjamma had remained. Ayyanavaru came to the shed and tried to administer the syrup to Akkamma. She flatly refused and did not open her mouth no matter how much he tried. It seemed she had decided that she ought to die.

At ten in the night, Kallesha came. Ayyanavaru reported to him all that happened. He too shed tears for two minutes. Now, they had to think about what needed be done further. Kallesha suggested: 'Vishwa has been inoculated. Nagalapura has also been vacated. There is no need to be worried or scared, even if he stays here. Let him stay here until his mother's obsequies are over. Later, I will come and take him. Akkamma has been affected by the disease since she had been sitting for so long in the vacated village. She was stubborn and, did not take the inoculation. Now, I will take her to Nagalapura by cart.'

No one was in the state to say anything against this. Ayyanavaru accepted his suggestion. But Akkamma was obstinate. She struggled and said, 'I won't go there. I too must be burnt where my granddaughter was burnt.' But Kallesha did not heed her words. He told Honna to spread straw in the cart, and then spread a gunny bag and a saree on it. Akkamma was carried and placed on it; she was covered with Nanjamma's blanket. The same night, Kallesha asked Honna to harness the cart and left with Akkamma.

Next morning, Appannaiah returned to the village. He had not been aware of the village being vacated due to the plague or his sister-in-law's death. He entered the shed, sat and shed tears. After Parvati's marriage, he had developed a certain affection for his sister-in-law. After she lost her two children and he went with her to Sringeri, he had developed respect for her. He used to eat sambar and rasam cooked by her every day when he had given up the company of his mother. Now, he felt as if there was no one for him in the village. He went to Narasi's house and brought Vishwa to the shed. Except for Ayyanavaru, there was only this uncle who Vishwa was intimate with in this village. Revannashetty's wife, Sarvakka, and many other women came to the shed, pulled Vishwa's cheeks, kissed him, cried and left. But nobody could bring back his mother. It was said that she had been burnt in the cemetery. Once somebody was burnt into ashes, she or he would never return. Vishwa wondered why these people burnt her. *If they had kept her from burning, couldn't she have gotten back to life again?*

Now, the obsequies of his sister-in-law were to be performed, Appannaiah said to his brother: 'I have sixty rupees with me. You give whatever you have. Let us perform the rites according to tradition. She was a meritorious woman. Her rites should be performed with faith and devotion.'

His brother retorted, 'Oh, that widow of a donkey built the house with whatever money she had. What headship had she left to me to have money?'

Ayyanavaru said, 'After the medicine was brought, thirty rupees still remains with me. Take that too. Somehow, manage the ceremony on a low scale; any donations you offer to these Jois, will not reach that amma who is dead.'

The same day, the headmaster of Kambanakere came. He handed over a hundred and twenty-five rupees as remuneration from the night school to Channigarayaru and asked him to acknowledge it in writing, as the person who had to take this money was dead, that he, her husband, had received it. The headmaster took his signature and left. Appannaiah asked his brother to give that money for the expenses of the shraaddha rites.

Maadevayyanavaru said, 'Don't spend that money. It can be used for the boy—for his clothes, to purchase his books and other things.' Then Appannaiah said, 'If so, give that money to Ayyanavaru.' But Channigarayaru did not give it to anybody. He secured it in a piece of cloth, tied it to his waist and walked away.

Vishwa had not undergone the ceremony of Upanayana. Appannaiah performed all the rites as a son would for his mother, changing his sacred thread from left to right. He was taken near the garden well and tonsured. He had to sit quietly when the rites were being performed. Annajois recited the mantras and instructed the rituals to be undertaken. There were vessels and glasses in Nanjamma's house and they were generously gifted to Brahmans on the day of Vaikuntha samaradhana[33].

8

Kallesha came ten days after Vaikuntha samaradhana was over. He informed that Akkamma had died the very second day she reached Nagalapura. Kallesha searched for Kantijois in Hassan, Kaushika, Goruru Hebbale and many other places, finally located him and brought him

---

[33]The ritual of offering food to the community on the thirteenth day following the death of a person.

to complete Akkamma's shraaddha. He had come to take back Vishwa.

Vishwa stopped crying after his mother's shraaddha was over. He sat quietly before Ayyanavaru in the shrine on the tank bund. He did not feel like eating. Ayyanavaru would force him to eat a little ragi ball and sambar he had brought from kantebhiksha. When not in the shrine, he would visit Narasamma's shop. He would ask her, 'Narasamma, if I go and search for her, wouldn't my Amma be there? Are not all these people telling lies that she is dead?' Not knowing what answer to give, she would say: 'No child, I don't know. Come, take this biscuit, eat it.' She would then give him a biscuit from her shop, but he would ask, 'No, I don't want a biscuit. Tell me, is not my Amma at home?'

One day, without being noticed by anybody, he went to the village, looked at his locked house and returned quietly.

When his uncle came to take him back, Vishwa boldly said, 'No, I won't come.'

'Oh, why?'

'You beat me. I'll go to school in this village.'

But who was there to look after him in this village? Gangamma said she would keep the child with her. But what was the guarantee of her words? Ayyanavaru told him, 'No child, you go with your uncle.'

'No, Ayya, he beats me like cattle are beaten,' Vishwa said in front of his uncle.

When Kallesha assured him, 'I'll not beat you for sure', all the others compelled him. He set out as there was no other way out. To bid them farewell, Ayyanavaru and his uncle Appannaiah walked for a mile. When these two were about to return, Vishwa called Ayyanavaru and stopped him. He came running to Ayyanavaru and said: 'All of you say, that my Amma is dead; perhaps it is a lie. After all the villagers leave the sheds and go to the village, she will return. Then, tell her to come to Nagalapura and take me back.'

'Yes, child. I will do so,' Ayyanavaru said and stopped walking. Kallesha held Vishwa's hand and walked ahead. Vishwa turned back and was dragging his legs behind his uncle. These two had waited until the child and Kallesha climbed the mound in front and vanished. Ayyanavaru reflected—*How bright and active Vishwa was before he was sent to Nagalapura! Now, gloom has struck his face. His hands and legs have become stiff; there are wounds caused by dampness. Perhaps his uncle* may, as the boy said, beat him as the cattle are beaten. Till now, there lived the old woman. How will that aunt look after the boy? Besides the beatings, Kalleshajois may take good care of the child. Only Shiva should take care of such motherless children...

Appannaiah came to the shed. Till now, he had not thought about anything. Now, he remembered that his cooking utensils were in the room on the platform of Beeregowda's cowshed in the village. The village had been vacated. He would have to put a separate shed for himself alone. He felt it to be a wearisome task. The villagers would stay in the sheds until it rained. Then, they would go into the village. So, he decided it would be better if he trekked through some region, and set out the next morning.

That night, after serving his meal, Gangamma said, 'When she was alive, she carried tales about me, and instigated you to quarrel with me. Now, why should you stay separately? You stay with me.'

All of a sudden, Appannaiah was furious: 'Hey, she did not carry tales to me; it is you who is a harlot widow!'

'Do you call so the mother who gave birth to you? You pariah bastard!'

'Yes, I call you so, you widow! I won't stay with you. I won't perform shraaddha if you die!' Appannaiah said; then taking his dhoti, shirt, blanket and gunny bag at once, he left the shed.

The moon was shining outside. He had not yet decided in which direction he would move. For five minutes, he mulled over the matter. More or less, every village had been vacated in this ragi region. It would be better to go to the irrigated areas. The place was filled with moonlight. It was eight miles to Bendekere. He decided to go there, sleep on the platform of the temple outside the village and proceed post daybreak. Appannaiah walked on.

While Appannaiah, who had no family, went again for mendicancy, Channigarayaru was discussing about having another family, sitting in Annajois's shed. On the very day Nanjamma's Vaikuntha samaraadhana was over, the Jois had a proposal for Shanubhoga's marriage. There was a bride in Bevanahalli, three miles to Tiptur. The girl had no father and the mother's circumstances were very poor. Her only wish was to marry off her daughter to a Brahmin and fulfil her duty. The Jois encouraged Channigarayaru: 'Oh, after all, what is your age? Marry again. There is a newly built house and the hereditary post of the Shanubhoga. What else is needed? The girl has good features. Moreover, how long will you be alone?'

Channigarayaru was enthused: 'Oh, you arrange for a girl. I'll surely get married.'

The Jois said that he had to meet the girl's mother and speak to her. When he went for the negotiation, he had to take a new saree for the girl. If he had to present Channigarayaru as this big Shanubhoga, the Jois should also cover himself with a fine shawl. All of this would require at least seventy-five rupees. The Jois asked for money. If he wanted the girl, the Shanubhoga had to shell it out. The hundred and twenty rupees of Nanjamma's remuneration from the night school was still in his waist. If the Jois had not known about this, he would not have proposed this. Channigarayaru took out the small packet of cloth tucked within his waist, opened it, counted seventy-five rupees before the Jois and gave it to him. The Jois was well aware of how much still remained.

The next day, the Jois went to Tiptur by bus. He had bought a shawl for twenty rupees and had put it on his shoulders. Channigarayaru too saw it. Was it not evidence that the Jois had given a saree of fifty rupees to the girl? After two days, during an auspicious lagna, these two left for Tiptur by bus. Following meals in a hotel, they slept on the platform of the choultry. As instructed by the Jois, Channigarayaru had brought his dhoti, coat and turban from the jamabandi, which were cleaned with washing soda. Now, that morning itself, the Jois had the clothes ironed and brought a barber to the bank of the tank. Being a Vaidic Jois, he ought not to go into the salon. He sat Channigarayaru on the bank and asked the barber to shave the grey beard and grey hair off Channigarayaru. The Jois himself stood close to him and saw to it that not even a stub of white hair was visible on his cheek. He told Channigarayaru to bathe in the tank. After bathing, he donned the pressed dhoti, shirt and coat and then tied the turban, as when he went for the jamabandi. Then, the Jois said, 'Come now, let's go to the hotel. Isn't there a big mirror there? You look at yourself in that and see how you are looking.'

In the hotel, until the masala dose was baked and supplied, Channigarayaru looked and looked at himself in the mirror; he felt astonished. Never in the past had he donned the coat and turban so nicely. *That 'slut' who had been his wife had never sent him to the jamabandi in a dhoti, shirt, coat and turban so neatly and nicely ironed.* After they finished the masala dosa, idli-sambar and Mysore pak, and drank coffee, the Jois hired a jatka, for eight rupees, to take them to Bevinahalli, wait there and bring them back to Tiptur.

Bevinahalli was a petty village in the middle of a jungle. There was only one Brahmin's house there, which belonged to this girl. Though she owned little land, the widowed mother of the girl could not cultivate it on her own; she would take whatever the tenants gave her and was somehow managing a hand-to-mouth living. When a jatka stood before her house, she was so excited that she could not move her limbs. The girl was fourteen years old. The mother said, that the girl had not yet attained puberty. Channigarayaru would have given his consent even if he had not seen the girl. But after looking at the girl, there was no question of refusal.

The Jois explained on behalf of Channigarayaru: 'Our Channigarayaru appears so because of having to always write the revenue accounts as part of his responsibility of being a Shanubhoga. He has not yet crossed thirty-two. He owns a house, has the post of a Shanubhoga and four acres of dry field. These days, it is enough if there is the post of Shanubhoga to maintain the family. Your girl will wash her hands daily in milk after her meals, not in water.'

The marriage was fixed. The Jois wrote the lagnapatrika, too, on the white paper he had brought with him. The horoscopes matched perfectly.

'There is a good muhurtha in the month of Vaishakha. You may celebrate the marriage without spending much money and by cooking simple rice and tamarind rasam.' When the Jois spoke thus, the girl's mother felt very happy, since it felt like a burden had been lifted off her shoulders. Somehow, she managed to cook ghee-rice and payasam and served Annajois and Channigarayaru. These two took betel leaves and areca nuts and returned to Tiptur by the jatka. Though there was a bus ready to go towards Ramasandra, none of the two were eager to start. The hotel food was very tasty. They decided they will set out the next morning. The Jois bought a pair of dhoti and a saree from a textile shop. He had not brought money with him. Channigarayaru himself paid the bill of twenty-two rupees to the cashier in the shop.

Everyone in the village knew the news of Channigarayaru's marriage. Narasi mocked him: 'Oh look at the addiction of this fellow. Would he really rule his wife?' Sarvakka interjected, 'Avva, that docile woman somehow managed with this fellow! How could any girl tied to him, manage or spend her days?'

Revannashetty met Channigarayaru one day and encouraged him, 'Well, you have made an excellent decision Shanubhogare! You marry again. If not, who is there to cook for you and serve you?' His mother, Gangamma, expressed her disinterest in this matter: 'What is it to me which slut comes? None will offer any service to me.'

Within a week, the month of Chaitra was over and Vaishaka arrived. The marriage had to occur this month itself. The first wife's earrings and nose studs were still there. Besides, there was the gold of the mangalya that was searched for from among Nanjamma's ashes and taken out. If hundred rupees were arranged, it would be sufficient for the marriage. He sold a cow that had been in the house, for hundred rupees and managed the amount. But nobody from the bride's side came to discuss matters further. The bride's mother had said she would send a relative from her parents' side, a Siddhavalli Venkataramayya. But nobody came. Only six days were left for the ceremony. Channigarayaru could not control his anxiety. When he enquired from the Jois, he answered casually, 'Who knows what the matter is. I don't have time. You go and find out what has happened.' So, the Shanubhoga himself went to Tiptur, got a shave like the last time, donned ironed clothes and reached Bevinahalli. There was an old man in the house. By the time Channigarayaru introduced himself and began speaking, the mother of the girl came out from inside and burst out rapidly: 'If I cannot get any other bridegroom, I will push my daughter into a well. But I won't give her to a fellow like you!'

The Shanubhoga Channigarayaru, unable to understand anything, sat blinking his eyes and staring at her. The woman spoke, 'I believed that scoundrel Joisa—that widow's husband—as he was a distant acquaintance. He got twenty rupees from me, said he would fix a bridegroom for my daughter, and now he has cheated me, showing an unmanly, coward of an old man. Fortunately, a virtuous man informed us of everything before the marriage.'

Channigarayaru gathered courage, and stuttered 'Wwwwhat iiis mmmmy mmmmistake, tttell me, amma.'

'How dare you ask what the mistake is! What kind of care did you take of your wife? What support did you provide her in terms of earning a livelihood? Was it not her earning a livelihood by joining the leaves of the flame of forest trees? Then the post of the Shanubhoga? It was being maintained because it was she who was writing the revenue accounts. My daughter does not know all these things. Where are the lands the Jois said you have in the village? The house too was built by your wife and it will be inherited by her son. Didn't you say you had only one son? Is it a lie that a son who had undergone the ceremony of Upanayana and a daughter who was married, died last year?'

'Wwwho tttold you aaal ttthis, amma?' he stuttered again.

'You ask me who said these to me? He is of your own village, an old Jangamayyanavaru. He had come to our house and told me all. Is it true or false? Tell me the truth! Is your age really thirty-two?'

'Oh, look at that fellow, f... his mother!' uttering those words, the Shanubhoga felt tremendous anger at Maadevayyanavaru.

'Oh, look at the words coming out of your mouth. We were told you used to speak in this manner with your first wife also. We should not offer even a glass of Gangaajal to people like you. Now, get up and go away from here!'

Channigarayaru went out of the house. Feeling scared to sit anywhere in that village, he directly went to Tiptur. *Tut-tut, this Madevayya, f... his mother! What the hell was up with him that he came here and told all these tales? It is said, that you should help a marriage take place even if you have to tell a thousand lies. But this old fool has impeded the marriage that had been fixed. Let his lineage be destroyed!* Abusing Maadevayyanavaru so, Channigarayaru entered the hotel and sat for his meals. He did not feel like returning to his place at once. Ninety rupees still remained from the money he had got from selling the cow. He stayed happily in Tiptur for twenty days. There was the platform of Dewan's choultry to stay at and there were many hotels in the town for food.

After he exhausted all the money, he returned to his village. By then, the monsoon had arrived. The villagers had vacated their sheds and returned to their houses. The Shanubhoga did not know to which house he had to go. Straightaway, he went to the temple of Hanumantharaya, which was his mother's home. Gangamma scolded him: 'Fie, you dunce, mud-headed bastard! You lost your post of the Shanubhoga!'

'Where did it go, mother?'

'You had not written accounts since your wife died. You have not given the list of collection, though two instalments are over. When the Shekdar came to enquire about it all, you were not in the village at all. So, Patel Shivegowda and Shivalinga met the Amaldar. The Shekdar came with the police, broke the lock of Gundegowda's house and handed the account books to Shivalinga. Now, he is the Shanubhoga.'

Channigarayaru sat down, his eyes wide as that of a corpse.

Gangamma said, 'You go and request the officer; say, "I have come now. Please arrange things in such a manner that my post of the Shanubhoga be given back to me, Mahaswamy".'

But whom should he ask? If they questioned, 'Where were you all these days?', what would he answer? Besides, who was there to write these accounts now? The accounts of grains—tut-tut, f... its mother—is very troublesome. He thought of a plan. He got up and went to Shivalinga's house. Shanubhoga Shivalinga knew the method of handling old accounts. But this new account of grains was cumbersome for him too. He sat writing, while it being instructed by Kambanakere Shanubhoga.

He questioned in the hauteur of a Shanubhoga, 'Hey what, why have you come?'

Channigarayaru humbly said, 'Shivalingegowdare, earlier too, you were looking after the post of Shanubhoga. Even now, you are doing that. But, do fix how much you are going to give me in the annual salary.'

'Hey, you have not given me the post of the Shanubhoga! You get lost! It has come to me from the government.'

'Then, can't you give anything?'

'No, not even a hair. Will you get up and get out or do I send for the village servant and ask him to push you out, holding your neck?'

He felt insulted. Foul words nearly came on the tip of his tongue. But he went away, scared that this Shivalinga might send for the village servant and harm him. His whole body was burning with anger.

Maadevayyanavaru's temple was on the way. Ayyanavaru sat on the platform and was rubbing tobacco on his hand. Coming across him, Channigarayaru's anger raised its hood. He too sat on the platform and asked, 'Ayyanore, I thought you were a righteous man. Since when did you learn this backbiting, this act of carrying tales?'

'Oh, are you saying this because your marriage was broken?'

When Ayyanavaru replied so coolly, Channigarayaru got angrier and said, 'Yes.'

'Do you manage your post of Shanubhoga by writing accounts independently? Are there any lands left to say that you get grains? The house is in Nanjamma's name and it belongs to Vishwanna. What is your age? How could you have taken care of that young girl?'

'Oh, I would have begged in some houses and looked after her. How did it matter to you?'

'Have we not seen how you looked after Nanjavva? Every woman will not be like Nanjavva. What will you do if your new wife becomes another Narasamma of the shop outside the village?'

Channigarayaru did not know an answer to this, but his anger did not decrease even a little. Ayyanavaru said, 'First, you understand your own nature. Why do you want to have that which you cannot maintain? You live like a sanyasi. If you want to do something, do it for Vishwanna. And now, had you been to Shivalingegowda's house? What did he say?'

'Fie, f...his mother! He refused to give anything from the annual salary.'

Ayyanavaru did not ask again. Patel Shivegowda was more or less the age of Ayyanavaru. Shivalingegowda was perhaps ten years younger to the Patel. Ayyanavaru wondered if these two would ever age. The world might continue in this manner only. Channigarayaru took a betel leaf, areca nut and tobacco from Ayyanavaru's bag, chewed them and went to his mother's home.

Channigarayaru stayed in the village for eight more days. Meanwhile, he sold away another cow and all the vessels that were in the house. He sold Nanjamma's earrings and nose bud, too, to Kashimbaddi. Then, he was absent for two months from the village.

After all, what was there in life? He decided he too should become a sanyasi like Maadevayyanavaru. Maundering through many places, he came to Malekallu Tirupati. He donned an ochre dhoti and shirt that he had bought in Arasikere, prostrated before the God Thimmappa and undertook the vow of sanyasa in his mind. He felt hungry by the evening. There were no families on the hill to offer bhiksha to sanyasis. He got down the hill, went to the nearby village and begged for alms. He cooked rice, sambar and ragi balls, and ate them. When he asked for a place on the platform to lie down on, the owner of the house—a gowda—agreed, gave him betel leaves, areca nuts and tobacco. He fell that the life of a sanyasa was not that bad.

But within two months, he was fatigued of this life. He was fed up of roaming around Metikurke, Kanakatte, Huliyar and Boodal, and raising bhikshaanna in several towns and villages. Daily, he had to go around a village. After he took on the vow of a sanyasi, he had discarded his feeling of Brahmanic purity and started taking food in the houses of all castes. People in some houses would reproach him, as if slapping him on the face. 'Hey, can't you work and earn your food?'

One day, he decided to return to his village out of weariness. *But who was there in the village? What was there?* He thought, *it would have been better if that slut of a wife was living. But let there be no one; my mother will never forsake me.* So thinking, he asked about the way and reached Tiptur through Halkurike and went back home.

Gangamma still lived in God Hanumantharaya's shrine. Now, she had to go alone around the villages begging. She could beg but could not carry what she received from the begging. It did not seem like her trusted son Appannaiah would ever come to her. She pined, 'Oh my fate itself is bad! It seems Shanimaharaya has climbed on my shoulders.'

One day, her elder son, Shanubhoga Channigaraya, stood before her shrine in a sanyasi's clothes—soiled ochre dhoti and even more soiled shirt. It was the same costume as that of Maadevayyanavaru. He used to shave his head and beard, but the hair on her son's head had grown and become longer. His beard was a bush of white and black. She could not recognize him for a minute. Then she shed heartfelt tears and said, 'Ayyo! What's this? What has happened to you? You bastard?'

'What else is there for me in life, Amma? Who is there for me? That's why I decided to give up everything and became a sanyasi.'

'Tut-tut, you son of a widow! Say "touch wood"! Am I dead? Come in, someone may see. Take off that ochre dhoti and wear another dhoti. Tomorrow, you may send for Rudranna and get shaved.'

Channigarayaru gave up sanyasa.

Mother and son were united. Channigarayaru was not used to carrying heavy loads. But the mother had a support. While she would be going round the houses begging for alms, he would sit on the platform of someone's house and chew betel leaf, areca nuts and tobacco, and enjoy a mouthful of its juice.

A new house had been built by Nanjamma. If he stayed in the temple, daily worship had to be performed. The temple and the enclosing place around the temple had to be swept daily and kept clean. So, the mother and son joined hands. They plastered and prepared the floor with red soil, and put doors and bolts. One day, Gangamma boiled milk in the newly built house.[34] She called the two Jois and said, 'It is not even a year since daughter-in-law died. We cannot perform the shaastra of entering a new house. I am a poor widow. You must please accept this,' she said. She had cooked payasa and other dishes, which she served them, gave them each a dakshina of two rupees and prostrated in front of them.

Now, nobody lived in Gundegowda's house, in which Nanjamma had lived till before her death. Kurubarahatti Muddayya of Ramasandra was Gundegowdaru's relative. He told Gundegowda's son that he would use that house and brought the key. But he was scared to live in the house in which plague maari had consumed three lives one after another. He decided not to live in it until some rituals and charms to keep away evil were performed by an expert Jois, and locked the house.

---

[34] A ritual that is performed, after entering a new house, for prosperity.

S.L. BHYRAPPA

CHAPTER SIXTEEN

1

It was more than forty-five years since Maadevayyanavaru had come to this village. He had started his life here, wishing for nobody's acquaintance or friendship. But as time passed, he was acquainted with several people and he came to know many villages around. There was no reason for him to feel weary here, as he lived without causing any trouble to anyone, and he had not developed an attachment to anyone. He never had any, bitter experience, no matter where he stayed. Yet once, he had felt a little disgusted, left this village and gone to Kashi. However much a holy city it was, he could not adjust to it and returned to this village. Often he would ruminate: *Why did I come back? What was here in this village that was not there?* Though it was true that in Kashi, the weather did not suit him, it was not the only reason for leaving it. He knew Hindi, the language of that region. It was convenient because of the opportunity of boarding and lodging in the Jangamavadi Mutt. There was no other town or village where one could recite bhajans or listen to them twenty-four hours a day, as one could in Kashi. Yet, a strong desire to return to Ramasandra arose in him. Whether it was the shrine, streets, tank, bund and the surrounding village where he had spent several years, had pulled his mind back to it or the people of that village occupied his memory, was not clear to him. Anyway, he came back.

After he returned, he came to be entirely accustomed to this place. He was spending time by going for bhiksha in the surrounding villages, he was helping people as far as he could, and he would sing bhajans like a ritual. But of late, he was finding whiling time away to be very difficult. And a feeling that there was nobody here for him, had seized him. So to say, who was there earlier? Who should have been there now? Though he asked himself these questions, the loneliness he felt in his mind did not go away. Once or twice he thought, *why stay in a place where there is no attachment?* It had been a few days since that feeling had been gaining strength. And, more or less, a decision had taken hold in his mind: 'No, this place is not what I want. I must go to Tiptur, Tumkur or somewhere else.'

While Maadevayyanavaru was thinking on these lines, one day, Appannaiah returned. He too did not have anyone in this village. After his sister-in-law's death, this place seemed empty to him. All these days, he had been begging around the irrigated fields.

While coming here, he had brought a quintal of rice, twenty seers of tovar dal, and ten seers of chillies and masala powder. He had stored all these in the room on the platform of Beeregowda's cowshed, and cooked for himself daily. There was no one as close to him as Ayyanavaru. As such, he would come to the shrine to pass his time, after cooking and eating. No matter what the topic of discussion would be, it always turned to the subject of his sister-in-law. Again and again, he would say, 'Ayyanore, this vile fellow harassed, tortured and devoured my sister-in-law!'

One day, Ayyanavaru said, 'Whatever happened in the past is over. At least, now your elder brother, mother and you stay together.'

But Appannaiah flatly refused, 'Tut-tut, let her lineage be destroyed! Oh Ayyanore, shall I stay with that widow? I am a man. I have earned a quintal of white rice from the channel-irrigated areas. You come and see, if you'd like.'

Ayyanavaru was silent. Appannaiah stayed in the village for twenty days. Not even for a day did he meet his mother or brother. He would flare up in anger if anybody spoke about them. He was totally fed up of this village. What could he do, sitting idly? In the surrounding villages, his mother and brother would have already gone round begging. People wouldn't give twice if he too went. So, he locked his room on the platform of Beeregowda, and left again for the irrigated areas.

Ayyanavaru was remembering Nanjamma's family the night on which Appannaiah left the village. All the incidents of her life appeared before his mind as if in a play: Her coming to this village as a daughter-in-law at a tender age, the many tortures in the house of her in-laws, her children, her setting up a separate family, bringing up her children, celebrating her son's Upanayana, her daughter's marriage, their death, and finally her own death. Now, he realized to what extent he had been attached to that family. When he was sighing about the fate of this woman's family, he remembered Vishwa, the only surviving child. Vishwa was very close to Ayyanavaru; he used to sit on his lap and eat the food he brought as kantebhiksha. *Very smart boy, oh, he had a tiger's courage. If he studied further, he would become intelligent. Nanjamma desired to educate him very much. How might he be in his uncle's house? How might the boy be faring in his studies? Perhaps his mischiefs would have lessened now. His aunt and uncle have no children. How would they be looking after him?*

He decided to visit Nagalapura once and see the boy before he left Ramasandra.

2

Two days later, one afternoon, Maadevayyanavaru finished his meals and was rubbing tobacco on the palm of his hand, sitting on the platform of the shrine, when Narasi came as if in search of him and sat at a distance. Sorrow was written all over her face.

'What Narasavva, you were not to be seen here for almost eight days. Where had you been?'

'I had gone to visit my relatives in Shantigrama, Ayyavre.'

'Why do you look so pale?'

'What shall I say, Ayyavre? I was coming by cart, when on the tank bund of Nagalapura, I met Viswappa. Seeing him, I cried.'

Ayyanavaru was at once interested. 'How is the child?'

'Oh, do you ask me "how is the child?" The boy, who was like a shoot of a young plantain, has now become like the dried-up twig of a castor oil plant. He had brought a copper pot to carry water from the tank. He recognized me as I sat in the cart. I could not recognize him at all. He has become emaciated. I stopped the cart, got down and asked: "How are you, child?" He simply started crying and did not stop, no matter how much I tried to comfort him. He asked: "Will you take me also to our place with you?" How could I bring him? You tell me, Ayyavre. He told so many things. He filled water and left soon after, saying his aunt would beat him if he was late. She had sent such a little boy with a copper pot to bring water—what a butcher-like slut she is! What do you say, Ayyanore?'

'Why didn't you go into the village and ask Kalleshajois? Are you not acquainted with him?'

'The boy left. I told the cartman to untie the oxen there itself. A woman was washing her saree. I went near her and said: "See, Avva, I belong to Ramasandra. This boy is from our village. Does Kalleshapparu take proper care of him?" That woman informed me about everything. Her house is near Kalleshappa's house. All the domestic chores are done by the boy. His aunt eats rice rotis and gives ragi rotis to the boy. That too, she sometimes does and sometimes does not. The boy has to wash her saree also. She hits the top of his head with a ladle.'

'Kalleshajois says nothing?'

'Oh, that man is a mad guy. If he is happy, he takes the boy to the fair and buys him some sweets or candies. When he gets angry, he hits the boy with a piece of firewood. How could the man know what the woman does inside?'

Ayyanavaru did not question Narasi again. He did not have any illusion about the state of that motherless child, Vishwa's happiness. But he could not have imagined that the boy was suffering such hardship and sorrow. He had heard enough about Kalleshajois's wife; he knew she was a bad woman, a termagant. He felt that the maternal uncle should have taken more care of his younger sister's son. If his mind was steady, he could have taken perfect or, at least good, care of the boy. Narasi too was thinking to herself and asked, 'Ayyanore, I will tell you something. Would you listen to that and accept it?'

'What is it? Ask away.'

'God did not grace my womb with a child. You bring that boy and give him to me. I will bring him up as my own son. My shop, my money—everything will be his. That boy was losing his life. He lay down on my lap and survived. His mother herself had said: "Narasamma, he is not my child, he is your child. You bring him up." You go to Nagalapura and bring back the boy. I will take care of him in such a way that no one will be able to lay a hand on him.'

She repeated the same, reminded him to 'think again', and left.

Ayyanavaru began dwelling on the matter. He did not get any sleep the whole night. Nanjamma's memory haunted him.

It was midnight when the tumour had appeared on her body. Though he had tried to prevent her from speaking, Nanjamma had said whatever was in her mind: 'When Parvati and Ramanna died, you told me the story of Gopamma. She was scared to give up her life and stood on the bank of that whirlpool. The same night, I had gone to drown myself in the crematorium well. I would have courageously plunged into that well, but came back worried about Vishwa. Now, I myself am going to die. Who will take care of Vishwa? Akkamma will cook something. I don't trust my Annayya. Food for the boy is not that important. But shouldn't the boy become an intelligent, educated man?'

He remembered all her words. If Akkamma had lived, there would not have been any problem as far as food for the boy was concerned. And his aunt would not have tortured him so at home. But she too died with her granddaughter. Ayyanavaru reproached himself: *Oh, while sending the boy with his uncle, I did not think about this at all. Oh, I am not intelligent at all! What could be done now? Should I bring him here as Narasamma has asked, and should he be given to her? She said that she had nearly ten to fifteen thousand with her, and the shop was running well. She would bring him up with love.* He thought, this would be better than that maternal uncle's house.

But again, he remembered Nanjavva's words. If Nanjavva was alive, would she have put the boy under Narasamma's care? She had said: 'Food for the boy is not that important. But shouldn't the boy become an intelligent, educated man?' *But who could get him educated? What was the father worth? What wisdom did the boy's uncle have? If the grandmother Gangavva had been a prudent woman, why would the family be this way? Now, what will happen to this boy?*

These thoughts haunted him for seven or eight days. One night, while lying down, suddenly a plan came to him: *I am leaving this village. I should take Vishwanna also with me. Let him eat ragi balls twice a day from the kantebhiksha I bring. I will send him to school. He is a clever child. Let him study in an English school. If he has any luck, let him study in higher classes also. Yes, that will be fine.*

When he decided upon this course of action, Maadevayyanavaru was thrilled with joy, though he could not understand why.

But then, another thought came to cloud his mind: *I am of an advanced age. If I take the boy with me and die myself, what will happen to the boy?* For a couple of hours, these thoughts tormented his mind. But it was difficult to find solace. *The boy is very smart. If at all I die, how would it matter? Let the boy work as a coolie and earn his livelihood. But let him not live in his uncle's house shuddering in fear. How do I know whether I will die at this very moment or in the near future? Even when a woman like Nanjavva—she, who would be of my granddaughter's age—could die, I am as strong as the round rock of a linga—I won't die until Vishwanna is a grown man.*

Maadevayyanavaru had another thought: *What if Kalleshajoisaru refused to send the boy with me? What should be done then? Anyway, if the boy sees me, he will stick to me. Then I will smuggle him and bring him here. What could Kalleshajois do about that?* Determined, Maadevayyanavaru set out for Nagalapura one day.

3

Maadevayyanavaru stopped on the way in Katigehalli, and reached Nagalapura the next day at ten in the morning. He bathed on the way in a tank, donned the same ochre dhoti and shirt, wound a red turban around his head, smeared vibhuti on the forehead and, meditating on Shiva, went directly to Vishwa's school. It was the hour for the boys to be let off from school. As soon as the bell rang, Vishwa came out. Recognizing Ayyanavaru, he came near him and said, 'Ayyanore', as he hugged Ayyanavaru's thighs.

'Come here, child,' Ayyanavaru said, held his hand and, taking him near the banyan tree behind the school, sat him near. Like Narasamma had said, Vishwa had indeed become like a dried-up stick of the castor oil plant. Ayyanavaru asked, 'Will you come with me?'

'To our place?'

'Whether to our village or some other village, it doesn't matter. Come with me. Let us go to some big town. I will bring kantebhiksha and serve you. You may attend the school there and study hard. Would you come with me?'

'Oh, Ayyanore, you simply tell lies.'

'No, child. It is true.'

'If so, swear it.'

'Yes, I swear on you, child,' he said, putting his hand on the boy's head.

'Then move, let us run away from here itself.'

'No, let's go home and ask your uncle.'

Vishwa began crying as soon he heard this: 'No, he won't leave me, Ayyanore.'

'Let us ask him first. If he refuses to send you, I'll come here tomorrow. I'll take you directly from here.' To convince Vishwa, Maadevayyanavaru had to swear three times, holding his casket of linga in his hand.

He sent Vishwa first. After ten minutes—by the time he entered the house, asking for the address—Kalleshajois was scolding his nephew. 'You rascal! Why did you come late?' He became silent once he saw Ayyanavaru.

While they were speaking about some usual matters, a red horse came and stood in front of the house. Kantijois got down from the horse. It was the first time he had come home since he had performed the shraaddha rites of his mother and left the place. He had known before he left, that Kallesha would bring Vishwa here. Kallesha himself had said so. Now, there was a turn of mood, and he had come home. He desired to see his grandson. He came in, called Vishwa, and gave him the packet of Mysore pak and vadas. He asked Ayyanavaru regarding Ramasandra and the house his daughter had built.

After a little while, Kallesha asked Ayyanavaru, 'Will you have food with us or will you cook for yourself or shall we send word to a family of your caste?'

'Send word to a family of my caste.'

Kallesha sent word, through Vishwa, to Mallashetty of the village. Mallashetty came and took this Jangama to his house for bhiksha. When Shetty's wife was cooking, Ayyanavaru enquired about the condition of Vishwa in Kalleshajoisa's house. Mallashetty said, 'Oh Shiva, such children should not be living. It is better if they die!' His wife, too, voiced the same thoughts from the kitchen.

Ayyanavaru said, 'Shettare, will you go and bring Kantijois here?'

Kantijois came with Mallashetty within ten minutes. He sat on the wooden seat Mallayyashetty placed in front of Ayyanavaru, leaning against the wall. Ayyanavaru explained the reason behind his coming here, to Kantijois, and said, 'If you want, please ask this Shettaru and the sister inside. You may inquire with anybody in this village. You yourself look at the boy, how thin and weak he has become. Your daughter-in-law's nature is what it is. You send the boy with me. I will educate him and look after him.'

Jois felt so angry that he wanted to break his daughter-in-law's waist. But Ayyanavaru said, 'The inauspicious spiral hair will not be destroyed by shaving it off. Her husband himself is unable to correct her. Besides, Kalleshajois too does not know how to look after children. You send the boy with me.'

Jois thought for a while and asked, 'What will you do by taking him with you?'

'I don't know what I will do, or where I will stay. If you have trust in me, just give me the boy.'

Kantijois did not respond immediately. Anger was seizing his mind. *The boy's grandfather, I, am still alive, and the maternal uncle, Kallesha, is here. This Jangamayya has come here and is asking to send the boy with him, saying that the boy is not taken proper care of. Oh, he has some nerve!* He had almost opened his mouth to abuse Ayyanavaru, but another thought came to his mind and he restrained his tongue. For ten minutes, he sat like a dumb person pondering over the state of Kallesha's family. *Fie, that Kamali, the slut, is not a good woman! She has made the boy so feeble by not giving him proper food. Kallesha too beats him. What if I took the boy and kept him with me, under my personal care?'* But what would he accomplish by doing that? Tasty, sumptuous food in hotels, horse-riding, black magic charms, medicine—is that what he wanted to give the boy? These things are all unwanted. His mind refused to entertain such a future. *Yes, there is nobody in this situation who can bring him up properly. This Ayyanavaru is a trustworthy person. Nanju, too, was saying, that he was a godlike man.* Kantijois was thoughtful and asked openly, 'Look, Ayyanavare, my coming here today is a pure coincidence. If I was not here, you would have to ask Kallesha. He would not have sent the boy with you. What would you have done then?'

'Now that you yourself have come, why these questions?'

'Perchance I hadn't come. What would you have done then? Tell me the truth.'

'Shall I speak the truth? Tomorrow, when the boy would have gone to school, I would have taken him directly from the school, holding his hand. If anyone had come to prevent me, I would have responded appropriately.'

For half a minute, Kantijois was looking at Ayyanavaru unblinkingly. Then he got up, patted his shoulder and said, 'Wah re wah Ayyanore, you are really a man, shabash. You take the boy. I will convince Kallesha.'

And he went home.

By the time Ayyanavaru finished his lunch and nap, and came a little late purposely, Kantijois had persuaded Kallesha to agree to send the boy with Maadevayyanavaru. The Jois himself went to school on the same day and got the boy's certificate. The next morning, Ayyanavaru bundled Vishwa's clothes and books and put them into his bag, saying, 'Child, touch the feet of Ajjayya, Maava, Attemma and do sharanu.' Kamalu stood like a stone while Vishwa was prostrating in front of her. Kallesha maava's eyes were filled with tears.

Kantijois had been very gloomy since last evening. He had not had his meals at night. Though both of them had laid down on the platform, he had not spoken to Ayyanavaru. He, too, came with Kallesha to take leave of these two, holding the reins of the harnessed horse and walking it till the outlet of the tank. After crossing the outlet, he told his son, 'Kallesha, you return. I'll walk for half a mile with them and then return.'

Before going back, Kallesha told Ayyanavaru, 'See, I had kept a strict eye on him. He is very mischievous. Nanju herself had asked me to keep him in control. If not, he would have been spoiled. You also bring him up in a way that he is scared of you.'

'Yes, it is correct, correct. Is it not that only under a thousand strokes, a stone moulds into a Shivalinga? But you should strike it at the proper place and with the right amount of temper. What you did was for his good.' Listening to Ayyanavaru's reply, Kallesha's made a long face. He left without uttering another word.

After all three of them and the horse had walked more than a hundred steps, Ayyanavaru said to Kantijois, 'You go back. We will walk faster.'

Though the Jois was trying to say something, the words were not emerging. He stopped with the horse. Ayyanavaru too stood close by. Between them, stood Vishwa, who had grown as tall as their waists. For five minutes, nobody spoke. Ayyanavaru asked, 'Shall we move?' Then Kantijois said, 'Listen to me, Ayyanore, you are really a man.'

Ayyanavaru did not understand. 'What is it you say?'

'Nothing. Take this,' he said and put his hand in the pocket of his inner shirt, and took out a bundle of notes. He shoved them into the pocket of Maadevayya's ochre shirt and said, 'There is one hundred and fifty rupees there. You take the boy wherever you want. Then drop a letter to me. It is enough if you write to this address: Nagalapurada Kantijoisaru, Ghost house, Behind the mosque, Channarayapatna.' Then he bent down his big body, kissed on both the cheeks of his grandson, stroked his body, face and back gently with his thick palm, turned around and mounted the horse. Ayyanavaru saw tears in the edges of the Jois's eyes. Hinting that the horse move, with a slight push to the horse's lower abdomen with his leg, Kantijois rode away without turning back. Vishwa turned and stood still, looking at the speed of the horse. After a little while, Ayyanavaru held Vishwa's hand and walked further.

They had walked half a mile when Vishwa was seen brooding over something. Without his knowledge, his lips moved as if he was muttering to himself. Ayyanavaru asked,

'My child, what are you thinking?'

'Will you get me a horse like the one Ajjayya has?'

'Why do we need it, child?'

'If I get such a horse, I want to go galloping, trot trot trot, faster than Ajjayya.'

'What else do you want?'

'I want to swim a long distance.'

'Don't you like to study?'

'I do. I'm first in my class in arithmetic.'

'In which other subjects do you come first?'

'I could not study at all in uncle's house. Otherwise, I would have stood first in every subject. My teacher said so.'

'Hereafter, you will study how much ever you want. I'll bring you a bagful of slates and books. Let's go.'

'Where shall we go from our village?'

'I have not yet given that a thought. Let's go to Gubbi or Tumkur.'

'Ayyanore, wherever we go, I want a tank to swim in. You get a horse someday from anybody. I feel like riding.'

'Yes, let's see. Come,' he turned and looked at Vishwa's face. At once, he remembered Kantijois.

4

They reached Ramasandra the same day. Gangamma was not in the village. Ayyanavaru sold the ragi, pulses and chillies he had with him that evening itself. He got a hundred and twenty rupees from it. Apart from that, he had forty silver rupees. In the pocket of his inner shirt, there was the hundred and fifty rupees that Kantijois had given. He tied the money to his waist and engaged a servant to carry the aluminium vessels, clothes and blankets. Before leaving the village in the morning, Vishwa asked, 'Ayyanore, is my Amma really dead?'

'Yes, child.'

'I must look inside our house.'

'What is there for you to see?'

'I must see,' he insisted.

Ayyanavaru knew that after the house was vacated, the key of that house was with Kurubarahatti Muddayya, who was a relative of Gundegowdaru. He sent for Muddayya and asked him to open the door. Since it had been uninhabited, it was filled with dust and the smell of stale air was coming from inside. Vishwa went into the house and entered the kitchen. Then he went into the room where the grain bins were stored and fumbled in the darkness. He climbed to the attic from the pillar and searched. Then finally, he shouted loudly, 'Oh, hey Amma, are you not here?' There was no answer.

He came down and asked, 'Ayyanore, then did my Amma really die?'

Muddayya, who had come to open the door, stood like a stone. Ayyanavaru comforted the child, 'Yes, child, your Amma is really dead.'

Vishwa started howling. Ayyanavaru hugged him and tried to console him by saying, 'Now, move, let's go.'

Vishwa simply followed Ayyanavaru. The servant walked in the front, carrying the sack of their vessels, blankets and clothes. Ayyanavaru walked, holding his ektaari and one more instrument used for the rhythm. As Vishwa had grown to be bony, no one in the village recognized him walking behind Ayyanavaru. Neither had Ayyanavaru informed anyone about his leaving the village. If he had, everyone would have asked what, why, where, and the like. How could he explain to them all?

They had to go through the Kambanakere road and reach the bus route. The servant was further off, carrying the luggage. Ayyanavaru, unable to walk at par with him, remained behind. Though he had held Vishwa's hand, he was immersed in thought and was walking slowly, with his head lowered. They had come a mile away from the village. Channigarayaru was lying beneath a tree, by the roadside, with his head placed on a small bundle of ragi. His mouth was full of tobacco juice.

Lying on his back, he was adjusting his lips so that the juice would not spill out of his mouth. Ayyanavaru spotted him. Channigarayaru sat up, listening to the sound of their steps, and turned towards them. Ayyanavaru did not speak to him. Perhaps, Gangamma must have gone to relieve herself behind the nearby pool. Ayyanavaru walked fast, thinking that if Gangamma saw them, she may ask, 'Where are you taking my grandson?' Channigarayaru had too much tobacco juice in his mouth to speak or ask anything.

Vishwa immediately asked, 'Is it not my Appa?' Channigarayaru recognized his son. His mouth tried to articulate something, but if he spat out the tobacco that was at present oozing out juice, there would be no other piece for him. By the time he decided what he should do, these two had already moved thirty or forty steps forward. Vishwa was turning back again and again and looking at Channigarayaru.

Ayyanavaru said, 'Don't turn and look in that direction; just walk forward, child.'

Channigarayaru could not spit out the juice of betel leaves and tobacco from his mouth at all. So, he could not speak. He wondered, *Oh this Jangamayya, though he saw me, went away without speaking to me. Let me find him again; I'll take him to task!*

As the two walked down the mound, they had vanished from his sight by then.

aachamana: A ritual of drinking a spoonful of water from one's right palm.

aapooshana: The ritual of taking a spoonful of water on one's palm after meals.

Amaldar: Assistant commissioner of provinces

ambode: A flat snack with soaked channa dal roughly ground with green chillies and spices that is deep-fried.

angadi: Shop

arisina: Turmeric

aarati: Ritual performed in functions by placing lighted lamps in a tray.

avare: Pulses

baraavardaar: Original claimant

bikkalam: Writing on behalf of the illiterate

bhikshanna: Begging for alms

bhikshapatre: The boy who undergoes thread ceremony should have a silver bowl for the ritual of seeking alms.

Bombai bonda: A fried snack stuffed with mashed potatoes and peas, with gram flour as its base and spices added to taste.

Brahmagantu: A knot in the sacred thread (worn by one who has undergone the Upanayanam) representing Brahma.

chandali: Wicked woman; meant also as an abuse.

chakkuli: A deep-fried, round, rough-surfaced snack that is prepared by mixing urad dal powder and rice powder.

chikkina unde: A deep-fried sweet dish that is a mixture of boiled jaggery and coconut, covered with ground urad dal.

chitranna: Boiled rice seasoned with dals, asafoetida, groundnut seeds, copra scrapes, along with lime juice or tamarind.

chitrahuti: A ritual of putting a few grains of boiled rice on the right side of one's plate five times.

Chowdamma: A mean deity

copra: A piece of dried coconut

Dafedar: Security personnel

dakshine: Pecuniary offering

darkhast price: Price paid for lands granted by the government

Dewan: The then-equivalent of Chief Minister.

firka: Subdivision

Gangajal: Holy water from the river Ganges

gangodaka: Sanctified name for potable water

Godaana: Cows given away in charity.

Goodemarammanavaru: Priest carrying village deity called Goodemaramma announces the arrival of plague in the village.

gowda: Villager

Gowri Festival: Festival that is celebrated before Ganesha festival.

grihapravesha: Ceremony to consecrate the entering into a new home.

gurukarunya: Begging alms in the name of Gurus

Halumatha: A religious tradition followed by the Kurubas. Kuruba is a community of Hindus who have long been known to have practised vocations like shepherds and farmers.

hanchi: It is a kind of grass out of which brooms are made.

Hobali: A cluster of adjoining villages under a single administration

homa: Fire ritual

honagone: A sort of green used for making a variety of curries and rasam.

Jamabandi: Land records/ record of rights of a village.

jangama: Ascetic moving from place to place

japa: Meditation where a mantra is repeated

jatka: Horse cart

Jois: Individuals who perform pujas and ceremonies

Jolige: A sack for begging

Kaalabhairava: Another name for Lord Shiva

Kamboli: Name of rituals performed after completion of the marriage ceremony.

kanda: A kind of poetic meter consisting four lines.

kantebhiksha: Begging for alms among Veerashaivas

karunya bhiksha: Alms given to an ascetic, a man of God.

Kasaba Shanubhoga: Accountant of various hobalis

khaneshumari: Enumerating houses of a village, census of population and livestock, revenue accounts and government documents

kharashev: Deep-fried spicy snack prepared from gram flour

khata: Ledger account book

kodanda: Hanging one upside down while exposing him to chilly smoke from beneath.

kodubale: A deep-fried snack that is prepared using rice powder, coconut scrapes, chilli powder and asafoetida. It usually resembles the shape of a bangle.

kumkumarchana: Worshipping deities with kumkum chanting mantras

Lagnapatrike: Writing of the wedding invitation

Lambanii (banjara): A tribe

Lavani: Folk songs or ballads

madi (saree): Washed saree worn after taking a bath

mahamangalaarati: A worshipping ritual

mangalyam/mangalya/mangalasutra/tali: Golden pendant with thread tied around the bride's neck by the groom.

mantapam: A stone canopy

moorti: Statue

muttaide: A woman whose husband is alive

Mysore Pak: A popular sweet dish prepared with gram flour, sugar and ghee (clarified butter).

naagoli: Ritual performed in a wedding, following kanyadaana

Nadaswaram: Musical instrument like that of a shehnai.

nagaru: An ornament resembling a cobra.

Nonabanna, Nonabagowda and Banajiga: Sub-castes under the Veerashaiva (a Shaivism sub-tradition within Ligayatism) sect.

obbattu: A chapati-like sweet dish stuffed with a mixture of boiled tovar dal and jaggery.

paap: Sin

paada: Part

pahani: Revenue record that contains details of owners, their lands, etc.

patala: Netherworld

Patel: Village head

parishechana: The action of sprinkling water around the meals that are served in plate or leaf.

payasa: Rice pudding

punya: religious merit

prarabdha: Fate or destiny

prasada: Devotional offering

preta: A spirit of the dead

ragi balls: Ragi flour well-boiled and then made into balls; a staple food in rural south Indian homes.

rave unde: Sweet laddus prepared with fried rava (semolina) and sugar solution.

Rishipanchami Vrata: A vrata or vow performed by women after three years of menopause. It is done either by a woman with her husband while he's alive, or by a tonsured widow. In this vow, seven great rishis are worshipped on a particular day. The observance is usually accompanied by fasting and the ritual continues through the night, along with appropriate chanting of matras and mangalarati, offering fruits as naivedya to the rishis, once every three hours.

roti: A flatbread similar to a chapati.

rudrakshi: Sacred bead

runaanubandha: A bond or relationship from a previous birth

rustum: Brave, strong

saadu: Home-made preparation used by men to apply on forehead.

Saaligrama: Small stones meant to be representative of gods

samaaraadhana: Feeding in mass

sandhyavandana(m): Ritual offering to Sun God thrice a day by a person who has undergone the thread ceremony.

Shanidevaru: Saturn

Shanimaharaya: Lord Saturn

Shanubhoga: Village accountant

Sharanas: Veerashaiva devotees

shaastra: Work or treatise on religion, divination or science.

Shirastedar: Part of the revenue department, he receives and checks court pleas in cases arising out of the record of land rights.

shraadh: Ritual of paying one's respects to one's dead parents

shruti: Base musical note

Sunkalamma Maari: Name of a mean deity

Sunkalamma: An evil deity

tapasya: A spiritual pursuit of self-realization; penance

tambittu: A sweet dish that is prepared with rice powder, coconut scrapes mixed with thick, boiled jaggery solution, along with cardamom.

tambula: Chewed betel leaves

tatvapadas: Philosophical songs

Upanayanam: A rite of passage, it is the sacred thread ceremony that precedes a young boy's beginning to acquire education.

usuli: Boiled sprouts or pulses seasoned to taste.

vade: A snack with soaked urad dal, nicely ground and deep-fried; it is round in shape.

vaara: Fixing a day for offering a free meal for poor students

vibhuti: Sacred ash

Vokkaliga: A community of farmers

vrata: A religious observance of a vow (vrat) that includes fasting, chanting prayers and other religious activities

Seasons:

Vasantha (Spring)—Chaitra, Vaishaka
Greeshma (Summer)—Jyeshta, Ashada
Varshaa (Monsoon)—Shravana, Bhadrapada
Sharad (Autumn)—Ashvayuja, Karthika
Hemanta (Winter)—Margashira, Pushya
Shishira (Winter)—Maagha, Phalguna